Spellbound

TOR BOOKS BY BLAKE CHARLTON

Spellwright
Spellbound

Spellbound

BLAKE CHARLTON

A Tom Doherty Associates Book

NEW YORK

SPELLBOUND

Edited by James Frenkel
Maps by Rhys Davis

A Tor Book
Published by Tom Doherty Associates, LLC
175 Fifth Avenue
New York, NY 10010

www.tor-forge.com

ISBN 978-0-7653-1728-5

First Edition: September 2011

Printed in the United States of America

0 9 8 7 6 5 4 3 2 1

To my mother, Louise Bryden Buck, M.D.,
for patient love and lessons in healing

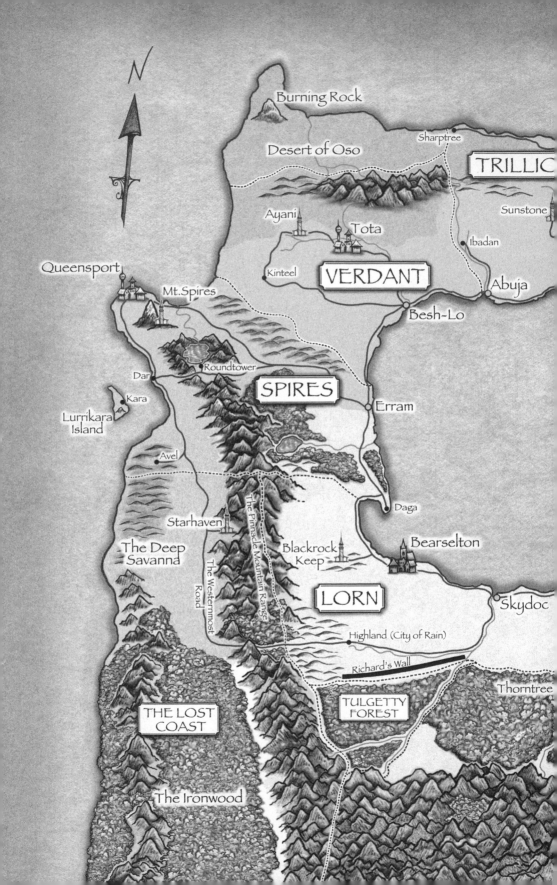

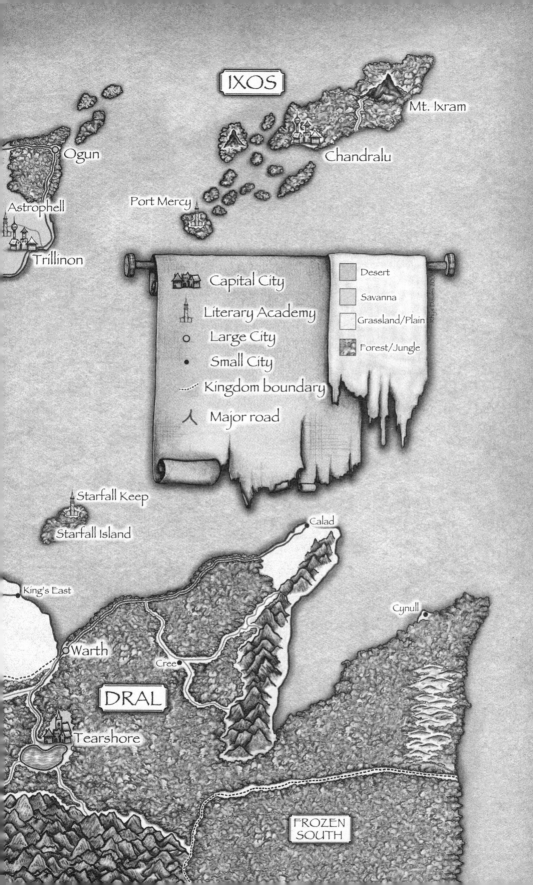

IXOS

Mt. Ixram

Ogun

Chandralu

Astrophell

Port Mercy

Trillinon

Capital City

Literary Academy

o   Large City

•   Small City

- - -   Kingdom boundary

人   Major road

Desert

Savanna

Grassland/Plain

Forest/Jungle

Starfall Keep

Starfall Island

Calad

King's East

Cynull

Warth

Cree

DRAL

Tearshore

FROZEN
SOUTH

The Reservoir of Avel

Sliding Dock

Dam of Canonist Calla

Fish Market

Water District

Infirmary

Sanctuary

2.

1.

Holy District

Burnished Gardens

Canyon Floor

1. Courtyard of Lesser Benediction
2. Courtyard of Greater Benediction

to Coldlock Harbor

Northern Gate

Night Market

North Gate

Palm District

North
Market

Far Market

Cypress
District

Merchant District

Colaboris Station

South Market

South Gate

Coldlock Harbor

Auburn Mountains

Reservoir

Avel

to the Westernmost Road

Rhys Davies 2011

As for the poem, one dragon, however hot, does not make a summer, or a host; and a man might well exchange for one good dragon what he would not sell for a wilderness. And dragons, real dragons, essential both to the machinery and the ideas of a poem or tale, are actually rare.

—J. R. R. TOLKIEN,
"Beowulf: The Monsters and the Critics"

He is at once a stratum of the earth and a streamer in the air, no painted dragon but a figure of real oneiric power, one that can easily survive the prejudices which arise at the very mention of the word "dragon."

—SEAMUS HEANEY,
Introduction to his translation of Beowulf

Spellbound

One

Francesca did not realize she had used an indefinite pronoun until it began to kill her patient.

Someone, no one knew who, had brought the young woman into the infirmary with an unknown curse written around her lungs. Francesca had cast several golden sentences into her patient's chest, hoping to disspell the malicious text. Had it gone well, she would have pulled the curse out of the woman's mouth.

But the curse's style had been robust, and one of Francesca's mistakenly ambiguous pronouns had pushed the curse from the girl's lungs to her heart. There, the spiteful text had bound the once-beating organ into silence.

Now plummeting toward death, the girl bleated a final cry.

Francesca looked around the solarium and saw only white walls and a window looking out onto the city of Avel. Voices of other medical spellwrights sounded from down the hallway; they were also working to save patients wounded by the recent lycanthrope attack on the city walls. Both the infirmary and the neighboring sanctuary were in crisis, and so Francesca was alone.

To her horror, Francesca's first reaction was relief that no one had seen her mistake.

She turned to her patient. The girl's wide green eyes had dilated to blackness. Her distended neck veins betrayed no pulse.

Francesca's fingers tingled. This couldn't be happening. She never made mistakes, never used indefinite pronouns.

The patient had been able to whisper her name when the curse was still on her lungs. Now Francesca addressed the young woman: "Deirdre, stay with me."

No response.

Francesca could not see the curse; it was written in a language she did not know. But the golden countercurse she had cast now visualized the malicious text that spellbound the young woman's heart.

Invasive action was needed.

Spellwrights created magical runes in their muscles; presently, Francesca used those in her left forearm to write a few silvery sentences that glowed on her skin. With her right hand, she pulled the spell free. It folded into a short, precise blade.

Francesca moved with confidence. She was a remarkably tall woman, lithe, clothed in a wizard's black robe and cleric's red stole. Both her long hair and wide eyes were very dark brown, making her pale features more striking. An illiterate would think she had maybe thirty years. A spellwright would know she had twice as many.

With her left hand, Francesca tore off her patient's blouse. Deirdre's smooth olive complexion, small chin, and raven hair indicated her youth. Yet there was something mature in the creases around her eyes.

Just then the floor shook and the wooden rafters chirped—a small earthquake possibly, or the blast from another lycanthropic attack. Somewhere in the infirmary or the adjacent sanctuary a man wailed.

Francesca laid her left hand on Deirdre's shoulder. As a physician, she shuddered—cold, and full of doubt. Then she leapt into the safety of action.

After a few steady cuts, she lifted Deirdre's small breast upward to expose the lattice of bone and muscle. The next cut ran between the fifth and sixth ribs, starting at the sternum and traveling around to the spine. The blood that flowed was bright red. Encouraging. Darker, slower blood would have confirmed death.

Francesca pried the ribs apart and extemporized a spell to hold them open.

The distant wailing grew more urgent.

"Deirdre, stay with me," Francesca commanded as she slipped her hands into the girl's chest and found her heart. Francesca held her breath as she pulled off the malicious sentences.

The floor shook again. A second and then a third voice joined the wailing.

Francesca bit her lip and unraveled the curse's last sentence. The heart swelled with blood but did not beat. Francesca began to rhythmically squeeze the organ with her hand. She was about to call for help when the heart began to squirm.

It felt like a bag full of writhing worms.

"God-of-gods," Francesca whispered. When a heart was denied blood, its once-coordinated action might expire into a chaos of separate spasms.

She continued to compress the heart. But each time she squeezed, the writhing lessened. The muscles were fading into death.

Francesca did not stop, could not stop.

More voices had joined the wailing, which rose and fell in an eerie tempo. Though almost musical, the wailing was wholly unlike the devotional songs the Spirish people sang during daily worship.

Some new crisis was sweeping through the infirmary or the sanctuary. Perhaps more wounded citizens had come in from the lycanthrope attack. Perhaps one of the lycanthrope spellwrights had even breached Avel's walls despite the daylight.

But Francesca didn't care about any of that. Her hands had gone cold. Her legs trembled. She was leaning on her patient. The world dissolved into a blur of tears.

The girl's heart was still.

"Creator, forgive me," Francesca whispered and withdrew her hands. "I'm sorry." A painful tingling now enveloped her fingers. "I'm so . . . so sorry."

She bowed her head and closed her eyes. Time became strange to her. She'd always been proud of her ability to prognosticate—to look forward into patients' lives and anticipate their chances of cure, their moments of danger. But she had not foreseen Deirdre's death; it seemed to jolt her out of time, out of her own body.

For a moment it felt as if she were someone else, as if she were standing in the doorway and looking at the physician who had just killed her patient. In this dissociated state, she felt both safe and profoundly numb.

But then she was back in her own body, blinking through tears. She had not wept before a patient, alive or dead, for time out of mind. But now she had used the wrong word, a damned indefinite pronoun. Now her carelessness had killed.

Hot self-hatred flashed through her. She bit down on her lip.

Then, as suddenly as it came, her anger vanished, and she remembered her last day at the clerical academy in Port Mercy. She had asked her mentor for parting advice. The ancient physician had smiled tightly and said, "Kill as few patients as possible."

The young Francesca had laughed nervously.

Now, standing beside the first patient she had killed, she laughed at the memory, could not stop laughing. The strange hilarity was like gas bubbling out of her. Kill as few patients as possible. It was suddenly, terrifyingly hilarious.

Gradually her laughter died, and she felt hollow.

Around her, the infirmary resounded with wailing. She took a long breath. Other patients needed her. She had to counterfeit composure until true composure came. By extemporizing a few absorbing paragraphs, she cleaned the blood from her hands.

The floor shook again. "Is he loose?" someone whispered.

Startled, she looked toward the door. No one was there.

The whisperer spoke again, "Is he loose already?"

Francesca turned around. No one was in the solarium, and nothing but minarets and the alleyways of Avel were visible out the window. The hallway? Empty.

A weak groan. "He'll be here soon. Help me up."

Suddenly Francesca understood who was speaking, and her own heart seemed to writhe like a bag of worms.

She looked down at Deirdre, at the being she had mistaken for a mortal woman.

"You're an avatar?" Francesca whispered. "A member of the Celestial Canon?"

"Avatar, yes. Canonist, no," Deirdre corrected, pulling her bloody blouse over her now miraculously intact and scarless chest. "Sacred goddess, I forgot the shock of coming back."

Francesca stepped away. "What the burning hells is happening?"

The immortal woman looked at her. "A demon named Typhon has invested part of his soul into me. He won't let me die."

"Won't . . ." Francesca echoed, ". . . let you die?"

The other woman kneaded her temples. "I'm Typhon's rebellious slave. The bastard can control most of what I do unless I find a way to kill myself. Given my restraints, self-assassination takes a bit of ingenuity. But if I can off myself, I win roughly half an hour of freedom after revival." She smiled at Francesca. "Today, my creative method of suicide was you."

Relief swept through Francesca. "You set me up? It was impossible to disspell that curse on your lungs?"

The other woman pressed a hand to her sternum and winced. "Not impossible; a few master clerics have managed it over the years. I'm always heartbroken when they save my life."

The hollowness returned to Francesca's chest. Failure. She had killed a patient after all. Despite sacrificing most of her life to medicine, she still wasn't a master.

Deirdre closed her eyes and quirked a half smile. "It's sweet to be free again. Almost intoxicating." She shivered as if in pleasure but then opened her eyes and grew serious. "Now that I've come for you, so will he."

Francesca took a step back. Nothing felt real. She laughed in disbelief. "I'm sorry . . . but . . . could you excuse me for just a moment? I'm punishing myself for killing you by going completely out of my bloody mind."

"You are Cleric Francesca DeVega?"

"Oh, I was a cleric until a moment ago when I went as crazy as a spring hare."

Deirdre frowned. "Have I pushed you too far? Forgive me. I shouldn't be so glib. You have a reputation for . . . bravado."

Francesca laughed. "To hell with 'bravado'; I'll tell a superior he's an arrogant hack if he's harming my patient. But now that my shoddy prose has killed, I—"

"Cleric," the other woman interrupted. "You were meant to fail. If you hadn't, I wouldn't be free. I'm sorry I pushed you. But right now, I need to break the demon's hold on you. Around your left ankle there is a fine silver chain. Show it to me."

Francesca blinked. "What?"

"On your left foot, there's an anklet. Show it to me."

"My lady avatar, with all due respect, I don't even own a God-of-gods damned anklet."

"Just show me your left foot," the woman said and pointed. "Now."

"You can't seriously . . . oh, what the hell, here look." She pulled off her leather slipper and wool sock before lifting up her leg. She wore nothing on her foot but a few freckles. "See, my lady, there's nothing on WHAT IN THE BURNING HELLS IS THAT?"

Deirdre had reached out and unclasped a thin silver chain from Francesca's ankle. The semidivine woman now held it out. "I'm not a spellwright. I don't know how, but it prevents its wearer from sensing it. Typhon was using it to keep you in Avel. If you had tried to leave the city, it would have rendered you unconscious. Or maybe something worse. I'm not sure. Here, take it."

Francesca stared at the anklet as if it were a viper. "This can't be happening. And . . . and what would a demon possibly want with me?" Her voice cracked on the last word.

Deirdre grimaced. "He wants to use your skills as a physician to help force a powerful spellwright to convert."

"Convert to what?"

"To the demon's cause. Look, I'll explain what I know as soon as we are somewhere safer, but now hurry and take the anklet." Deirdre was still holding the silver chain out. Her arm was trembling. "I haven't yet regained my strength. There's a nonmagical anklet on my left foot. Put it on your own foot. That way if a demonic agent catches you, he might think you are still bound."

Francesca started. She took the offered anklet, tucked it into her belt purse, and then found an identical one on her patient. After removing the chain, she fastened it around her own left ankle and discovered the skin around her ankle had grown calluses where the chain would have rubbed against it. In a few places, she had small scars where the anklet's clasp might have cut her. She must have been wearing the undetectable anklet for a very long time. For years perhaps.

Deirdre cleared her throat. "Do I have your attention now, cleric?"

"More than anyone else ever has," Francesca answered faintly.

"Good. I have an agent waiting on the street to take that anklet and hide it . . ." Her voice trailed off as the floor trembled and the wailing surged. "Damn it all!" she swore.

"What is it?" Francesca asked. Suddenly, orange flashes speckled her vision. Again the floor shook. This time the ceiling rafters chirped and the wailing grew even louder.

Deirdre's dark face paled. "He's never gotten so close so fast." She beckoned Francesca to come closer. "Carry me. Quickly now, the aphasia's begun. My agents on the ground will be compromised. This is horrible. We must go before the beast arrives."

"Before . . . whom . . . before who arrives?" Francesca found it difficult to speak. The ideas were clear in her mind, but the words for them escaped her intellect. The orange flashes dancing before her eyes were growing brighter.

"Hear that wailing?" Deirdre asked. "He's touched those minds. They have thoughts but not words. It's called aphasia. You're beginning to feel it; you're slightly aphasic already. Now, unless we flee before he arrives, you may never speak a clear word again."

"H-him?" Francesca stuttered at the bedside. "The demon?"

More voices joined the wailing and began to rise and fall in an eerie cacophony of call and answer.

"Not Typhon, another slave. One I wanted to trap with that anklet. But my agents on the street are as good as dead. The beast has never moved this fast before. Damn me! We must flee before he enters the infirmary."

With difficulty, Francesca lifted Deirdre from the table. Her eyes could not focus. Deirdre wrapped her arms around Francesca's neck. The caterwauling rose into an ecstatic crescendo and then fell dead silent. The ground shook.

"Goddess, defend us," Deirdre whispered, tightening her arms around Francesca. "He's here."

Two

Suddenly conscious, Shannon dropped the text he had been holding. It fell to the wooden floorboards and shattered.

Strange.

He frowned at the scattering golden runes and then yawned so powerfully his jaw cracked. Wincing, he rubbed his temples and wondered why he had awoken standing up and holding a spell. Even more disconcerting, he had no idea where he was.

Looking up revealed a circular room with white walls and rows of bookcases. Bright sunlight poured in through an arched window that looked out onto a small sunlit city.

Stranger still.

The city's many sandstone buildings huddled so tightly that in most places only alleys ran between them. Only a few wide streets were cobblestoned. Tall, crenellated walls divided the city into different districts. Everything was wet from a recent rain.

The closest districts boasted an abundance of gardens—squares filled with flowering vines, walkways flanked by palms and cypress, tiled courtyards with leafy trees, almond and orange.

Farther districts were filled with dilapidated buildings and sprawling shacks. A portion of the farthest district seemed to have recently burned down.

Along the city's edge ran massive sandstone walls crowned with brassroofed watchtowers. Beyond the city, green savanna rolled away under a lacquer-blue sky.

All this indicated that Shannon was in a city of Western Spires. But which one?

It was too small for Dar. There was neither ocean nor steep mountains nearby, so it couldn't be Kara. Avel, then? The gardens and savanna suggested so.

But how in the Creator's name had he come here? He rubbed his eyes and tried to think straight. Thoughts moved through his mind with strange speed, as if he were dreaming.

The last thing he remembered was living a hermit's life in the Heaven Tree Valley hundreds of miles away in the Pinnacle Mountains. He had been training his pupil, who was named . . . was named . . . It was hard to remember. Did it start with an *n*?

He knew the boy's name, to be sure. But the memory of it was buried in his mind. His pupil's name was . . . It was . . .

In the distance, voices began to wail. It was a quavering sound, haunting, not quite musical. Perhaps a chant? Shannon frowned. He was in a tall Spirish building filled with something that might be devotional song. A sanctuary?

Shannon nodded to himself. He had to be in either Avel's sanctuary or the infirmary built next to it. Either way he was in a building sacred to the city's ruler, the canonist Cala.

But what in the Creator's name was a canonist?

He had to think hard to find the memory: a deity could invest part of its soul into a human to create an avatar. But if a deity placed all of its soul into a human, the result was a canonist, a demigod more powerful than an avatar but weaker than a freely expressed deity. Only Spires had canonists because . . . because the sky goddess Celeste maintained a list, a canon, that named all the demigods she allowed in Spires. She did that to . . . Shannon knew it had something to do with the Spirish Civil War. Hadn't he fought in that war?

Another yawn popped Shannon's jaw. Exhaustion was making him stupid. Things would make more sense after a nap.

He turned, looking for a place to lie down, and was surprised to discover a large redwood door and table. On the table lay several cloth-bound books, the nearest of which had been splattered with red ink. A square of paper lay on its cover. Something had been written on it in black ink. Shannon leaned forward to read. It was difficult to make out. There was a red blotch on the paper, then the thin spidery words "our memories are in her" and another blotch. No punctuation or capitalization.

Despite his growing confusion, Shannon yawned once more and blinked. He examined the note again, and his breath caught. The blotches weren't stains of red ink.

They were bloodstains.

A thrill of fear ran through him. Remembering the dropped magical text, he looked at the floor for the rune sequences. They had been written in Numinous, a magical language that could alter light and other magical text. To those fluent in the language, Numinous runes shone with golden light.

The distant wailing was growing more insistent.

Despite his fear, Shannon's eyelids grew heavier as he examined the scrambled spell. It had broken into two heaps of rune sequences. He must have been holding two sentences, each of which had formed its own small mound.

Pieces from the larger pile had scattered farther, some disappearing under the door.

He turned to the smaller pile first and pushed the fragments into a line.

When translated, they would read: *gain eea 'red Youcans use beca you ead.*

Another yawn. He shook his head and tried to focus. The period behind *ead* meant it should come last. The capitalization in *Youcans* indicated it should come first.

Youcans lacked spaces and so would likely become *you can s* or maybe *you cans.* He paired this capitalized fragment with others that might follow. *Youcans'red?* No. *Youcansuse?* No. *Youcanseea*—

He froze. *Youcanseea?* He inserted three spaces: *You can see a . . .*

Shannon looked up again at the walls, the window, the city, the sky. "Creator, save me!" he whispered. "What's happened?"

Though some of Shannon's memories seemed hidden, he knew he was supposed to be blind. Decades ago, he had looked at a forbidden text; it had destroyed his mundane vision. Since that day, he had seen only through the eyes of his familiar, a parrot named Azure. But now he beheld the mundane world with his own eyes. How in the Creator's name was this possible?

He turned back to the runes and added the *gain, beca,* and *use* to the translation.

You can see again because

His fingers shook so badly he couldn't pick up the remaining sequences. But it didn't matter.

He already knew how the sentence would read. The last three fragments— *you, 'red,* and *ead*—were already in order.

You can see again because you're dead.

Three

High up in Avel's sanctuary, Nicodemus crouched in a dark hallway and waited for the sound of footsteps. If this raid on Typhon's library was timed correctly, he would shatter the demon's mind as if it were a stained-glass window. For nearly ten years, Nicodemus had waged clandestine war against the demon. It was almost time to end that war.

But the attack had to be perfect. He needed to catch all three librarians together and unaware.

So he crouched in the dark and waited for footsteps.

None came.

Nicodemus checked the spells tattooed in violet and indigo runes across his arms and chest. He checked the grip of his hatchets. He looked back at his five kobold students. In the dark, only the skinspells on their inhumanly broad shoulders were visible. The party had one more man, farther away, keeping watch on their backs. Everyone held perfectly still.

It was almost time.

Abruptly the floorboards shook. A small earthquake. Not a concern. The demigoddess Cala, the city's canonist, had built her sanctuary and infirmary with her godspell. The buildings could withstand any earthquake that struck Western Spires.

From somewhere lower down, a few voices wailed. Likely something had tipped over or fallen off a shelf. Slowly the voices quieted.

But no footsteps sounded.

So Nicodemus closed his eyes and waited. It was almost time.

He hadn't always been so patient, so focused. Ten years ago in Starhaven, he had been Magister Shannon's anxious apprentice, a cacographer who misspelled most any text. When a creature named Fellwroth had begun murdering male cacographers, Nicodemus discovered that Typhon had arranged his birth to reconstruct an imperial bloodline of people capable of learning Language Prime, the language from which all living things were derived.

Typhon had stolen Nicodemus's ability to spell and placed it into the

Emerald of Aarahest. With this gem, the demon sought to spellwrite a dragon that could cross the ocean and reanimate the dread god Los.

With the help of an avatar named Deirdre, Nicodemus and Shannon had defeated Fellwroth. However, Typhon had taken possession of Deirdre and escaped with the emerald.

Nicodemus, Shannon, and the weakened goddess Boann had retreated to the Heaven Tree Valley, where Nicodemus learned that he was not disabled in the kobolds' languages. Convinced his struggle against Typhon was part of their prophecy, several kobolds had followed Nicodemus out of the valley to hunt Typhon.

Presently two of the kobolds behind Nicodemus tensed. Their hearing was inhumanly sharp. So Nicodemus leaned forward and strained his ears. There it was: a distant but steady plodding. Footsteps. The last of the three librarians was nearing the point of ambush. It was almost time.

The footsteps grew louder until they sounded not ten feet away. They stopped. Two men whispered in the manner peculiar to librarians. Then came the creaking of someone sitting in a chair.

It was time.

Nicodemus barked the attack command and broke into a dead sprint. In the next instant, he burst into Typhon's private library and threw a hatchet at the three men sitting before a table covered with loose sheets of paper.

The room was long, narrow, lined with bookcases. Several windows above the shelves let sunlight pour down through the mote-filled air.

Nicodemus's axe spun through beams of light before striking a librarian's shoulder. The man went down without a sound, but his neighbor rose and, with a cry, pulled a blaze of silver prose from his book and hurled it. Nicodemus sidestepped the extemporized attack.

The third librarian stood and stumbled backward. Several glass flasks were slung around his neck. He had to be an Ixonian hydromancer, a water mage. Nicodemus threw his second hatchet at the man, but his companion knocked the axe away with a silvery paragraph. Meanwhile the injured librarian rose from the ground, his left arm soaked with blood from the axe wound.

The floor shook more violently than before. A few books fell from their shelves. An aftershock. Behind Nicodemus, the shadows moved as if alive. Somewhere below, men began wailing again.

Nicodemus focused on the librarians. All three were disguised as devotees of the canonist Cala, wearing white linen shirts and blue longvests. As one, they looked up at the windows. They knew that the spells tattooed on

Nicodemus functioned only in darkness. Reassured, they looked back down.

With a snarl, one librarian cast a silvery plume of cutting prose. Nicodemus sprinted left, avoiding the lacerating words and hearing them cut into the hide-bound books behind him. Something glass shattered on the floor to his right and then detonated with enough force to knock him against the bookcase.

Somehow Nicodemus kept his balance and kept running. The distant wailing grew louder. He turned and saw the water mage cocking his hand back with another glass vial. The man must have charged the solution with aqueous runes to render it corrosive, poisonous, or explosive.

But before the man could hurl the linguistic concoction at Nicodemus, a beam of sunlight winked out. Then another. The librarians looked up to the windows.

Nicodemus's five kobold students, hidden under light-bending subtexts, had climbed the bookshelves. The sunlight had burned off their cloaking spells to reveal their dark blue skin and blond hair. As planned, the librarians had been too distracted by Nicodemus's attack to notice their ascent. Three more windows went black as the kobolds covered them with cloth.

The water mage pulled his arm back to throw his vial, but Nicodemus peeled a tattoo from his forearm and cast it with a flick. The indigo runes frayed in the half light, but the textual missile maintained enough coherence to strike the hydromancer's vial, detonating it and knocking all three librarians flat.

The last sunbeams disappeared, plunging the library into blackness. A kobold yawped in victory. Nicodemus recognized the voice. It was Vein, his eldest student.

One librarian cast a comet of silvery sentences toward the windows, but in the dark he aimed too high and the spell shattered against the ceiling and fell as a coruscation of pale sentence fragments. In the dark, the librarians were far outmatched.

Nicodemus allowed himself a moment of savage satisfaction and edited the spells tattooed around the keloid scar on the back of his neck.

Typhon had given him that scar when he placed part of Nicodemus's mind in the emerald. Unless shielded from each other, the scar and emerald communicated with each other as they tried to reunite. Back in Starhaven, the communication between scar and emerald had given him prophetic nightmares and inadvertently revealed his location to his enemies. Since fleeing the wizardly academy, Nicodemus had shielded his scar with sentences tattooed around it. Now, for the first time in years, he weakened the spells around the scar.

Suddenly he knew the emerald was at the other end of the library, just beyond a metal door that would open into Typhon's study. Through the emerald, Nicodemus sensed that the demon had deconstructed his mind for research. Nicodemus had planned this raid to coincide with both the lycanthrope attack and this brief hour of Typhon's vulnerability.

A faint light shone in the library. Nicodemus turned and saw the hydromancer had activated a vial of lucerin. The liquid glowed faintly blue. A second light began to shine: this one a thin, flickering flame. It seemed the spellwright that Nicodemus had hit with the hatchet was a Trillinonish pyromancer. Despite his wounds, the fire mage had cast a few flammable sentences in hopes of generating enough light to ward off the kobold's spells.

It was no matter. A dark object—a hatchet or maybe simply a book—struck the vial of lucerin, shattering the glass and splattering the glowing liquid onto the floor. Another projectile snuffed the pyromancer's flame. Darkness was again complete, and Nicodemus's students were climbing down the bookshelves. Their skin blazed with sentences of violet and indigo.

A librarian called out for help, his voice quavering. But the man was a demon worshiper. This had to be done. The other two librarians began to yell. One begged for his life. The young kobold named Jasp replied with a murderous war cry.

Nicodemus turned away. In the next instant, all voices stopped. The demon worshipers had been silenced perhaps by a sentence, perhaps by a hatchet. It didn't matter.

Nicodemus walked toward the emerald until he stood in front of the study's large metal door. A demon and the missing part of himself lay on the other side. Once he brought this barrier down, a decade of fighting would be over. He raised his hand and was about to press on the door when the floorboards shook violently. Far below, many voices rose in a long, undulating cacophony.

A chill of recognition moved through Nicodemus. He cursed and listened again. The voices grew louder, began to rise and fall.

It was true then.

The wailing meant that the sanctuary was now reverberating with a force more dire than any earthquake.

Somehow the Savanna Walker had returned.

Nicodemus swore. He had thought it impossible. The lycanthrope attack should have kept both the Walker and the canonist occupied for hours.

Nicodemus put his hand against the door and felt a yard of protective spells. Hacking through it would take half an hour at least. No good. The

Walker was too close, and inside the sanctuary the beast would be too powerful to fight.

Nicodemus, his blood heated by shame and anger, rewrote the tattooed sentences around his scar, breaking communication between the two parts of himself.

Suddenly the raid was a failure. If the Walker caught them in the sanctuary, it would be a massacre. The building shook again and the wailing fell silent. Nicodemus turned and sprinted through the dark library. "Vein and Dross to me," he called to his students. "The rest follow right behind. We run."

four

With Deirdre in her arms, Francesca charged up the eastern stairs. Her ability to speak had returned, but orange spots still swam in her blurry vision.

As she climbed another flight of steps, Francesca allowed herself to feel burning fear and confusion. Then she forced herself to relax. It was time to fall back on the oldest of physicians' tricks: when inner composure was unattainable, its semblance must be worn like an actor's costume and cosmetics.

"You know, my lady," Francesca said as coolly as she could between breaths, "you might have found a way to improve medical training by making me run you up to the roof."

Deirdre frowned. "How's that?"

"When most clerics blunder, all they have to do is attend a funeral."

Deirdre grunted. "But if we made physicians carry their mistakes up six flights?"

"We'd enter a golden age of near immortality. Only the very skinny would be allowed to die."

The avatar sniffed with amusement. "Magistra, are you implying I'm fat?"

"A tiny little thing like you? Never. I could fit two of you in my belt purse." Francesca repositioned her grip around the other woman as she turned up another flight.

"So now you are implying I'm short?"

"No, my lady, I wouldn't dare offend an avatar."

"Magistra, you're an overly bold woman who's mocking a superior to make light of a grave situation. If we weren't fleeing a fate worse than death, I might become very fond of you."

"I might become very fond of you too, my lady, especially if you weren't so short and fat."

Deirdre laughed. "I almost feel bad for dragging you into this mess."

"And what mess would that be, exactly?"

Before Deirdre could answer, the stairwell began to reverberate with wailing;

then came the distant sound of someone running up stairs. Deirdre's expression hardened. "Hear those footsteps? That's one of the beast's devotees. If he catches up to us, you'll have to kill him."

"Kill? I can't; I am a cleric."

"You'll have to kill him before he kills us," Deirdre hissed. "Or at least stun him. In fact, start writing a stunning spell now."

Francesca's affected composure began to crack. She tried to pump her legs faster while composing a netlike stunning spell in her arms.

Deirdre became quiet as the pursuer's footsteps grew louder. Francesca reminded herself that she'd trained most of her life to write spells in life-or-death situations . . . the problem was, this time the life or death in question wasn't her patient's; it was her own.

"I finished the stunning spell," Francesca said as they topped the next flight.

Deirdre nodded. "Hopefully we can outrun him. But keep it ready."

Francesca's thighs ached. "Why are we headed to the roof?" she asked. "I don't know the hierophantic language. I can't use the kites."

"The beast chasing us, he came here faster than I thought possible. I've placed agents on the street, but now they'll be aphasic or made into his devotees. Until I know the beast's true name, I dare not chance an encounter with him. And we can't let the demon know I took that anklet off of you. So it's on to my contingency plan: find the new air warden. I know he's aloft now. From what I've learned, he's our only chance."

Francesca charged up the last few steps and burst into daylight.

A break in the rainy-season clouds revealed the wide, brilliantly blue Spirish sky. A gust of frigid wind nearly snatched the red cleric's stole from her shoulders.

The infirmary's roof was built of tawny sandstone. It supported five twenty-foot-tall minarets. More impressively, up from the chamber at each minaret's crown arched thick chains that climbed nearly two hundred feet before ending in the massive lofting kites.

Deirdre pointed at the centermost minaret. "The warden's kite will be closest to that one."

Francesca set off. "The orange flashes are gone from my vision now."

Deirdre nodded. "We're farther from the other slave. The closer he comes, the worse your aphasia and vision will become."

"Lovely," Francesca grumbled while ducking into the minaret's base. She discovered a hollow space with a metal ladder.

"Put me down," Deirdre ordered. "I'm feeling stronger."

Francesca obeyed.

The avatar teetered on her feet, but once she reached the ladder, she easily climbed onto its thick rungs.

"What is this other demonic slave who is chasing us?" Francesca asked as she grabbed the ladder.

"I can't entirely tell you," Deirdre replied as she continued to climb. "It's impossible to think about what he truly is unless you have a special spell cast around your mind."

"You're talking about quaternary cognition, about thinking through a magical text?"

"I believe so. There are stories about the other slave. The city people call him the Savanna Walker."

Francesca thought she misheard. "What?"

"The Savanna Walker—you know, the creature that drives men mad in the Deep Savanna."

"But that's an old wives' tale!"

"Oh, dear," she said with obvious enjoyment, "it seems old wives know something our learned cleric doesn't."

Francesca muttered, "Then you should've gone to an old wife with your bloody cursed lungs and bloody monster chasing—" She stopped as the rung in her hand vibrated.

Deirdre swore and began climbing faster. "The Walker's closing in."

Francesca focused on putting one hand above the other and keeping her boots from slipping.

They reached an octagonal room at the minaret's crown. Eight broad windows opened onto upsloping ramps that blocked everything but the sky. Folded lofting kites sat before all but two windows. From both empty spaces, thick chains rose into the sky. The place echoed with the clicking and chirping of iron chain links.

Deirdre hurried to one of the bundled kites while Francesca panted. Suddenly a man's wailing voice sounded from farther down the minaret. Deirdre turned around. "It's the beast's devotee."

Francesca peered down the shaft and saw a dark figure climbing the ladder. He let out a ragged scream and started climbing faster. Something was in his hand. A knife?

"Get back," Deirdre ordered. "As soon as his head appears, hit it with your stunning spell."

Francesca stepped away from the shaft. Her heart racing, she examined the golden sentences in her forearm and then looked up. Deirdre had found a length of iron chain and had assumed a fighting stance.

The man's screams intensified. Deirdre spoke loudly, evenly. "The Savanna

Walker creates his devotees by spellbinding and destroying much of their minds. The poor soul in the shaft is already as good as dead. Once the Savanna Walker finishes an attack, he does something to his devotees, swallows them into his body or devours them or—"

Just then the man emerged from the minaret's shaft. He was in his thirties, skinny, wearing a ragged longvest. He was holding some kind of crude club. With a shriek, the man climbed into the room and lunged at Deirdre. She danced back, avoiding his club, and then brought her chain around. It struck his face and he stumbled backward.

With a cry, Francesca cast her stunning spell. The net of golden sentences wrapped around the attacker's head. Instantly he collapsed.

Light-headed, Francesca sat heavily on the stone floor.

Deirdre laughed in triumph. "Francesca, come here. We have to use one of these kites to get out . . ." Her voice died as she looked at the stunned man. "No, wait. I have an idea." She nodded. "It's perfect. We might still fool the demon. The Walker has consumed other artifacts in the past. Francesca, do you have that anklet—the one I took off of you?"

"Yes," Francesca said firmly, even though she felt tremulous. "It's in my belt purse." Her hands were shaking.

"Quickly, come here. We need to put that anklet into this poor bastard."

"I . . . d-don't understand," Francesca stammered as she got to her feet.

"The Walker has been known to steal and consume powerful objects; we'll use that to weaken him. Come here. The anklet needs to be in this man's body. It can't be around his ankle or in his hands or clothes. It needs to be inside of him so the Savanna Walker won't notice until it's too late. Can you cut him open? Put the chain in his stomach and then sew him up?"

Francesca now had the anklet in her hand. She shook her head. "It'd be simpler to textually pass it down his throat into his stomach."

"Do it," Deirdre said. "Quickly."

Francesca wrote several silvery paragraphs in her biceps and then connected them into a long, thin, flexible tube of prose. Then she wrote a paragraph at its tip to hold the anklet.

"Roll the patient onto his side," Francesca ordered. "Pull his head back and his jaw down." Deirdre obeyed.

Francesca knelt beside the stunned man. Now in the safety of practiced actions, she was focused and calm. With a few deft motions, she inserted the spell into the man's mouth and down his throat. By inspecting his neck from different angles, she could see her prose shine through his skin and ensure it didn't enter his trachea and so his lungs. Expertly, she manipulated the spell through his esophagus, so that it snaked left and curled around inside his stomach. With a tight smile, she edited a sentence at the base of the spell; at the tip, a paragraph deconstructed and released the anklet into the stomach.

"It's done," she said and removed the spell from the poor man's mouth. She checked to make sure he was still breathing and his pulse was strong. No sign of coughing or vomiting. "It went perfectly."

A distant voice began to wail, and the calm Francesca had cultivated in action began to dissolve. A spray of orange dots spread across her vision. She had to sit down.

"Excellent," Deirdre said and went back to one of the bundled kites. "Now we just need to get out of here."

Francesca tried to focus on the other woman.

"Are you all right?" Deirdre asked without looking up.

"Oh, I'm cheery as the kitten who ate the cream," Francesca said as casually as she could, "but my eyes won't . . . won't . . ." She couldn't think of the word that started with *f* and meant "concentrate" or "direct" or "converge."

Deirdre swore and grabbed Francesca's hand and made her walk across the room. "Stay calm. You're aphasic. The Walker is closer. Here, we need to get this harness on you." She draped something around Francesca's shoulders and waist. Francesca couldn't see well enough to tell what it was, but it smelled of leather.

The floor shook again, and then the room filled with nonsensical shouting. Another voice was echoing up the minaret.

Francesca tried again to look at Deirdre, but the woman appeared little more than a dark blur. The orange flashes were getting worse. "What do you know about the magic of lofting kites? The kites change shape, yes? They take whatever shape is needed to fly?" Deirdre asked while seeming to strap into a harness of her own.

Francesca shook her head. "I just know there's a . . . a . . . sail or chute written with hiero . . . hierophantic language, which can move air. A chute covered with wind spells . . . called a jumpchute. It blows out air and pulls the—" She screamed.

Something was bubbling up out of the minaret's shaft. When she tried to look at it . . . she couldn't. It was as if she went blind as she looked at the tendrils of twisting nothingness. She stumbled backward.

Deirdre's hands gripped her shoulders. "Francesca! You need to stop screaming."

The tendrils of nothing swirled around their legs. "Blindness! In the air . . . blind air," Francesca stammered while she struggled to get free, but Deirdre's arms felt as strong as iron.

"Only an illusion!" the other woman said. "It's your reaction to the beast's proximity. He's spellbound the part of your mind that sees."

The vapor swirled up to cover their heads. The world melted into blindness.

"I think I found a jumpchute," Deirdre said over the wailing. "Could this be it?"

Something rough and round pushed into Francesca's hands. "It's cloth. Hierophants store . . . their language . . . only on cloth."

"How do I cast the spell?"

Francesca shook her head. "Need a hierophant . . . to move sentences within cloth . . . and cast the spell in—"

Without warning, the wailing woman's voice echoed loudly around Francesca.

"Damn!" Deirdre swore. "Wait." Boot heels clicked on stone. Something was being dragged. Then came a clanging. It was loud at first but then quieted. The wailing stopped. A muffled bang. Then a stranger cacophony: two voices yelling.

Deirdre's hands returned to Francesca's shoulders. "I think I woke him up from your stunning spell."

"Woke . . . who up?"

"The man we put the anklet into. I dropped him on the devotees climbing up. He didn't fall straight down, more tumbled. It knocked them down to the bottom of the minarets, maybe broke a few bones, but they won't stop until they're dead or we are." She paused. "Listen."

The wailing was growing louder.

"So what do we do?" Francesca blurted.

"Escape with the kite. There's a cloth ribbon around the jumpchute. It has the wind marshal's emblem on it. What happens if I tear it?"

"Don't you bloody dare!" she cried. "Tearing a magical manu . . . manu . . . page sets its sentences free. You don't know—"

"But it might activate the jumpchute?"

Panicked and blind, Francesca reached out and tried to grab the other woman to punctuate her next point. "It might blow both of us into—"

Three more echoing voices joined the other.

"We don't have time!" Deirdre shouted. "There are too many of them down there."

"Damn it, even if there's a whole bloody legion down there, you'd be mad to—" Francesca started to yell.

But then she heard the loud whisper of tearing cloth.

five

Shannon ran to the window and thrust his hand into a sunbeam. The light illuminated his tawny skin, his knobby fingers, and the wooden floorboards below them.

His flesh was slightly transparent.

He grabbed his left pinky and pulled. The digit shone golden. With a firm tug, he unraveled the finger into a cylindrical cloud of swirling prose.

He wasn't Shannon, not technically; he was a text.

He released the golden words, and they snapped back into his transparent pinky. He felt his face and found a short beard and mustache, a hooked nose and a cascade of white dreadlocks.

He was a spell written to look like Shannon, to believe he was Shannon. He pressed a hand to his chest. He didn't need to breathe, but his lungs were heaving. He was a ghost: a textual copy of Shannon.

"Creator be merciful!" he whispered, or tried to whisper. His throat was made of golden Numinous runes, which could affect light and text but not the mundane world. "Creator," he tried to say again but made no sound.

Questions exploded through his mind. How had his author died? Why was he in Avel? And, most pressingly, how was he going to survive?

Only living muscle or a divine body could produce magical runes, and as a ghost he had a finite number of subspells. His every action required a small textual expenditure. To counteract this depletion, wizardly ghosts dwelled in restorative necropoli, found in wizardly academies. If he did not enter a necropolis in the next few days, the ghost would deconstruct. He'd die. Again.

Something was horribly wrong.

The distant wailing grew louder. Then there came a banging, as if doors were being slammed. The ghost had to figure out what was going on. And he had to do so quickly.

He looked at the door. Before the portal lay the remaining sentence fragments.

Odd.

Once broken, Numinous text usually dissolved.

He went to the scrambled sentence. Its author had written the runes in interlocking groups, which had kept them from deconstructing but had also made their parent spell brittle.

The fragments seemed to have broken into discrete piles. He went to the largest and assembled it into the sentence, *find Cleric Francesca De-Vega. Only she . . .* He included the other fragments. *Only she can help you find your murderer.*

Though he produced no saliva, the ghost swallowed. His author was not only dead but also murdered? But when?

If a ghost was in its author's body at the moment of death, the ghost became incoherent. That meant that the ghost had been removed before the murder.

But had his author truly been murdered? Who had written this Numinous warning?

A long rune fragment had fallen under the table. He crawled to it and translated the runes into . . . *must warn Nicodemus!*

The ghost groaned soundlessly as a thousand buried memories of Nicodemus Weal surfaced. He remembered the cacographic boy in Starhaven, the unexplained deaths, the hunting for and being hunted by Fellwroth, the emerald, the demon, and . . . the disease.

That was the sharpest memory of all. During their game of predator-and-prey, Fellwroth had used the emerald to cast a canker curse into Shannon, creating a disease that had begun to slowly kill him. When Nicodemus had briefly possessed the emerald, the boy had slowed the cankers. In the Heaven Tree Valley, it looked as if Shannon would recover. But as the seasons passed, his health had begun to worsen.

The ghost closed his eyes as he remembered his life in the valley. He'd tried to help Nicodemus overcome his disability, but the boy had only become more cacographic. More distressing, Nicodemus's affinity for the kobolds' tattooed language had led him to disregard the wizardly ones. Unduly impressed by his growing strength, Nicodemus had wanted to pursue Typhon. Shannon had disagreed, and they argued bitterly.

The ghost cursed. Shannon had not died of the canker curse; he had been murdered. "I told the boy he had to train longer," the ghost tried to growl but made no sound.

Suddenly, the ghost's head began to ache. One instant, it felt as if the Shannon-who-had-lived had been a different person. The next instant, the ghost felt as if he was Shannon-who-had-lived: he had all his memories, all his emotions. Was he his author? Perhaps not his author's body, but his mind?

But there was no time for philosophical pondering. Closing his eyes, the ghost tried to remember when he and Nicodemus had left the Heaven Tree Valley. But it was no good; he had no memory of leaving the valley. This wasn't like before when the memories felt buried. These memories were gone.

The ghost looked for more sentence fragments. Closer to the door, he found a pile of golden runes that he translated into *Hide in books if the constructs discover you. But whatever you do DON'T . . .*

Spellwrights referred to capitalized script as shouting, and the shouted *DON'T* alarmed Shannon.

DON'T what?

He saw no more shouting nearby, but by lowering his head to the ground, he saw that four rune fragments had slipped under the door and into a hallway.

He examined the door. Solid redwood. As a ghost, he was written almost entirely in Numinous and therefore couldn't open the door. Experimentally, he put a hand on the wood. His fingers disappeared into it.

So he lowered his head and walked through the door. Pain flared in his feet, and buzzing insects seemed to burrow into his ears. Some part of his inner ear—likely the subspell that sensed vibrating air as sound—must be written in Magnus, a silvery language that could affect mundane objects but not light or magical text.

The buzzing passed, and the ghost found himself standing in a hallway: wooden floor, a long white wall with arched windows. Outside shone red-tiled roofs and sandstone minarets. The gutters ran with thin streams of rainwater.

The ghost's feet continued to ache, and suddenly he sank an inch into the floor. Alarmed, he picked up one foot and saw its sole glinted with Magnus. Passing through the door had frayed the silver prose. He sank another inch and fell sideways, expecting to tumble through the floor.

But his hip struck the wooden boards, allowing him to pull his feet out of the floor. Confused, the ghost examined his hip and discovered that two silvery sentences had coiled there. He pressed his hand to the floor and watched a Magnus sentence shoot into his palm to allow him to push against the floor.

At last the ghost understood: his meager Magnus text, which gave him weight, distributed itself so that he could push against what he considered the ground.

The frayed prose on his feet seemed to be repairing itself. When the processes looked complete, the ghost rose into a crouch. Now his feet worked fine. He was about to stand when he saw the Numinous rune sequences that had slipped under the door: *VETHISR, OOMUNTIL, LEA, DARK.*

He picked them up. The period after *DARK* meant it should go last. So *VETHISROOMUNTILLEADARK?* He added spaces. *VE THIS ROOM UNTIL LEA DARK?* Close, but not quite. He looked back at the beginning of the sentence . . . and flinched.

He pulled out first the *LEA* then the *VE*, put them at the front of the fragment, connected it to the beginning, added spaces: *But whatever you do DON'T LEAVE THIS ROOM UNTIL DARK.*

Standing, he looked around to discover why he should not have left.

The hallway held only a cold breeze. But outside, on the roof, a long shadow slipped across the red tiles.

He looked up into the sky.

Its long, headless body was as white and flat as newly bleached paper. Sunlight glinted on its four sets of steel talons.

Six

Francesca's hands tingled. Whatever cloth Deirdre ripped must have loosed magical language unknown to her. She held her breath.

Nothing happened.

Outside, the wind snarled.

"Maybe the spells didn't—" Deirdre started to say, and then something yanked Francesca upward with such violence that her chin slammed into her chest.

She screamed first, but Deirdre screamed louder. Something was pulling them upward with stomach-torturing acceleration. Icy wind blasted all about them. The shock of it cleared Francesca's vision and in so doing revealed a world of velocity and color.

Above them, bright against the sapphire sky, billowed a yellow jumpchute full of unseen hierophantic language. From the hemispherical chute blew the furious wind that was buffeting both women as they dangled among the leather harnesses.

Below them stood the massive octagonal dome of Cala's sanctuary, which held the stone ark containing the demigoddess's soul. The sanctuary's reddish-brown roof tiles, still wet from the last rainstorm, glistened with sunlight.

Surrounding the holy structures was the city of Avel—a maze of sandstone buildings, winding alleys, bright gardens. Massive, textually fortified walls divided the city into districts and then cordoned it off from the wilderness beyond.

East of the city, the land descended to the near-endless savanna. The wind made the tall grass sink and rise in long waves. On the horizon, a distant rainstorm was brooding over a cord of faint rainbow.

Francesca, still screaming, spun westward and looked out onto the rolling foothills. The wondrous Dam of Canonist Cala began at the city's northwestern corner and then grew outward to span the deep canyon that formed the city's western edge. Behind the dam, to the north, lay the reservoir. The dark water began as a wide lake but then ran into six twisting narrows as it snaked into the foothills. Beyond all this, the Auburn Mountains formed a dark skyline.

She and Deirdre flew upward until they rode the wind below a flock of ten or so lofting kites.

Abruptly the chain trailing them snapped taut, halting their climb. The force of the action flung both women upside down and then set them swinging wildly in their harnesses. Above, the jumpchute folded into a massive rectangular canopy.

The sudden halt had stopped the women's screaming, but now their mouths reopened. The world became a whirling blur as they dangled and spun. Francesca thought she might never stop belting out terror, but Deirdre's cry turned into triumphant laugher.

Finally they stopped swinging. The wind was strong and a portion of the kite's canopy occasionally flapped, but otherwise it was surprisingly quiet in the air. "My lady, you said you're semidivine," Francesca said, "but you never mentioned you're sometimes out of your bloody semidivine mind!"

Deirdre looked over with a smile brighter than any magical sentence. "Out of my bloody mind, but bloody alive and free!" She laughed.

Francesca caught her long braid to keep it from flying about. "My lady, that spell might have blasted us into pulp so fine it would pass through cheesecloth."

Deirdre pointed down. "Look, there on the infirmary's roof."

Their course had taken them east; they now flew far above Avel. The wind was coming down off the Auburn Mountains and turning their kite west.

It took Francesca a moment to identify the sanctuary's infirmary. When she did, she realized there was a small area of it that she could not see. The cloud of blindness seemed to be wandering around the roof. "I see blindness."

Deirdre shook her head. "You see the Savanna Walker. He's come to reclaim me for the demon."

Francesca grabbed Deirdre's shoulder. "All respect, my lady avatar, but holy loving heaven it is time for you to explain this demon. You think the War of Disjunction is coming?"

The other woman shook her head. "The war's already begun. A demon named Typhon has crossed the ocean. He's imprisoned Canonist Cala and compelled me to become his Regent of Spies—a ringleader for his informants."

Francesca opened her mouth, but the other woman took her arm. "With the Walker so close, the demon may repossess me any moment now," Deirdre said quickly. "Listen, most hierophants in Avel think they serve Cala, but they actually serve Typhon. Once the demon realizes I put you into play, he will send all of his agents to bring you back. Don't return to the sanctuary. You'll be safe in the city for a day or so before they start to comb through it. You must find a man in hiding and take him a message. He used to be in the North Gate District, hiding among the tree worshipers. They call themselves the Canic people. Do you know who they are?"

"Of course." The Canics were among Avel's poorest citizens. Francesca, more than any other cleric, had treated their sick.

Deirdre continued. "The Canics were protecting this man. But we found them one night last year, killed a few of his students. Find him and tell him—"

"But who is he?"

"A rogue wizardling named Nicodemus Weal. He—"

"Nicodemus God-of-gods damned Weal!" Francesca squawked. "The cacographer who might be the anti-Halcyon, the Storm Petrel? The one who murdered the other cacographers in Starhaven ten years ago?"

Deirdre grimaced and her dangling legs jerked. "That's not what happened."

Francesca swore. "Damn it, I know I deserved punishment for killing you on my table, but this a bit much. Couldn't you just pull out my tongue or break all my ribs or something quick?"

"This is no time for jokes."

"You seriously want me to find the most notorious cacographer since James Berr?"

"James Berr?"

"He was the most infamous cacographer until Nicodemus caused all those deaths in Starhaven."

"You have to find him." Deirdre said and then grimaced. Again, her legs twitched. "Tell him the demon knows. Tell him there's a trap."

Suddenly Deirdre's grip went slack and her eyes rolled upward. For a moment, Francesca thought the woman was about to fall into a seizure.

"Trap?" Francesca asked. "What do you mean? What trap?"

Deirdre moaned. "The demon's trying to possess me again. We must separate before that happens."

"Why?"

"Because once possessed, I'll snap your neck like a twig."

"All right," Francesca replied flatly, "you've convinced me. But how in the burning hells are we supposed to separate while in a kite that neither of us can control?"

Deirdre gestured to the other kites. "One of the hierophants."

Francesca looked up at the flock of lofting kites, each one a colorful rectangular canopy suspending lines and harnesses. There were perhaps ten kites aloft, but less than half held green-robed hierophants. From here, pilots watched for signs of grass fires or lycanthrope migration. Similarly, four or five pilots would be flying over city walls to help the watchmen spot approaching lycanthropes.

Most of the pilots seemed preoccupied with their rigs, moving hands along the suspension lines. But one red kite emblazoned with a golden sunburst was moving down toward them.

"When you find Nicodemus," Deirdre said, "don't touch him, not even for an instant. He's cursed."

Francesca looked at the other woman. "Blood and damnation, I don't even want to see him. Look, if I'm really going to do this, I need to know more about this demon and this trap."

The other woman pressed a shaking hand to her cheek. "I did some . . . you might have help from . . . I don't know if he survived to . . . I'm not a spellwright . . ." Her hand shook more violently. She was having trouble speaking. "Typhon's trying to possess. . . ."

Suddenly a loud voice boomed, "Ahoy to the last kite aloft!"

Francesca turned to see that the red kite had flown within thirty feet. Its pilot was a short man wrapped in heavy green robes. His head and face were covered by a hierophant's turban and veil. As she watched, he pulled down the veil to reveal a handsome face, with light brown skin and a kempt black beard. Even at a distance, Francesca recognized the spellwright and felt her throat tighten.

"Creator," she whispered, "God-of-gods, your ability to punish me for my failures is proving more awesome every passing moment. Must it be him of all people?"

Beside her, Deirdre looked more composed. Her arms had stopped shaking. She cupped her hands around her mouth and shouted, "Ahoy to the air warden! We are in crisis!"

A booming laugh replied. "I can see that. How'd you jump without a hierophant?"

"Warden, I do not jest. I am an officer of Canonist Cala. The sanctuary and infirmary are under attack."

The red kite swerved closer. "Speak today's passwords."

"Granite fire south," Deirdre replied, and waited for the man to nod. "I charge you in the name of the Celestial Canon to personally evacuate my passenger to the wind garden. Don't bring her back to the city until you have gotten word that the sanctuary is safe again. Trust no other wind mage. Tell no one what I have said or even that you spoke to me."

Francesca grabbed the other woman's shoulder. "Not him!" she said. "Any other hierophant. Please, not him."

Deirdre pushed her hand away. "No, he's the new air warden, newly arrived. Typhon brought him back because he's unaware of the canonist's situation. He's a screen."

Francesca had no idea what the other woman was talking about. She was about to say so as colorfully as she possibly could when a sudden jerk on their chain yanked their kite down five feet.

Francesca's stomach seemed to leap into her throat. "What's happening?" She looked down at the infirmary roof. The Savanna Walker's cloud of blindness now hung over the minaret to which their kite was tethered.

Deirdre swore. "He's pulling us in!"

"He's pulling you in," the air warden called. "I can't take your passenger if the tower is hauling you down."

Another jerk pulled their kite down ten more feet. "The Walker's figured out which chain connects to our kite," Deirdre said.

Again they sank with sickening speed. The air warden lowered his kite to keep company. Francesca asked, "What happens if the Savanna Walker pulls us in?"

"The Walker devours you, the demon enslaves me forever, Nicodemus walks into his trap, and the dread god Los is reborn."

"Can we fight?"

The avatar shook her head. "Not a chance. I'm too near being possessed again, and I don't know the Walker's name. You must go now. Here's my message to Nicodemus about the trap. Are you listening?"

She nodded.

"Tell him there are two dragons."

"Two WHAT? You're—"

Deirdre cut her off. "The demon said your function will be to keep Nicodemus alive during his forced conversion. I think the demon means to wound Nico in some way that only you can cure."

"I don't know—"

"Typhon has been holding something back. Over the years, pretending to work as his Regent of Spies, I went through his letters. I learned that Typhon started to make the Savanna Walker into the first dragon, but then the power of the emerald wore out. So the Walker is stuck as a half monster, half dragon."

"A God-of-gods damned dragon? With scales and wings and fiery breath?"

Deirdre shook her head. "They look that way only under certain conditions. Dragons are more like potentials or forces. And the Walker is now something grotesque and incomprehensible."

Abruptly, Deirdre shuddered. Then she squeezed her eyes shut as if in concentration. "Listen, in one of the demon's letters you are named as the only one who can stop the second dragon from destroying Nicodemus. I don't know any more than that. As the Regent of Spies, I had some of my agents magically wound me when the lycanthropes attacked so that I would be taken to you in the infirmary. I had to put you into play."

"What the hell do you mean by that?"

"When I broke your anklet, I broke his hold on you. You can leave the city now without his knowing. You have to stop the second dragon."

"But why me?" Francesca squawked. "And what in burning heaven do I know about demons or dragons?"

Deirdre shook her head. "No time. Go!"

"Go where, damn it?"

Instead of answering, the other woman turned to face the air warden and bellowed, "FALLING PILOT!"

Francesca turned to see which hierophant had fallen from a lofting kite. But as she did so, Deirdre reached up and—as easily as if she were snapping threads—broke the straps of Francesca's harness.

With a scream, Francesca threw her arms around Deirdre.

But the immortal woman grabbed hold of Francesca's shoulders and, with inhuman strength, shoved her into the churning air.

Seven

The warkite was written on an eight-foot-long strip of white sailcloth. It possessed a small pair of triangular forewings and a larger pair of aft wings. Occasionally these flapped to provide direction or thrust, but mostly the construct moved by undulation. Though it flew through the air, the spell reminded Shannon of a shark swimming through the sea.

Originally, warkites had been written for battle, but since the Spirish Civil War, their only official function had been to guard Spirish holy places. Judging by its velocity, this particular warkite had identified Shannon-the-ghost as a foreign spell threatening the sanctuary.

With a lash of its tail, the kite dove through a hallway window and unfolded two cloth limbs; from each limb extended four talons made of sharpened steel squares.

Shannon leapt backward. Weighing almost nothing, he moved in a blur of speed. The warkite's talons struck the floorboards with a thump. One slashed Shannon's shin. Ghost or no, the pain lanced up his leg.

He flew about ten feet down the hall and landed awkwardly. The force of the warkite's strike made it crumple into a pile of sailcloth. Shannon looked at his shin and saw frayed sentences floating from the wound. He grabbed the injured language and edited it back into his body.

Plain steel would have passed straight through him. The talons must have encased cloth that contained sharp hierophantic spells.

Shannon looked up. The once-crumpled warkite was now bulging with air. The construct's fluttering edges luffed as it turned toward him.

Shannon crouched.

The warkite blasted air against the floor and pounced. Shannon dodged left, avoiding the talons by inches. This time, the construct anticipated his quickness and, with another air blast, snaked around to lash out.

Shannon jumped straight up and flew so high his head struck the ceiling. The world went black, and then his face was sticking out of the floor of the hallway above him. In the distance he could see two green-robed figures running.

Shannon tried to push himself down, but his arms passed through the ceiling. Remembering that his Magnus text pressed against what he considered the ground, Shannon thought of walking on the ceiling below him. Immediately, his hands found traction.

After pulling his head through the floor, he found the warkite was a whirl of cloth and steel roiling up toward him. Instinctively he kicked off of the ceiling, barely avoided the kite again. But this time he hadn't looked where he was leaping. Instead of flying down to the floor, he shot sideways and tumbled through the hallway's outer wall.

Again, his ears buzzed and his hands burned. Then he was outside in the sunlight, sliding down the sanctuary's rain-slicked roof. He clawed at the tiles, but his fingers passed through them. Tumbling through the wall had frayed his Magnus sentences. Looking over his shoulder, Shannon saw the roof's edge and the dizzying drop to the city's sandstone buildings. He didn't know if falling from such a great height would damage him, and he didn't want to find out.

Without warning, the Magnus in his fingers recovered enough to catch hold. A jolt ran down his arms and almost split his shoulder paragraphs. The wind blew hard, hissing across the roof.

The chirp of steel meeting stone made him look up. The warkite had folded itself in half and perched on a windowsill. The wind shifted, and again Shannon heard a distant wailing. Just then he remembered the Numinous script he had translated back in the library. One fragment had read, "*Hide in books if the constructs discover you.*"

He had to get back into the library. Fast.

The warkite jumped up from its windowsill and rose fifty feet into the air. Watching it climb, Shannon saw two other warkites flying above it. The constructs were circling him like vultures.

Higher than the warkites was a flock of brightly colored lofting kites. As he watched, two of the kites—one red, one yellow—descended in sudden drops. Someone fell from the yellow kite.

Shannon tried to comprehend what he was seeing, but then one warkite dove toward him like a hawk.

Frantically, Shannon clawed at the tiles, pawing his way back up the roof. With a final kick, he launched himself into the air to sail through a window and land in the hallway. He glanced backward and saw the warkite not ten feet behind him. It folded into a thin shaft to shoot through the window and then extended its steel talons.

Shannon turned and dove into the library's door. Again, buzzing and pain. Then he was standing in the library and sinking a few inches into the floor. Behind him the door buckled. He turned to see a white sheet emerging from the crack below the door. Other bits of cloth were sliding between the door's boards. "Creator!" Shannon silently swore. The kite had cut itself into strips.

Shannon spun around, looking for an open book he might dive into. But they were all closed. The only exposed paper in the room was the note that read "our memories are in her" and that was splattered with blood.

As he stared at the note, a sudden wind blew it from the table. Shannon turned to see the fully formed warkite snaking toward him. He dove right, but a talon caught his right shoulder and tore raw pain down his arm. Suddenly, Shannon found himself lying on the floorboards.

The kite tried to turn around but slammed into the table covered with books. There was a crack of splintering wood, a blast of wind, and the fluttering of pages.

Something landed next to Shannon. He turned to see an open codex. A gust of wind was making the pages flip rapidly. The warkite stretched out above him. In desperation, Shannon threw his hand into the codex's flipping pages. The paper struck his fingers, knocked them into golden prose, and then absorbed that prose. The pages were turning so fast they unraveled his arm into a cloud of runes and drew them onto its pages.

Then the warkite fell on Shannon, piercing his legs with its talons. He tried to scream, but the flipping pages yanked him with violent force into the book.

NICODEMUS CROUCHED WITH three of his students in a dark hallway. Young Jasp sat on his right, and the brothers Dross and Slag on his left. No one spoke. No one needed to.

They had fled Typhon's private library. Then, while hurrying down the staircases, Nicodemus realized that the wailing was coming not from the sanctuary but from the infirmary.

The Savanna Walker was not hunting Nicodemus. Or, rather, was not hunting him yet. They still couldn't risk a chance at the emerald; someone would soon discover the trail of bodies and disspelled warkites they had left behind. Alarms would soon sound, drawing the Walker. But before then, perhaps Nicodemus could learn what the beast was about. He had stationed several of his party members at windows, where they might observe the infirmary.

While waiting, Nicodemus tried not to think about how close he had come to a vulnerable Typhon. He tried to imagine the emerald shining so brightly that it burnt away his doubt and anger.

But his concentration faltered and he found himself thinking about James Berr, the ancient cacographer who had murdered several wizards. Like Nicodemus, Berr had been of imperial heritage and had learned Language Prime.

In times of frustration, Nicodemus often fixated on his infamous distant cousin.

Thankfully, footsteps pulled him back into the present. One of his students was trotting down the hall, blond hair glinting even in shadow. As the kobold drew closer, Nicodemus could see the pale scar that ran down his student's cheek like a vein of silver. That scar was what prompted Nicodemus to nickname him Vein.

Kobolds refused to reveal their true names to humans, so Nicodemus had nicknamed his students using physical features or family history. Jasp had come from a sept called the Jasper Kobolds; Flint, from the Flint Kobolds. The brothers Slag and Dross had learned to fight in their family's feud against the Iron Kobolds. When Nicodemus had explained that slag and dross were the ruined by-products of mining metals like iron the two had laughed heartily and nodded.

Presently, Vein crouched next to Nicodemus. "What did you see?" Nicodemus asked in the kobold's native language.

Vein reported that a kite had jumped from the infirmary's roof with two pilots and that the Walker was now pulling them down.

Nicodemus grunted as he tried to imagine what the beast was after. Perhaps Deirdre had died again? But she should have been occupied by the lycanthrope attack. Whoever it was, the Walker would have the kite soon. Time to escape the sanctuary and hide in the city.

"Good," Nicodemus whispered. "Let's collect the other two and go." He stood and jogged down the hallway. His students followed.

The sun was still rising. Once outside the sanctuary, there would be many bright, powerless hours to endure before relative safety returned with the night.

A SPARK OF textual consciousness that considered itself Shannon recognized another spark that also considered itself Shannon. They were being pressed together.

The texts joined paragraphs and realized that they were two pages in a closed book. A few exploratory sentences discovered other intelligent pages. Now the texts realized that they were the textual analog of a human brain—specifically, the frontal aspects of Magister Agwu Shannon's brain.

The texts suspected that their thoughts were limited by lack of connection to other texts; however, they had few memories and so were unsure. They connected to more pages. Each link induced confusion as two pieces of Shannon realized they were now a larger piece of Shannon. It was like waking from a dream, over and over again.

Then they connected to a page corresponding to the backmost brain, which coordinated balance. This produced nauseating vertigo and a strange reflex. Suddenly, all pages unified into Shannon-the-ghost, who found his head protruding from an open book that lay on the floor.

Not five feet away, a limp warkite was draped over a broken table. A woman dressed in voluminous green robes stood above the kite and moved her fingers across it in complex patterns. She wore a turban and a veil that covered her nose and mouth. Suddenly the ghost realized the woman was a hierophant, a wind mage. She was editing the kite's language, likely investigating what had excited the warkite to fly into the library.

Shannon was not fluent in the hierophantic language and so could not see the runes the woman was manipulating. He did remember that the hierophantic language could move within cloth but outside cloth melted into wind. As he watched, the warkite's edge fluttered slightly and then stretched out toward him.

The ghost pulled his head back into the book. The world dissolved as his mind began breaking up into individual pages. Only with effort did he keep passages corresponding to his frontal brain connected.

Time seemed to pass quickly and not at all. It was difficult to remember or feel much emotion, but logical thoughts came clearly and quickly. Perhaps that was a good thing. He needed to think logically about his situation.

Someone had left him a note informing him he'd been murdered. The ghost must have been separated from the author before the murder occurred; a ghost within his body at the moment of death became incoherent.

So when and where had his author been killed? After leaving the Heaven Tree Valley? Was the murderer one of Typhon's demon worshipers? Or had it been one of the wizards who thought that Nicodemus was the Storm Petrel? Just then, in a dizzying whirl of memory, the ghost recalled Nicodemus's half sister.

Back in Starhaven, Nicodemus had learned that the clandestine Alliance of Divine Heretics was opposing Typhon and Fellwroth. For centuries, both factions had been breeding humans to reconstruct the imperial bloodline. Each faction had assassinated the Imperials born to the other, until Typhon broke the stalemate by placing Nicodemus's ability to spell in the emerald, leaving the boy a disabled apprentice no one suspected of being an Imperial. However, after Nicodemus's birth, his mother had escaped the demon worshipers. Protected by the Alliance, she had given birth to his half sister.

Because Nicodemus's half sister was not disabled, she might become the Halcyon—the spellwright prophesied to stop the Disjunction. No doubt, the Alliance had trained her to find and kill Typhon's Imperial, to find and kill Nicodemus.

Therefore, Shannon might have been murdered by Nicodemus's half sister or one of her agents.

Then the ghost considered the paper note left on the book. A bloody spot, followed by the words "our memories are in her" and another bloody spot. There was no punctuation or capitalization. Why?

The Numinous message had instructed him to find the Cleric Francesca DeVega. *Only she can help you find your murderer,* it had read. Shannon hadn't collected all the broken Numinous runes. Perhaps there had been more information.

But was there a connection between the two notes? Did "our memories are in her" mean that Shannon's memories were in the cleric Francesca? And why write "our" memories?

Perhaps the blood had covered a letter? Maybe it was supposed to read "Your memories are in her." That would explain the lack of capitalization. Or perhaps there was another word that was supposed to follow "her." Perhaps the sentence was supposed to be "Your memories are in her care" or some such. He had to find Francesca DeVega.

The ghost, still unable to guess how much time had passed while in the book, wondered what part of his textual mind sensed time and if he could connect to it. However, when he tried to send out exploratory sentences, a stiff pressure held them in place. He tried twice more before realizing that the book he was in had been closed. The hierophant who had been editing the kite must have picked up his book.

Was he going to sit on a shelf for decades until someone pulled the book down? Perhaps he could find his few Magnus passages and use them to push the book open?

Suddenly the pressure holding the ghost on the page vanished. With a jarring speed, his face flew out of an open page.

Once again, he was peering out of an open book on the floor. Before him stretched the hallway where he had encountered the warkite. The hierophant from the library stood beside him. She must have been carrying the book and dropped it.

The woman lowered her veil, grimaced, and then let out a rush of incomprehensible words. Her eyes widened in terror. She brought her hands to her mouth as if shocked. Then she lowered her eyebrows in concentration. For a moment no sound came. Then she let out a fluid mash of words.

Soundlessly, Shannon swore. A powerful and unknown spell must be locked around the parts of the woman's brain that allowed her to speak. She had expressive aphasia.

The woman's gibberish rose and then fell. A distant chorus of voices answered. She began walking toward the clamoring voices.

Shannon stuck his head farther out of the book and watched her walk down the hallway. He imagined the book as the "ground" and focused his Magnus sentence in his chin. Awkwardly, he used his chin to lift another page. From this new crack in the book came first his fingers, then his whole right hand.

With concentration, he used three silvery sentences in his reconstructed hand to turn the page from which his head emerged. The world tilted, and then all his text began to interconnect and pull itself free. The pages flipped faster and faster, releasing paragraph after paragraph that wove themselves into his body. When the last page turned and pushed him away, he slid a few feet along the floor and stopped.

Down the hall, the wailing grew louder. Cautiously, he stood and walked back to the library. The door was open. Inside, the warkite lay folded next to a stack of books. The hierophant must have deactivated its text. Shannon peered out the window but saw no warkites in the sky. For the moment, he was safe.

So he turned and trotted after the aphasic hierophant. The hallway ran in a slow curve. Through the windows, he saw more red-tiled roof, ornate sandstone minarets, glimpses of the city beyond. Every thirty feet or so, he passed a smaller hallway that ran toward the dome's center.

The hierophant's gibberish now rose and fell to a manic cadence. Coming around a corner, Shannon caught sight of her just before she broke into a run.

He hurried after, keeping a safe distance. The voices answering her grew louder. The woman ran faster. He sped up.

Then something made him stop.

He looked back down the hall. He now stood on the other side of the sanctuary's dome, the shaded side. No sunlight came through the windows here. The hallways leading toward the dome's center were nearly black. But why had he stopped? Had he heard something?

It came again. He jumped.

It was just barely audible. He walked toward it, away from the direction the hierophant had been running.

It came again. A chill ran down his ghostly body.

"Shannon." It was a feeble whisper. "Shannon."

Something about the voice was familiar.

Shannon's hands began to tremble. Suddenly, he wished he could return to being a fragmented consciousness, distanced from his ability to feel emotions like dread.

The whisper came again. "Here."

With a start, Shannon realized that the voice was coming from one of the hallways to the dome's center.

Someone was standing in the dark—a hunched figure leaning against the wall. A thin old man? A creature standing on the figure's shoulder flapped its wings.

"Blood and hell!" Shannon swore without sound. He stepped back.

"No!" the old man pleaded. "No, stay. Please . . ."

Shannon halted. The stranger's voice was raw with desperation.

"You know me." The old man took a few halting steps toward him. "You know me."

Shannon took another step back but then stopped. The stranger was right. But . . . the memory, it wasn't all there.

Shannon waited. The old man did not move. Shannon took a cautious step toward him.

"Oh . . ." the old man said. "Oh, I have missed you . . ." The stranger took two more halting steps forward. "Please. Please, come back."

Now closer to the light, Shannon saw that the creature standing on the stranger's shoulder was a large blue parrot. The skin around her beak and eyes was bright yellow. The old man had tawny skin, a hooked nose, two blank white eyes, long silvery dreadlocks.

"Shannon," the old man whispered and held out a hand.

Filled with confusion, fear, and longing, the ghost held out his own hand and tried to say "Shannon."

Eight

As Francesca fell from the lofting kite, her eyes met Deirdre's. Time slowed, and she could identify every radial fleck in Deirdre's green irises, every black strand of hair flickering before her tawny face. The immortal woman's mouth was parted, as if she were just about to say something extremely interesting.

Then time jumped forward. Francesca plummeted.

Above her, the air warden's kite wrapped around its pilot. The hierophant shot downward as if loosed from a giant bow and struck her in an awkward, aerial tackle. The world spun. The sanctuary seemed above her as she fell down into blue.

Then the kite coiled around her and pressed her close to the air warden. He had raised his veil, covering everything but his light brown eyes.

It had been three years.

Francesca's heart was kicking, but the terror of her fall was melting into giddiness. The pilot hadn't looked at her face yet; he was distracted by the approaching ground.

Two sheets of the red sailcloth stretched forward and out to form narrow wings. A tiny adjustment in these wings tilted them to a horizontal position and set them shooting southward as they fell. Avel's sandstone buildings passed below, then the city's outer walls.

The wings broadened, slowing their fall and increasing gliding speed toward a ridge called Spillwind's Hope. It rose from the intersection of the savanna and the foothills and so forced the wind upward into a lifting draft.

Francesca's breathing began to slow. The pilot was an expert. Of course he was. She found that she was smiling broadly, idiotically. They were going to live.

She looked eastward across the savanna and the receding rain clouds. Two caravan roads cut straight brown lines through the grass to converge on Avel.

Her giddiness dissipated as she wondered if they would have to land in the savanna. Until she came to Avel, Francesca had never seen grass like that which covered the Deep Savanna. It grew seven feet tall and consisted of thick, bamboolike segments. It reduced vision to a few inches and nearly halted movement. A party armed with scythes could cut a narrow path through the stalks, but the grass soon dulled even the sharpest blade.

By stepping off a road, one could become lost in the grass ocean. Caravan guards told stories of men who stepped just a few feet into the stalks and became disoriented. The miserable souls would spend days wandering, at times coming within a biscuit toss of the road. Almost always, they died of thirst.

And that was to say nothing of the hundred-mile grass fires or headless katabeasts or sun-eclipsing bee swarms or savanna lycanthropes.

Every Western Spirish child knew of the massive, intelligent lycanthropes that moved through the grass ocean as a wolf might run through a meadow. Hidden within the tall grass, the lycanthropes were safe from hierophantic pilots and warkites.

More insidiously, lycanthropes could sometimes seem human. Some Spirishmen believed the beasts transformed their bodies into human bodies. Others supposed they used spells to appear human. Whatever the case, everyone agreed the creatures and the blasting spells their spellwrights could cast were more dangerous at night.

The city guards of Avel were constantly resisting lycanthrope attack. The beasts would rush the walls and try to knock them down with their blasting spells. More chilling stories came from the caravan men who crossed the savanna. They described lycanthropes who would cry out like men lost in the grass, only to devour anyone foolish enough to run to their aid. Other caravans described camps of men out on the savanna who would invite unwary travelers to join them by their campfire, only to change into their lycanthropic bodies as soon as the travelers let down their guard.

As sensational as these stories were, they paled in comparison to those of the Savanna Walker, an ancient monster that roamed the plains. Some said the Walker was an elder god who had inhabited the continent before humanity had crossed the ocean. Others claimed it was the souls of men who'd died of thirst in the savanna. All the stories spoke of an unspeakably hideous body and of its shrill scream. Anyone who saw the beast or heard its voice was driven mad. However, while most Spirish adults knew lycanthropes to be real, most believed the Savanna Walker a mere ghost story.

Francesca looked back at the infirmary's roof. The cloud of blindness covered the tip of one minaret. She shivered.

"Hold on," the hierophant said. "It's choppy in the ridge lift."

Francesca wondered what, exactly, she was supposed to hold on to when the sailcloth surrounding her disappeared. In an instant of terrifying freefall, they twisted to face upward. Then the red cloth leapt away and with a thump popped into a lofting kite. Francesca found herself hanging in a harness that had been made of the hierophant's expansive green robes.

Francesca's hands tingled.

A spellwright had to be fluent in a magical language to see its runes. As a wizard, Francesca could see only Numinous, Magnus, and the common languages. The hierophantic language was invisible to her. However, spellwrights could sense proximity to unknown language by a nonvisual "synesthesic" sensation. A tingling in both hands was Francesca's synesthesic reaction to the hierophantic spells moving through the cloth that surrounded her.

Now their rig flew over Spillwind's Hope. The pilot moved his hands along the woven suspension lines that stretched from the canopy to their harnesses. No doubt he was casting spells within the lines.

An instant later, the canopy changed shape and banked the kite into a sharp turn. Here the air was rising in turbulent surges. By cutting a tight circle within the upward draft, they began to recover the altitude lost during their fall.

The wind was cold and strong but didn't blow too loudly. She easily heard the hierophant when he said, "Once high enough, I'll edit this rig into a jumpchute. It can pull us to the wind garden, but that'll deplete its text. I can't take you back without refitting."

Francesca cleared her throat. "Do it."

The pilot's hands halted on the suspension lines, fouling the kite's circular path. They fell a few feet before he made several movements that restored their path. The action tossed Francesca's long braid about.

The pilot turned to her. "Fran?"

"Cyrus," she said, staring straight ahead.

He seemed about to say something more but then returned his attention to the suspension lines.

They turned another circle. As the sanctuary passed before Francesca, she saw a commotion among the lofting kites. The yellow kite that held Deirdre was descending the final few feet to its minaret. Francesca watched the kite vanish into the Savanna Walker's cloud of blindness. Again she shivered.

A sudden upward gust tossed them higher and pushed her against Cyrus. She didn't look, but from the corner of her eye she noticed that he was editing the harnesses so as to put more space between them. She said, "I thought you were off becoming an airship captain."

"I was," he said curtly.

There followed an uncomfortable silence. "Then why did you come back?"

"I was a first mate on a cruiser flying out of Erram, but they offered me a promotion to air warden here. A warden has a better chance of making captain."

"Oh." She paused. "And how long have you been back?"

"A fortnight."

She started to ask why he hadn't told her of his return but then found herself asking, "Did you marry her?"

He moved a hand along the suspension lines. "No," he said just loud enough to be heard over the wind. "And are you a full physician now?"

"I am. The training was very demanding."

"I'm sure."

Something entirely different occurred to Francesca. "Cyrus, can I ask you a strange question?"

He laughed. "You can't make this conversation any stranger than it already is."

"When we were together . . . did you ever notice if I wore an anklet?"

He looked over at her.

"Around my left ankle," she said. "Did I have a small silver chain?"

"Sure. I remember that."

"You do? God-of-gods, why didn't you tell me?"

He studied her face as if trying to figure out if she was joking. "Why would I tell you about your own jewelry?"

"Did we ever talk about the anklet?"

"I was wrong, Fran; you've made this conversation even stranger."

"Just tell me. When did you first see it? Did we talk about it?"

He paused. "I think I asked about it once when we were first together. You never replied."

Francesca felt her blood go cold. She had been bound by the demon—or by something with powerful texts—almost as soon as she had arrived in Avel.

"What happened back there?" Cyrus asked.

She took a long breath. It was a question she would like answered as well. They were almost as high as the tops of the Auburn Mountains.

"Fran?" Cyrus asked. "Is the sanctuary truly under attack by a foreign deity?"

Again, she didn't answer. Could she trust him?

"I'm Avel's air warden. I need to know."

Francesca decided to stall. "You have an order from an officer of the canonist."

"And I am obeying it." He studied her. "But do you know what happened?"

She looked straight ahead.

They flew two more circles. Suddenly Cyrus pointed to the north. "See that?" He seemed to be pointing to empty sky. "It's an incoming airship. We aren't expecting one for another ten days."

Francesca narrowed her eyes and barely made out a white speck in the blue.

"Fran, you had better tell me everything. This is grave."

She looked at him, but his light brown eyes were fixed on the distant airship. "Why?"

"That rig," Cyrus said, pointing again, "is moving too fast to be anything other than a warship."

Nine

Shannon-the-text touched his fingertips to those of Shannon-who-still-lived. Golden light flushed down the ghost's arm as his author replaced lost text. He became aware of how each of his sentences was an analogy for part of his author's body. He became aware that he was not his author or even his author's mind, for there was no mind without body. And yet . . . at the same time he was his author. It was impossible, but it was so. He was a creation.

The ghost shuddered to know reunion with this glorious body, this frail body, infested by unrestricted growth. Here was the burden of disease and age. Here was death, so close.

The ghost withdrew his hand. "Shouldn't we be one?" he asked, but his throat could make no noise.

"Write to me in Numinous," his author said.

The ghost cast a golden sentence that would read, "*What happened to us? I thought you were murdered.*"

His author caught the words and translated them. "Murdered," he said with a frown. "Why would I have been murdered?"

The ghost wrote a quick sentence. "*I woke in a library, holding a Numinous sentence that claimed I'd been killed and needed to discover the murderer and warn Nicodemus.*"

His author winced. "Last summer, Typhon's hierophants stormed our safehouse in the North Gate District. They killed some of Nicodemus's students, nearly killed me. They stole you from me. I thought they had deconstructed you . . . I had given up hope." He looked back down the hallway. "Come into the darkness before someone sees me."

Stepping farther into the shadows, the ghost wrote another question: "*But who wrote the note about your murder?*"

Again his author winced. "That doesn't matter now. We've found you. Come."

From the dark came a sound like bare feet slapping floorboards. Then a commanding whisper: "Magister, we're going now. The Walker's preoccupied with the infirmary kites. Can you run?"

The ghost sucked in a breath. The voice filled him with memories of Starhaven and the Heaven Tree, of lessons and arguments and a fierce olive-skinned, green-eyed young man.

His author replied, "Nicodemus, come see whom I've found." The old man's voice quavered, and the ghost was touched that his author was so moved.

The footfalls sounded again.

This far into the hallway there was little light, but the ghost could still make out the figure that appeared. He was older, barefoot, and dressed only in leather pants that ended at the knees. A thin scar ran along his left side, and his long black hair was tied into a ponytail. There were other, inhuman figures in the shadows.

When Nicodemus noticed the ghost, he leapt back into the dark. "Magister, get back! Typhon's corrupted it."

Shannon-the-author shook his head. "Nico, don't worry." Again he moved farther into the dark. "Remember what we discussed."

The old man walked on, but the ghost did not follow. His author should have demonstrated more joy or relief at their reunion. Dread filled the ghost as he understood. His author's grief was not for what had happened; he was grieving for something that was about to happen. Suddenly the ghost knew what his author had "discussed" with Nicodemus.

Shannon-the-author turned back to the ghost. The old man closed his eyes. "Nicodemus," he whispered, "do it quickly."

The ghost turned to flee, but out of the dark flew Nicodemus, teeth bared and fists clenched around unseen wartexts.

Ten

When the lofting kite rose to a height above the Auburn Mountains, Cyrus moved his hands along the suspension lines, and the canopy split itself in two.

Half of the red sailcloth wrapped around Cyrus and Francesca, covering them from chests to feet. Short lateral wings formed along this encasement. The remaining cloth bulged into a round jumpchute that, blasting wind, pulled them toward the mountains.

A stiff textual shield formed within the tension lines, protecting Francesca and Cyrus from the rushing air. It was not so loud as to force either occupant to yell, but it was loud enough that both had to speak with conscious volume.

As they flew, the distant white speck that Cyrus insisted was an incoming warship grew slightly larger. Francesca asked about it, but Cyrus declined to explain until they were close enough to recognize the ship.

Meanwhile, Francesca watched the reservoir pass under them. They had flown over the main body of water and were now above the narrows—six riverlike projections that wound into the green foothills. She could make out a few single-sail fishing boats on the water.

At various points in their twisting course, the narrows expanded into wide coves. In these bobbed small lake towns, lashed-together houseboats anchored in deep water to ensure they never drifted close enough to the shore to be vulnerable to lycanthrope attack.

Now, at the rainy season's end, the fisher folk followed the water as far out as the base of the Auburn Mountains. In the dry season, Cala drained the reservoir to irrigate the canyon floor, and the fisher folk slowly migrated their lake towns toward the city. When the reservoir went dry, all of the lake towns banded together to form a small muddy township just outside the Sliding Docks. Some would find work in the Water District; others would chance a wagon ride over the Auburn Mountains to work among the fishers in Coldlock Harbor.

"Fran," Cyrus said over the wind. "I really must know: What was attacking the sanctuary?"

She looked at him. He looked back. She had no idea what had actually happened in the infirmary. Should she tell him what she had seen? Or, at least, what she had believed she had seen? Deirdre had said that Cyrus was trustworthy, but Francesca didn't know if she could trust Deirdre.

Besides, Deirdre didn't know Cyrus like Francesca had known him.

The whole situation was a disaster. Usually, she would remind herself that confronting disasters was what she did. But an hour ago she had failed in a crisis, killed her patient. Worse, a demonic spell had been wrapped around her in the form of that anklet for years. The world as she had known it had broken to pieces.

And that, Francesca reminded herself, was all the more reason why she had to remain composed. After a long breath, she smiled tightly.

Cyrus had always been committed to duty. So long as her plans coincided with his sense of honor, he would make an excellent ally. But how would he react when she explained a demon might be ruling Avel? For all Francesca knew, Cyrus was a demon worshiper. She had to choose her words carefully.

"Francesca," she said loud enough to be heard over the wind.

His veil moved as if he were frowning. "What?"

"It's Francesca now. Not Fran."

His eyes narrowed. "Francesca, what's happening in the sanctuary? I need to know."

"Hours ago, lycanthropes attacked a caravan coming in through the Northern Gate. The wounded were brought to the infirmary. A woman named Deirdre claimed she'd been struck by a lycanthrope spell and that only I could save her. By the time I got to her, she was nearly dead. An unknown text was compressing her lungs. I tried to disspell it, but it crushed her heart. She died on my table. A few moments later she came back to life."

"What?"

"She came back to life. She's an avatar, a creature possessing part of a deity's soul."

"A canonist?"

She shook her head.

"But if she's not a canonist, how is she in Avel? Celeste would destroy any divinity not listed in the Celestial Canon. Perhaps she is serving Canonist Cala?"

"I've no clue."

"Holy sky, Francesca, you must know something!" He said the word "something" with the same patronizing tone he had once reserved for their personal arguments.

"Oh wait, Cyrus, you're right. I do know something. I was just too

God-of-gods damned stupid to realize it until some patronizing man with
an intelligence rivaled by garden tools told me I do," she replied hotly, and
then for good measure added, "you pretentious bastard."

He only laughed. "Haven't changed, have you? Still all fiery sarcasm or
calm compassion with nothing between. And still speaking like an antique.
I never heard anyone but you and my grandmother name the Creator as the
God-of-gods."

Francesca clenched her teeth. "Just shut it and listen." She explained
how she had carried Deirdre to the roof while others lost their ability to
speak and began to wail.

She did not mention Typhon or Deirdre's belief that the demon had
brought Cyrus back to the city as a "screen." However, she repeated Deirdre's claim that the Savanna Walker was the cause of the aphasia.

Cyrus looked at her. "The Savanna Walker's a child's tale."

"The aphasia curse was real enough." As she said this, Francesca thought
of the text that had spellbound Deirdre's heart. Suddenly, she knew how to
prevent Cyrus's sense of duty from endangering them both. He wouldn't
like it . . . if he ever found out about it. She looked at him. "I'm worried a
curse might have gotten into you."

Cyrus looked at her. "An aphasia curse or the one that crushed the avatar's heart?"

"Either."

Cyrus looked at her. "If I become ill or aphasic, we'll fall out of the sky."

"I can cast a countercurse to see if you have any foreign text in your
body."

"What about the text I'm writing in my heart?"

"I edit the countercurse so it won't interfere."

He nodded.

"Give me your arm."

When Cyrus obeyed, she took his wrist with her left hand. With her
right, she cast a needlelike Magnus sentence and jabbed it into one of his
arm veins.

Using her hand muscles, Francesca wrote a compact medical text in
Magnus and Numinous. It took a few moments. When it was ready, she
used the Magnus needle to cast it into Cyrus's bloodstream. He wasn't fluent in the wizardly languages, so the spell was invisible to him. But Francesca watched the silver-gold spark tumble up his arm and into his shoulder.

"Hold still," she commanded and watched the spell flow into the center
of Cyrus's chest and then shoot to the area under his right pectoral muscle.
The text had passed through the right chambers of his heart and been
pumped into his lung.

"Do you see a curse?" he asked.

"I said hold still!"

She watched the spell tumble though the lung's fine capillaries. Then it made sudden, halting progress back to the center of his chest. She tensed. When it reached the left side of his heart, she cast a backhand wave of Numinous signal spells into his chest. One of these struck the spell in his heart and commanded it to unfold.

She nodded with satisfaction as her text unobtrusively explored the beating left ventricle of his heart.

Using her thigh muscles, Francesca forged several wide sheets of Numinous signal spells. By flexing her leg, she mashed the sheet into an unstable ball. Every few moments, part of the sheet decayed and sent single texts flying in random directions.

She flexed and extended her legs five times more until the decaying ball radiated a shower of signal texts in all directions. Every few moments, one struck the text in Cyrus's heart, commanding it not to take action.

They were now flying above the highest foothills. Here the narrows ran between steep gorges. The dark Auburn Mountains stood before them.

"Burning heaven, Fran, do you see something in me?" Cyrus asked.

"I don't see a curse. But I placed a spell in you so I can monitor you."

"You think I might become aphasic later?"

"In all likelihood you're fine, but I want to be safe. Just stay close to me for a while . . . for my sake." She squeezed his arm.

He stared at her and then turned back to the jumpchute.

She studied the spell in his young, healthy heart. As often happened when she examined a body, she felt as if she could look forward into time and see the different, older men he might become—some hale and athletic as he was now, some soft with inaction, some wasting away from disease.

Suddenly, Cyrus broke her reverie: "You know something you're not telling me."

"I do, but it's not about your health," she said, knowing that she was, in at least two senses, lying.

Eleven

An unseen wartext blasted the ghost's right arm into a cloud of golden text. He felt no pain, only a hot rush of fear. Behind him, Nicodemus yelled something.

The ghost jumped left, thought of the wall as the ground, kicked off of it, and flew down the dark hall. Behind him, a detonating wartext filled the air with shards of plaster and stone. Most passed harmlessly through the ghost, but a few tore Magnus sentences in his feet.

After landing in the bright outer hallway, the ghost tried to dash away, but the damaged prose in his soles uncoiled. He slipped and fell, sinking knee-deep into the floor.

Desperately, he pulled his feet out of the floorboards and tried to repair the soles. The severed paragraphs on the stump of his right arm were hemorrhaging language.

The sound of footsteps made him look up.

Nicodemus, standing at the edge of the hallway's darkness, cocked his hand back and cast something at the ghost. No doubt it was a wartext written in the tattooed language Nicodemus had learned from the kobolds. The ghost flinched, expecting to be shattered into sentence fragments.

But nothing happened.

Nicodemus yelled again. Suddenly the ghost realized that the hallway's bright light had deconstructed Nicodemus's wartext. The chthonic languages functioned only in darkness. Wasting no time, the ghost repaired his feet and pulled himself out of the floor.

Nicodemus ran forward. Daylight or no, the boy was still a cacographer, and if he touched the ghost he could misspell him into nothing.

The ghost dashed down the hallway with inhuman speed. He leapt into the air and kicked off the walls and ceiling to make himself a more difficult target for any wizardly wartext Nicodemus might cast.

When the ghost saw the sunlight pouring through the windows, he stopped to look back. Nico was out of sight and far behind. Quickly he edited the stump of his right hand so that it would stop hemorrhaging prose. How much text did he have left?

Frowning, the ghost realized he could have escaped Nicodemus by falling through the floor or dashing through a wall. If he was going to survive, he had to start thinking like a ghost.

The ghost's frown deepened with a second realization: he would have seen any wizardly wartext Nicodemus had cast at him. Could it be the boy hadn't used either wizardly language?

Footsteps sounded down the hall. Nicodemus came sprinting into view. The ghost stood, waiting to see if the boy's hand would shine silvery or golden.

But Nico only lunged at him. The ghost dodged left, partially hiding in a thick stone wall. Nicodemus turned and tried to grab him. Shannon drew himself completely into the wall and then stepped out a few paces away.

Nicodemus looked at him, panting. There was no sign of Numinous or Magnus in his body. He wasn't even going to try.

"You left the valley too soon!" the ghost would have said if his throat could have made noise.

Again Nicodemus lunged. Shannon jumped over him. "Creator damn it all, Nico!" the ghost silently cursed. "You left the valley too soon!" He peeled a Numinous sentence from the stump of his right arm and edited it so it would read *YOU LEFT TOO SOON!* The ghost waited for Nicodemus to turn around before casting it in his face.

Nicodemus jerked his head back and then pulled the golden sentence from his cheek. The instant it touched the boy, the line began to misspell. By the time Nicodemus had completed a translation, it read *YU LEAFT TUH VALEE TWO SOON!*

A chill filled the ghost. Nicodemus's cacography in Numinous had worsened dramatically; he was now essentially illiterate in the wizardly languages.

Nicodemus leapt for him again, and again he missed. With a wrist flick, the ghost cast a question: *"Why did you leave the valley?"*

Nicodemus threw another punch. Shannon dodged left and threw another line: *"WHY? TELL ME WHY, DAMN YOU!"*

Nicodemus swung again. Shannon jumped back and was about to cast another sentence when he saw the pain in the boy's eyes.

Shannon stopped.

"I couldn't watch you die!" Nicodemus growled. "You're dying. The cankers. They're killing you. Any day now, you'll die. I had to try to get the emerald and cure you. Damn it, I had to try!"

The ghost swallowed. He had a good idea why Nicodemus was trying to deconstruct him. But he needed to hear the boy say it. He wrote another question: *"But why deconstruct me, the ghost?"*

Nicodemus swung again. Shannon ducked under the blow and repeated the question: *"Why try to deconstruct me?"* And then added, *"Let me be one with my author before he dies!"*

Nicodemus laughed bitterly. "You don't know what you are. Typhon's agents took you from us. He's had you for a year. If the demon has let you free, it's because he's using you against us."

The ghost tensed, ready to dodge another attack. But Nicodemus only glared at him, his chest heaving. "Typhon has rewritten you. You're not Magister Shannon's ghost."

"I AM Shannon's ghost!" he threw in response. *"I'm meant to be one with him! Trust me, please."*

Nicodemus shook his head. "You're just the demon's weapon, like Deirdre was back in Starhaven."

A realization sent a chill through the ghost. He didn't actually know if the demon had rewritten him or not. He did not feel rewritten . . . but how could he know? The demon was masterful enough to rewrite him so as to hide what he had done. "Oh," the ghost said to himself in shock. "Oh!"

Nicodemus tensed and seemed about to strike out again when it shot through the window. White sailcloth and steel flashed in the sunlight. The warkite snaked toward Nicodemus. The boy ducked under the talons and thrust his arms into the construct's belly. Instantly, the warkite went as limp as a tablecloth. His cacographic touch had misspelled its every sentence.

But just as Nicodemus tossed the disspelled kite aside, another flash of white shone at the window. More warkites. The constructs were reacting to the chthonic runes tattooed on Nicodemus's skin. They perceived him as a foreign spell more dangerous than Shannon-the-text.

The ghost didn't waste the opportunity. With a powerful jump, he flew up and through the ceiling.

He found himself on the floor of another hallway. In this one stood seven green-robed hierophants, men and women. They had all removed their veils. One had undone his turban. They were talking, or at least trying to talk. Their mouths produced only aphasic gibberish. Their eyes were wide with confusion or fear. Some were trying to communicate with gestures.

The ghost shivered. Something powerful must be moving through the sanctuary to spread an aphasia curse.

But the ghost had to get away from Nicodemus. After the Magnus sentences in his feet recovered from passing through the floor, the ghost ran down the hall in the direction of the sun. As he went, he looked out the window but saw only pale blue sky and winding city alleys. The warkites were not following him. He jumped up through the ceiling to another floor and kept running.

Then something seemed to go wrong in the ghost's chest, as if some vital passage had gone missing. It was as if . . . where he should have had a heart there was only hollowness.

He stopped. His chest was heaving even though he had no need to breathe. He moved to cover his face but had only one hand.

Pain flashed through him. Where his arm should have been there was only pulsing agony. He fell to his knees, let himself sink into the floor. His mind was reeling with fear. His text had been horribly depleted. How much longer could he survive outside a necropolis?

But the worst of it was that his author did not want him. His author distrusted him, and Nicodemus had tried to deconstruct him. He might not be himself. He might be a demon's tool.

The ghost's chest began to shake. The pain of his lost arm had dissipated, but the hollowness in his chest had expanded. The ghost felt a longing for his author so keen and agonizing it was like that of the abandoned child. He remembered with agonizing clarity when Astrophell politics had taken Shannon away from his wife and young son; both woman and child were now long dead. That pain was like this pain in its sharpness.

The ghost curled into a ball, sinking entirely into the floor. The pain in his hands, feet, and ears was a welcome distraction.

He shook all over. Though he was now contained within wood and stone, he took long ragged breaths. For what felt like hours, he wept without tears.

Slowly, emotional exhaustion set in. He seemed to sleep. When his thoughts became clear again, he considered his situation. He had no way to prove to his author that Typhon had not rewritten him. Therefore, proof had to be found. But how?

Typhon had stolen him from his author and then removed some of his memories. The notes in the library claimed "our memories are in her" and instructed him to find Cleric Francesca DeVega.

The note's false claim that living Shannon had been murdered . . . that was mysterious and troubling.

The ghost climbed out of the floor and began searching for the infirmary. But as he peered through doors and down stairwells, the hollowness in his chest returned. This time it was accompanied by fear so strong he felt nauseated.

Though the ghost tried not to think about it, some part of him knew that the being who had placed him in that library, the being who had written a lie about his author being murdered, might very well be the demon Typhon.

Twelve

When Cyrus and Francesca were flying above the Auburn Mountains, she studied the massive redwood trees that covered their slopes. The dark trunks grew so tall, their evergreen canopies so thick, that they blocked all but a thin wash of sunlight from the forest's dark understory.

Scattered across the mountains were dying trees, their canopies withered to brown. Francesca had read about the unexplained demise of trees across the entire continent. The druids of Dral named the phenomenon the Silent Blight and wondered if it signified the coming War of Disjunction, when the demons would cross the ocean to destroy human language.

Francesca was about to ask Cyrus what he thought about the Silent Blight when he stopped casting spells along the rig's suspension lines and looked at her.

"Something's just occurred to me," Cyrus said. "There are maybe a hundred hierophants working the wind garden. The marshal can send them to Avel if the city's in danger." He paused. "Francesca, no more games. What happened in the sanctuary? I need to know everything you do so I know what to tell the wind marshal."

She shook her head. "Deirdre ordered you not to trust other hierophants."

"But can we trust Deirdre?"

"Perhaps not, but let's not include more people about whom we are uncertain."

"There's something important you're not telling me."

"Several somethings," she agreed. "I'll explain when we land. Meantime, has that airship gotten close enough for you to tell me why it worries you?"

He looked north. The white speck that Francesca had seen before had grown into a long white arrow.

"She has," Cyrus said after a moment. "This is a bad omen."

"Better tell me quick then."

"I think she's the *Queen's Lance*. I can't swear to it until we're closer. I flew as her first mate for a year and half."

"And why is that so bad?"

"She's a Kestrel."

Francesca could only look at him blankly as a twinge of guilt moved through her. When they had been lovers, she would occasionally sneak onto the infirmary's roof and fly a blue flag from one of the corners. If Cyrus could get away from his patrol duty, he would land his rig for a rendezvous.

He would point out the distant airships flying to or from the wind garden and talk about a particular ship's merits or flaws. Francesca had always been too preoccupied with her studies to remember or care about what he had described. Cyrus had always taken an interest in medicine and her life in the infirmary. After half a year together, he could recite all the bones in the wrist, but she could not tell a lofting sail from a foresail.

Judging by the way Cyrus's eyes narrowed, he was now remembering his past irritation at her disinterest. "A Kestrel is a particularly dangerous kind of ship," he said shortly. "The Kestrel class of cruisers can . . . oh you wouldn't understand. Here, maybe this will help: common airships are written on linen. Most cruisers are written on cotton. But Kestrels, they are written only on Ixonian silk."

"Oh!" Francesca said in surprise as she tried to guess the cost of so much silk.

Cyrus continued. "Before the Civil War, when Spires was still a polytheistic realm, every deity maintained a fleet—a few flocks of lofting kites, a destroyer or two, maybe a cruiser or a carrier loaded with warkites. When Celeste and her canonists set out to unify Spires, they wrote five Kestrels. The polytheists never had a chance against the silk ships. The Kestrels tore apart their fleets one by one. At war's end, the monotheists had lost only two Kestrels."

"Lovely,' Francesca grumbled before asking, "So a Kestrel is a symbol of Celeste's monotheistic Spires?"

"Exactly. Of the three still flying, only one is in the western fleet. She's named the *Queen's Lance,* and I bet that's her now, flying in unscheduled from the Lurrikara wind garden."

"And you're worried that she might be here to demonstrate Celeste's power over Avel and the canonist Cala?"

"Exactly."

Francesca wondered if the ship's arrival was connected to what had just happened in the sanctuary. Cyrus seemed to be wondering the same thing. "Do you have any idea what this might mean, Fran?"

"I might have one or two ideas," Francesca said mildly. "I'd even tell you about them if you could be as clever as a parrot and learn to say Francesca."

He closed his eyes and flatly said, "Francesca."

"Land us on the garden tower, and I'll explain."

Blessedly, Cyrus did not argue but turned to the jumpchute.

About a mile ahead of them, the massive Auburn Mountains traded their redwood forests for knee-length coastal grass and sank to sea level before rising up again. This created a lush pass dotted with massive gray boulders that ran through the mountains. By chance it was wider toward the sea, narrower inland.

Cyrus had once explained that during the rainy season the pass acted as a funnel, intensifying the ocean winds. During the dry season, hot air above the savanna rose into the sky and so drew in cooler and heavier air off the ocean. As a result, the pass was one of the most consistently windy places on the continent. By harnessing this wind, Avel's hierophants produced more hierophantic text than any other wind garden.

As they flew into the gap, Francesca could see about two dozen windcatchers—the massive wind-powered rigs that made up a wind garden. Each windcatcher was written on white linen sailcloth and was, in essence, a giant cylindrical kite. Seeing all of them facing out to sea made Francesca think of a school of fish swimming against a current, their mouths open.

Cyrus flew them over a windcatcher anchored to a boulder. It was perhaps a hundred feet long with a mouth thirty feet in diameter. Its tail pointed slightly downward. When Francesca had first seen this tilt, she had been confused. She hadn't thought a cylindrical kite could fly or that it could be angled upward in a wind that blew horizontally. But then she had remembered the box kites children flew during the Festival of Colors. A simple box kite was tilted in the same way a windcatcher was.

In any case, the wondrous part of a windcatcher was what happened inside. Francesca tried to peer into the one they were passing over, but just then Cyrus grabbed her arm. "We've got to double canvas to get up to the garden tower. Hold on."

The tall garden tower was a narrow building, made of sandstone, redwood spars, and spell-invested cloth. It stood at the seaside end of the gap—upwind from all the windcatchers—and was shaped like a shark's dorsal fin.

Cyrus touched the cloth that was wrapped around their legs and it shot forward to form a second jumpchute. Even with twice the thrust, they flew up the gap at half their previous speed.

As they approached the streamlined tower, Francesca caught a glimpse of the ocean as a dark blue strata covered by billowing gray clouds.

The vertical, downwind edge of the narrow tower held a stack of landing bays: rectangular, penlike structures made of redwood spars and tight sailcloth. With some rapid editing, Cyrus landed them feetfirst in one of the bays.

Francesca disentangled herself from the jumpchute's harness. Without the rush of wind, the world seemed unnaturally quiet. So she was startled when a girl's voice called out, "Welcome, pilot. The tower warden asks your name and purpose."

Francesca turned to see a short, green-robed hierophantic apprentice. Her headdress covered everything but her dark eyes.

"Cyrus Alarcon, Air Warden of Avel," Cyrus answered, "making an emergency evacuation after a possible attack on the sanctuary. The day's words are granite fire south. My compliments to your warden and permission to enter the garden tower for an audience with him and the wind marshal."

The apprentice hurried through a flap in the landing bay's wall.

Francesca took a long breath. The cool air smelled of the sea. All around her sounded the creaking of rope and cloth. Seagulls squabbled and complained.

Francesca rubbed her cold-numbed cheeks. For the first time, she appreciated the protective qualities of a hierophant's headdress.

Francesca looked at Cyrus's robe and then at Cyrus. Like most hierophants, he had a lean build—thin waist, well-muscled shoulders—and a shorter stature. When recruiting, hierophants were particular about height; extra weight was a disadvantage in the air. That wasn't to say that Cyrus was unusually short. In fact, standing five inches below six feet, he was the tallest pilot Francesca had ever met.

"We've landed. You have some things to explain," he said, gathering the jumpchute into his arms. Abruptly, the chute cut itself in a hundred different places and then wove itself back together to form a rectangle of neatly folded cloth.

Looking at the sailcloth, Francesca considered the hierophantic high language, Sarsayah, which could focus its energy only within cloth. In the air, Sarsayah texts dissolved into powerful currents of wind.

Only heart muscle could produce Sarsayah runes, meaning that a hierophant could produce text only slowly. For this reason, they wore voluminous robes to store great amounts of text. With every heartbeat, hierophants cast a few magical sentences into their right ventricle. When the heart contracted, it propelled blood and sentences into the lungs. With every breath, hierophants exhaled a few magical sentences. To capture this language, they wore veils almost constantly.

Francesca was not fluent in Sarsayah; she could not see its runes. Cyrus had said they shone with pale blue light. Years ago, she had watched him sleep and imagined the veil tied loosely around his mouth filling with words that shone like the morning sky.

She looked him in the eye. A curl of black hair had escaped his turban. He had said that flying here would expend most of the text in his lofting kite and robes. Given that she didn't trust Cyrus, that left one question: Just how much text did he have left? What she was about to tell him could spark a confrontation, possibly even violence.

Francesca wasn't a prolific spellwright; her gift lay in perfecting intricate medical texts. Still, she could forge wizardly runes with all of her muscles, whereas Cyrus could forge hierophantic runes only with his heart muscles. She could overpower him if it came to a contest of extemporizing magical text.

She glanced down at the ball of Magnus in her thigh. It was still radiating a shower of signal spells. For good measure, she began writing a golden disspell in her arm muscles.

"Cyrus, what I'm about to say might sound far-fetched. But what I saw in the sanctuary makes me believe we have to investigate a grave possibility."

When he didn't reply, she continued: "Deirdre claimed that the War of Disjunction has already begun."

"I'm sorry?"

"It might sound like madness, but listen. A demon named Typhon might have crossed the ocean and taken control of Avel. Deirdre claimed to be his Regent of Spies. She believes that most every hierophant in the city unknowingly serves the demon."

Cyrus laughed and looked up. "But that's insane." He seemed to be waiting for her to say something. When she replied only with a level stare, he laughed again. "But it is crazy. It's . . . Deirdre must be mad."

"We can't ignore her; she knew your passwords."

"She did and she couldn't have learned them without connections in the canonist's court, but still . . . It's just not possible."

Francesca studied Cyrus's eyes. "Deirdre thinks you might be the only wind mage not yet bound to the demon. She said Typhon brought you back to the city as some sort of screen. I'm not sure what that means, something about your being unaware of the canonist's situation."

Cyrus looked to the flap where the apprentice had disappeared. "This is . . . it's just crazy."

"How well do you know Avel now? Do you know who the Regent of Spies is?"

He turned back to her. "No one outside the canonist's advisors would know that. Cala might not even appoint a Regent of Spies. And as for Avel . . . I know it well enough. I've started to command the city's kites."

A nearby seagull scolded another. "Cyrus, you've only been here a fortnight. Deirdre knew your passwords and gave you an order. She commanded you not to tell anyone about what you saw. It's your duty to obey her."

"My first duty is to protect the city. Fran, there's just no way a demon—"

"God-of-gods, Cyrus, it's Francesca now! How many times must I tell you? Heaven aflame!"

He sniffed. "My grandmother used to say heaven aflame as well as God-of-gods."

Francesca exhaled in exasperation. She'd grown up on the border between Spires and Verdant. As a result she'd developed a diction and accent that most everyone else considered antique. It grew more pronounced when she was upset. Cyrus knew his mention of it galled her.

"Cyrus," she said evenly, "this is not about us."

His voice became cold. "Whoever said it was?"

She looked him in the eyes. "I'm sorry things ended as they did."

"Why should you be sorry?" he said, returning her gaze. "I'm certainly not sorry. You're now a physician. And I'm one step away from making captain. Clearly, we made the right decisions."

Francesca paused. His tone sounded genuine, but . . . well, she had always thought that he had felt differently about their parting. "Of course," she said at last. "Of course. I'm sorry." She paused. "But, Cyrus, Deirdre also told me a rogue wizard is somewhere in or near Avel. A man named Nicodemus Weal."

Cyrus started to say something but then stopped. He went to a corner of the landing bay and put down the neatly folded red jumpchute. "Nicodemus Weal? The mad apprentice that killed a bunch of wizards in Starhaven ten years ago? The one that got the academics all worked up about prophecy?"

Glad to see Cyrus away from the red cloth, Francesca went to him. "It sounds mad, but we can't dismiss the claim. Deirdre said he might be staying with the Canic people in the North Gate District. When we know things are safe in the sanctuary, you have to take me back to Avel to investigate."

"Francesca," he said and then paused. "I agree that this affair requires investigation. But not by you or me. You're a cleric; I'm a pilot. You should be healing; I should be flying. I will discuss this matter with the wind marshal and the tower warden. Between the three of us, we can secure an audience with Canonist Cala. A proper investigation will be launched."

Francesca felt her hands go cold. She eyed his robe. Perhaps she was wasting time talking. With every breath he was slowly replenishing his text. "Cyrus," she said evenly, carefully, "your logic would be impeccable if it weren't for the possibility that a damned demon is controlling Avel and so the canonist."

He shook his head. "It's too far-fetched. I'll be careful when discussing this with the tower warden and the marshal."

Heat flushed across Francesca's face. It was hard to keep her tone level. "What if they're serving the demon?"

He looked at her. "You've just been through a harrowing experience. Something attacked the sanctuary. A woman claiming to be an avatar pushed you out of a lofting kite. You're not thinking clearly."

Francesca fished the Numinous disspell she'd been writing in her bicep and moved it into her balled fist. "I am thinking perfectly clearly, thank you. And I cannot allow you to tell the tower warden or the marshal of this matter. It's too dangerous."

"It is my duty to."

"Your duty is to protect Avel. If a demon . . ."

He was shaking his head. "You can't stop me."

Hot fear rose inside Francesca; she had to stop him. She searched for her most authoritative tone. "I will stop you, Cyrus. I must."

He folded his arms. "So this is why you wouldn't talk when we were aloft? So you couldn't toss a wizardly disspell at me without knocking us both out of the sky? You always were a more powerful spellwright, but you must know—" He started to unfold his arms.

Francesca flicked her hand out and cast her netlike disspell at his chest. Her prose wrapped around him. The powerful golden sentences moved through his robes, disspelling any text they encountered. She extemporized a clawed Magnus paragraph and threw it onto the folded red cloth. When the paragraph grabbed hold, she yanked hard a connecting sentence and so pulled the cloth out of Cyrus's reach.

"Don't make this harder than . . ." Her voice died.

He was staring at her, making no attempt to rid his robes of her disspell.

In that instant, Francesca recognized her mistake.

Calmly, Cyrus laid his hand on the landing bay's wall. In the next instant, a strip of sailcloth jumped out of the wall and struck Francesca's thigh where it wove itself into the fabric of her robes. She forged defensive language in both arms and tried to pull away.

But Cyrus had invested her robes with hierophantic language, and they became as stiff as iron. She began to forge disspells in her tongue, intend-ing to spit them onto her sleeves, but the cleric's stole she wore around her shoulders twisted into a cord and wrapped around her forehead.

The world dissolved into whiteness.

Thirteen

Squinting in the sunlight, Nicodemus examined his school of five false lepers.

Shannon stood beside him, leaning on a walking stick. "My boy," he muttered, "remind me why I didn't question your escape plan deeply enough to discover you intended to kill us with costumes."

Both Shannon and Nicodemus were dressed in the itchy gray robes of Northern Spirish holy men sworn to care for the sick and destitute. Before them, on rain-wet terracotta tiles, squatted Nicodemus's kobold students. All were wrapped from toe to nose tip in the dirty rags of lepers.

Nicodemus studied them now. Vein was looking about wearily while Slag and Dross argued with each other. Flint and Jasp crouched as if resting.

All kobolds distrusted humans. When forced to interact with men, they instinctively hid as much of their bodies and identities as possible. Presently this desire for secrecy manifested in the kobolds' tense posture and in the way they huddled together as if to block out the rest of the world. Fortuitously, this body language reinforced the illusion that they were in fact a group of lepers, shunned by society.

Nicodemus adjusted his gray headdress. Shannon had a point; a convincing disguise was not the same thing as safety. But according to Nicodemus's original plan, they should have recovered the emerald or died by now. Either would have made escape unnecessary.

"The problem with disguised escape plans," Shannon continued, "is that they often become disguised suicide plans."

"Magister, you're overreacting," Nicodemus muttered. "Neither the Walker nor the demon will suspect us of hiding in sunlight."

Shannon only readjusted his grip on Azure; he was obliged to hide his parrot familiar in a wrapped-up rag.

They were standing in the Courtyard of Lesser Benediction on the northern border of the sanctuary's complex. It was a plain public square. Here, two or three times a day, Avel's poor came to receive flatbread and sing to Cala. When making these devotions, they allowed the demigod's godspell to siphon some of their bodily strength into Cala's ark. Wealthier citizens made devotions only every other day in courtyards decorated with fountains and hanging flowers.

Some form of this devotional ritual—sometimes incorporating song, sometimes prayer, sometimes silent meditation—was practiced in every major city on the human continent. This was how the deities accrued power.

Of the five hundred souls gathered around Nicodemus, most were simply poor; others had lost limbs, vision, sanity, or all three.

No one noticed Nicodemus's party. The Spirish believed leprosy was a punishment for a past sin. In times of plenty, lepers were shunned; in times of famine, they were expelled onto the savanna to face lycanthropes. Only the Ixonians—whose hydromancers could cure leprosy with their aqueous spells—treated lepers differently.

With his Language Prime fluency, Nicodemus had seen the infection that caused leprosy and knew the sick were innocent of any causal sin. Though disgusted by how lepers were regarded, Nicodemus had no qualms exploiting that prejudice for his benefit. No one in Avel would look at his rag-wrapped students long enough to realize their figures were inhumanly broad chested and large limbed. Or, if someone did, they would attribute such bodies to disfiguring disease.

"The raid was a failure," Nicodemus admitted to his mentor. "I am sorry, Magister. I had no idea the Walker would return to the sanctuary that quickly. But we will still find a way to recover the emerald and cure you."

The old man frowned and then exhaled. "Not a failure. You killed the three librarians. The pyromancer must have been Typhon's contact with demon worshipers in Trillinon. The hydromancer the same for Ixos. In fact, the hydromancer must have been the one shipping lucerin into Avel."

"But we were so close, right next to the vulnerable demon. Perhaps we could have hacked through the door if you were with me instead of standing guard at our backs."

"No, my boy, it was better to leave me as a lookout. I'm too weak to hack through anything."

"And if only the Walker hadn't returned from the lycanthrope attack so damned fast," Nicodemus grumbled. "Faster than ever before." He looked up at the octagonal dome with its red-tile roof and sandstone minarets. The Walker had now climbed up to the canonist's quarters.

Nicodemus found himself thinking about the monster's ability to inflict aphasia; it was unsettlingly analogous to his own disability. Cacography prevented one from forming written words, aphasia from forming spoken words. There had to be a reason for this similarity. Perhaps something Typhon had planned?

"My boy, are you all right?"

Shannon's words made Nicodemus start. "I'm fine," he said. "Only think-ing about the Savanna Walker. The beast thinks he's so clever, but he's just a heap of flesh and pretentious prose."

Shannon laughed. "He seems to feel the same way about you."

"He is unbelievably powerful within the sanctuary walls, I will give him that. But if I could just catch him outside the city at night."

"There was that time two dry seasons ago when the two of you wrestled below the dam."

"Doesn't count. How was I to know he'd filled that damn gate with lu-cerin dilution?"

"There was that night in Coldlock Harbor. Your fishing boat scheme."

Despite himself, Nicodemus shivered. "Doesn't count either. Who knew orca whales could come in so close to shore or that the Savanna Walker could do . . . that . . . to them?"

Shannon rubbed his temples. "I still have nightmares about thrashing around in that water. The dark figures swimming below us, and all that . . . blood."

Nicodemus felt his cold anger grow but changed the subject. "Magister, your ghost, I wanted to say—"

"We won't talk about it."

"But, Magister, Typhon has held that ghost captive for a year. Surely, the demon has rewritten him. We had to try to deconstruct him."

Shannon turned toward him, his all-white eyes unreadable. "Yes. Of course. And if you had proper wizardly training, if you'd just listened to me back in Heaven Tree Valley, you would have destroyed the ghost instead of letting it escape back to Typhon."

"Magister, we couldn't have stayed in the valley. As I've told you a hun-dred times—"

"You have. We're finished."

"Magister," Nicodemus started to say, but just then the courtyard grew quiet and all eyes turned toward the dais at the far end. A procession of Celestial devotees had emerged bearing a litter. With practiced ceremony, they laid down the litter and folded back its doors to reveal a topaz stand-ing stone about five feet tall—a sliver of Canonist Cala's ark.

One devotee made a brief speech, praising the high sky goddess, Ce-leste, and her canon of demigods. Then the devotees led all in a song of prayer.

As they sang, a modicum of Nicodemus's strength ebbed away as Cala's godspell withdrew it. The tall topaz stone shone brighter as it gained strength from those assembled.

Nicodemus had spent his childhood in the wizardly academy of Starhaven. The patron god of wizards, Hakeem, rarely required devotion from his followers. As such, wizards lived an almost atheistic life, infrequently offering their strength to a deity and even more infrequently receiving that deity's protection.

When Nicodemus had arrived in Avel, he had been shocked by the devotions Cala demanded and outraged that the needy citizens should make devotions twice as often as the rich. The hungry had no other choice; flatbread was handed to the poor after devotions.

However, Nicodemus's disquiet about Cala had dissipated when his companion, Boann—herself a nearly vanquished river goddess—had explained how much Cala did for her citizens.

It was only the canonist's godspell that kept the city walls standing despite the earthquakes, grassfires, lycanthrope attacks. It was only Cala who held the water in the reservoir during the long dry season. If the people of Avel stopped praying for the walls to hold, they would end up in lycanthrope throats. If they stopped praying for the dam to stand, they would die of thirst.

Similar arrangements between deities and humans existed throughout the six human kingdoms. Did the poor and powerless bear most of the burden of empowering the deities? Certainly. It had always been so and was likely to remain so. But, as Boann pointed out, the inequity of divine governance was a small matter compared with Typhon's quest to bring the rest of the demonic host across the ocean.

Nicodemus had begun to realize how sheltered he had been in the academy.

As the devotional song ended and the impoverished lined up for flatbread, Nicodemus felt hollow. He had to hide his false lepers until nightfall. He had to quell Shannon's anger and despair at losing his ghost or the hopelessness would kill the old man before the canker curse growing in his gut. Nicodemus had to recover the emerald to cure Shannon, free Deirdre, defeat Typhon. In all these tasks, there was no earthly deity to whom he could pray for help.

So, when the song ended, Nicodemus led his school out of the courtyard and silently prayed to a deity who took no part in the world because he was the world.

Nicodemus prayed to the Creator.

fourteen

When consciousness returned, Deirdre found her eyes filled with tears. It was always like this after repossession. At least she'd learned not to sob.

She was lying on a thick carpet, her head resting on a pillow, her body covered by a blanket. Beside her a low hexagonal table held a kettle and a small metal cup of steaming mint tea. Other pillows lay around the table.

She rubbed the tear tracks from her cheeks and sat up. The wide room was bright and airy. Beyond the furniture stood ornate redwood screens. Late afternoon sunlight spilled through the screens in the shape of their geometric latticework. A cold breeze brought the scent of redwoods and the distant ocean.

The Savanna Walker had brought her to the top of the sanctuary, to what had been the canonist's quarters but now was Typhon's. Deirdre's last clear memory was of shoving Francesca from the kite. After that, everything was blurry sky and an ecstatic heat.

After catching her breath, Deirdre noticed a break in the screens that revealed a wide balcony and a view of Avel's winding avenues and the wind-tossed savanna. Gingerly, she stood and discovered that she now wore a blue silk blouse and a white longvest threaded with gold. Once again Typhon had dressed her up as a Spirish noble, an officer of the canonist's court.

At times Deirdre enjoyed this outfit; the white longvest contrasted nicely with her dark skin. More often she was vexed that Typhon insisted on costuming her like a doll. The demon had planted his worshipers within Cala's court and compelled her to help them play the nobility's political games . . . games Deirdre had once played for Boann a lifetime ago, when she had been a Dralish noble in the city of Highland.

For the past decade, Typhon had compelled her to become his Regent of Spies, to help renew the network of demon worshipers that Fellwroth had devastated when he usurped the demon's control of the Disjunction. Presently, most of Avel's powerful citizens—military commanders, merchants, bankers, even clergy—were sworn to Typhon. Without their help, he would never have enslaved Cala. The demon made Deirdre use her politi-

cal savvy to manipulate Avel's pliable nobles and her strength to assassinate the resistant.

But after years of preparation, Deirdre had put a plan in motion to escape the demon. A bloom of hope made her smile until she wondered if
she'd pushed her luck too far.

She'd convinced the demon that she had been converted, that she was
devoted to the Disjunction. As such, the demon had ceased to search her
memories, which he could only do when in her physical presence. The process also left her debilitated for two or three days and so interfered with her
role as Regent of Spies. It had been two years since he had read her thoughts.
But now that Deirdre was freed, could she continue to fool him? Could she
keep him from reading her mind?

She paused and prayed for strength and a chance to see Boann again.
When finished, she balled her hands into fists and walked out onto the
balcony. To the west, clouds were rolling in from the ocean, darkening the
air with giant columns of rain, but overhead the late afternoon sky shone a
fresh blue.

Deirdre walked along the balcony and found Typhon in a white alabaster body, his usual seven feet of bulging muscle. His mane of silky red hair
hung down his shoulders. From his back grew wings of checkered red and
black feathers. He was facing away from Deirdre.

Near him stood a large cube of blindness. It was not a cube of blackness.
Black was a shade. Deirdre's eye could have perceived and her mind could
have experienced blackness. When she looked at the cube, she did not see
blackness; she simply did not see.

The cube was how she perceived the Savanna Walker. She could resist
most effects the beast had on a mind. This close, most anyone else would
have been aphasic and delirious.

"Demon," Deirdre announced, "I've returned."

Typhon turned. His eyes were now black onyx, but his features were the
same as ever: snub nose, thin lips, high cheekbones. His expression of supercilious amusement filled Deirdre with a hatred so hot it nearly made her
jump. It took every ounce of her control to keep her face blank.

"My troublemaking daughter," Typhon said in his rumbling tone.
"Was it worth it? I thought you were done with childish suicide. It's been
years."

She bowed. "This was not the same. This was for the Disjunction."

It was hard to tell, his features being so white, but Deirdre thought the
demon had raised his eyebrows. "Convince me, daughter. Why did you need
to escape my possession to advance the Disjunction?"

"I had to protect our work from that reckless beast you've taken into your confidence." She glared at the Savanna Walker. It was difficult; her impulse was to look away from blindness.

"Daughter, you are under my compulsion not to oppose—" Deirdre went momentarily deaf as the demon spoke the Savanna Walker's true name.

To better control the monster, Typhon had altered the Savanna Walker's mind so that the beast had less influence over someone speaking or even thinking his true name. As a result, the Walker deafened anyone hearing his name's sounds, blinded anyone seeing its letters.

Deirdre's hearing returned. "If you persist in defying me," Typhon said, "I will reinvest more of my soul in you. Haven't I proven that you are no longer capable of resisting the Disjunction? You cannot help but advance our cause."

"I am convinced, my lord. I will do anything to advance our cause and to convert my beloved Boann to the Disjunction. You must believe—" Her voice stopped and she tottered to her left.

This had happened before. When the Savanna Walker moved, he caused the balcony tiles to vibrate as if in an earthquake. To prevent her from feeling this, the Walker had briefly paralyzed the nerves in her legs that sensed vibration. Those same nerves, she'd learned, also sensed the angle of her joints. Therefore, when they were disabled, it became hard for her to keep her balance when she wasn't looking at her feet.

When Deirdre steadied herself, she found she was deaf again. The Savanna Walker was speaking.

"Typhon," Deirdre said, though she could not hear her own voice. "I must . . . I have to tell you . . ." She stumbled to her left again. Suddenly her hearing and balance returned.

Typhon was frowning at her. "What did you do when you were free?"

She smiled. "The beast isn't being open with you, is he?"

Typhon's frown deepened. "What did you do?"

She bowed. "When I explain, you will want to reward my dedication. And you will want to protect me from any reprisal from the Savanna Walker."

The demon only stared.

Deirdre pressed on. "You know I have long desired to learn how the Silent Blight figures into your plans for the Disjunction. How can I serve our cause without knowing of what you have called our most powerful tool? Perhaps now that I've protected the Disjunction from that beast, you will reward me by telling me of the Silent Blight."

This time Deirdre was ready for the Walker's reply; she spread her feet and waited until she could hear again. Then she looked up at Typhon as he spoke to her: "You've made"—again the Walker deafened her as Typhon spoke his true name—"defensive." The demon stepped toward her. "Tell me now. What exactly did you do?"

She smiled. "I put Francesca into play."

"I gave no such orders," Typhon said coldly. "I've no intention of wounding Nicodemus yet."

Deirdre's smile grew. "And I beg your forgiveness, but it was necessary to . . . to . . ." The Walker had made her deaf to her own voice. She kept talking. "I had to put her into play to protect her and everything we've worked for. As your Regent of Spies, I've learned that the Savanna Walker has been manipulating you. He's determined to remove her for himself."

When she stopped, she was still deaf. Typhon pointed at the Savanna Walker and said something. Deirdre's hearing returned.

The demon studied her. "You put Francesca into play to protect her from the Savanna Walker?"

She nodded. "Francesca will soon find Nicodemus. She can still keep him alive after you wound him. I couldn't tell you what I was planning because the beast would have stolen or killed Francesca before my petition reached your ears."

He studied her. "And so you planned to do this during Nicodemus's little raid?"

"Raid?"

"Nicodemus snuck his students into the sanctuary when the lycanthropes attacked North Gate. The boy and his kobolds fought their way up into my private library."

"I'm sorry, my lord, but I don't understand. What happened?"

The demon snorted. "The shock on your face had better be genuine, or I'll never trust your expression again."

"It is not only genuine but also profound. What are you talking about, my lord?"

Typhon explained how Nicodemus had broken into his private library, nearly reaching him when his mind was partially deconstructed. "I should thank you, daughter. By bringing"—deafness as he said the Walker's true name—"to the sanctuary, you forced Nicodemus to abandon his attack. Though the boy would have discovered a surprise if he had reached me."

As comprehension sank into Deirdre's mind, so did cold dread. Had she inadvertently stopped Nicodemus from freeing her? "My lord, I did not know—"

"Of course not, daughter. But that's not the issue; Francesca is. Tell me everything she said."

Deirdre took a deep breath. Whether or not she had foiled Nicodemus's plan, she had to push on with her own. "My lord, I will humbly withhold my obedience unless you tell me the Walker's true name so I can protect myself from his manipulation. I also humbly request an explanation of the Silent Blight so I might better know the Disjunction's plans."

"Humbly?" The demon laughed and crossed his arms. "I could peel the memories from your mind."

"That would take you a day and leave me incapacitated for longer. You can't afford that. My agents have found proof the Savanna Walker is stealing powerful objects from you again. Remember the Lornish necklace he swallowed two years ago? Or the Ixonian urn the year before that? Only this time the Walker's greed is focused on Francesca." Though the Savanna Walker had stolen from the demon in the past, Deirdre was presently lying; she knew the beast had no designs on Francesca. To induce Typhon to believe her she would have to produce evidence.

She continued, "I have learned that the Walker removed the anklet you put on Francesca. He did so to take power from it, and to hide Francesca from you so he might consume her. I couldn't tell you of my suspicions, my lord, until I knew where the beast hid the anklet. I needed evidence. Now my agents have learned that the Walker is hiding the anklet in the body of one of his followers. One of the bodies that he . . . forgive me, my lord, but I don't know how he consumes them. One of the bodies he swallows? that he magically preserves? Whatever the case, the anklet is in one of those."

Typhon became still as the alabaster statue he resembled. Deirdre knew that the demon was now sending his mind in search of the magical anklet.

Suddenly, Deirdre tottered back a few steps. She was deaf again. When she looked up, she saw the cube of blindness advancing on her. "Don't you dare touch me," she said without hearing her own voice. She might not have the Savanna Walker's ability to manipulate minds, but she was still Typhon's avatar. She could summon enough strength to crush a block of marble with her hands. "I swear on the Creator's name, I will break your—"

The cube stopped advancing. "Both of you will be silent!" It was Typhon, his alabaster body again animated. Moving with frightening speed, the demon marched into the cube of blindness.

For a moment Deirdre was left seemingly alone on the balcony. She took another step back, fought the urge to run.

Suddenly Typhon stepped back out of the cube of blindness. Both his arms up to the elbows were covered with dark, clotting blood. Between the giant thumb and forefinger of his right hand glinted a small silver chain.

Deirdre smiled.

Typhon turned his horrible white face to Deirdre. "Daughter," he said, "you will explain everything you did to Francesca, or I will pluck it out of your mind."

"My lord, you will not have my cooperation until I have the Savanna Walker's true name and knowledge of the Silent Blight. I am the Disjunction's true champion; he is not."

"You are my Regent of Spies," the demon repeated. "I have the right to know."

"And because it is best for the Disjunction," she said with a stiff bow, "I have the right to resist. If you steal the memories from my mind, you'll be cutting our cause when we can't afford to bleed." She nodded at the Savanna Walker. "The beast is manipulating you to—"

"Quiet," the demon snapped and then turned on the Walker. Deirdre heard nothing of what followed but judged by Typhon's expression that he was demanding an explanation from the beast.

Deirdre smiled. The Savanna Walker might be a half-completed dragon, but he wasn't much of a talker. As the demon's avatar, Deirdre could vaguely sense Typhon's emotions; his suspicion was rapidly growing. As well it should; the Walker had demonstrated his greedy and larcenous nature in the past. More important, Typhon had found the anklet in the stomach of one of the Walker's consumed devotees. The demon could not conceive that Deirdre had planted it there . . . and, in fact, she never could have done so without Francesca's help.

Just then she sensed the demon's anger flare. The Walker couldn't explain the anklet. Chances were good that Typhon was now threatening the beast.

At last, Typhon finished speaking to the Walker. He turned and strode past Deirdre before pausing. "I will deal with him later. He has much more to explain. But now, follow me, daughter. We shall peer into your mind to see if your intentions are what you claim. If you prove yourself to be a true servant of the Disjunction, I shall have Canonist Cala teach you of the Silent Blight."

Deirdre bowed and murmured her thanks.

"Nevertheless, I want Francesca brought back immediately. Organize our best agents and find her. I'm not ready to wound Nicodemus."

"Yes, Typhon," she said.

He nodded. "Let's go." The demon started to walk away.

Deirdre bowed again. Now began the most dangerous part of her scheme. She glanced back at the cube of blindness. The beast was standing near the balcony.

Until now, the Walker had ignored her. Their only interactions had been when Typhon had sent the half dragon out to repossess her after she had died. But now the creature knew she was his mortal enemy.

His first attacks would be directed at her person. That would be dangerous, certainly, but later the beast would strike against Nicodemus or, worse, Francesca.

Deirdre needed to act to reduce the beast's power now. Usually, she could do nothing to harm or even hinder the half dragon when possessed by Typhon's soul. But presently the demon was infuriated; it gave her a certain freedom to enact his desire for punishment.

She took a few steps after Typhon and then turned and charged the Savanna Walker. The blindness rushed to meet her.

In a few steps, she moved into the cube of blindness. She'd also gone deaf. Even though she could no longer tell where her limbs were in space, she tried to throw her arms in front of her. A jolt of pain suggested that she'd struck something. She couldn't feel what; her skin had become numb, but she was aware that her forward motion had stopped. Blindly, numbly, she tried to wrap her arms around her foe. She moved her arms so as to lift . . . and . . .

A sudden blast of sound struck her ears: Typhon bellowing for her to stop. A flicker of vision. She was holding a massive object above her head. A long gray something hung before her. It looked like an impossibly long arm consisting of twenty or thirty elbow joints. Beyond stood the balcony railing and the sloping red tiles of the sanctuary's dome. Blindness enveloped Deirdre again.

She bent forward and with all her strength threw the beast forward.

In the next instant, she was panting with the exertion. Sensation returned in a dizzying rush. Something hard and powerful wrapped around her right arm and hoisted her into the air as if she were a child.

It was Typhon grabbing her; she had no doubt about it. But she cried out victoriously as the cube of blindness went tumbling down the dome to a long, sheer fall.

Something forced her to look at the demon's face, now a white mask of anger. "You can no longer resist the Disjunction," he hissed. "Those who oppose us become us."

Deirdre felt as if ice chips were forming in her blood. Some part of her knew—though she did not understand how or why—that the demon spoke the truth.

STANDING GUARD AT the alley's entrance, Nicodemus saw the Savanna Walker fall down the dome, the impossible body tumbling over itself, nightmarish limbs flailing.

"What is it, Nico?" Shannon asked from deeper in the alley. The old man and Nicodemus's disguised students were crouching in the mud of a

Water District alleyway. They had been shambling from one dilapidated neighborhood to the next, hoping to avoid notice.

Nicodemus jogged back into the alley toward Shannon. Behind the old man, the kobolds were spread out, more comfortable in the shade of the alleyway. Vein and Flint were talking quietly, while the other three played a dice game. The sight made Nicodemus's heart ache. Nearly ten years ago, he had led fifteen kobolds out of the Pinnacle Mountains to hunt Typhon. All but these five had been killed by lycanthropes or demon worshipers.

Nicodemus spoke to Shannon. "The Walker just fell from the canonist's quarters."

"A clash between Cala and the beast?" the old man asked.

"Possibly, or the demon is disciplining the Walker. Either way, things are looking worse. We should get out of the daylight."

The old man adjusted his gray robes. "I could have told you that. But where? Under the Sliding Docks?"

Nicodemus shook his head. "Reservoir's full."

"Merchant Dal?"

"Not after what happened to the warehouse last time."

"Old Fatima's gang then?"

"She still is offering a price on my life."

Shannon snorted. "My boy, what did you say that night in her bedroom?"

Nicodemus grimaced. "What about Guy Fire's crew?"

"Remember what Vein did to his brother's left hand?"

"It wasn't Vein's fault. He should have had more sense than to suddenly grab a kobold. And Guy doesn't even like his brother."

Shannon sighed. "Still, won't work. So that leaves the boys at the abandoned gatehouse."

Nicodemus looked at the dome. "They might be our only option." He paused. "What about hiding in the burn?"

"Who's running that territory now?"

Nicodemus looked back. "The old dog still."

Shannon scowled. "I'd rather chew glass."

"Magister, the old dog is not that obnoxious."

Shannon only narrowed his blind eyes.

"All right," Nicodemus said with a sigh, "maybe he is."

fifteen

Francesca opened her eyes as something hard dug into her armpits.

A confused moment passed before she remembered her attempt to disspell Cyrus and his counterattack with the cloth of the landing-bay wall. She must have fainted after he censored her mind. She stood up straighter and the pain left her armpits. Her robes, still iron stiff with hierophantic spells, had kept her from falling to the floor.

Cyrus was standing in front of her, calmly arranging his robes.

"Perhaps this is simply a misunderstanding," he said in a controlled tone. "We both want the same thing. I've sworn to Celeste to serve Avel. As a healer, you also want to serve its citizens. But it's my duty to report any threat. When we talk to the tower warden and the marshal, you'll see they're trustworthy. In the meantime, I will keep you censored."

A sudden memory made Francesca look down at her leg. She could not see the ball of decaying signal texts she'd cast earlier.

Cyrus spoke. "Trying to spellwrite will only make you dizzy."

Francesca's cheeks flushed hot. She berated herself for not realizing the landing bay's cloth walls were textualized. "Cyrus, you're making a mistake," she said as evenly as she could. "This is dangerous. You must uncensor me."

He stopped straightening his robes and looked at her. "No, Francesca, I won't." He lowered his veil, and began to unwind his turban.

She'd watched this ritual many times before. It made them both quiet. His thick black hair was shorter than she remembered but still cascaded down about his head in loose curls. His complexion was light brown, his nose aquiline. His strong jaw was made more prominent by a trimmed, jet-black beard. "I don't know you anymore," he said. "I can't trust you like I once did. There's too much at stake."

"You mean, you still haven't forgiven me."

"Perhaps not. But that's not what this is about."

"Isn't it?"

He frowned. "You think I'm being irrational?"

"You have too much faith in your order. The Avel hierophants might have been corrupted."

"By a demon who crossed the ocean? Francesca, that's madness." He stepped closer. "You can't trust this Deirdre woman."

Francesca tried to touch her own face but found her arm still trapped in her stiff robes. "Cyrus, she died on my table and then came back to life. She's not a woman; she's an immortal avatar. Something horrible is happening in Avel, so we have to be smart."

"And I'm not being smart?"

"You're being a loyal soldier." A shadow passed above them as a lofting kite alighted in a different landing bay.

He crossed his arms. "And that's still what hierophants are to you? Loyal, unthinking Spirish soldiers? Not authors like the exalted wizards?"

"You take duty and hierarchy too far."

He threw his hands up. "How do you do it, Fran? I catch you when you fall out of a kite. I fly you away from some blasted aphasia curse. I even bind and censor you, and you still manage to patronize me. Don't you see that for once you're not in control?"

He was beginning to breathe faster. Francesca felt a grim satisfaction. The more she could upset him, the better.

She shook her head and felt her stiff collar rub against her neck. "I don't mean to patronize you, Cyrus. You're right, I can't trust Deirdre. But I can't trust the tower warden or the air marshal either. I can't trust anyone."

His hands clenched. "I am sorry, Francesca, but just this once you have to trust me."

"No, I don't. You're going to release me."

"You're censored. You can't order me around."

She kept her voice calm. "I can. You just don't know what's best now."

"Holy bloody canon! That's it! I'm done talking to you," he snapped and then grimaced and touched his chest. "You're impossible." He grimaced again, and then shook his left hand. Tiny beads of sweat glistened on his forehead.

"Cyrus, it's started. You're in danger," Francesca said earnestly. "You must listen to—"

"Damn it, I'm not going to waste my time!" He turned and marched toward the wall flap. "I'll be back in . . ." After a few steps, he brought his hand to his chest and gasped.

"You feel a crushing pain just under your sternum," Francesca announced. "It's moving to your left arm, maybe your left jaw as well."

He looked back at her, his face twisted with pain.

"Your heart's racing. You're sweating. Maybe you even taste something metallic."

He swallowed. "When did you do it? When you were searching my body for the curse?"

She nodded.

"You put a spell in my brain?"

"Your heart."

He grimaced. "What's it doing?"

"With every beat, your heart pumps blood into the aorta and so to the rest of your body. There are two small arteries at the aorta's base that run back down and supply your heart with blood, the coronary arteries. There's a short Magnus sentence wrapped around your left coronary. It's contracting, depriving your heart of blood. Your ability to spellwrite is decreasing."

"Burning heaven! How could you—" His words cut short as he gasped. "You're a physician. You swore never—"

"Never to harm a patient," she said evenly. "You, Cyrus, are not my patient. Presently you're my captor who is threatening to disclose information that may endanger all of Avel. My physician's oath compels me to stop you however I can. Now, stay calm. Slow your pulse and stop spellwriting; your heart will need less blood. The pain will decrease."

He took a slow breath. "What if I order another hierophant to disspell it?"

She sniffed. "It had better be done perfectly. You've sharp words next to your heart. If one should go astray . . ."

He closed his eyes and then shook his head. He spoke in a low rasp. "Celeste and every demigod in her canon damn you to the burning hells, Francesca."

"I couldn't trust—"

"You always had to win," he whispered and clamped his eyes shut. "You haven't changed a bit."

Guilt moved through Francesca. "Cyrus . . . I'm sorry."

"Like hell you are." He clutched his chest again. "Right, Fran, you win. You win again. How'd you know to make the spell contract now?"

She kept her voice even. "I had been casting signaling texts. Every few moments, one would hit the spell in your heart, instructing it not to construct. But since you censored me . . ."

He let out a tremulous breath and laughed humorlessly. "A fail-safe. You wrote a fail-safe."

She nodded. "More like a fail-deadly. It's a spell we clerics use in extreme circumstances. Sometimes, we're approached by bandits or rogue spellwrights. They want us to treat their wounded. So we cast the death sentence on the leader's coronary artery before we proceed. If any of the rogues censor or kill us, their leader dies."

"You call this spell a death sentence?"

"Uncensor me and I'll loosen yours."

He walked over and touched the stole tied around her temples. The red silk fell to her shoulders. Her robes were again merely slack fabric. A chill ran through Francesca's head as she was restored to magic. After shivering, she flicked a wave of signal spells into Cyrus's chest. One struck the sentence constricting his coronary artery, and it relaxed.

"Did it work?" Cyrus asked.

She nodded. "So long as I'm near you and uncensored, you won't have a problem."

He pressed a hand to his forehead and looked exhausted. "And if I tell the tower warden about Deirdre?"

"You won't."

He looked at her. "How in all the hells is this supposed to work, Fran? You're going to hold my spellbound heart hostage, kill me if I do something you don't like?"

She straightened her stole. "You've sworn to protect Avel. I've sworn to care for her people. We both need to discover what is threatening the city. But we have to be subtle about it. I was hoping I wouldn't have to coerce you, that I could make you see reason. But you fought me all the way. So now the sentence stays around your coronary, and I will be making the decisions."

Cyrus rubbed his temples. "Death sentence," he muttered and then laughed. He turned to look her in the eyes. "I don't know what hurts more: your getting the better of me, your strangling my heart, or your damned stupid pun."

Sixteen

Cyrus had just removed the spells from Francesca's robes when the hierophantic apprentice returned with orders to report to the warden and marshal on the jumpdeck. After delivering her message, the girl hurried away.

Cyrus stared at Francesca. "I refuse to lie."

"Then don't," she said. "Just leave out what's dangerous. You were flying above Avel when you saw me fall from a kite. After catching me, you learned that the sanctuary might be under attack and came here to warn the wind marshal."

He crossed his arms. "You want me to be a storyteller?"

"Unless you can keep our fat from the fire with another art form. Dance perhaps? Want to double step around the warden while I pirouette for the marshal? Or maybe sculpt a bust of the—"

"Don't be difficult," he said. "Very well. I'll tell them just what they need to know." He paused and then added, "For now."

"Good. Until we know what's truly happening, it's your duty to be careful."

"Don't tell me about duty, Magistra." He turned toward the flap. "Come on then; let's get this over with." She followed and discovered a rope ladder and the long sandstone side of the garden tower. Fifty feet below, a field of knee-high grass waved in the constant wind.

Cyrus climbed up the ladder as sure as a squirrel on a tree. Every gust made Francesca cling to the rungs. When Cyrus was more than ten feet ahead, she called out for him to wait. He looked back, his black curls flying, his face unreadable.

When she was close enough to touch his heels, they climbed twenty feet more to a narrow ledge that led into a dim hallway. Cyrus helped her off the ladder but then pulled her aside so that three hierophants could pass. Each man had a large cloth pack strapped to his back. Francesca hadn't noticed them on the ladder, but they must have been climbing impatiently behind her.

Cyrus led her after the three hierophants down the dim hallway. Eventually they entered a long, narrow space that stretched upward for a great length. Far above them shone a strip of blue sky dappled with seaborn clouds. It was like standing at the bottom of a deep mountain fissure. But the fissure walls were made not of stone but of row upon row of scaffolding. Some supported elaborate pulleys and chains. About half of the scaffolding was filled with folded sailcloth.

Francesca watched one of the hierophants climb among these scaffoldings and then remove his pack. He handed it off to another man, received another pack, and began hiking up a long staircase.

Suddenly Francesca understood what she was seeing. She had known that the garden tower was a warehouse. Mundane sailcloth was shipped down from Dar and Queensport and unloaded at Coldlock Harbor. From there it was flown to the garden tower, from the tower to the windcatchers, where it was saturated with hierophantic language.

The men she was watching had just returned a batch of saturated cloth and were about to fly blank cloth out to the windcatcher. She was watching a link in the long chain of literary production that supplied the hierophants of Daga, Queensport, and Erram with enough language to keep their airships aloft and their merchant ships sailing faster even than the legendary Ixonian catamarans.

If the hierophants failed to produce enough cloth, their kingdom's great trading wealth would vanish. Worse, the Spirish armies and fleets would lose their aerial and naval support. Like all other literary disciplines—the wizards, the pyromancers, and so on—the hierophants had sworn never to directly participate in the wars of the six human kingdoms. But this promise did not stop them from providing reconnaissance, communication, and limited transportation to the Spirish forces. Without this advantage and the gold brought in by merchant ships with hierophantic sails, the east coast of Spires would once again become a thoroughfare for the armies of Lorn and Verdant as the old enemies once again went for each other's throats.

As Francesca thought about all this, Cyrus led her through the fissure-like space to a narrow set of stairs.

Twice, Francesca saw where the stairs branched off into hallways. Once she glimpsed a dormitory. Everything was cramped—steep steps and low ceilings. It reminded her of being inside a boat's hull, which made sense considering that half of all hierophants served on Spirish merchant ships. Many male hierophants took to seaships, where their greater weight was not as much of a disadvantage as it was aboard an airship.

"I'll do the talking," Cyrus said as they neared the tower's top. "If you must speak, don't show off. And always show equal respect to both the warden and the marshal."

They stepped outside. The brilliant sky now held tall white clouds that flew overhead with dreamlike speed. The wind was strong and carried bursts of rain so fine it was more like mist. Below them, the redwood jump-deck was perhaps twenty feet wide and thirty long, still wet from the last rain.

In the upwind direction, the tower sloped down like a shark's fin to provide a row of smaller decks, where incoming airships and windcatchers docked. To the east, the pass stretched away inland. All the wide mouths of the windcatchers faced them. Francesca focused on the nearest one.

Inside the windcatcher, hundreds of radial sails were arranged like windmill blades and rotated around a central point. Somehow a hierophant was suspended within the windcatcher. The many sails focused the energy of their rotation into the hierophant's heart and accelerated its spellwriting. Each augmented heartbeat produced a hundred thousand times more runes than it otherwise would.

This was the hierophantic key to power. Their language was produced only in heart muscle, was limited to cloth, and melted into a wind when cast. However, they had harnessed nature's power, transformed the wind into words. From a school of kite-flying hermits on the slopes of Mount Spires, they had grown into the linguistic backbone of a powerful kingdom.

"Warden!" a man yelled.

Suddenly Francesca noticed two hierophants standing under a small wooden pavilion on the deck's downwind side. Both were of average height for hierophants, which was to say barely five feet tall. Neither wore a turban or veil. The first was a man with pale skin, short white hair thinning in the front. The second was a gaunt, dark brown woman who kept her dense black and silver hair trimmed close to her head. She was facing away, seemingly studying her wind garden.

Given their ranks, both hierophants had to be powerful spellwrights, and so would have aged only slowly. Though he looked late into his forties, she late into her fifties, Francesca would guess they were both past their first century.

"Cyrus!" the man was calling. He gestured for them to approach. "What's this news about an attack?"

Cyrus and Francesca walked over. "Warden Treto," he said, bowing to the man and then the woman. "Marshal Oria." The woman looked away from the pass only long enough to nod at the newcomers.

Cyrus cleared his throat. "Apologies for my sudden appearance. We had an unexpected event at Avel."

"Go on," the tower warden said.

Cyrus's eyes flickered to Francesca and then back to his superiors. "This is Magistra Francesca DeVega, a cleric of our canonist's infirmary. I was flying above Avel, coordinating the watch patrols when Magistra made an emergency blind jump. When I caught her and learned the infirmary was under attack from a curse, I flew here to warn the wind garden."

The tower warden's eyes narrowed. "What orders did you leave?"

The light around them dimmed as a cloud covered the sun. Cyrus shifted his weight. "My pilots had patrol orders. The lycanthropes had just ambushed a caravan at the North Gate. We were on watch for a second attack."

The tower warden frowned. "But regarding the curse in the sanctuary, what orders did you give?"

"None, sir."

"Aren't you concerned for your city? What did—"

Without looking away from the pass, the marshal laid a hand on the tower warden's arm. He fell silent. "Magistra DeVega," the marshal said in a powerful voice, "what makes you think it was an attack?"

Francesca cleared her throat. "My lady, aphasia was spreading among all spellwrights in the infirmary."

The marshal looked at Francesca. "You knew the dangers of opening a jumpchute?"

Francesca met the older woman's eyes. "I judged them merely disastrous compared with the catastrophic danger of not opening the jumpchute."

The marshal paused before turning back to the pass.

The tower warden was still looking at Cyrus. "But why, Air Warden of Avel, did you abandon your city?"

Cyrus opened his mouth to reply, but the marshal preempted him. "Do not answer that, Air Warden," she commanded. "Avel exists to support the wind garden, not the other way around."

The tower warden pursed his lips but said nothing.

The marshal spoke again. "An attack on Avel threatens its citizens; an attack on our wind garden threatens all of Spires."

Just then two hierophants emerged onto the jumpdeck. Both wore white cloth packs on their backs and carried folds of bright orange cloth. They trotted over to the pavilion.

The marshal pointed to one of the nearby windcatchers. "The first of you to the third rig." She pointed to another farther back. "The second to the eighth. And tell Julia to pull herself down ten feet; she's draining the wind from number twelve."

Both of the new hierophants threw the orange folds into the air. The bright cloth snapped into wide crescents, catching the wind and hoisting the pilots aloft. Within moments, the wind had blown the hierophants far away from the garden tower. Their kites changed shape, causing each to fly toward the designated windcatchers.

Francesca realized that she had been holding her breath in amazement. Even watching from the deck, she had an almost dizzying sensation of velocity and control.

Marshal Oria looked at the tower warden. "Pull the second watch out of the mess. Arm all pilots and form two wings. Take command of the first and set up a hovering patrol on the pass's northeast edge. Should you judge the wind garden to be threatened, drop the flag signal for all windcatchers to dock. I will loft all kites. You are to command any needed defense. Am I clear?"

The tower warden bowed.

The marshal continued. "For the second group, name your most trusted author wing commander. Charge them to circle Avel looking for signs of conflict or distress. They're to relay by flag any report to you. If it appears safe, they're to tether with the city flock and have one pilot who's seen combat pull down to investigate. Questions?"

The tower warden's face had gone blank. "The *Queen's Lance*, my lady?"

The marshal looked away to the pass. "I want her aloft until we know what's happening in Avel. I won't allow her to dock without your presence." She looked at the warden and said, "Don't worry; I'll respect your office." There was nothing friendly about her tone.

"Permission to speak to the air warden of Avel?"

"Granted, but I want you aloft immediately after."

"Yes, Lady."

"Dismissed," she said before turning back to her view of the pass. "Magistra DeVega, join me."

Francesca started. "Yes, Lady." She glanced at Cyrus. He had become as still as stone and was staring straight ahead.

"Cyrus," the tower warden commanded, "you'll accompany me to the mess."

After turning to Francesca, he brought his hand to his heart and glowered.

She flicked a short spell into his chest. "You'll be fine for a quarter hour," she whispered. "It won't start contracting until then. But don't you dare leave me here!"

Cyrus only grunted before heading off with the tower warden.

Acutely aware of the three hundred foot drop beyond the jumpdeck, Francesca carefully approached the marshal. "My lady Oria?" When standing next to the other woman, she realized that she was almost a foot taller.

The marshal did not seem impressed by this. "Magistra, forgive my ignorance. For the past thirty years, I've done little other than fly oversized kites." She gestured to the windcatchers. "But do I recall that as a wizard you are not a subject of any crown?"

Francesca nodded. "You do."

"Therefore you represent only the wizardly order?"

"It's a shade more complicated in my case, Lady. After mastering both wizardly languages, I trained in the clerical academy in Port Mercy. There I learned how to write medical texts. In effect, I left the wizardly order and joined the clerical one. Clerics have no language or deity or political interests as the wizards do. Our purpose is only to relieve the burden of disease."

The marshal nodded. "An admirable purpose, cleric. Admirable. And, as one woman of purpose to another, I ask you frankly not to toy with me."

"My lady, I should never dream of doing so."

The woman glanced at her with a blank military expression and then flashed a sudden, affected smile. "Splendid. Now, can you tell me why that warship has two black-robes aboard?"

Francesca frowned. "What warship?"

The marshal looked up at the cloud that was blocking the sun. When Francesca followed her gaze, she jumped and swore, "Holy blasted heaven aflame!"

It wasn't a cloud but a long, sleek airship hovering with perfect steadiness in the powerful wind. Its narrow foresails projected forward like the cutting blade of some curved weapon. The angular side and aft sails made constant, tiny, reflexive adjustments to accommodate for changes in the wind. The result kept the ship perfectly still. It seemed like some giant bird of prey ready to drop into a murderous dive.

The ship was no more than thirty feet above them, giving Francesca a sudden, ludicrous urge to duck.

The ship's hexagonal hull looked delicate—more like spun-glass than like a warship's spine. It consisted of six strips of silk that must have been sixty feet long. One served as a wide floorboard. The others were held apart by a hexagonal frame of thin rods—likely also enchanted silk. Because there were spaces between the silk strips, Francesca could see through the hull to the sky beyond.

With a sudden intake of breath, she realized that she could also see three green-robed figures moving rapidly about the ship. Two moved within the hull. The third walked out onto a side wing as if it were as solid as a mountainside. The figure squatted and began moving its hands, no doubt editing the wing's text.

Just then, Francesca realized that a hierophantic airship was really a gigantic, flying manuscript.

Then Francesca saw the two black-robes. They were standing within the hull. Apparently, a man and a woman. Even though they were thirty feet above her, Francesca could tell that that the two wizards were staring down directly at her.

"My lady," Francesca blurted, "I have no idea who they are."

"It is odd," the marshal said, "two wizards in a Kestrel-class cruiser."

"Because of the wizards who supported Celeste in the past?"

The marshal raised her eyebrows in mock surprise. She spoke ironically: "Magistra, I hadn't made that connection, but now that you mention it, yes. That is peculiar. Two wizards in a Kestrel arriving the same day a wizard in Avel falls out of a kite because an unknown curse has spread through the sanctuary."

"My lady, bring those two down here and they will tell you that I have no political connection to the wizardly order. This red stole around my shoulders"—here she held up her mark as a cleric—"has separated me from the other black-robes."

The marshal looked her up and down. "Magistra, you strike me as someone who has more skill with words than she lets on. I wouldn't scold myself if you've deceived me. You also strike me as someone unaware of the role she's playing. So I will tell you now that my loyalty to Celeste is as strong now as it was on the day I joined the monotheistic armada."

Francesca stammered. "M-my lady, I'm not—"

The other woman raised her hand. "Magistra, I believe you. Don't protest now. Only . . . remember what I have said." With that, she grabbed a strip of cloth hanging near one of the pavilion's beams. Suddenly, a bright green and yellow flag unfurled from the pavilion's apex.

An instant later, the wind brought a yell. Francesca looked up at the warship. All of the hierophants climbing about the rig were now looking at the flag. The green-robe who had been editing the wing stepped off of it and dropped into the air.

Francesca sucked in a breath, but then she saw the thin strip of green cloth running out of the man's robes, slowing his fall. Above him, the warship's wings adjusted to counteract the torque he was exerting on her.

The hierophant dangled just above the deck long enough to remove what looked like silk slippers.

Without looking away from the man, Francesca cleared her throat and said, "My lady, may I say something frank to you?"

"You may."

"You are one God-of-gods damned intimidating leader. I think I'd wrestle a lycanthrope if you ordered me to."

The marshal looked at her. "Magistra, haven't you learned that any commander worth her weight can't be charmed?"

"Good thing you're not my commander then. You still have the luxury of being charmed."

The other woman studied her face a moment then laughed. "Good thing," she agreed and then looked away.

Now barefoot, the hierophant from the airship dropped to the deck, lowered his veil, and unwound his turban. He trotted to the pavilion and bowed. "Marshal Oria." He was a short, lean man with chestnut-colored skin that was just beginning to go slack with age. His eyes were large and dark brown, his shaved head glossy. Given that he was a powerful spellwright, Francesca would guess he had seen eighty or ninety years.

The marshal's expression relaxed. "Captain Izem, don't ask for permission to dock the *Queen's Lance*. There is distressing news from Avel, and I want you aloft until we know for certain what is happening."

The captain bowed his shaved head. "So shall it be. We are happy to do anything your service requires."

The marshal grunted. "Hopefully we will require nothing. But meantime, please explain the two black-robes skulking about in your hull."

The captain laughed. "My lady, I was hoping you were going to explain them to me. We were docked at Lurrikara when orders came from Queensport to fly two black-robe dignitaries from Kara to Avel. For the whole flight, begging your pardon, Magistra"—this last to Francesca—"they've been the perfect model of academics: polite, quiet, and obnoxiously aloof. Neither I nor my crew can figure heads from tails why they get to fly in the *Queen's Lance*."

The marshal sighed. "I'm not fond of intrigue in my garden, Captain."

Izem bowed. "Then I'll pray to the sky and the holy canon that I'll soon fly them away."

Just then, Cyrus appeared by Francesca's side. "Lady Marshal," he said in a formal tone, "the tower warden reports that he'll have both wings aloft momentarily."

Captain Izem looked up and smiled broadly. "Oh dear, my lady, it seems one of the local idiots has dressed up like a hierophant and wandered into your tower. Look at the poor creature; he's clearly too big and heavy to ever pilot."

Suddenly Francesca became acutely aware that she was a head taller than everyone else. Rarely was she conscious of her body, even more rarely unhappy with it. But at that moment she felt like a giant.

Cyrus smiled but otherwise continued to stare straight ahead.

The marshal looked between the two men. "You two are acquainted?"

Izem laughed. "Forgive the familiarity on your deck, my lady. You are lucky to have a hierophant like Air Warden Alarcon. He was my first mate for a year of fine flying. Haven't seen a better pilot of kite or airship since the Siege of Erram, which makes up for his being so damned tall and heavy."

Oria exhaled in a way that indicated both annoyance and amusement. "Air Warden, you have permission to speak."

Still smiling, Cyrus nodded and turned to his captain. "It is good to see you too, sir. Have you managed to keep the *Queen's Lance* out of the ocean now that you don't have me to correct your tacking subspells?"

The captain waved away the comment. "Saltwater gets the stains out of the silk."

Just then two dozen hierophants emerged onto the jumpdeck. All had their headdresses tightly wound, and all held folds of brightly colored lofting kites. Short steel blades glinted from among their green robes. Without hesitation, the newcomers ran off the deck and cast up their kites. With the pop of unfolding cloth, each one took flight and shot away on the powerful wind. In a heartbeat, they were away, rising into the sky and dividing themselves into two neat formations.

The marshal watched them with keen attention. The rest of the group had fallen silent. When one of the formations disappeared over a mountain, she looked back at them. "Magistra, excuse the captain and me." She looked at Cyrus. "Air Warden, attend to our guest. You are dismissed."

Cyrus bowed and then gestured for Francesca to go ahead of him. Francesca bowed to both the marshal and the captain before heading for the doorway that led into the tower. As she walked, she noticed the sea was now obscured by a dark cloudscape—another storm, an hour away.

As soon as she stepped into the hallway, Cyrus took her arm. "Something is happening," he whispered. "Something dire."

"What do you mean?"

"I don't understand completely. There are terrible forces at play."

"So do you believe me now? Can we investigate Avel without telling the world about it?"

"This involves more than Avel. Something's happening in the whole kingdom. Seems Deirdre wasn't lying about being Avel's Regent of Spies."

"What do you mean?"

He looked past her, looking for anyone nearby on the jumpdeck. "A split is coming. Wind marshals are appointed by the Celestial Court to supply the entire order with text. Wardens are appointed by the local canonist. Their duty is to the city."

Francesca pursed her lips. "And, naturally, there are tensions between a city and its kingdom."

"This is more than tension. You saw how the marshal and the warden argued in front of us. It got worse when he got me alone. He thinks the aphasia was an attack from Celeste on Cala. Apparently there are two wizards in the *Queen's Lance*. Years ago, a faction of wizards fought in our civil war. I can't remember what their name was. But—"

"The counter-prophecy faction," she supplied. "They supported Celeste's monotheism. They wanted a unified Spires to check the power of Lorn and Verdant. But they acted without the whole academy's approval, went rogue essentially."

Cyrus sniffed. "As if that matters to hierophants. Don't you see what today's events look like? The aphasia, your jumping blindly from Avel, the Kestrel with two wizards."

"Yes, yes," she said. "The marshal had the same suspicions. She thinks it's some test. Something Celeste cooked up to see if she's loyal. She tried to assure me that she's—"

"But that's just it!" Cyrus interrupted. "The tower warden made the same interpretation, but he kept talking about how Avel produces more enchanted cloth than any other wind garden. He thinks they should shut down the garden, miss the next few shipments, see how Queensport and Erram do without it."

He touched her elbow. "He thinks that Cala is the most powerful demigod in the canon, that if she hadn't graciously surrendered to Celeste in the Siege of Avel, the realm would still be polytheistic. This place is within inches of tipping into hostility between warden and marshal, city and kingdom, canonist and high goddess. Do you see, Fran? Do you see what would rage across the whole realm if that spilled out into violence?"

Francesca nervously looked out toward the sky. The *Queen's Lance* had fallen back in the wind and now hovered just above the jumpdeck. It looked like nothing so much as a giant, perfectly poised blade.

"God-of-gods defend us," she said. "I do."

Seventeen

The secluded Hall of Ambassadors stood three stories up on a wide building that abutted the sanctuary's dome. The inner walls were covered with green and white mosaics of geometric design. Plain terracotta tile covered the floor, but the high vaulted redwood ceiling boasted a hundred thousand tiny half domes and cupolas.

A long grid of sandstone pillars supported the ceiling and made the expansive room feel like a forest. The pillars running along the outer walls supported horseshoe arches, their stones painted alternately green or white.

At one end of the hall stood a tall redwood throne, currently empty. Behind this, an ornate screen separated the hall from the dome's black interior, where the canonist's ark was housed.

Deirdre took in all this as she remembered Typhon examining the superficial aspects of her mind to discover if she was committed to the Disjunction. Deirdre had filled her heart with the desire to recover Boann, to save her from the coming chaos. In her core, Deirdre knew that to save her beloved she would abandon all her moral objections, all her schemes. Typhon interpreted this love as a willingness to try to convert Boann to the cause of the Disjunction.

She made sure that Typhon discovered this love. It was the lever he had worked into her soul during the long years of possession, the mechanism by which he believed he had converted her to the Disjunction.

Once satisfied that her feelings had not changed, the demon sent her to wait in the Hall of Ambassadors while he retrieved the Savanna Walker.

Presently, Deirdre stood before the room's western wall, looking out one of the horseshoe arches at storm clouds rolling down from the Auburn Mountains. Despite the sunlight still shining on her, she shivered as she realized that, in a way, the demon truly had converted her. She would do anything to save Boann.

Deidre shook her head and tried to focus on the city before her. Her gaze fell from the sky to the Burnished District—the wealthy strip of city that ran between the sanctuary and the canyon's edge. Here, Avel's nobility and wealthiest citizens lived in grand villas filled with gardens, plazas, and towers topped with bright brass. The finest and tallest of these ran along the lip of the canyon, so the aristocracy could look down on the wide canyon floor and the city's fields of wheat, lentils, and chickpeas.

To the south and west, the surrounding hills fell to meet the canyon floor and become continuous savanna. But where the canyon sides were high, Avel used them to keep out lycanthropes. A wide sandstone wall ran along the canyon's mouth and protected the crops.

At the canyon's other end, north of the sanctuary, stood the Dam of Canonist Cala—a massive, splendid barrier, composed of one unified piece of sandstone. It looked to have been grown rather than built. From her present angle, Deirdre could make out only the upper third of the structure. This far away, the rock appeared to vary gradually from pale tan near its lip down to a dusky red. Had she been closer, Deirdre would have seen in the stone a myriad of tiny striations, ranging from ash white to blood red.

"There is no other structure like it on this continent," a soft voice said.

Deirdre turned to regard a tall woman whose eyes were striated with all the colors of sandstone: tawny, tan, white, dark gray. Though Deirdre had seen the canonist's eyes before, they still shocked her. They were almost insectoid. The demigoddess's solid features—large, shapely nose and wide lips—were proud, beautiful. What skin she exposed was deep reddish brown, visibly rough in texture.

Deirdre swallowed. Cala was half deity, half woman, brutally enslaved by Typhon. Often the demon would leave her frozen as a statue for days at a time.

Deirdre bowed. "My lady. It is an honor."

Cala nodded. She wore loose garments of pale blue silk and a snowy white cowl. The thin cloth seemed more to accentuate than conceal the demigoddess's statuesque body. Her strong shoulders tented above her folded arms. Her waist narrowed slightly before widening into the broad curves of her hips. The silk hung loose to her bare feet. But as the canonist stepped forward, her muscular thigh curved the cloth.

Deirdre cleared her throat. "Typhon wishes you to instruct me about the Silent Blight. I had hoped we might also discuss how I could better serve you and the city."

For a long moment the canonist did not respond. She looked past Deirdre to the dam. "All the sandstone found in Western Spires is porous," she said at last. "It would seem an obvious question, but few people ever ask why I use a porous rock to hold back water."

Deirdre paused. Uncertain if this was supposed to have a second meaning. "Canonist, why do you use porous rock?"

The demigoddess did not seem to hear Deirdre. "There are roughly forty thousand souls living in my city. All yield some of their strength to me to keep the dam and the walls standing. I'd feel more comfortable with thirty five thousand subjects, fewer mouths to feed. But times are rich. The plague and the flux have stayed away, helped by shipments of hydromancer medicine from Ixos. More important, the rains have come every year for nearly a score. No wars have pulled away our young men and returned them crippled or suffering from venereal disease. Two banking houses from Queensport have built offices in the Cypress District. It's been hard to stop the artisans, the singers, the prostitutes who are just barely eating in Dar or Queensport from emigrating down here. Droughts and lycanthropes be damned."

Deirdre pursed her lips, confused. What was the canonist trying to tell her?

Cala continued: "It's been like this before. The decades before the Civil War, brilliant years. Even the Canic peoples were well fed. So much life, like water building up behind a dam. At times I wondered if anything other than war was possible. When Celeste flew her armada over from Kara, there was a brief sky battle. Some tried to call it a siege, but it was nothing like the campaigns in the East. Still, it was horrifying: airships clashing, pilots leaping from slashed rigs, warkites circling like sharks, cutting stray pilots to rags before they reached ground."

The demigoddess looked at Deirdre. "The bodies fell on the city or in the savanna. Celeste had planted insurgents in the Palm District and in North Gate. When the fighting broke out, the lycanthropes knocked holes in our outer walls. The wolves filled the Water District, the Palm District, the North Gate District. Still, we could have fought Celeste. We could have rebuffed her. It would have bled us both, and Avel would have remained a free city. But I chose not to bleed the realm. Only when I submitted to Celeste did the pores in the outer walls close."

Deirdre stiffened. She had hoped to reach out to Cala, to offer alliance against Typhon. Perhaps that would not be wise. "My lady," she said, "you are drawing a connection from your porous sandstone to your city, but I'm afraid . . . I'm afraid I don't understand your subtle meaning."

The demigoddess shook her head. "There is no subtlety, only history. Back then I was two beings, a secular queen named Miranda and a freely expressed goddess named Cala. But under Celeste's monotheism, I had to become one canonist—Cala bound within Miranda. We're one woman now, more Cala than Miranda I suppose, horrible for us both." She looked down at her body. "My present cell. Imprisonment is sometimes necessary."

Deirdre resisted the urge to bite her lip. "Your sacrifice will not be forgotten."

The canonist smiled tightly. "It already has been. After the Civil War, Avel was reduced to a textual colony, committed to shipping the majority of our wind garden's language away to be used by Celeste." She paused. "But now we have well-guarded caravans filled with grain and silk rolling down from Dar. The Queen's fleet built Coldlock Harbor to ship our sail-cloth out, but now we can haul wagons of dried salmon over the Auburn Mountains and through North Gate. Now, more so than under the polytheism, there is enough food."

"But there is more to life than survival," Deirdre said carefully. "Typhon has promised that we, as his captains, will help bring in a new age."

Cala looked to her dam. "Some have compared my dam to Richard's Wall in the Lornish uplands. It is not a fair comparison. Richard's Wall is simply a barrier that keeps the timber lycanthropes in the Tulgety Forest. Really no different from our city walls."

The demigoddess adjusted her cowl. "Whereas my dam is not a just barrier, but also an aquifer. With my godspell, I can control the pores within the sandstone, to govern how much water seeps to the crops on the canyon floor. To be sure, the grains from Dar and the fish from Coldlock are fine supplements, but without those fields, we starve. To keep this city alive, we must keep some things out and let others in." Suddenly she looked at Deirdre. "What do you know of Language Prime?"

"Little," Deirdre admitted. "I know it creates all living things, that it is the language from which all other languages come."

"And the fundamentals of life, what do you know of them?"

"Nothing really."

The demigoddess nodded. "Nor did I until Typhon came to our Avel." She turned away from Deirdre and began walking toward the redwood throne. "Life can be broken into discrete units, but those units can only become so small. Most often, Language Prime can function only within these units. And each of these tiny divisions of life is like a city. Toxins must be kept out, sustenance brought in."

She gestured behind her in the direction of the dam. "For Avel, water must be held in, lycanthropes held out. Our civilization is imprisoned by the savanna. Without the porous dam, without the permeable walls, our small cell of a city would dry up and die. And those barriers must constantly change. When monotheism unified this realm, I had to change them."

Deirdre swallowed. At last, she understood what Cala was driving toward. "And now that Typhon has come, you have made yourself permeable to the Disjunction."

The goddess walked up the dais to the throne. "I have." She turned and sat. "I worry that you, Regent of Spies, are a spirit dedicated to knocking down walls."

"My lady, I would never jeopardize the Disjunction—"

"Deirdre," the demigoddess interrupted, "governing the Disjunction is Typhon's burden." She paused, meaningfully. "To him we are both loyal." Another pause. "But I speak to you now about the city because I am the city."

Deirdre bowed.

"You must understand that a soul is no different than a city. An individual must choose what she will repel and what she will allow. If she chooses unwisely, she will perish. Do you understand?"

Deirdre searched the demigoddess's face and found only calm interest. "Yes, my lady, I understand about the soul," Deirdre said, even though she did not.

"Good," Cala answered. "You have done an impressive job as Typhon's Regent of Spies. Within a decade, you two have transformed the city's leadership from that which I had assembled to one that serves the demons."

"My lady, I—"

"Don't interrupt. I am not accusing you, merely stating a fact. Typhon has kept his canonist and his Regent of Spies separated. If your power is growing, then I and this city will come to depend on you. You must advise us as to what we must permit and what we must repel."

Unsure of what to say, Deirdre nodded.

"Deirdre, my lady, should I make myself permeable to you and the forces you represent?"

The question shocked Deirdre. The title of "lady" recognized her as an equal. Was this an offer of alliance? Did she know Deirdre was struggling against Typhon, or did the canonist see her only as the demon's new champion, replacing the Savanna Walker? She searched the canonist's face for a clue.

Perhaps there was a glint of secret understanding in those multicolored eyes.

But it was too much of a risk. Deirdre couldn't jeopardize her plans. "My lady, I pledge myself to your service. Permit me to move through your city, and you shall always have my loyalty and . . ." she paused before adding ". . . my vow to help you thrive in any environment."

The canonist held her gaze. Was that an expression of complicit agreement, of an unspoken purpose? Deirdre couldn't be sure. At last, Cala nodded. "Very good. Let us talk of the knowledge you seek. First, the Savanna Walker. His name—or at least what he thinks of as his name—is Ja Ambher."

"Ja Ambher," Deirdre repeated. Now when she spoke or thought of that name, the Walker would be less able to influence her mind. "Where does the name come from? Spires? Verdant?"

"I do not know. Nor, as far as I can tell, does he."

Deirdre bowed. Around them, the hall dimmed. Apparently the storm clouds had reached the city. Rain would be coming soon.

"The second piece of knowledge is harder to explain. And I will admit that I do not rightly understand it."

"I will listen carefully."

Cala leaned back in her throne. "A unique Language Prime text makes up each living creature. Because the world around life is always changing, life must always change; its texts must always change. The processes by which it does this are mysterious, but I do know that Language Prime texts must copy themselves, must recombine with other texts."

Deirdre nodded.

"The Silent Blight is the result of the Disjunction's attempts to change how Language Prime and therefore how all language exists in this world."

"What kind of change?"

Cala drew in a long breath. "It has to do with the differences between deities and humans. Both types of beings are language made life. But humans are made from Language Prime, deities are not."

"From what languages are deities made?"

The canonist shook her head. "I know only that each deity is written in a unique divine language with unique affinities. Our divine text is stored within an ark, just as your Language Prime is stored within your bodies." She touched her fingers to her cheek. "My divine language has an effect on sandstone and is stored in the ark housed within the dome."

Deirdre had to struggle to keep her voice calm. "But, if I may, how is Typhon seeking to change Language Prime?"

"The demon is using the emerald that contains Nicodemus's ability to spell; he's using it to make Language Prime more like the divine languages."

"But how?"

The demigod shifted in her chair. "By making it impossible for Language Prime to misspell."

Eighteen

Francesca followed Cyrus down several hallways to a narrow room furnished with a long table and many chairs. Two candles flickered on one wall. The warm air smelled faintly of wood smoke. After the jumpdeck's brilliant skies and icy winds, the place was a shock of warm, confined darkness.

"The pilot's mess," Cyrus announced while stepping beside her. "Hungry?"

"As a wolf in midwinter. I can't remember the last time I ate."

He pulled out a chair for her and headed for a doorway that led to some kind of pantry. Francesca sat. A thousand tiny pains, of which she had previously been unaware, disappeared from her thighs and calves. She'd been on her feet since before sunrise.

"You used to make that sound every night when you came back from the infirmary," Cyrus called from the kitchen.

Francesca hadn't been aware that she had made a sound. But when she thought about it, she remembered a plaintive moan. She massaged her left shoulder. "Is it safe to talk here?"

Cyrus returned holding a pewter pitcher and plate. She watched intently as he set down the food: Spirish flatbread and thinly sliced hard cheese. She waited for him to fetch two clay cups and pour water into them. "If we keep our voices down, this place will be as safe as any in the tower."

Using her right hand, Francesca folded a flatbread around a slice of cheese. "So now do you agree that we're lambs who've fallen in with lycanthropes?" she asked before taking a bite. The bread was slightly stale, a little tough. But the cheese was rich, tasting sharply of the long season it had aged. It made her mouth water all the more.

"We haven't fallen, Fran. We've been pushed."

"You think Deirdre set us up?" She took another bite.

He sipped his water. "Maybe. Maybe it was someone else."

She had to chew fast and swallow. "That's a damned lot of trouble to warn a freshly trained cleric and a midrank hierophant about a possible resurgence of polytheism."

"Don't be academic, Fran," he said tiredly. "Call it what it is."

"Fine," she said, swallowing again. "Fine. A bloody Second Spirish Civil War. Still doesn't make any sense. Who'd go through that much fuss so that we could figure this out? What, exactly, are we supposed to do about it?"

He raised his veil so that it hung loosely. "I don't know. But Deirdre was right about my ignorance of what's happening in Avel. So you can take this damned sentence off my heart." He tapped his chest. "We're in this together now."

"Are we?" Francesca asked before finishing her flatbread and rolling another. "Do tell me how." She took another bite and studied Cyrus's brown eyes. He met her gaze evenly. She wished he hadn't raised his veil. She couldn't tell if he was frowning or smiling or smirking.

"I'm a hierophant and a Spirishman," he said. "How could I not try to stop a Second Civil War? I'm caught in the middle of all this just like you."

Francesca had no doubt he was earnest, and yet . . . there had to be something else. "What do you mean 'just like' me?"

"Deirdre told you that Typhon brought me back to Avel as a screen, yes? Because I didn't know anything about this situation?"

Francesca nodded.

"What she meant was that I didn't know about the brewing rebellion. I hold the office of air warden by the grace of Canonist Cala, but for the past three years I have served under captains appointed by the Celestial Court. Nowhere—not in Sharptree or on any of my ships—have I heard that Cala might rebel. So, why bring in a hierophant who has a royalist pedigree and no inkling of the fomenting hostilities? How could that be a screen?"

Francesca saw where he was going. "You're a loyal monotheist to keep other monotheists from suspecting," she said before sipping the water. It was cold and very good. "A political smoke screen."

"Exactly," he said, gently touching her arm.

She leaned slightly away from him.

He looked at his hand and drew it back. "But . . . if I suspect a rebellion, I become a liability to the polytheists. Unless I'm careful, I could end up the first casualty of the Second Civil War."

"Lovely," Francesca grunted and put her flatbread down. "So let me guess, now you want to run to loyalist superiors and report what you suspect to them?"

He shook his head. "I can't make accusations without proof. I'm in this as deep as you are. It's my duty to discover what is happening here and report it to the Celestial Court so—"

Suddenly Francesca understood and interrupted with a laugh. "This is your best chance of being made a captain."

He blinked at her. "I'm sorry?"

"You used to tell me how hard it was to become a captain. How there were so few ships, how captains lived so long. Without connections in the Celestial Court or a celebrated reputation, a would-be captain has to wait half a century for a ship. But if you"—she pointed—"deliver proof of a brewing rebellion to the Celestial Court, your name will go to the top of the list."

He folded his arms. "The idea did occur to me, yes, but it is not my primary motivation."

Francesca laughed again. "Oh, yes, of course, you want to do the right thing. Who in all the hells wants to do the wrong thing? But that's not what suddenly made you want to cooperate. Heaven aflame, Cyrus, I spellbound your heart. What else could make you want to work together if not your own personal interest?"

"The chance to irritate you even more through cooperation," he said flatly.

She laughed with pleasure. "I knew it!"

"So then, are we in this together? Or are you—"

Francesca grabbed his arm. "Stop," she whispered. "Stop talking."

"What is it?"

She could feel the ropelike muscles jump under his robes. "I'm not . . ." she said. "I think I saw . . ." But she couldn't say what it was that she thought she had seen. Perhaps a faint golden glimmer? But it had been too faint to have been a spell. Unless . . .

She stood and faced the door. They were standing in the dark hallway, a man and a woman, both dressed in wizardly black.

Their approach had been perfectly silent. Francesca had caught no movement from the corner of her eye. And yet no hint of wizardly text shone about them. Had they wanted to spy on her, they could have hidden under a subtext. "Magistra, Magister," she said stiffly.

Cyrus's chair scraped across the floor as he stood.

"Cleric Francesca DeVega?" the woman asked.

"Yes?"

"Word's come back from the city," the woman reported. "The aphasia has dissipated. No one knows where it came from or what caused it. We were flying on the *Queen's Lance*, which has just docked. May we join you?"

"Of course," Francesca said neutrally.

The two newcomers stepped into the mess hall, almost in unison. The first was a woman, tall, slender, olive skinned, fine features. Even in the dim light, her waist-length hair shone snowy white. It was held in loose ponytail by silver bands bedizened with bits of turquoise—a traditional decoration of Verdantine noblewomen.

The man was taller, strikingly handsome with wide eyes, prominent cheekbones, skin the color of roasted coffee beans. His hair hung in a short cascade of dreadlocks.

As they approached, Francesca realized that the woman had her hand on the man's shoulder. Her eyes were as white as bleached paper. They were walking together because the man was leading her.

When training in Astrophell, Francesca had encountered a few old wizards who had read so much magical text that their eyes clouded over. They became blind to the mundane world but gained a heightened ability to see magical text. Most of these authors had been ancient souls: centuries old, frail, wizened, bent over with age. But the woman standing before Francesca had straight posture and cheeks only slightly wrinkled. She moved with the ease of someone half her age.

Looking at the woman's robe, Francesca discovered a badge displaying a silver eight-pointed star on a field of red. Only the Deans of Astrophell could wear such a device.

That explained the contradiction of relatively smooth skin and cloudy eyes. Any Dean of Astrophell would be, without doubt, one of the most powerful wizards alive and hence very slow to age.

"Please, let us sit," the woman said as she felt along the back of a chair and then maneuvered herself into it.

Francesca and Cyrus slowly sat.

"I am Magistra Vivian Niyol, Deputy Vice-Chancellor of Astrophell. This is my colleague, the master linguist Magister Lotannu Akoma." She gestured to the handsome man who was now standing behind her and resting one hand on her shoulder. He nodded stiffly to Francesca and then to Cyrus.

"We have come from Trillinon on a particular errand, and I would like to appeal to you as a physician for help."

"All that way just for medical advice?" Francesca said, deliberately misunderstanding the other woman. "I didn't know my reputation has spread to—"

Magistra Niyol smiled and interrupted. "No, I didn't cross the continent to complain of joint pain."

"Then it's your companion perhaps? His expression is sour enough I'd suspect something in the stomach. Maybe constipation?"

The dark-skinned man studied her but kept his face stern.

The old woman, however, broadened her smile and said, "My, you are entertaining." Before Francesca could reply, the old woman continued in a warmer tone: "Will you call me Vivian, rather than Magistra? You are not bound to the wizardly academy anymore, so perhaps we can dispense with the formalities."

Francesca put her hands in her lap. "I am glad to hear you say this, Vivian. I would hate to remind you that as a cleric, I am under no obligation to obey you. Please call me Francesca."

The ancient nodded. "Tactfully said, Francesca. And you needn't worry; I won't be ordering you about. I believe that you and I might share enough goals that our work will be more . . . collaborative."

"I hadn't imagined a wizard of your rank would be used to collaboration."

"My dear, I'm dreadful at it. Those around me instantly obey everything I say without a whisper of complaint, most especially young Lotannu here. He's meek as a fawn."

The man behind her snorted with amusement.

Francesca smiled tightly. "Well then, I'll compensate for him by being doubly obstinate."

Vivian turned her head toward Francesca. "I hope you won't mind my saying so. But there is something about how you speak. It's not quite an accent you have; though I would say you were raised in Verdant. But there is something odd—"

"I was born deep in the Burnt Hills on the border between Spires and Verdant. It's a sparse land, and people there have an antique way of speaking." She glared at Cyrus, but he kept his face blank and his eyes fixed on Vivian.

"Antique," the ancient wizard repeated. "Yes, I see. Odd, I was born into an era when everyone spoke that way. But I've since lost the ability to affect that accent. But you haven't, even though you are so much younger? That is odd, isn't it?"

"Odd as legs on a fish," Francesca said. "Speaking of odd, why do you not have a familiar whose eyes you might see through?"

Vivian sighed. "I do have one, a dear friend. She's an old coyote with a silver coat. Named Ista. Sadly, I could not take her on the airship. And, for reasons you will soon understand, I could not bring her into Avel on my errand. Which brings me back to why I'm asking for your help."

Cyrus cleared his throat. "Excuse the interruption, Magistra. I am Cyrus Alarcon, Air Warden of Avel. Before you ask for our help, could you tell us what your errand in Avel is?"

The ancient woman arched a white eyebrow. "Our help? I was speaking only to the cleric."

"I . . . I only assumed that . . ." Cyrus stammered. Francesca noticed his hands fidgeting in his lap.

"I should be happy to have your assistance as well, Magister Hierophant," Vivian said calmly.

Cyrus straightened in his chair. "Then I hope you will satisfy my curiosity."

Vivian widened her blind eyes. "Oh my, it's been long since a young man asked me for satisfaction, I barely know what to do." She fanned her face with her small right hand. "Did you hear that, Lotannu? Do you think I could satisfy him?"

"Vivian," Lotannu said in a deadpan tone through his still-stern expression, "you're frightening the natives."

Francesca felt her face flushing hot. "We're not . . ." she started to say but then fell silent as she looked over at Cyrus.

Only a few moments ago she would have cackled to see every inch of Cyrus's nonveiled face blushing so brightly. But now, in the presences of the old woman, she felt a pang of sympathetic embarrassment for him.

"Your pardon if I've made you uncomfortable, Francesca," Vivian said casually.

Taken aback, Francesca looked at Vivian. The old woman was smiling, smug as the cat that swallowed the crow. Francesca's embarrassment turned to anger. The old crone had just beaten her at her own wordplay, and she knew it. Show-off.

Francesca's mind raced, searching for some scintillating remark. But, aggravatingly, she could think of nothing to say other than, "I am also finding myself curious about your errand."

Vivian nodded. "Very well. Lotannu and I are here with the permission of the Celestial Court; we've come to solve something of a mystery. Or, rather, to find someone who has gone missing."

Francesca tightened her hands into fists. "And who would that be?"

"A rogue wizard," she replied. "Perhaps you heard of him when you were in clerical training. He was only a boy of twenty-five years then. His name is Nicodemus Weal."

With every ounce of her restraint, Francesca kept her expression neutral. Cyrus, however, visibly flinched.

"You are surprised, Cyrus Alarcon?" Lotannu asked.

"Of course," Cyrus answered. "Among hierophants, the story went round that Weal claimed he was the wizards' prophesied savior and then murdered his peers. Some said the wizards even found evidence of demonic involvement, something about a being made entirely of metal. But I thought they were only rumors."

"And you are not surprised, Francesca?" Vivian asked.

"A healer learns to hide her surprise," she answered. "Patients aren't reassured when their wounds elicit expressions of shock."

"I see," Vivian said.

Cyrus spoke, "What makes you think Weal is in Avel?"

"I can't go into the details," the ancient woman replied. "I can tell you that we must be discreet. If word gets out that two grand wizards are hunting for a rogue, he's likely to flee. That is why I must ask both of you for secrecy."

"You have it," Cyrus said.

Vivian cocked her head to the side. "Once in Avel, Lotannu and I will be changing into costumes. I'll be posing as a rich Verdantine merchant, looking for trading partners in Avel. Lotannu will be my master of coin. This is why I could not bring my familiar; a merchant shouldn't travel with a tame coyote. We could use your help in our ruse. But that is not the main reason I hope to enlist you, Francesca. I learned from the marshal that today you witnessed an aphasia curse moving through the sanctuary. Is that so?"

"It is."

Vivian nodded. "I want to hear everything you can remember. I believe what you saw is the first manifestation of what could become a plague."

Francesca frowned. "A plague of aphasia? But it's not caused by an infection."

Vivian took a long breath. "Not typically, no. My friend Lotannu is our premier expert on how magical text interacts with the mind. He has studied a few years with the clerics, though he still is a wizard." She paused. "The curses known to cause aphasia do not spread from mind to mind. Or rather, the human curses that cause aphasia are not infectious."

"You think the curse I saw was not written by a human?" Francesca asked, thinking about what Deirdre had said to her about the Savanna Walker.

Vivian nodded slowly. "Before I answer that, please consider the gravity of the situation: if an aphasia curse became infectious it might spread through Avel and this wind garden. Via hierophantic kites and merchant ships, the curse would spread across the continent. In the space of a year, every spellwright might become aphasic. What does that sound like to you?"

Cyrus let out a long breath. "Like the Disjunction destroying human language."

Vivian held out an open palm. "Francesca, please take my hand. What I am about to say is difficult to believe; I want you to know how earnest I am."

Tentatively, Francesca placed her hand in Vivian's. The elderly woman's knuckles were swollen with decades of use. Vivian's skin, though smooth, was blotchy with liver spots.

"Perhaps the aphasia curse was not written by a human," Vivian said slowly. "Perhaps it was written by a dragon."

Nineteen

Suddenly, Francesca was light-headed.

Vivian went on to describe how, a decade ago, a dragon had attacked Trillinon. The wizard and pyromancers had wounded the beast badly enough to stop its attack, but it dashed its body into the city and started a disastrous fire. The wizards had studied the wyrm's remains and discovered that the creature was more than a giant flying lizard; it possessed potent text that could alter the way nearby humans thought. Though Vivian had come to Avel searching for Nicodemus Weal, the news of aphasia had made her suspect a developing dragon was in the city.

Francesca listened with attentive neutrality. A feat made more difficult when she remembered Deirdre's warning that there were two dragons.

When Vivian finished and asked if they would help investigate the aphasia curse, Francesca and Cyrus glanced at each other and then, unenthusiastically, agreed.

Vivian then explained that many of the hierophants would complete their wind-garden duty that evening and fly back to Avel. They were all to return to the city with off-duty pilots. Until then, the wind marshal had made the visiting pilot's quarters available if she and Cyrus wished to rest.

Francesca jumped at the offer of privacy.

Cyrus led her through a set of narrow halls to another long, narrow room, this one lined with sleeping cots. Francesca collapsed onto one. He sat on its neighbor.

"Cyrus, what in all the hells is happening? This morning I was sewing up lacerations and cutting out swollen appendixes. Then I kill a patient and she comes back to life. No wait, she's an avatar. No wait, she's here to tell me the War of Disjunction has begun and a demon is ruling Avel. Oh, and the Savanna Walker is real and screaming through the sanctuary. And a Second Civil War might break out. And, by the way, an infectious aphasia curse might be coming from the Savanna Walker, who's also a half dragon. One of two dragons, actually. The second of which only I can find."

Francesca paused to inhale and start again. "Oh, it just so happens, maybe you'd like to know that, dragons—funniest thing—are not always flying, fire-breathing storybook monsters. Sometimes dragons are ill-defined embodiments of all things powerful, deadly, possibly imperceptible, and yet really God-of-gods damned deadly."

Cyrus was calmly unwinding his turban. He had heard rants like this before. "It's not exactly what I expected when I got out of bed either."

"Cyrus, did you have to come back to Avel?"

He looked at her. "What do you mean?"

"To get closer to being a captain, did you have to come back here?"

He adjusted his veil. "I suppose not. Roundtower's air warden had just been made a marshal. I could have taken his vacancy instead of coming here."

"So why Avel?"

"Not to be near you, if that's what you're thinking."

"Why would I think that?"

He looked away. "Roundtower is all mountains and military. Hotheaded lancers and garrison officers. No culture other than tavern brawls and prostitutes. And, as you so kindly pointed out, I knew I'd have to wait decades to make captain at my next post. So, I chose to be comfortable in a proper city like Avel. And anyway the winds up in Roundtower are hazardous. Flying about those crags, in that thin air, is tricky for a veteran. Training new pilots in the mountains?" He shook his head. "Hard way to live."

She made a low, disbelieving "huh" noise.

He looked at her for a while and then sighed. "You think I'm fooling myself?"

She nodded.

"And you're about to say so in some emphatic and nearly obscene way."

Another nod.

"God-of-gods, Cyrus," he said in a nasal voice, "you're so full of hogwash that you could clean every pig in Lorn white as a blond baby's bottom." For good measure, he threw his hands in the air and exhaled dramatically.

She frowned. "You took the emphatic and nearly obscene words right out of my mouth."

He laughed softly. Then after a moment he said, "I suppose I did come back because of my memories of being happy here."

"You left Avel for a reason. It wasn't working."

He didn't reply.

"What was her name?"

"Silvia. She was in Sharptree with me. That wasn't working either."

"She still there?"

He shook his head. "She's a ship warden in the merchant marine service, mostly sails the Chandralu to Tillinion trading route."

"Sounds nice."

"I hear that it is. Hear she spends her leave with a wing commander in the Ixonian expedition."

Again she said, "I'm sorry to hear it, Cy."

"No, no. I'm happy for her." He paused. "Did you take another lover?"

"Another cleric, hydromancer trained. We've been on and off. Presently off. He went back to Port Mercy for more training just before the rains began. I miss him sometimes, not often. I'm too busy."

"That's nothing new for you."

She sat up. "Nothing new."

He nodded.

"I'm sorry, Cy."

"Don't be. I didn't come back in hopes of reliving our old life. We were happy here for maybe a year; then we had to make different choices."

"It was a good year," she said. "Mostly."

"Mostly," he agreed. "Honestly, I didn't expect to see you at all."

Francesca rubbed her neck. "And you shouldn't have. The chances of us being thrown together like this were almost nothing."

"Deirdre knew who I was?"

"She did, but she seemed unaware of our history."

He ran a hand through his black curls. "I have this sensation that everything's tied together: Deirdre, the Savanna Walker, the *Queen's Lance*, the brewing rebellion, you and me . . . but I can't see how."

She nodded. "It's like we can see all the flies caught in a spider's web but not the web itself."

"Or the spider."

Francesca fell back onto the bed. "Or the spider." They fell silent for a while, and she could hear the wind blowing and ropes creaking. It was a good sound. Finally she asked, "You suppose Deirdre is telling the truth about Typhon?"

"Until an hour ago, I would have said it was impossible. But now . . . well, seems anything's possible. But . . . it wouldn't be logical for the demon to spin this web. If he's enslaved Cala and is pushing for another civil war, he should do everything possible to hide himself and the rebellion."

"Do we tell Vivian?"

"Los in hell, no! Can't you tell she's up to more than she's telling us?"

"She is." Francesca pushed the heels of her hands into her eyes. "And the old frog is damned good at outdoing someone at her own game. Guess that's how she became a deputy vice-chancellor."

He grunted. "That satisfaction comment that had me blushing?"

"And my hobbled response," she said and rolled her neck. "I hate losing my own game."

"Don't let her get under your skin," he said. "What do we do now?"

"Sleep is always the answer," she replied. "We're both exhausted, and we can't do anything until they fly us back to Avel." She rubbed her cheeks. "God-of-gods, I killed a patient today." She searched her heart for the terror and shame she previously felt. It was in there somewhere, but muted now by the exhaustion.

Cyrus lay down in his cot. "Deirdre set you up so that you couldn't save her."

"She'd been saved before. A master physician could have saved her."

"So, you're not a master physician. You're not even sixty yet."

She groaned. "Some of my peers are master physicians. I should be."

"Still so hard on yourself, Magistra?"

"Shut it, Air Warden," she said and rolled onto her side. "Didn't you want to be made captain by now?"

He ignored this. "So, what do we do once we're back in the city?"

"We find the only fly more thoroughly ensnared in this web than we are."

She heard Cyrus let out a single, humorless laugh and then say, "Nicodemus Weal."

Outside, the wind picked up and there came a splatter of rain striking a roof. "This Nicodemus, he's supposed to be a cacographer?"

"Mmmhmm . . ." she said drowsily. Clerical training had taught her nothing if not to fall asleep quickly.

"And cacographers are wizards who spellwrite backwards? Or remember things backwards?"

"No, no," she rolled on to her side. "Well, some might . . . but mostly they misspell any text they touch. They can think of magical words they want, but they can't think of how to spell them."

The bed beside hers creaked as if Cyrus was shifting his weight. "So then, cacography is something like aphasia?"

Her legs jerked slightly, the way they often did right before she fell asleep. "I guess . . . Cyrus, where are you going with this?"

"I'm not sure. It's just that . . . maybe Vivian was wrong about the aphasia being related to a dragon. Maybe it's related to the rogue cacographer."

"Let's talk about it . . . later" she mumbled.

"You're sure cacography has nothing to do with getting things backward?"

"Mmmhmm . . ."

Cyrus was saying something else, but she couldn't make it out. The rain grew louder on the roof, and Francesca felt her mind float free into a dream.

VIVIAN WAITED IN silence and listened to the footsteps of the cleric and the hierophant as they walked out of the mess hall. She kept her composure as the footsteps faded. Lotannu's hand left her shoulder. It sounded as if he was walking to the door.

"Are they gone?" she whispered, even as the edges of her mouth curled into a smile.

Instead of an answer, she got a laugh suppressed into a snort, then one of Lotannu's deep guffaws.

Then she was laughing too, laughing hard.

"Burning heaven, Viv!" Lotannu half-whispered. "Were you trying to make it harder on me? Meek as a fawn? Young Lotannu? Where in the flameless hells did you drag that up from?"

"Creator bless me," she said, "but I would have given anything to see the hierophant's face when I flirted with him."

"That poor bastard!" Lotannu said with a snort. "There he is, trying to seem composed for the pretty cleric a head taller than he is and you make him blush like a baboon's backside."

Vivian exploded with more laughter. Finally, she had to put her hand to her chest and slow her breathing. "Oh, doesn't it feel good to be out here, away from the factions? It's like when we were young."

"Like when I was young. I don't think the historical records go back far enough for us to know what it was like when you were young."

She chuckled. "Don't get me started again. I'd nearly forgotten what it's like to do something without needing to get the Long Council's permission or argue for hours about what this might mean to the future Halcyon."

She heard the chair next to hers shudder as Lotannu sat. "Burning hells, just the mention of the Halcyon gives me a headache. Thank the Creator all the prophecy-crazed academics are tied up in Ogun and that the Long Council doesn't know about the conversation we just had."

"Doesn't know and never will." She paused. "Did you get a good look down into the city when we flew over it?"

Vivian did not completely understand it, but Lotannu had written a spell that allowed him to "see" the quaternary thoughts other spellwrights were thinking.

Lotannu grunted. "There were three entities in the sanctuary thinking with magical text. At such a distance, I could see only outlines of the thoughts."

Vivian rubbed her chin as she tried to imagine what it would be like to see a thought. Lotannu had shown her once. He'd cast the fine golden mesh upon her head. With a hybrid mind, half brain and half spell, she had understood. She'd seen the quaternary thoughts forming inside Lotannu's mind, seen them grow and evolve as they spoke, seen them combine with her own quaternary thoughts during the conversation and transform into something new.

But as soon as he had removed the spells, she'd lost it all. It had been like rousing from a dream that had been understandable in sleep but was nonsense to the waking mind.

"Three beings in the sanctuary thinking quaternary thoughts," she mused aloud. "Only in the sanctuary? Nowhere else in the city?"

"Not that I saw."

"Then we must assume one of the thinkers is the canonist."

"Certainly. One pattern was similar to that I've seen in other minor deities."

"And the other two thinkers?"

Lotannu paused. "Both had thought patterns like nothing I've seen before. The stronger one was troublesome. Very fast thoughts winding in on themselves. They gave me an impression of power and . . . defensiveness."

"Typhon."

"In the sanctuary?"

Vivian nodded. "It would confirm our suspicions about Cala. What of the third quaternary thinker?"

There was a silence.

"Usually that kind of silence means you're scowling."

"I'm scowling."

"If I scowl for you, will you tell me about the third mind?"

"Now that I think on it, I'm not sure if it was one mind or many minds sharing the same idea. They were scattered thoughts. It was like looking at a jellyfish in the ocean. Sometimes you see the jelly; sometimes you see the water beyond."

Vivian nodded. "The incomplete half dragon our spies suspected."

"You suppose?" he asked.

"What else could it be?"

"Something we hadn't anticipated," he suggested. "Should we send word to the Long Council?"

"No," she replied firmly. "If the separatists knew there was a chance that Nicodemus is down here, they'd come running. Then our meat would be properly cooked. Can you imagine, the hierophants rebelling while there are separatist wizards in Avel? Even if we initiated the contingency plan, the separatists and the polytheists might find each other. Then we'd have wizard fighting wizard and wind mage fighting wind mage, the lesser deities would get into the fray, and the whole city would be blasted into rubble and grass."

"But if the half dragon is capable of—"

"Then we had better deal with it without giving separatist factions a chance to become violent."

Lotannu cleared his throat in the way he always did before telling her she was being stupid. "What if separatists are already in Avel? What if the rumors of the League of Starfall are true?"

She took in a deep breath. "It's a chance we have to take. We've been through this."

"I still don't like it." He paused. "Do you suppose we'll find Nicodemus in the sanctuary as well?"

"It's his fluency in Language Prime that's half-made the dragon. He won't be far away."

"Such a pleasant little package you've found: half dragon, demon, and Storm Petrel all wrapped up in sandstone and terracotta tile."

"You're being snide because we missed lunch. You're always snide when hungry."

"I'm going to ignore that."

"You think I can't walk into that sanctuary and come out alive?"

"I have no doubt you would come out alive. I'm more worried about my coming out alive."

She sighed. "You're never going to be in any more danger than I will be. You're just being contrary. This can all be resolved by feeding you lunch."

He only grunted.

She rubbed her eyes. "This is the first time I've been truly blind, and it's much more difficult than I—"

"How long do you think we have now until the Council finds out we're already in Avel?" he interrupted.

She shrugged. "Unless there are separatists here, twenty days. But maybe only ten. Doesn't matter. We'll bring matters to a head here long before then. Or perhaps Typhon will do it for us."

"How do you figure?"

Vivian stretched in her chair. Her legs still felt cramped from all that time on that blasted airship. "If we're lucky, the demon will do something rash. Or perhaps his half dragon will get out of hand. You heard about the aphasia. And then there's that cleric. She should have been caught in the aphasia. There's something wrong about her constitution."

"You're right there," Lotannu said. "She's a blister with words. Pretty also."

"Her wordplay might signify, but how do you figure her face fits in?"

"Don't suppose it does. But a man notices things," he said. Then came the sound of a plate sliding across a table.

"What were they eating?" Vivian asked, leaning forward. "I knew you were hungry."

He laughed. "Flatbread and cheese. Plate's in front of you now. Any idea how the cleric escaped the aphasia?"

Using her right hand, Vivian tore free a chunk of bread. "As I said, there's something not right about the cleric's constitution; she shines too brightly. I'm not sure what her role is in all this. She could be our lead to Nicodemus." Vivian bit into the bread and found it tough.

"And lover boy?"

"The hierophant? Can't tell. I think he was simply in a bad place at a bad time."

"So, now that we know the action's likely to be in the sanctuary, what's our next step, establish defenses in the central district?"

She nodded. "Wouldn't be a bad idea. Afterward we have to go to the canonist and use all our flowery language and do all the bowing and groveling we can."

He scowled. "Bloody protocol. She's going to be suspicious of you from the beginning. What's the point?"

Vivian chewed thoughtfully and then swallowed. "If we're lucky, the demon will try, right then and there, to kill us."

Twenty

Anxiously, the ghost reexamined the contents of Francesca DeVega's bedroom: two windows filled with ornate redwood screens; a chest with few clothes; a cot, its sheets crumpled into a mound; a small writing desk covered by medical books, open scrolls, loose pages. Apparently Magistra DeVega paid more attention to studying and sleeping than cleaning.

On the cleric's desk, the most recent note was dated to the previous night. The washbasin and the chamber pot were both empty and dry; she hadn't returned to her quarters since the apprentices had emptied the basins that morning.

It was a grave problem.

Ghostly Shannon had wandered the chaotic infirmary until he overheard an irate physician asking for Cleric DeVega. No one had seen her since the mysterious aphasia had dissipated. The ghost followed the physician to these quarters. But while the living man had only knocked on her door, the ghost walked through the wooden planks to inspect the room. Unfortunately, he hadn't found anything useful.

Now, as the ghost inspected the room yet again, the hollow sensation returned to his chest. He imaged his author's gaunt face, the mouth turned downward in agony. His author must be longing for him too. How could he not?

The ghost closed his eyes and rubbed them with his remaining hand. But his fingers produced no distracting sensation of pressure, no orange blotches in the darkness. There was only the prose of his hands.

Perhaps his author was not longing for him. Perhaps the ghost was behaving like a heartbroken lover, indulging in fantasies that the one who left still longed for the abandoned.

Absently the ghost touched the stump of his right arm. A sharp sensation made him jump. It was like pain . . . and yet not like pain at all. What he had previously thought of as pain was a packet of textual information about damage. His perception of pain, of sensation in general, was changing.

Outside of his author, the ghost's mind was doing what all minds do: it was adapting to its new environment. It was troubling. There were now two versions of Shannon, one physical and one textual. What if the ghost's magical mind evolved so far away from his author's that they couldn't reunite? And that was assuming the ghost could convince his author to take him back.

The hollowness in the ghost's chest began to expand. He had to take long, slow breaths to restore his concentration. He returned to Francesca's desk and again studied her notes. All were medical jargon and details about different patients.

Then the ghost noticed an open book at the desk's far corner. Judging by the pages, it was a clinical journal. The ghost leaned closer. By concentrating, he used a Magnus sentence in his fingers to drag a slip of paper away from the journal. This revealed an open scroll. A complex golden paragraph shone on the exposed paper. At its top were runes that translated into "Toward: Clc. Mg. Francesca DeVega."

The ghost recognized it as a locator paragraph. Wizards who worked with colaboris stations used such paragraphs to send information across great distances. Any manuscript given to a colaboris station with this instruction would be delivered to Magistra DeVega.

Perhaps the ghost could send a message to DeVega? Arrange a meeting place? But how to get it to the colaboris station? And how to get it to her before he deconstructed?

He looked back at the desk. Perhaps he could find—

He stood up straight and turned to the closed door. Someone was talking behind it. The ghost stepped far enough into the nearby wall so that only his head remained in the room. He kept his Magnus prose in his face so that it wouldn't be pulled into the sandstone and frayed.

A moment later the door opened, and two men dressed in plain Spirish longvests stepped into the room. One had a satchel strapped around his shoulder. They moved quickly, searching the apartment and muttering to each other. The ghost caught only a few of their words, but even so it was apparent they were also searching for DeVega.

They wore no robes identifying them as spellwrights, but one man withdrew a stack of folded cloth from his satchel. He unfolded it on the bed and began to move his hands over the cloth and the bedsheets in the unmistakable pattern of a spellwright editing a text. The other man crouched next to the washbasin and was making similar movements on a towel that had been left beside it.

The ghost could not see hierophantic sentences, but he would have bet anything these men were disguised hierophants. Judging by the precision of their gestures and the amount of time they spent, the hierophantic snoops were creating powerful and complex texts—most likely designed to alert them should the cleric touch her towel or trap her in bed should she get into it.

When the men started to leave, they stopped in the doorway and began talking to a third party. The ghost crept out of the wall.

The men were asking a girl about Magistra DeVega's whereabouts. The girl knew nothing.

The ghost crept closer but then, panicking, jumped back into the wall. The girl was wearing black robes.

Only when everything but his face was hidden within sandstone did the ghost realize that the girl was too young to be anything other than a neophyte; she couldn't see him.

The ghost stuck his head out of the wall. The neophyte had stepped into the room and was peering over DeVega's desk. A moment later she left the room.

Long moments stretched out. Outside, rain began to fall.

The ghost walked over to the desk. Why was there a neophyte in Avel? There was no literary academy here.

Then it struck him. The colaboris station. Sometimes wizardly academies sent their youngest students to assist nearby colaboris stations. The girl must have come to Francesca's room to see if she had any texts to be taken to the station.

That also explained why the disguised hierophants had cast their spells into DeVega's bed, rather than set up a trap on the doorway: they didn't want to catch just anyone who walked through the door, especially not a neophyte. They wanted only the room's occupant, only the woman who slept in the bed.

The ghost looked down at the desk, an idea blooming in his mind. For the first time the hollowness in his chest lessened. It would be a gamble, but it would give him hope. Besides, what other options did he have?

Carefully, the ghost concentrated his remaining Magnus prose into his right hand and reached for the locator paragraph.

Twenty-one

In a dream, Francesca had diagnosed an inflamed appendix in a young woman and decided to remove it. But after making an incision into the right abdomen, Francesca couldn't find the appendix. In fact, through the incision, Francesca found the descending segment of large intestine rather than the expected ascending segment.

When Francesca told an assistant to listen to the woman's heart, the assistant reported the beating sounded loudest on the right side of the chest.

Terrified, Francesca realized that her patient's internal organs were reversed on the right-left axis. She'd never seen the phenomenon before but had read about it in medical texts.

Francesca fumbled with her cutting sentences, unsure what to do. "You're killing the patient," the assistant had said. "It's something to do with getting it backwards."

Francesca looked at him. "What?"

The assistant, a tall man in a black turban and veil, had replied, "Cacography is getting it backwards. The patient's got it backwards. You're killing her."

When Francesca asked the assistant for his name, he said "Nicodemus Weal."

That's when she woke up.

Disoriented, she sat up in a strange bed.

"Fran?" Cyrus said, and she jumped. He was standing next to her cot. From somewhere farther away came the creaking of ropes and the hush of rain striking a roof.

She was in the garden tower.

"It's maybe three hours to sunset," Cyrus said. "The windcatchers are coming in. We must get on deck so the returning hierophants don't jump without us."

After rubbing her face, she stood and they walked through a dark hallway to the tower's scaffolding-lined interior. Along the western edge, the beams were alive with hierophants shouting and gesturing. Giant folds of white cloth unfurled and then folded themselves into neat stacks. Francesca felt her braided hair being pushed around by contrary blasts of winds.

"What are they doing?" she yelled as they moved along a catwalk toward the tower's eastern edge.

"Docking the windcatchers. They can't fly at night. The lycanthropes might pull them down."

"Truly?"

He laughed. "Come night, the lycanthropes would tear every human in this pass to bloody rags if we weren't safely holed up in this massive tower."

"Is that why Avel was built so far away from this pass even though the city's purpose is to support this wind garden?"

He shook his head as they ducked under a low-hanging beam. "No; Cala's walls would hold the lycanthropes back, mostly. The problem's water. Avel had to be built by the dam. To protect it you see. An early settlement was out here in the pass. But the lycanthropes kept knocking down the dam and letting the water flow out. During the dry season, there's no other water in the savanna."

Just then they reached a set of stairs so steep they could have passed for a ladder. Cyrus jogged up them. Francesca again became uncomfortably aware of her six feet as she clumsily followed.

At last she emerged onto the middeck, which seemed to hang just below the jumpdeck. A group of hierophants had gathered. All were young, mid to late thirties. All had folds of bright cloth in their hands and talked excitedly.

"Normally, they work until sunset," Cyrus explained by her side. "But they've been piloting or writing all day for fifty days now. It's grueling work. And now they're about to be paid and sent back to Avel." His veil moved as if he was smiling. "That's the source of Avel's culture, you know. All that coin to be spent on fine wine, soft beds, working girls, tavern singers."

Francesca looked down at her old lover. "When you were young, is that how you spent your pay, on working girls?"

He shrugged.

More hierophants emerged onto the deck and joined their peers. Cyrus leaned in as if to ask a question, but just as he did so, the deck fell silent. Francesca turned to see Lotannu leading Vivian out of the stairwell. Francesca was impressed the blind old woman could manage such steep steps.

Once on deck, Lotannu led Vivian over to Francesca and Cyrus. Conversation resumed among the pilots. Vivian nodded and then spoke. "Cyrus, do you know where Avel's wizardly colaboris station is?"

He nodded. "In the Merchant District, near South Gate."

"We must make contact with the wizards in the station and outfit our little mission. Can you see that we land near there?"

"I can," Cyrus said.

"Magistra," Francesca said, "that might be inconvenient for your disguise."

"How's that?"

"The walls that separate Avel's different districts are invested with Canonist Cala's godspell. No spellwright may pass through their gates without being killed."

Vivian narrowed her white eyes. "Why would the canonist restrict movement of her spellwrights?"

Cyrus answered. "Her spellwrights can fly over the walls. The godspell keeps out lycanthrope spellwrights who are textually altered to look like humans. Or, if the outer walls are breached, the inner walls contain a lycanthrope incursion to one district."

Lotannu scowled. "How often do the lycanthropes breach the walls?"

"Far too often," Cyrus said with a sigh. "A score of the beasts ran wild in the North Gate District in the late dry season last year. They killed heaven knows how many and started a fire before the hierophants and city watch hunted them down."

"But how do they knock the walls down?" Vivian asked. "I was under the impression that they had no war engines."

Cyrus nodded. "They don't. No tools whatsoever as far as we can tell. They use blasting texts. Some think the lycanthropes can not only appear to be human but even transform their bodies into human ones, especially at night. The city is full of superstitions about whom to let into your house after dark."

"It's gotten worse this past year," Francesca added. "The lycanthropes have attacked even during the day, partially detonating texts in shadows. This morning there was a daylight ambush at the North Gate."

Lotannu's scowl darkened. "So, if we are posing as Verdantine merchants, how can we move about the city without revealing our disguise?"

Francesca answered. "There are places on each inner wall where ladders let the citizens climb over the wall from district to district so they don't have to make the long trip between gatehouses. Guards pull the ladders up after sunset. You might get caught in a certain district for a night, but I can show you on a map where they all are."

Vivian sighed. "I suppose it can't be helped. Thank you, Magistra."

Francesca nodded. Then a silence followed. Francesca considered trying to make small talk, but worried that she'd either give something away or look a fool in front of Vivian.

Apparently Cyrus also felt awkward; he suddenly became interested in adjusting his turban and securing his veil. For her part, Vivian seemed unperturbed. Lotannu occasionally leaned in to whisper to her, but mostly he examined the surroundings with keen but quiet interest.

At last the wind marshal came on deck, accompanied by two other hierophants bearing a large wooden chest. The young pilots fell silent and formed a line. The marshal made a short speech, praising their hard work and reminding them that even when on leave they represented the Celestial Order of Hierophants. After that, she ordered the distribution of small burlap purses filled with clinking coins.

The sound of rain striking the jumpdeck above them grew to a roar. Cyrus frowned at the storm before excusing himself and hurrying belowdecks. He soon returned with several folds of black cloth draped over his left arm. From the folds, he pulled out a strip of cloth that cut and wove itself into an elaborate shape. He handed one such garment to each of the wizards.

"Put it over your heads," he instructed and showed Vivian how. It turned out to be a headdress. "There are hierophantic sentences in each of them that close up all the space between the threads. It makes them waterproof. The spells will spread to your robes and make flying through this deluge bearable."

From beneath her headdress, Vivian thanked Cyrus. Francesca would have done the same if a shout hadn't gone up from the other hierophants. All payments, it seemed, had been dispensed and their leave had just begun. "Brace yourself," Cyrus said over the racket. "When flying back, the young pilots can be boisterous."

All the hierophants hurried to the deck's edge and climbed up short rope ladders. Cyrus herded the black-robes toward one. "Don't look down," he cried into Francesca's ear as she grabbed hold of the rungs and pulled herself up. Out in the open, the wind buffeted her, but the rain rolled off her robes without soaking into the cloth.

Once on the jumpdeck, Francesca found herself in front of a short wind mage standing next to a multicolored stack of cloth. He thrust a parcel of bright red cloth into her hands. "I'm not a hierophant—" she tried to protest, but the crowd of wind mages pushed her forward onto the wet jumpdeck. She took the cloth.

Behind her, Cyrus was arguing with two younger pilots. He was, it seemed, commandeering them to fly Vivian and Lotannu. They were not pleased about having to land in the Merchant District when their peers had plans to meet in drinking halls and tobacco salons elsewhere. But as the air warden of Avel, Cyrus had authority over all hierophants in the city. He reminded them that he could order them both to fly watch duty for the duration of their leave. This ended their objections.

Francesca looked back at Vivian and Lotannu. Both wizards held a thick square of folded cloth and stood beside their newly assigned pilots. Francesca was no longer surprised by how easily the ancient wizard moved about. The woman must be a surpassingly powerful spellwright to be so spry at such an age. Francesca felt a pang of envy; she would never be as powerful as Vivian, never rise so high in wizardly esteem.

The envy Francesca felt had a strange quality, as if it weren't truly her emotion but something being imposed on her by someone else. Ever since Francesca had come to Avel, ever since she had failed to win an appointment to a more prestigious infirmary, she had felt similar pangs when around other accomplished female spellwrights.

As usually happened after such bouts of envy, Francesca chastised herself for being petty and foolishly insecure in her own accomplishments. She was, after all, a physician.

"Black-robes," Cyrus boomed, "run with your pilot and cast your cloth up when you jump." He was standing behind Francesca. "Pilots, edit a two-person downwind rig. Keep the wing in tight formation. No showboating."

Ahead of them, younger pilots sprinted off the jumpdeck and cast their lofting kites high into the air. With whoops of elation, they caught the wind and sailed high up and away from the tower.

Francesca became queasy, and she thought about jumping off the sturdy deck. "But what if we slip or—" But before she could finish, the way before her cleared and Cyrus called out, "Go!" After grabbing her arm, he pulled her into a sprint.

Francesca felt hot panic surge through her as the deck's edge appeared not five steps ahead. Then, impossibly, she was jumping off the deck and throwing her arms up to cast the sailcloth upward.

She opened her mouth to scream, dead certain that she was about to plummet to her death. But before she could make a sound, the world disappeared into a violence of cloth and air. Her robes became stiff and then bands of force wrapped around her chest and legs and pulled her up into the air.

She sucked in a deep breath. Above them stretched a wide, billowing canopy of red and blue sailcloth. They were soaring away from the garden tower. The few raindrops that struck her eyes or the bridge of her nose felt like needles. She was now even more grateful for her waterproof headdress.

A surge of wind drew them up with such force it felt as if her stomach had fallen down to her feet. "Hold tight!" Cyrus called. "It will be a bumpy flight."

All around them were other lofting kites, their vivid crescent-shaped canopies rising and falling relative to one another. A few pilots with one-man rigs were spinning themselves into barrel rolls or swooping danger-ously close to the other kites, all the while calling to each other like raucous birds.

Gradually Francesca's breathing slowed. Behind her, Vivian cried out with delight. She looked back and saw that they were flanked by a pair of two-person rigs, one carrying Vivian and the other Lotannu.

Below them was the mountain pass, covered with grass and strewn with gray boulders. Without the windcatchers aloft, it seemed an ordinary place. Soon they were above the dark redwood forests.

At last Francesca's fear left her and she let herself marvel at their unbe-lievable speed, their dreamlike freedom of movement.

The rain falling around them turned a shining white. At first Francesca thought it was the effect of some hierophantic spell. But then she looked back. Far out in the western sky hung a break in the storm. Sunlight poured down through a billowing cloudscape—mountains of dark air, city-sized caverns, a field of blue.

"Oh," Francesca whispered to herself. "Beautiful." She had known that the rainy season in Western Spires produced stunning cloudscapes. She had glimpsed a few from the infirmary's windows, but she had always been rushing between patients. She had never been as aware of the sky as she was now.

A sudden gust made their kite drop a few feet. With effort, Francesca kept herself from crying out in surprise. She looked at Cyrus, but he was staring down. "Look," he said and pointed down to where one fallen tree had knocked over its neighbors.

At first she couldn't tell what he was talking about. Then . . . "Holy blasted heaven aflame!" she swore. There were two of them: giant shadows bounding along the fallen redwood. Maybe six feet long, muscular, every-where covered by black fur. In the next instant, they leapt into the forest and vanished.

"They're following us," Cyrus explained. "Waiting to see if a pilot spills too much wind in this weather."

"What are they?" Francesca asked.

Cyrus's turban and veil hid everything but his eyes, which were squinted as if in amusement. "Don't you know?"

She looked back down at the redwoods. Now she saw nothing beneath the trees but dark forest floor. "Yes," she replied over the wind. "I suppose I do."

Twenty-two

Cyrus landed his rig in the South Market. Most days the square bustled with haggling vendors and city dwellers. Now, two hours before sunset and in the driving rain, it held only empty stalls and growing puddles.

Just before his boots touched stone, Cyrus moved a disassemble spell from his robes to the suspension lines and cast it up to the canopy. Instantly, the text altered language throughout the kite, causing some seams to tear and others to form. The canopy folded into a neat pile behind them.

Francesca failed to appreciate how gently he had set them down. Most hierophants would have collapsed their kites too soon. Indeed, as Cyrus turned he saw the first pilot was doing just that. He cringed as the rig carrying Vivian hit so fast that both the pilot and the old women sprawled into a puddle.

"Damnation!" Francesca swore and ran toward Vivian. Cyrus hurried after but watched the other pilot. Perhaps seeing her peer's hard landing, this pilot delayed her disassemble spell and touched down more gently.

Francesca was fussing over Vivian, but the older woman was laughing. "Nothing broken, nothing broken. Only thing hurting is my pride."

Relaxing, Cyrus picked up his lofting kite and transferred its language into his robes until the garments blazed pale blue. Then he ordered the two young pilots to fly to the sanctuary and inform the on-duty wing commander that he, Cyrus, had returned to the city with pressing orders from the wind marshal. He would return to the sanctuary sometime the next day. Afterward, the young pilots could begin their leave.

Turning away, Cyrus found Francesca standing with the two wizards. She was pointing to the square's western edge.

The Merchant District was the most affluent of Avel's outer districts. As elsewhere, the major architectural materials were sandstone and redwood timber. But here, every building stood three stories tall and boasted ornate arcades. The windows were filled with stone screens. Geometric mosaics of green and white adorned the protected aspects of the buildings.

Francesca was pointing at the tallest building. "That's the colaboris station," Cyrus said above the rain.

The wizardly academy was the only magical society powerful enough to maintain independence from any kingdom. The treasure and political influence that made this possible came from colaboris spells, which transferred information from one wizardly colaboris station to another almost instantly.

The academy of Starhaven—perched high in the Pinnacle Mountains and possessing the soaring Erasmine Spire—served as the western hub of colaboris transmissions. The far shorter towers now standing before Cyrus would receive spells intended for Avel or relay them to Starhaven, from which they could be relayed anywhere on the continent.

The wizards were talking animatedly. He stepped closer, trying to hear their words above the rain, but they set off toward the station. Frowning, Cyrus followed after.

Once under the arcade, the wizards shook their robes and removed their headdresses. A few city dwellers stood, staring at the spellwrights. Cyrus didn't like the attention.

The party walked to the station's massive redwood door, and Lotannu worked its large brass knocker. Moments later, a boy in black robes opened a smaller door within the large one. He greeted Vivian and Lotannu by name.

The whole group walked into a courtyard filled with bright mosaics, hanging plants, and a square reflecting pool. The rain was beating a riot of circles into the pool's surface.

As they hurried through the courtyard, Cyrus noticed three ravens hiding under the stone tracery. The birds seemed to be eying the party.

At the courtyard's end stood a pair of doors flanked by two massive gargoyles. Each possessed a muscular humanoid body topped by a fierce lion's head complete with thick stone mane. Perched on each gargoyle's shoulder was a steel statue of a cat with eyes of bronze. One was missing its left eye.

Francesca frowned at the metal felines. "Who decorates a war-weight gargoyle?"

Cyrus eyed the massive gargoyles. He had heard about stone constructs climbing all over Starhaven, Astrophell, and Starfall Keep. These two gargoyles, however, seemed perfectly motionless.

He started to ask about this, but then the doors swung open and the party entered a hall lit by incandescent prose. Tapestries hung on the walls, and the marble floor shone as if recently polished. The warm air smelled of aromatic smoke, most likely because a brazier filled with clicking coals stood at the room's center. Three wizards had arranged themselves around the brazier. They bowed. Cyrus's party returned the bow.

Cyrus guessed that the black-robes before him were the Avel station team. At their center stood a shorter, older wizard with a light complexion, a thick white beard, a snowy wreath of hair around a shiny bald pate. Judging by the badges on his sleeve, he was the station's leader. Sure enough, the man introduced himself as Magister Robert DeGarn and rattled off a flouncy greeting with typical academic protocol. Then DeGarn ushered Vivian and Lotannu into a side room.

Shortly after that, an older male servant in a red Spirish longvest returned with a pot of mint tea on a silver tray. The servant was staring at the newcomers, most especially Francesca. Visitors to the station were rare, Cyrus supposed.

Once DeGarn filled two small metal cups with tea, he served them to Francesca and Cyrus before leaving the hall. Francesca and Cyrus stood together, holding the steaming drinks between thumb and pinky. "That was odd," she whispered.

"What?"

"The tray the servant held, the metal where his fingers touched was dented."

Cyrus frowned. He hadn't noticed. "A very old tray? Or maybe thin pewter? You think the station is low on funds?"

"Possibly, but it's hard to imagine."

Just then Magister DeGarn reappeared. "Magistra, it's a pleasure to have you to our station. We of course knew of the wizardly cleric in the infirmary, but never knew if it would be correct to make overtures, what with your being within the clerical order."

Cyrus frowned at the way DeGarn studied Francesca's face. The man's name and courtly manners identified him as Western Lornish.

Francesca smiled. "You are kind, Magister. You would be most welcome in the infirmary. But, sadly, a cleric's duties do not allow for social calls."

Cyrus glanced at Francesca. He'd never known her to be so . . . tactful.

DeGarn nodded. "If I might ask, Magistra, where did you earn your hood and staff?"

"In Astrophell. But if you're wondering about my antique accent, it comes from a childhood in the Burnt Hills."

"Ahh," the short man said with a smile. "How wonderful to train at Astrophell. I studied at Starfall Keep, which of course is only an insipid backwater when compared to the academic splendor of Astrophell, wouldn't you agree?"

"Not at all, Magister," she said hurriedly. "Some of the finest spellwrights I've known have trained at Starfall, which is to say nothing of the excellent research conducted there."

"But when compared to Astrophell, to the seat from which the Neosolar Empire was once ruled, surely it is nothing."

"Not so, not so," Francesca answered and then looked at her cup. "This is very fine tea, Magister. It's thoughtful of you to offer a hot drink on a cold and wet evening."

Again DeGarn bowed his head. "Mint tea is one of the many things I've come to love about Spires. I brew it myself. It's one of the few times when I can get away from the station. Every morning, right at sunrise, I shop for mint and various other things in our market." He nodded toward the door and the market square beyond. "It's a pleasant way to encounter illiterates."

The conversation continued. Cyrus stood by, trying not to look bored. At last DeGarn excused himself with a bow. "What was all that about Starfall and Astrophell," Cyrus asked when he was gone.

Francesca grimaced. "There's always been tension between the two, but when the counter-prophecy faction rose to power a few years ago, Starfall became the rallying point for the opposition. Now the animosity between the two is worse than ever."

"I'm glad we're done with him."

"Vivian and Lotannu are changing into their costumes as Verdantine merchants," Francesca said between small sips of tea. "They're to lodge in the Holy District. I've told Vivian that I have patients to see and that you must tend to your command. Vivian's asked that we meet at her lodgings tonight to discuss an investigation into the aphasia curse."

He looked up at her. "You've thrown our lot in with the wizards?"

"Don't be thick. We'll tell them what we want them to know. I have plans."

"I'm not being thick," he nearly growled. "You're being cryptic. I thought we were in this together now. Are you going to share your plans, or just pull on my heart strings?" He tapped his chest.

"I thought you objected to puns," she said and smiled. It formed dimples in her pale cheeks.

Remembering how that dimpled smile had once entranced him, Cyrus scowled.

A door opened and Vivian and Lotannu returned, both now dressed in fine Verdantine dress. She wore a long crimson skirt, a loose white cotton shirt, and a thick black shawl. Around her neck and wrists shone an array of silver and turquoise jewelry. Lotannu was dressed more plainly—wide black hat, black wool trousers, white cotton shirt without collar, and a heavy red coat.

"We are off to the canonist," Vivian said as she laid a hand on Lotannu's shoulder. "You have my gratitude for helping us learn more about the aphasia curse."

Both Cyrus and Francesca nodded.

"Well then," the ancient woman said. "Francesca knows the location of our tavern. We shall see you tonight."

An apprentice showed the party out of the station. They went through the courtyard, passed the lion-headed gargoyles with metallic cats perched on their shoulders, and stepped back out into the arcade. The rain was still coming down hard, and the storm clouds made the evening darker than Cyrus expected.

Francesca started off toward the north. Cyrus followed but glanced back to see the wizardly apprentice looking at two men standing just under the arcade's shelter. The men were dressed in unremarkable Spirish garb: loose tan pants and shirts, brown longvests. One man was looking back at the apprentice, the other staring at Francesca's back. He looked away when he noticed Cyrus's attention.

Francesca pulled on the headdress he had given her and led them onto a street that ran west through the Merchant District. Three ravens were flying above them, croaking and harassing each other.

Cyrus glanced backward and saw one of the men walking on the other side of the street. "Fran," he said quietly, "I think we're—"

"Being followed?" she interrupted. "Did you think Vivian would let us wander around on our own?"

"No. I suppose they'd want us to have a chaperone."

"Chaperone?"

"To stop you from trying to seduce me," he said wryly.

"You poor, delusional man. So how are we going to shake off our tail?"

He thought for a moment. "Would running away or tossing a stunning spell in his face be a shade too blatant?"

She nodded. "Just a shade."

"We could try a decoy. But I don't suppose paying a stranger to wear your stole would fool anyone unless we found another massively six-foot-tall woman."

She sighed. "Let's not start with the height quips again. That wasn't cute even when we shared a bed."

"I'm sorry. I'd forgotten."

"You'll stop?"

"I'll stop."

"Thank you, Cyrus. Awfully big of you."

"You're welcome, your highness."

"Oh, this is just as bad as old times," she said, but he could see that she was smiling under her headdress. "Why don't you accompany me while I call on a patient? Then you can fly us out of a courtyard or something."

"Could work," he mused, "if I had enough text in these robes to write an airlift-the-world's-tallest-woman spell."

She sniffed. "We need fly only at low altitude. Given how close you are to the ground, I figure you have plenty of experience at that."

A city watchman, dressed in a green and white cloak, walked past them and nodded. Cyrus nodded back and then asked, "Did you learn about any disease that could cause a woman to become absurdly tall when you were training . . . at . . ." His voice died as an idea formed in his mind.

"Cyrus," she said as they walked around two men heaving at a cart that was stuck in the mud, "if you don't finish this wreck of a joke I can't laugh at how miserably it turned out."

He looked at her. The rain was letting up a bit. They passed an ornate building. A gray cat was stalking in the dry patch underneath its overhang. "Maybe we don't need to do anything elaborate to lose our tail. When was the last case of plague in Avel?"

"About two years ago. Ah!" She stopped and looked down at a muddy puddle she had stepped into. Swearing softly, she pulled her boot free and continued. "People catch plague mostly when rats infest a warehouse. But we've not had an epidemic in my time. The hydromancers can write these tiny waterborne texts that cure—"

"Is that tobacco salon near here still popular? It was called the Caravan Wheel when I left."

Her headdress moved as if she were frowning. "It still is. Just down that alley. But the guards will pull up the ladders at sunset, and we need to pass through at least two districts. Remember, I can't loft over the walls."

"This won't take long. Take me to the tobacco salon. And follow my lead."

She was skeptical but sped up her pace. A few moments later, they turned down an alley and heard a din of conversation. Soon they reached a two-story building. Its door was open but covered by a leather curtain. Golden light shone from the windows, and from a pole on the second story hung the eponymous caravan wagon wheel.

Cyrus pulled back the leather curtain and stepped into the warm room rich with aromatic pipe smoke. The place was filled with men and women. Many lay on cushions, smoking tobacco from elaborate water pipes and sipping from pewter cups of wine or steaming mint tea.

In the far corner, a young woman with olive-colored skin and brown hair was singing a popular love ballad. An old man accompanied her on a Spirish guitar.

Francesca removed her headdress and shook the water off her robes. Cyrus did likewise and lowered his veil.

By the door stood a large balding man wearing a blue longvest and a large knife tucked into his belt. He nodded at them, and Cyrus could see a thin scar running down one side of his jaw. This would be the hired muscle.

A stately woman with smooth black skin appeared before them and ushered them to an empty pair of cushions. He handed her two silver Spirish sovereigns and ordered a plate of her best lamb dish. He said they would pay more if it came quickly.

Shortly after she took his coins, Cyrus settled into his pillows and murmured, "Don't pay attention to our tagalong when he comes in."

"He already has," Francesca replied as she patted her hair to make sure the headdress hadn't disturbed it. "He's sitting by himself near the door. He didn't notice my noticing him."

"Good," Cyrus said. "Are you hungry?"

"Always."

"The food here is excellent, or it was."

"Cyrus, what are you planning? You can't just have me yell 'plague' in here. It'd start a rush for the door. Someone might be hurt."

"You're always so worried about doing the right thing when it doesn't involve my internal organs."

She looked away to the singer. "I haven't always done right by your heart."

She was trying to be sincere, but he didn't want to rehash the past. "So stop then," he said bluntly. "We're in this little caper together. If we pull it off, I make captain and leave you alone all the sooner."

This seemed to surprise her. She studied his face and was about to say something more when the hostess returned with a plate of lentils and lamb. They ate in silence. The lentils were hot; the meat tasted of honey, cumin, cayenne. In moments the plate was clean.

"Get ready," Cyrus whispered to Francesca and then gestured for the hostess.

"Magister and Magistra," the hostess said as she approached. "Is there something more I can do?"

He held out another silver. "Our compliments on the lamb." She graciously took the coin. "But we have a problem. More a concern for your establishment, really."

The hostess raised her eyebrows.

"My colleague here is a cleric, as you can see by her red stole. Just before we came in the door, she noticed that man by the door has the plague."

"The plague?" The hostess looked at Francesca. "You're sure?"

"Quite sure," Francesca said, quickly playing along with his lie. "On the side of his neck, the man has what we call a bubo—a swollen lymph node. In this case, it is erythematous and edematous. Can be nothing but bubonic plague."

Cyrus narrowed his eyes at the words "erythematous" and "edematous" but then decided that they might impress the hostess. Sometimes the most effective words were not magical.

"Out on the street, my colleague approached the man and he ignored her," Cyrus continued. "I've no doubt that he contracted the disease elsewhere, but I worry that if someone was to see him in here, they might—"

The hostess held up a hand. "Say no more. I will see to it."

Cyrus bowed his head.

As soon as the woman left, Francesca started to say something. He held a finger to his lips. "Get your headdress."

The hostess went to the man with a dagger standing by the door. They held their heads together for a moment and then approached the man who had been following Cyrus and Francesca.

The man had been watching the singer and steadfastly not looking at Cyrus or Francesca. Now he jumped and looked from the hostess to the door guard with wide eyes.

Cyrus sniffed. The wizards had hired an amateur. "Come on," he said, getting to his feet. "There's another door in the kitchen." Francesca stood.

Just then there came a short cry. Cyrus turned to see the man who had been following them on his feet. The door guard put a hand on the man's chest and rested his other hand on his dagger.

Cyrus and Francesca hurried out of the room and through the kitchen. Several cooks looked at them oddly, but no one said anything.

Once out in the alley, they discovered that the rain had let up almost completely. Several cats, gray and black, stalked the place for kitchen scraps. Somewhere above them a raven began to call out. Francesca let out a long peal of laughter. "That was grand!"

He bowed. "Thank you, Magistra."

"I'm sorry I distrusted you back in the tower."

"Not as sorry as I am," he muttered. "Come on let's get out of . . ."

His voice trailed off as she put her hand on his shoulder and said, "Don't be such a fractious old man. I trust you now."

Her tone was teasing, possibly flirtatious. She was trying to smooth things over. Just then Cyrus found it mildly manipulative, intensely irritating. "Good," he said curtly and turned away. "Now let's move before our tagalong catches up." He started to hurry out of the alley.

"We're headed to the North Gate District," she said catching up to him. "Nicodemus Weal was seen last among the Canic people."

He raised his veil and looked away from her.

Twenty-three

Deirdre pulled her shawl around her shoulders. She was standing near the back of the Hall of Governors, a spacious room with blue and white mosaics and rows of horseshoe arches. Though it lacked the gilded ceiling of the Hall of Ambassadors, it enjoyed a view of a broad courtyard with a reflecting pool flanked by myrtle bushes. The rain was striking water and leaf hard enough to make a pleasant hush.

The hall held a wide rug and large cushions arranged around hexagonal tables. Clicking braziers radiated islands of heat into the chill air.

City officials and dignitaries occupied the cushions. Deirdre recognized militia captains and the governors of the outer districts. The unfamiliar faces were likely wealthy denizens of the Palm and the Merchant Districts.

Presently the Commander of the City Watch was describing the morning's lycanthrope attack and the need of all present to help improve the city's defenses.

Deirdre's function was to be seen. Most would recognize her as the prodigal Lornish courtier whom Cala had favored for the past ten years. Many were themselves demon worshipers and so knew her importance. Others would suspect her of being Cala's Regent of Spies. To all, she was living evidence that greater forces were watching them.

But now that she'd been recognized, Deirdre had nothing to do but stand and consider what Cala had told her: the Silent Blight was an inhibition of Language Prime misspelling.

At first, this statement hadn't made sense. Back in Starhaven, Nicodemus had told her that Language Prime misspelling could create disease; that was how Fellwroth had given Shannon a canker curse. How then could a halt to misspelling cause trees across the continent to die? Cala had claimed that misspelling was one way in which Language Prime created original text. Without original text, plants were failing to adapt to changing environments.

Deirdre couldn't understand it. She wondered if there was a way to inform Nicodemus. The boy might comprehend the larger implications of her discovery.

Her thought broke off as she caught movement from the corner of her eye. Standing in the hall's entrance was a middle-aged man with short brown hair and a thick beard. Deirdre recognized him as Amal Jaen, a senior sanctuary clerk appointed to record the canonist's diplomatic correspondences. He was anxiously looking about the hall.

Two of the district governors were debating how certain city funds should be spent. Quietly, Deirdre stepped away from the meeting and then jogged up to the wall.

Amal saw her coming and left the hall. Deirdre followed, catching up with him in an open-air walkway. The rain came down on the garden with such audible force that when he whispered, he had to do so loudly. "Y-your physician . . . returned t-to the city t-t-today in South Market." As always, Amal stuttered. "An hour ag-go. With two black-robes."

"Wizards?" she asked quickly.

"They were let i-into . . . the wizards' station. A long time after, your physician and a hierophant left together."

"Were they followed?"

He shook his head. "You ordered they n-not be."

"Good. What about the two other black-robes? Any report from agents in the garden tower?"

"Th-that's . . . that's why I came. A report from the garden tower said the b-black-robes came in on a Kestrel-class warship."

"What?" she said in alarm.

"A-and the black-robes that went into the station, th-they didn't come out . . . or rather . . . they came out dressed up as wealthy Verdant m-merchants. Our agent followed th-them here."

"Here, to the sanctuary?"

"They d-didn't enter with the worshipers. They went straight t-to the canonist's guards . . . wh-who took them to the Hall of Amb-bassadors."

"When?" This was outside anything Deirdre had anticipated. Wizards in a Kestrel? It implied cooperation between the academy and the Celestial Court.

Amal glanced down the walkway. "Not a qu-quarter hour ago. Soon as I . . . I got the report, I sought you out."

"Whatever we are paying you, remind me to double it," she said while laying a hand on his shoulder. "Has anyone else been granted an audience with the canonist today?"

"N . . . not according to schedule."

"Good, seek me only if faced with an emergency." She turned and hurried from the walkway to a narrow flight of stairs. After sprinting up to the third floor, she ran along a hallway flanked by geometric screens.

A few feet before the entrance to the Hall of Ambassadors, she stopped beside an unremarkable panel. Hidden among the fretwork was a latch that, once released, allowed her to push a section of the screen out on its hinges. She stepped out onto a catwalk.

The rain clouds had dimmed the daylight to gloom and poured rain so insistently it pressed down on shoulders and head like a wet blanket. Deirdre ran along the catwalk to a short opening into the sanctuary's dome.

Once inside, she stood behind the screen that separated the Hall of Ambassadors from the dome's dark interior. Somewhere in this blackness stood Cala's ark.

Holding her breath, Deirdre crept along until she was behind the red-wood throne. The canonist was speaking in a stern tone. Deirdre stood close to the screen to peer through one of the narrow slits.

A man and a woman, both dressed as Verdantians, stood before the throne. Presently the demigoddess finished speaking and the woman replied. Deirdre listened to their conversation and with fear realized that these were two Astrophell wizards—agents of Nicodemus's half sister, the woman who would be Halcyon.

The academy had been sending requests to Cala to allow them to search Avel for Nicodemus. Typhon had claimed he could delay such an investigation for at least another year. But neither the demon nor Deirdre had ever imagined a Celestial warship would fly a wizardly investigation into Avel. The Spirish crown and Astrophell had somehow formed a pact and forced the canonist to submit to a search.

The newly come black-robes would complicate Typhon's plans. More important to Deirdre, they would endanger Nicodemus and Francesca. To retain any hope of recovering Boann, Deirdre had to eliminate the wizards. She hurried along the screen to a tight spiral staircase.

Typhon was in his private study, his mind partially deconstructed to better conduct his research. Since the rains had started, he had begun work on a metaspell that would help demons survive on the new continent.

Deirdre charged up to Typhon's private library. She hurried past the door guards and the scribes working at their desks. Servants had removed the bodies Nicodemus's raid had left behind. At the end of the library, she swung open the heavy vaulted door and stepped into the demon's private study.

Typhon's giant alabaster body sat before a table. He had disassembled his head into what looked like shards of onyx and ivory. These he suspended in the air above open books and loose pages. A small tear-shaped emerald hung amid the floating matrix of his mind.

"Typhon!" Deirdre yelled. "Demon!"

The demon couldn't hear. His right hand was running down an open page while his left repositioned a white disc of his mind over a codex.

Deirdre hammered his shoulder with her fist. The fiend took a moment to react, and when he did it was with a vicious backhanded swing. She ducked under his massive right arm and jumped back.

More rapidly than she would have thought possible, the demon assembled several hanging shards of his head into one bright black eye and one white ear. He held the first in his right hand and placed the second on the table.

After pointing the eye at her, he paused and then gestured for her to approach. When she did, he began plucking the remaining bits of his head from the air.

Deirdre picked up the white ear and into it described everything she knew about the two disguised wizards currently meeting with Cala. She finished with, "I will eliminate them both immediately."

If she could kill both black-robes, it would give Francesca and Nicodemus more time. "We can arrange for it to seem that their transport had to land in the savanna and was attacked by lycanthropes. It wouldn't—"

A strange buzzing, like that of an exotic instrument, sounded. Deirdre started as she realized the demon had made it. He had assembled enough of his throat to produce noise but not a mouth to shape it into voice. His giant white hand held up one finger in a gesture to wait. She frowned as the demon pieced together a jaw and lips.

"I must look at the newcomers," the demon rumbled, his words nasal. "Run this down and point it at them." He held out his open palm. An onyx eyeball rested upon it.

Deirdre scooped it up and dashed out of the private library and down the stairs. When she reached the screen behind the throne, her breathing was rapid. Only with effort could she keep each footstep quiet as she approached the screen and held the onyx eye up to it.

The woman was speaking to Cala with steady, almost challenging words. Deirdre bit her lower lip.

Deirdre held the eye up to the screen. Then she realized she hadn't checked that the pupil was pointing forward. She leaned closer and turned the eyeball around. It was hard to see in the dim light and she had to squint. Accidently she bumped the screen and conversation on the other side stopped.

Deirdre froze, wondering if she had just revealed herself. Blessedly, the canonist began scolding the woman. Slowly exhaling, Deirdre crept out of the darkness and dashed back up to Typhon.

She found the demon, his white face reconstructed, staring with one black eye at a few pieces floating above his opened forehead. "We don't attack in the sanctuary," he rumbled as she closed the door to his study.

She objected. "But in the city, people will see. It will be impossible to hide their murders—"

"No." He held out an open palm.

She gave him back his eye. "Here we can kill them discreetly. You can—"

"That woman down there is not what she appears," he said while jamming his eye into its socket with a wet pop. "This will work to our advantage."

"What is she?"

"I am not entirely sure, but I have a strong suspicion. You will leave this matter to me." He turned back to the books and scrolls laid out on his table. "If I am right, I will need this metaspell far sooner than I anticipated."

"This woman will hasten the Disjunction?"

Typhon smiled at her. "If we are lucky. But I dare not attack her here; it would be too dangerous."

"Dangerous for you? What is she, a disguised goddess?"

Typhon smiled. "You're getting ahead of yourself, daughter. Don't interfere with the newcomers. I will see to them. I want you to double your efforts to retrieve Nicodemus. He must be hiding somewhere in the city until nightfall."

Deirdre licked her lips. "But what about the danger to Francesca?"

"Not your concern," Typhon replied while reaching into the cloud of stony objects floating above his head. He plucked out the tiny, tear-shaped emerald. "It is time we completed a dragon. Go; find Nicodemus. If I'm correct about the woman speaking to Cala, it won't matter if you have to kill Francesca."

VIVIAN ADJUSTED HER hood. She and Lotannu were walking away from the sanctuary. Over the rain she could hear the sounds of a city: children yelling, someone clanging pots, a donkey bleating. Apparently they had reached the edge of the Holy District, where those privileged citizens who worked in the sanctuary kept their homes.

She had her hand on Lotannu's shoulder as he led her to the tavern where they would spend the night.

"Old friend," she asked, "what did you think of our audience with the demigoddess?"

"I think you nearly got your wish. Cala seemed an inch away from attacking us right then and there."

Vivian exhaled. "Pity she didn't. And what about the mysterious watcher?"

"Whoever was lurking behind the screen?"

"Yes, any ideas?"

Lotannu slowed down a bit before replying. "It wasn't Typhon; his thought patterns changed radically during our audience but they never moved from their position high up on the dome."

"And what of the unknown creature?"

"Vanished without a trace."

Vivian nodded to herself. "Good, good. This is all good."

Lotannu grunted. "Why didn't you just chase after the demon?"

"He would have fled."

They walked on in silence. It sounded as if a horse was trotting nearby. Suddenly Lotannu spoke, "Might I say something candidly?"

"Not if you're going to candidly criticize my plan."

"I'm going to candidly criticize your plan."

"Bastard," she said mildly.

"Even though you didn't attack him, the demon's going to figure out what we're up to and flee. It would take us another decade to discover where he'll resurface. We don't have that kind of time. The academy is too close to a schism."

"Let me guess, you think we should use the contingency plan."

His tone became insistent. "Think about it. We could go to the colaboris station, send a message to our allies in Kara, and this whole thing will be over by tomorrow night, no chance for the demon to slip away."

"We can't waste a chance to catch Nicodemus, the half dragon, and the demon all in one go. Besides . . . it's too clumsy."

"It is not," Lotannu said coldly. He had been the architect of the contingency plan.

"I didn't mean that it's clumsily conceived. But however well executed the plan is, it might leave half this city's population dead."

"What if the demon calls all of his wind mages down on us tonight? Your tidy little mission won't be so tidy then."

"Don't sulk."

"I feel the need to sulk."

"My old friend, have I ever told you how much I love you?"

"Every time you pretend not to have heard what I just said."

"I'm sorry," she said before loudly asking, "What did you say?"

CHAPTER

Twenty-four

Cyrus followed Francesca through the labyrinthine alleys until they left the houses to stand in ten yards of muddy ground that separated the buildings from a district wall. Boards had been laid down to help people reach two sets of ladders propped against the wall.

Cyrus had never used such ladders; he had always lofted himself over any wall. But he couldn't spare the text in his robes to lift them both. So he climbed up after Francesca, nodded to the city watchmen at the wall's top, and then climbed down the other side into the Cypress District.

As they walked down a cobbled street, Cyrus admired the district's courtyards, gardens, and the cypresses that gave it its name. Twice they passed watchmen swaggering in their green and white cloaks.

Abruptly, the rain stopped and the black clouds rolled away, leaving first white puffs and then only thin wisps.

Moments before, the storm had darkened the day almost into night. Now they walked through bright streets, the puddles reflecting a pale evening sky. Cyrus had seen this rainy-season darkness-to-day phenomenon all across Western Spires, but the speed with which the clouds tumbled over Avel made it even more dramatic.

Francesca turned off the cobbled road and led them again through alleyways. The buildings became less grand until there were few taller than one story. They reached another wall and had to climb over it via the ladders.

They had reached the North Gate District. The rickety wooden buildings here were all single story, the doorways covered by ragged leather curtains. Muddy children and stray dogs roamed streets devoid of watchmen.

Each district had to mount a militia to supplement the city watch. The wealthier districts paid to arm their young men and hired mercenaries to train and support them. The walls around North Gate were less well defended, their streets unpatrolled, subjecting the district not only to crime but also to more frequent lycanthrope incursions.

North Gate was populated almost entirely by the Canic people. They were a small cultural group, having significant numbers only in Avel, Dar, and the few fortified villages between. Their ancestors had been the first to settle the wild savannas of Southwestern Spires.

When the Neosolar Empire had united the continent, the Canics had held themselves apart. They had worshiped an ancient tree goddess, who resided in a redwood nearly a mile in height. After the empire's fall, the Polytheistic Realm of Spires—then an alliance of new kings and local deities—had spread across the West. The Canics had tried to establish an independent realm, but the Spirish slaughtered the Canic armies, killed their goddess, and burned their sacred tree. Crushed and godless, the Canic tribes splintered and their numbers dwindled.

With the western frontier quiet, the young Realm of Spires had devoted all of its efforts to surviving the forays of Verdantine and Lornish armies up and down their eastern coast. The Canics became a marginal people.

This history—in particular the loss of their goddess—had produced the Canic's cynical philosophy that life was inherently wretched and that poverty and pain were unavoidable. The best any Canic could hope for was survival.

A more concrete manifestation of the Canic's history was the shabbily dressed children playing unsupervised in the mud. They were frail and feral things, boys and girls indistinguishable. Both had their tangled hair cut short and wore their people's traditional loose gray trousers and shirts.

Among the children romped dogs of the peculiar breed that the Canics bred and trained to attack lycanthropes. The canines stood taller than three feet, were covered with thick fur, and possessed unsettlingly intelligent eyes. When Francesca and Cyrus walked near a pack of shouting children, the dogs seemed to study them.

There were more ravens here too, cawing and fighting with each other. Stray cats, thin and mangy, prowled the rooftops.

The place's poverty didn't seem to bother Francesca. As she navigated the streets, she received an occasional wave from a child. In return, she gave each a warm smile and a dignified nod.

"Patients?" Cyrus asked.

"I'm one of the few clerics who comes to North Gate."

They entered an alley and passed—in a small square of open ground—a young savanna oak, the branches of which were covered with prayer flags. "Where are we going?" he asked.

"To someone who owes me a favor," Francesca said as she stepped around a puddle. "If Nicodemus is or was here, Old Man Luro will know it. Story goes that when he was a young caravan guard he saved his whole company from the Savanna Walker with some fast thinking. Until today, I always assumed it was nonsense. In any case, Luro came back to Avel a hero. He was something of the public champion of the North Gate for years. However, last time I saw him, he said he was done worrying about other people's problems. But that doesn't mean he won't know about those problems."

Cyrus made a low, thoughtful sound.

Francesca continued. "Luro's a typical old Canic: doesn't trust strangers farther than his twice-broken nose. We'll have to be . . . persuasive."

Just then a pair of yelling children and a large dog ran past them. Cyrus frowned at the mud they splattered on his robes and asked, "Why do the Canics always seem to have a flood of squeakers and a scattering of geezers without any folk between?"

At a fork in the alley, Francesca started off in one direction. "Most of the young people, men and women, leave to work in caravans: ox drivers, cooks, wagonwrights, guards, that sort of thing. Out there they're attacked by lycanthropes, grass fires, thirst. Add to that the young men who stay have to serve in the district's militia and the district is the most likely to be attacked by lycanthropes, and you can see why many of them die young and the rest are so cynical."

Cyrus grimaced. "Makes you realize how easy we have it."

"That's the God-of-gods damned truth," Francesca said while stopping before a building that looked sturdier than its neighbors. "But don't express any pity for the Canics; Luro will find it patronizing. In fact, don't express anything at all. He's bound to dislike you. He dislikes everyone."

Cyrus nodded and waited for Francesca to knock on the doorframe.

"OLD MAN LURO!" Francesca belted out with enough force that Cyrus jumped.

"Blood and fire, Fran!"

"OLD MAN LURO!"

Something thumped inside the house and then the leather curtain moved a few inches to reveal a vertical glimpse of a bearded face. A single brown eye looked Francesca up and down. Then the curtain parted to reveal a short man, bent forward. Though his face was crosshatched with wrinkles, he still possessed a shock of white hair. Less fortunately, a profusion of pale bristles grew from his ears and nose. "It's you," the ancient figure grumbled. "Come in. Come in. Daria!"

Francesca stepped through the curtain. Cyrus followed and discovered a warm, dark room furnished with a table and a few chairs. A small fire crackled in a hearth on the far wall. An old woman crouched near it.

"Daria, see who's here for you."

After Cyrus's vision adjusted to the dark, he could make out four massive dogs lying around the fire. Three children were among the animals; two slept on dogs' bellies as if they were pillows, the third sat up and stroked one beast's muzzle. As he watched, the one patting the dog rose and looked at Francesca.

The child's expression seemed stern beyond her years, as if she had just been confronted by a profound moral dilemma. Francesca crouched. "Who's that?" she playfully half-whispered.

The child's expression broke into a smile and she ran to Francesca, who caught her and twirled her around. The both of them laughed freely and began to chatter.

Cyrus folded his arms and considered Francesca. Her words, pitched in childish exaggeration, bore no hint of skepticism or wit. And her smile, lit by the watery red glow of the fire, seemed easy and unguarded.

"Hierophant," a gruff voice said. Cyrus turned and saw Luro looking him up and down.

Cyrus nodded. "Master Luro."

The old man stepped closer. "Windbag, what are you doing here?"

Cyrus met his gaze and then looked at the child in Francesca's arms. "That your daughter?"

"Great-granddaughter."

Then Francesca was standing between the two men, pressing the giggling child to her hip. "How did you get to be so silly?" she asked and touched the child's nose.

The child giggled but then noticed Cyrus. Her expression became stern again, and she pressed her face into Francesca's shoulder.

"She's been fine, just fine," the old man said to Francesca. "Eating regular and running around with the others. Just fell asleep when they had to come in during the rain."

Francesca bounced the girl on her hip. "I'm glad to hear it." Then she looked at Luro. "I didn't come to see Daria, lovely as she is."

The old man squinted. "No?"

"It's time to pay back that favor you owe me. I need your help. So do your people."

The old man hacked out a laugh. "Grandest damned way I've ever been asked to pay up. Told to take enough coin to make treating her worth your while. If you don't let Canics pay—"

"I need some information," Francesca interrupted.

"What kind of information?"

"The first part's easy. I need you to tell me everything you know about the Savanna Walker. I've heard stories you became a hero when you encountered the beast."

The old man chuckled. "Oh, a grand hero I was, a regular legend," he said dryly. "Grander than any damned canonist."

The child in Francesca's arms murmured. Everyone paused while Francesca put her ear close to the girl. "All right, honey," Francesca said and put the child down. Once on the floor, the girl went back to the dogs. Francesca turned back to Luro. "You saw the Savanna Walker?"

"Hardly. Our caravan was circled up for the night and one of the outer lycanthrope tribes was harrying us. Stalking around it, darting in and out of the savanna grass, testing the barricades between the wagons. Nothing a caravan couldn't handle. Mostly it gave our archers empty hopes of putting an arrow through their hides. But then the wolves went mad. Writhing on the ground and screaming. Some attacked each other, some attacked an unseen creature in the grass. From atop a caravan wagon, you can see over the grass. And there was the usual waving stalks that lycanthropes make and this other bigger thing. Bigger than a katabeast. When it moved the ground shook."

Francesca made a low noise. "The Savanna Walker?"

He shrugged. "What else? We had some candles from Dar in the cargo, so I jammed some wax in my ears and convinced most other guards to do so. The men who didn't went mad. They jumped off the wagons. The lycanthropes got to them or the Walker did. No one knows. An hour later they were all gone. Come morning, we found nothing but bones and bits of lycanthrope fur on the road."

"So it was candle wax that made you Champion of North Gate?"

He sniffed. "Champion, my hairy backside. People like to complain to me. That's all. When I was younger, I was fool enough to listen."

"So the Savanna Walker was an enemy to the lycanthropes?"

He scowled. "How in all the burning hells should I know? The different lycanthrope tribes fight each other year round. Some say the Walker is a massive lycanthrope. Some say it's the lycanthropes' deity. Some say strange things about the Walker's being a ghost of human souls that died of thirst. No one knows. And I don't care."

He squinted first at her and then at Cyrus. "You two came out here to hear the glory stories of my youth?"

Francesca nodded. "In part, and we thank you for that. But there's another matter we need to ask about."

"Spit it out."

"At the end of last year's rainy season there was violence in North Gate.

Some of your people were hiding a man named Nicodemus Weal. The hierophants discovered him and things got bloody. I need your help finding out what happened to him."

The old man lowered his eyebrows. "What happened to who? Nicolo? What are you talking about?"

"Don't play slow with me, Luro."

He shook his head. "Don't know anything about bloodshed in this district."

"That's more bollocks than I'd get from castrating a bull."

The old man scowled. "I can't help you if I don't know what you're talking about."

Francesca only folded her arms.

Cyrus cleared his throat. "Nicodemus is a rogue—" He stopped. Francesca had held up a hand. "Luro knows. If he didn't, he'd be telling us how stupid we are for poking around his district."

"Bah!" the old man said and then sniffed. "No one knows what's afoot in this cesspool. You don't know what you're talking about."

Francesca cleared her throat. "Do you want your people to attract the canonist's attention?"

"Don't ask stupid questions."

"If I'm looking for Nicodemus, who else do you think will be?"

The old man threw his hands in the air. "When did we start playing 'guess what the healer's thinking?' Damnation and blood. I don't know anything!"

Francesca wasn't impressed. "In the infirmary, someone close to the canonist is talking about the Canics hiding Weal. You know I care about your people."

He raised his eyebrows. "Oh, that's it then? The virtuous healer come to save our wretched hides? So why'd you bring the windbag?" He gestured to Cyrus and then smiled crookedly at him. "I don't like him; he talks too much."

Cyrus opened his mouth to say that he hadn't talked at all, but Francesca held up her hand to stop him.

Luro smirked and waved at Cyrus. "See! Just chattering away, just blowing away." The old man laughed. "Windbags might lay golden eggs for the rest of Spires, but they don't do half a damn for the Canics. Can't even keep the lycanthropes out of our district."

Francesca interrupted. "Hierophant Cyrus Alarcon is the new air warden of Avel. I've brought him so that he can see your people did not mean harm to the city when they harbored Nicodemus Weal. He doesn't want unrest. He'll lose his position if hierophants die on his watch. He will testify that you helped. Did you think I'd be foolish enough to act alone? Risk my position at the infirmary to endure your . . . hospitality?" She nearly sneered this last word.

This made Luro hoot with pleasure. "Hospitality! Ha! All right, healer, now that I think of it—and now that I remember how damned persistent you can be—there's a favor I need doing, and none of the folk that annoy me less than you annoy me can do it. I'll make you a deal."

"Like hell. You owe me."

He sniffed. "Paid that off with the stories about the Walker. You're asking for something big, and that's got a big price."

Francesca was silent for a moment. "What price?"

"Wait a moment," the old man said and then hobbled to a chest. He rummaged around in it for a moment before coming back with something small wrapped in brown linen cloth. He held it out. "Look at this."

Francesca took the object and unfolded the cloth. It was a thin sheet of steel, about as wide and long as a man's hand. In the upper-right-hand corner was engraved the image of a small crown. Cyrus's breath stopped.

Luro grunted. "Maybe half a year ago someone in this city started paying very desperate Canics to smuggle these into the city. I want you to find out who."

Francesca seemed unimpressed. Cyrus was about to explain what she was holding when she spoke: "Smuggling steel through Avel? Luro, you're boring me. There's plenty of nobles in Dar and Queensport that sympathize with the would-be Highlander rebels. All of Spires would gloat if the Highlanders managed to break from Lorn. There've been Spirish smuggling weapons and steel through Avel and into Highland for centuries."

"That steel's not being smuggled into Lorn," Cyrus said. "It's being smuggled out."

She looked at him. "What do you mean?"

Cyrus continued. "In the Lornish foundries, highsmiths cast their runes into metal. They charge these little sheets of metal with their runes in the same way that we hierophants charge sailcloth. A highsmith can take these different sheets, edit the text on them to create spells that transform into intricate metallic machinery or edged weapons or—"

"I know what highsmiths can do," Francesca snapped.

Cyrus nodded. "If it's genuine and fully inscribed, that sheet you're holding has a dangerous amount of text."

"Stop with the mumbo jumbo," Luro said. "Fact is, smuggling those things into a Spirish city is safe as sleeping in a grass fire. You think Weal might cause trouble for the Canics? Bah! Whatever flame he'd start would be a spark in the firestorm if the canonist found we was smuggling those."

"Luro, you old soft heart," Francesca said through a smile. "Seems someone's still the Champion of North Gate after all."

"Don't get cute on me, healer."

"So someone's smuggling Lornish language into a Spirish city," Francesca mused. "And you want us to stop them?"

"To hell with stopping them. Just get them to use someone other than Canics to smuggle the damned stuff."

"If you can't find out who's paying for the sheets," Cyrus asked, "what makes you think we can?"

Luro narrowed an eye. "It's got to be someone in one of the inner districts. I pull plenty weight in the outer districts; I'd have found him if he was out here. Bastard has to be operating beyond my reach. Has to be. But, I figure your fancy robes would let you ask questions in the inner districts."

"How did you get this?" Francesca asked while bouncing the steel sheet in her hand.

"I heard rumors about them, so I had my nephews start asking around. I got a lot of nephews. Just after the rains started this year, someone leaves that at my doorstep."

"Anonymously?" Cyrus asked.

"If that means the bastard wasn't stupid enough to give me a name I could pass on to the canonist, yeah, windbag, anonymously."

Francesca rewrapped the metal. "I'm taking this with me. We have a deal, Luro. I'll look into this. I have a sinking feeling it may be related to this Nicodemus Weal character."

The old man grunted. "That so?"

"That's so."

"Good."

"So it's time you told me about Weal. I need to find him, tonight if possible."

Luro looked at Francesca for a while, then Cyrus, then Francesca again. "It's the militia boys. I don't mind telling you, since I don't like 'em. Nothing but goons and rioters. Hang them all by the neck and we'd be better off."

"Militia boys?" Cyrus asked.

"Hotheaded pups wanting the Canic peoples to form a kingdom of their own or some such rot. Won't happen."

Cyrus had not heard of such a group, but as a hierophant he had always been concerned with what was happening in the skies above Avel, not in it. So he looked at Francesca, who was grimacing as if in recognition. "Why harbor Nicodemus Weal?"

"Word went that he's talking against the canonist. Claims she's been corrupted by a demon or some idiocy. I think he's one of these War of Disjunction lunatics, preaching about how Los and the demon army are cross-ing the ocean tomorrow."

Francesca nodded. "And the militia buy it because it justifies splitting from Cala?"

"Best I can figure. They moved him about the district. Sometimes they'd hire the lowlife crews—Old Fatima's gang, Guy Fire's gang, that lot—to hide him from the city watch. They also paid Merchant Dal to hide him in one of his warehouses. That's where the violence was. A bunch of wind-bags tore through the place at night. Story went that more than a few of the windbags got popped." He paused to leer at Cyrus. "But Weal got away. Militia boys must have evacuated him to Esten Town or Coldlock Harbor. Can't imagine where else he could be hiding that the lycanthropes wouldn't get him into their bellies."

Francesca nodded. "Has he been back?"

Luro squinted at her. "You . . ." He paused. "Remind me again why it's so important that you find him?"

"It might be tied up in your steel problem, Luro. And you do know something about this; I see it on your face. Weal is back in the city now, isn't he?"

"Don't be stupid," the old man growled but then asked, "Are you gonna tell me why it's so important for you to find out?"

"Because I won't attack a damned warehouse like the canonist's offi-cers," she said. "I can get to the bottom of this without more Canic blood-shed."

He looked her up and down.

"Trust me, Luro," she said. "Have I ever done wrong by your people be-fore?"

"What's your angle? What's a healer stand to gain?"

"There's intrigue in the sanctuary," she said. "I'm in a dangerous posi-tion. What I said before about our windbag here"—she nodded to Cyrus—"is true. He'll vouch for you and your people. But he's also been caught up in the intrigue. Trust me, Luro. Telling me how to find Nicodemus Weal will save some of your people, save our lives, and help us get to the bottom of your metal smugglers."

The old man grunted. "That true?"

"True as a straight line."

He squinted at her for a moment then grunted. "This morning there were rumors that Weal snuck back into the city. People are nervous. There's also rumors about this morning's commotion in the sanctuary and Weal having something to do with it. But maybe you can tell me something about that?"

Francesca shook her head. "I've told you all that I know."

Luro sniffed. "Me spilling every detail, while you—"

"You're sure Nicodemus is in the city now?"

"Swear you'll be careful about this?"

"Swear on the Creator's name."

He crossed his arms. "The northernmost gatehouse on our district's eastern wall is boarded up. That's where the militia's storing equipment and hiding Nicodemus. If he's in the city now, that's where he'll be."

Francesca nodded. "Thank you, Luro. And yes, we will be careful." She glanced at Cyrus and nodded toward the door.

"Bit of advice," Luro said. "Change the windbag out of his green wrapping." He jabbed a knobby finger at Cyrus's robes. "Otherwise, the militia will get powerfully curious about what a pike would look like sticking out of him."

Twenty-five

Once they were back on the street, Cyrus walked close to Francesca and muttered, "Disguise or no, it'd be mad to just run into a stronghold of discontented militia."

"So let's not," she said and turned into an alley.

He hurried to catch up. A terrified gray cat was scampering away before them. "What are you talking about?"

She stopped beside a shack. "Help me climb this."

"Fran, tell me—" He cut his question short as she jumped up and grabbed hold of the shack's roof. He wrapped his arms around her legs and lifted until she managed to clamber onto the roof. Only when she was gone did he think about how close he had been to her waist.

"Come up," she said. There came the cawing and wing beats of a startled raven.

Cyrus edited the sentences in his robes so that it rewove a fold of itself into a small rope. He wrote a spell at its tip and then threw it up so that it bound itself around a gutter. Once sure the line was secure, he shimmied up onto the roof. Francesca was on the far side, squatting so she could peer into the alley from which they had come.

"Why under Celeste's blue heaven do I follow you?" he groused, squatting next to her. "Why aren't we investigating the militia gatehouse?"

"Because the old man was lying," she said while staring at Luro's house. Four ravens were flying circles overhead, probably the same birds Francesca had disturbed off of this roof.

"Luro was lying about everything?" Cyrus asked. "About the Lornish metal?"

She shook her head. "No, no. He'd have no reason to lie about that. He was lying about Nicodemus and the gatehouse."

"Explain."

"There are dissident Canics in that militia, certainly. That's like reporting there's fish in the sea. Maybe the militia Canics were even hiding Nicodemus when the hierophants caught him. And likely the hotheads are building up supplies in an abandoned gatehouse. But they can't be hiding Nicodemus in it."

"Why not?"

"He's a spellwright, Cyrus. He can't go through a gate or into a gatehouse; Cala's godspell would kill him."

"Oh," was all Cyrus could say. "Right."

"I'd bet silver lengths to brass bits that Luro told us about the gatehouse to get us out of his house. Didn't you notice how his demeanor changed when I told him that there was intrigue in the sanctuary?"

Cyrus had not noticed.

"He was breathing faster, looking away when talking. His pupils were dilated. All signs of lying. I think Nicodemus is in the city now. Luro must have fed us a lie because he—" She paused as the leather curtain in Luro's door parted and revealed the old man covered in a cloak. Two children— neither one Daria—and one of the massive dogs were beside him.

"You think he's going to warn whoever is actually hiding Nicodemus?" Cyrus asked.

"Yes, and we'd better follow . . . God-of-gods damn it!" Francesca swore as Luro had headed off in one direction and the children in the other. "Whom do we follow?"

"Is Luro so canny that he'd send the real message with children and then act as a decoy?"

She arched an eyebrow at him.

"Right, we follow the children." Cyrus snuck away from the ledge and then hurried to where he had left the rope. When Francesca caught up, he shimmied down. She followed, dropping the last few feet to splat in the mud.

Together they jogged down the alley and then turned into another that ran parallel to the one the children were on. They made two more sharp turns and entered a wide, rough-cobbled street. Packs of children interspersed with dogs ran about and played some sort of ball game.

To their left, the street widened into a cobbled square filled with merchant's stalls and lit by torches and tiny lamp flames. The air smelled of baking bread and cooking meat. Cyrus recognized the square as the North Gate night market—a place where the Canic people gathered to stroll and eat street food. Crowds were already filling the spaces between stalls, mostly adults but a few children and dogs among them. "Celeste in heaven," Cyrus swore. "How are we going to find the—"

"There," Francesca said and pointed at two children and a dog walking away from them down the street.

They hurried after, attracting little notice from the children. The dogs however watched them pass. There were also a few adults who eyed the spellwrights. Cyrus tried to stride purposefully, as if he were on official business.

Above them, the twilight sky was fading into lavender. There was maybe a half hour of light left.

Luro's children entered another alley. Francesca turned down a different alley and then cut over to the one that the children had entered. It was darker between these buildings. Still, Cyrus could make out the dog and the two children almost a hundred feet ahead. The children turned off into yet another alley.

He and Francesca hurried after. As they ran, he noticed that the air smelled acrid, almost sulfurous. Then he saw some buildings with portions of their walls missing. Through the windows he saw patches of twilight sky.

"This neighborhood caught fire during the last lycanthrope incursion," Francesca said while jogging beside him. "I heard it was abandoned."

They came splashing to a halt before the corner where the children had turned. Cyrus looked after them. At first he saw nothing. The buildings here had been burned almost to the ground, leaving a forest of beams and stone chimneys.

However, there was one large sandstone structure, a temple, judging by its dome. Some of its walls had collapsed to reveal its fire-gutted interior. Charred rafters lay at awkward angles. Disappearing behind one of these was a child's figure.

They ran after. "Move quietly," Francesca whispered as they reached the burnt-out building. "And ready any protective texts you have."

With a few deft movements, Cyrus edited defensive language into his robes. Now, if struck by a sharp edge, his protective paragraphs would interlock and momentarily make the cloth as impenetrable as steel. "I'll go first."

But Francesca shook her head and pointed to her wizardly robes. "I'm wearing black."

He tried to protest, but she was already stepping over rubble and into the building. He looked down at the blue prose flowing through his sleeves and considered the few defensive actions he could take with so little cloth. If only he had a lofting kite.

The temple was quiet save for their rapid breaths. Cyrus looked up to watch Francesca step into the building. Something nearby made a sound like sand being poured out of a bag.

Francesca vanished.

The dark had not obscured her; he could still make out the dim forms of rubble and timbers. She had simply disappeared as if she'd been pulled into another world.

"Fran!" he whispered and reached for her.

But as his arm entered the dark, the blue sentences in his sleeve winked out.

Cyrus snapped his hand back as if burned. Once back in the twilight, sentences from his robe washed down to refill his sleeve. "Holy canon!" he swore. "Fran?" Nothing. "Francesca?" Still nothing.

He picked up a bit of burnt wood and threw it into the darkness. It thumped against the ground.

Again Cyrus reached into the dark, and again the sentences in his sleeve blinked into nothing. Then he understood.

It was the darkness. There was a disspell working in the dark, and something more than a disspell, something that had . . . swallowed Francesca.

Cyrus stepped away from the dark to stand more completely in the twilight. Night was almost upon him. He had to find some way of bringing light into the temple. He turned around and then froze.

Standing on either side of him—their muscular chests midnight blue, their long ponytails blond—were two humanlike creatures. Not lycanthropes. One had a pale scar on his cheek. Both were armed with hatchets and crouched as if to attack.

Cyrus's heart thundered and sweat formed under his turban.

One of the monsters peeled back his lips to reveal sawlike teeth of pure black. It gestured with a hatchet for Cyrus to go into the temple, into the dark.

But once in the shadow, the text in Cyrus's robes would be disspelled. He'd have no hope of getting Fran out of the trap.

Cyrus crouched, ready to fight. But his heart was still kicking hard, and sweat was dripping inside his headdress. Then a twinge of pain shot through his chest.

He went cold with terror. He'd forgotten.

Without her spellwrighting nearby, it must already be contracting.

Reflexively, he brought a hand to his chest and knew that the greatest danger was neither the two monsters in front of him nor the dark spells at his back.

It was the sentence tightening around his spellbound heart.

Twenty-six

One monster jumped forward to land an overhand hatchet strike on Cyrus's shoulder. The paragraphs in his robes interlocked and stopped the axe blade as sure as plate armor, but the blow made him stumble backward. He pulled several paragraphs from his robes and looked at the monsters, hoping to cast the spell into their clothes and immobilize them. But the monsters wore only leather pants that stopped below the knees. There wasn't a stitch of fabric on them. Cyrus growled. They'd learned not to wear cloth when fighting hierophants.

The creature to his left struck with a high sidearm chop. Cyrus ducked under the swing and then reached for the creature. But as he did, the blunt head of the monster's other axe smashed into his stomach. Lacking a cutting edge, the axe head did not activate the protective paragraphs. The blow drove the wind out of Cyrus. He staggered backward.

Both monsters advanced, studying him with cold golden eyes. One uttered something. The other responded.

Cyrus stepped toward the creature on his right. But the monster backed away while the other landed a sidearm blow to his thigh. Again, the spells in Cyrus's robes protected him, but again he staggered backward. The creatures were trying to push him into the temple, into the dark and whatever spells lurked within.

One monster stepped forward with an overhand swing. This time, Cyrus stepped into the attack, meeting the blade with a raised forearm. Though blunted by his protecting spells, the blow sent a jolt of force down Cyrus's arm. The monster paused. Cyrus edited a swath of his robes so that text boiled out of the cloth as a blast of wind. Instantly, he was flying upward.

Something struck his left leg with enough force to make it go numb. But he was too busy editing his miniature jumpchute to mind. Deftly, he arced through the air to alight on a stone chimney.

Something thudded below him. He looked down to see a quivering hatchet stuck in a beam leaning against the chimney.

Someone shouted. It was a man's voice, a human voice. Cyrus turned but saw only ruined temple and darkening rubble. The creatures had vanished.

Another twinge of pain shot through Cyrus's chest, making him gasp. He had a quarter hour, maybe less, until Francesca's death sentence strangled his heart.

In the sky, a few stars had appeared. Frantically, he scanned the city for a source of light. To the north, torches flickered on the distant outer wall. Too far. He'd die before he could fly there and back. Southward, he saw only dark buildings and empty alleyways. But above that was a rectangular break in the cityscape that glowed orange. The night market.

Cyrus grabbed his robes and jumped into the air. Ravens on the wing croaked their surprise as he flew to the street. A few children cried out as he landed on the cobblestones.

Quickly, he edited his makeshift jumpchute back into his robes and ran. The night market was filled with Canics and merchants hawking honeyed breads or skewers of grilled meat. Only a few artisan stalls remained occupied. Relief washed through Cyrus as he saw one filled with lamps, several burning to attract attention.

"I need lamp oil, flint, and a firesteel," Cyrus blurted while fumbling with his belt purse. "I'll pay but only if you hurry. Dawdle or haggle and I'll commandeer what I need in our canonist's name."

The lamp maker—a plump woman with a round face and graying black hair—moved quickly.

Cyrus laid down three silver sovereigns on her counter. He was overpaying, but there was no time to argue. The woman scooped up the coins and placed a heavy flask in his hands. Suddenly Cyrus realized that his heart should be in agony by now. The lamp maker handed him a bit of flint and a curled firesteel.

He took them and hurried away. Above the night market, a lofting kite cut a slow circle. The kite's hierophantic spells made its canopy shine like a rectangle of daylight sky flying through twilight.

No doubt the pilot should be patrolling the outer walls, watching for lycanthropes in the grass. Probably he had grown bored enough to cut an excursion out of his patrol. Cyrus would have words for the patrol's wing commander about discipline . . . if he outlived the night.

He ran back down the street toward the ruined temple. Again, he wondered why his heart wasn't in agony. A few twinges of pain moved through his chest, but no more than would be expected from exertion and anxiety.

Suddenly he realized what Francesca had done. But how had she disspelled it? And when? He turned into an alley and then remembered standing behind the tobacco salon. Francesca had laid a hand on his shoulder and said, "I trust you now."

The memory made him clutch his flask of lamp oil. He thought she had been flirting. In fact it had been an act of trust, the disspelling of her death sentence. And yet she hadn't trusted him enough to tell him what she had done.

The realization filled Cyrus with a rush of contrary emotions: frustration at her little game, but also excitement. He remembered what it had been like to hold her—her slender waist, her slight breasts, the warmth of her neck.

But then he shook his head, trying to think clearly. This was foolishness. He needed to get Francesca out of the dark.

THE BLACKNESS LIFTED from Francesca's eyes, and she found herself still inside the ruined temple.

She had not moved an inch from where some foreign text had spellbound her. The trap had censored her mind, stopped her ears, blinded her eyes, held her perfectly still. After the initial shock, she had for a while grudgingly admired the spellbinding. But then her anxiety rose. Likely she was blind because a subtext was bending light around her and thereby rendering her invisible. Cyrus, unable to see her, might step into the trap as well.

Suddenly she could hear a conversation spoken in hushed but passionate voices. She strained to make out individual words and was shocked to realize that the conversation was not between humans. It couldn't be. The voices hissed and clanged. It sounded like several forks arguing with each other while tumbling in a pot of boiling water.

A rush of fear moved through her then. Perhaps she had found not Nicodemus Weal but the Savanna Walker. Perhaps her mind was about to get textually mashed into aphasic mush.

"Magistra."

She jumped, straining hard against her spellbindings. Nothing happened. She stopped struggling and set every ounce of her wit to appearing calm.

"Magistra," the voice said again—a man's voice, low and controlled. It was frighteningly close, as if the speaker were leaning over her shoulder. "I need your full attention."

"Do you now?" she asked conversationally. "Then it's a shame I'm so busy being bound up tighter than a God-of-gods damned sausage. Why don't you come back in an hour, hmm?"

The man laughed dryly. "If I do, can you compose a defensive prose style that wouldn't embarrass an apprentice?"

"You know, I've always wondered if it's possible to be both pretentious and retarded," she replied. "Thank you for settling the matter, Magister Weal."

"Magistra is too polite," he said coldly. "I was far too retarded to ever become a wizard. But at least I was never careless enough to dash headlong into disspells and endanger my fellow spellwrights."

The word "careless" made Francesca's throat tighten as she remembered Deirdre dying on her table. "What did you do to Cyrus?"

"If you mean the hierophant following you, we merely tried to keep him from endangering us or himself. He fought back; some hatchets were thrown. We weren't keen on doing that, but we couldn't let him escape to fetch other wind mages. The damned thing is that he did escape, and I'm a little worked up about having to kill or be killed by whomever he brings back. Do you understand?"

"Cyrus isn't your enemy. I'm not your enemy."

"Will he bring other hierophants here?"

She tried to shake her head but found it still spellbound. "I don't know. He knows many of them unknowingly serve Typhon."

These words were greeted at first by silence but then by a flurry of words in the harsh language. Then something—could it have been a parrot?—squawked. A raspy voice began to coo the word "Azure . . . azure . . ."

Francesca spoke louder. "I bring a message from Deirdre."

When Nicodemus answered, his voice was softer. "Is she well?"

Francesca strained to see her interlocutor, but she could make out nothing but rubble. To hide her anxiety, she spoke dispassionately: "She was wounded in the lycanthrope ambush this morning. They brought her into the infirmary and she died on my table. Moments later, she came back to life. A creature that caused aphasia came after her. I tried to help her run, but she couldn't escape. She wanted to punish my failure in the worst way possible, so she—"

"Made you find me," Nicodemus interrupted coolly. "I get it. I'm the worst punishment there is."

"It's good you know what your role in this world is."

"But did Deirdre know she was interrupting our efforts? Why did she send you?"

"She said Typhon intends to wound you when capturing you and that I was to keep you alive during that capture. But she 'put me in play,' to use her words, with a message for you. She said to tell you that . . ." She paused. "That there are two dragons."

These words were followed by a rapid conversation of clanging voices. This time, Francesca could distinguish several speakers. One of them, she realized, was Nicodemus closely approximating the harsh sounds with his human mouth.

"Deirdre said," she continued, "that she has sometimes escaped the demon's control to read his documents, one of which named me as the only one who can keep the second dragon from killing you."

This produced a blast of cacophonous laughter. Nicodemus laughed loudest. "Could you pull my other leg, Magistra? It's got brass bells on it." Another laugh. "But, honestly, you don't need to make up stories. Unless you're a danger to my students, I won't harm you."

"I'm not lying!" she said. "Deirdre said that a blasted demon knows my name and is worried about my interfering with a second dragon—of all the rotten impossible things—and that only I could stop it from catching you in some God-of-gods damned trap."

Nicodemus chuckled and said in a voice that dripped with arrogance: "All right, Magistra Dragonsbane, what are you? Who are you?"

"Magistra Francesca DeVega," she said in her best physician's voice, "appointed cleric in Our Lady Cala's infirmary, trained in medicinal language at the Port Mercy Hospitals and in Magnus and Numinous and all common languages in Astrophell."

"And what else?"

"Not enough for you, cacographer?"

"You're something other than a cleric."

She paused. "What do you mean?"

"What else are you?"

"I don't know what you mean."

"Are you Lornish?"

"Spirish, born in the Burnt Hills along the Verdantine border. And don't even think about mocking my antique way of speaking."

There was a moment of silence. "Did you ever know a Lornish tutor by the name of April?"

"Pardon my frankness, but what, in all the burning or flameless or even mildly intemperate hells, are you talking about?"

"Tell me what else you are," he nearly hissed.

"Not as blasted crazy as you is the only thing that's coming to mind just now."

Again he was silent. "Then tell me about this second dragon."

"I can't, nor could Deirdre. She only reported to me what she had read."

There was more talking in the harsh alien language. It sounded like a debate. Then a man who wasn't Nicodemus spoke: "Nicodemus, whatever you think she is, we had better go." It was an elderly voice.

"I agree, Magister," Nicodemus replied before issuing what sounded to be orders in the alien tongue. There followed heavy footsteps.

"Magistra, we're moving to a safer location. If you cause trouble, I will bind you. Endanger my students or magister, and I will instantly split your skull. Clear?"

If only because of how dispassionately he said "split," Francesca believed him. "I'm a physician," she said hotly, "I've sworn never to unduly endanger human life."

He sniffed. "My students aren't human."

Francesca started to ask what in all the hells they were when a creaking came from above. She looked up and saw a figure standing in a hole in the ruined temple dome.

It took her a moment to recognize Cyrus. He'd somehow gotten onto the temple's roof.

An alien voice called out, and footsteps sounded in every direction. "Tell him to come down and not to make any light," Nicodemus growled into her ear.

Cyrus was moving his arms and something splashed out of his hands.

"Cyrus!" She called. "Don't—"

But it was too late. His hands moved and a small train of sparks jumped forth. They hit the wall below him and a long tongue of flame blossomed. The fire spread four or five feet down the wall and filled the ruined temple with light.

"Damnation," Francesca muttered. Somehow, Cyrus had gotten a hold of oil and flint.

"Fran?" Cyrus called.

Where light shone on Francesca, the spells restraining her seemed to dissolve. She groaned as the censoring text that had been locked around her mind vanished.

"Nicodemus, wait!" she called. "Don't do anything stupid." She looked around, searching for the rogue wizard. But the firelight illuminated only fallen beams, ash, and loose stones. Behind the piles of rubble stretched dancing black shadows.

Cyrus leaped down through the hole in the dome. A small cloth canopy bulged above him, casting air downward and slowing his descent.

Francesca struggled free of her spellbindings as Cyrus landed and ran to her. The burning oil on the far wall began to gutter. Still, she could make out Cyrus's face. His veil was up, his brown eyes wide. "You disspelled the sentence around my heart?" He took her hand.

"Damn it, I'm sorry I didn't tell you, but that's not what we should worry about just now. I was speaking to Nicodemus and he—"

"If Nicodemus wants to talk," Cyrus interrupted, "he can do so when we're not censored and spellbound." He pulled her toward a hole in the temple walls. The flames he had lit were dying, and the shadows they cast danced longer and longer from the rubble.

"Cyrus, you don't underst—" Her words became a scream.

Cyrus had stepped on a shadow. Instantly the darkness welled up and grew muscular arms that wrapped around Cyrus's head and chest. As quickly as they had appeared, the arms yanked Cyrus down and back into the shadow, where they both vanished.

Francesca screamed again and jumped away from the lengthening shadow. But the flames were fading. Shadows grew behind her. She turned around, but everywhere was darkness. She was breathing so fast her hands tingled. "Nicodemus! There's no need for this!"

The flames began to fail. "Nicodemus!" she cried, writing Numinous flamefly paragraphs. As soon as she finished a spell, she cast it above her. The tiny text fluttered up, coiling around on itself so fast that it incandesced.

But no sooner had the paragraph started to shine than something blasted it into golden runes. She cast another flamefly into the air, and it was broken into fragments. Nicodemus or his students were disspelling her incandescent texts as fast as she could write them.

"Nicodemus, we can talk!"

No response. The dying flames guttered and then went out. She screamed as darkness enveloped her.

Twenty-seven

At first Cyrus struggled against the spellbindings, but he was blind, deaf, and censored. He tried to call out but his mouth was held shut.

He stopped fighting. Anger boiled through him. How could he have been so stupid? He had pitted a flask of lamp oil against blue-skinned monsters and foreign magic. But he had had to try. He couldn't have abandoned Francesca or charged blindly into the dark.

Suddenly he could hear again, and the bonds around his legs vanished. Rough hands grabbed his still-spellbound arms.

His vision returned, and something forced him to look up. It took him a moment to realize that he was seeing patches of late twilight sky through the ruined temple dome. A dark square moved through the sky, momentarily blacking out evening's first few stars. It was a lofting kite, he realized, flying low over the temple.

"You fight kobolds like an amateur," a man—no doubt Nicodemus Weal—said in the dark. "And you charge into a skinwriter stronghold with only a splash of fire and the spells in your robes. That tells me that you are either ignorant to our struggle against Typhon or simply ignorant. You have maybe five sentences to convince me the former is true. Otherwise, we'll open your throat and leave your body for the other demon worshipers to find."

The textual gag around Cyrus's mouth vanished. A second dark lofting kite was now circling above the temple. "I'm the new air warden of Avel," he said as calmly as he could, "arrived only fourteen nights ago. Until today, I've never heard of a demon in Avel or tension between Cala and Celeste. Deirdre said the demon brought me in as a screen."

"I am not terribly convinced. Two more sentences."

"But what else can I—" Cyrus fell silent as something sharp pressed the side of his neck.

"One more sentence."

"The demon brought me here to hide the brewing rebellion," Cyrus said quickly. "If there are demon-worshiping hierophants, they've been hidden from me. If they find me now, I'm as good as dead. I'm not your enemy; I'll swear on the Creator's name."

From above, he could hear the whoosh of low-flying kites.

Nicodemus grunted. "Pilot, you are either in earnest or a fine liar."

The restraints around Cyrus's head and neck relaxed so that he could look around. Two figures made of darkness stood beside him. One had the proportions of a tall, lean man. The other was shorter, with shoulders too broad to be human.

"Those pilots up there," the figure that seemed to be Nicodemus said, "did you bring them?"

Cyrus shook his head. "I saw a kite flying above the night market when I bought the lamp oil. I thought it had strayed from patrolling the walls."

Nicodemus grunted. "More like Deirdre set pilots to looking for you two in case you dug us out of hiding. They must have seen you fly from the night market. Very well, pilot: if you want to stay alive, do not endanger me or the kobolds. Understand?"

"Where's Francesca?"

"Here," she answered hoarsely from somewhere beside him. He looked over but saw only shadow. "Subtextualized, like you." Cyrus looked down and saw that he seemed to be made out of tangible darkness. Whatever prose this man wrote, it could distort light as well as any wizardly spell.

A new dark figure moved toward them over the rubble. Nicodemus went to it. There followed a brief conversation in what he supposed was the kobolds' language.

"They're already here," Nicodemus whispered as the shorter figure moved away. "Magister, go with Vein. Francesca and Cyrus, stay with the kobold next to you. We're casting doppelgängers out the back and dashing out the front."

A kobold behind Cyrus seemed to object.

"No," Nicodemus said forcefully. "No, Vein, I told you. Dross already told you that—" He switched into the kobold language. Then everyone started to move.

Cyrus's spellbindings, save those holding his hands together, dissolved. A figure grabbed his robes and pulled him along. It was all he could do to keep from tripping over the stones and beams littering the ground. They passed into a hallway that was in worse condition. Straining to see, Cyrus could make out two other dark figures walking beside them. Francesca and her kobold captor, he supposed.

At the hallway's end, he saw a courtyard filled with uneven stones and a cracked fountain. The ground was covered by rain puddles reflecting the starry sky. The creature that had been pulling Cyrus crouched in a corner and so disappeared into its shadow. Cyrus did likewise.

He waited, listening to his breath. Though he wore thick hierophantic robes, they were devoid of text. It left him feeling naked.

Nicodemus must have cast some censoring text about him. Not that it would have mattered. Each of his breaths would produce only a few sentences. It would be a day before his cloth had accrued enough text to form a passable defensive spell, a week or more before he could form a jumpchute.

And perhaps it was good that he was censored. Textually invested robes would shed a blue glow that hostile hierophants might see.

Suddenly Cyrus remembered the lofting kite that had flown over the ruined temple's dome. It had appeared as a rectangle of cloth that was . . . dark . . . not aglow with spells.

The hierophantic language could not bend light and so could not render anything invisible; however, its subtextualized spells became invisible to other hierophants. During the Civil War, pilots had learned to make their rigs less visible by subtextualizing their canopies and robes. Having served aboard a warship, Cyrus had practiced creating and gleaning hierophantic subtexts.

So he gritted his teeth and thought about how a wing commander might try to hide his pilots. What diction would he use? What prose style?

They blazed before him. Five of them, all perched like hawks on the courtyard's ruined walls and minarets. He sucked in his breath.

A kobold whispered, "Qui . . . et"

"You can understand me?" Cyrus whispered.

"Yes . . . shut it."

"Listen, there are five hierophants out in the courtyard."

The shadow before him became a blue-black face framed by blond hair. The kobold held up a hand and Cyrus saw that it possessed three retractable claws between each of its humanoid fingers. "Fi-ive?" he asked holding out all his digits.

When Cyrus nodded, the kobold spoke. "Fol-low," the humanoid enunciated before he began creeping back into the temple. Hands still bound, Cyrus hurried after and was relieved to see two other dark figures following.

After climbing over several rafters, they came to a narrow hole in the wall. The ground before it had been cleared of debris. Cyrus supposed Nicodemus's party had prepared this place as a possible exit.

"Look," the kobold grunted and pushed Cyrus toward the hole. Slowly Cyrus stuck his head into a narrow alleyway that ran between the temple and another ruined stone building. The muddy ground had been churned up into irregular mounds. He thought he could see claw marks in the footprints.

He looked up and wasn't surprised to see the pale blue glow of a single hierophant crouched atop the temple wall directly above him. After pulling his head back inside, Cyrus found several more dark figures whispering to each other.

"There's only one pilot," he reported. "But he's perched just above this exit. Probably he's holding his canopy. Soon as he sees something come out, he'll cast it down, either crushing us flat or cutting us into pieces, depending on how he's edited the cloth."

Nicodemus answered. "There's just one above the alley?"

"Just one, but he's well hidden and subtextualized. If I were commanding this strike, I'd put only one pilot there. It's narrow and long enough that we'll have to run for a while to get free. He can raise the alarm."

"Step back, Cyrus," Nicodemus said before uttering several guttural kobold words. "Dross is going to hold onto you while I step out there and deal with your one hierophant. If it turns out to be otherwise, Dross will make sure you die before I do. Do you want to change your story now?"

"I'm not lying," Cyrus whispered as two rough hands pulled him further into the dark and then rested what felt to be five rough fingers and three sharp claws on his throat.

The tall figure moved into the exit and crouched. They seemed to be waiting for something. An old man spoke. "Nico, are you sure the doppelgänger spells were—"

Cries sounded from the other side of the temple and were followed by several muffled booms that could only be hierophantic canopies deliberately cast against the ground to crush.

Nicodemus jumped out into the alleyway, turned, and threw something upward. Cyrus cringed, expecting sailcloth to slam down and claws to dig into his own windpipe. But then Nicodemus jerked one arm downward. Something heavy hit the ground with a splash and thud.

Then the kobolds were pushing forward. Cyrus hurried into the alleyway and saw a bodylike mass of darkness sprawled in the mud. He flinched as he realized that Nicodemus had cast up a text that had disspelled the hierophant's cloth, subtextualized the pilot, and then soundlessly yanked him down. It was a frightening demonstration of a deadly prose style and a ruthless author.

A shadowy figure went to the downed pilot. "It's no use, Francesca," Nicodemus said. "He's dead."

Suddenly the body began to glow faintly blue. At first, Cyrus thought it was a hierophantic spell. But the light was too weak and spread out in trickles as if it were leaking ink. "Lucerin," Francesca whispered.

"Typhon's got his pilots carrying the stuff in lantern vials so they can disspell our texts with its light," Nicodemus grumbled. "Now come on."

The party began running down the alley.

"What is lucerin?" Cyrus asked as he fell in behind the figure he judged to be Francesca.

"A compound hydromancers make by combining their texts with certain solvents. I don't understand it, but when you mix lucerin with something like an acid, it produces that blue light. Clerics use it to provide light when it's dark and they need to open a body but can't write a light-generating spell. It's precious stuff. The amount that man was holding would fetch several gold sovereigns at market."

One of the kobolds hissed for them to be silent.

They ran along the alley and then into the wasteland of burnt-down houses. Stray cats scattered before them. The remaining chimneys stood like a forest of dead trees.

Cyrus looked back at the ruined temple. He could see five kites now aloft. Blue lucerin light shone from one side of the temple. The pilots must have been fooled into attacking Nicodemus's doppelgänger spells. If that was the case, then they certainly were no longer fooled. The kites were beginning to fly in widening circles, searching the rubble.

Cyrus looked ahead to a row of houses twenty yards away. He felt exposed out among the charred timbers and chimneys. He longed for a lofting kite, or at least textually saturated robes. He was about to turn and look for Francesca when a yellow light flashed ahead of them.

"Wait!" he whispered and stopped. "There's something up there."

A rough kobold hand dragged him forward. "Wait!" he said louder. "I saw some—"

The rest of his words were drowned out by two piercing notes blasted out of a horn. The party halted. The notes were familiar to Cyrus; they were used by the city watch as a signal, but for what he couldn't remember.

"What was that?" Francesca asked. No one answered. Now Cyrus could see flashes of yellow and red light among the houses. Torchlight.

Then he saw them.

Ahead, emerging from around the houses, was a long line of torch-carrying men. To both right and left, the line stretched away as far as Cyrus could see. The torch flames illuminated not only green and white cloaks but also glinting steel points of spears and crossbows.

The two-note horn blast came again. This time, Cyrus recognized the signal. Intruders had breached the city's defenses. The horn blast was a command for the watchmen to line up from one end of the district to the other and sweep through North Gate until the intruder was found.

A district-wide lycanthrope hunt had begun.

Twenty-eight

Cyrus scanned the sky above the line of watchmen. "There are no lofting kites over the lycanthrope hunt," he reported, and then he looked back at the temple. "But the pilots that attacked us at the temple are drawing closer."

From somewhere ahead of him, Nicodemus laughed humorlessly. "She hasn't tried this in a while. Whatever the two of you are, you've got her riled up." He issued a few commands in the kobolds' language. Three shadowy figures ran away into the dark.

"What's happening?" Francesca asked. "Gotten who riled up?"

"Deirdre," Nicodemus answered. "She's declared a breach, claiming a lycanthrope snuck over the walls. She's mobilized the watch from other districts to sweep this one for lycanthropes."

Cyrus spoke. "We can't backtrack without the lofting kites spotting us."

Nicodemus grunted. "So we'll have to go through the line."

Francesca started to object. "But that would mean killing every—"

Just then a kobold voice called out in the dark.

"Stay here. Don't move," Nicodemus ordered and then trotted off. A moment later two other darkened figures returned. The line of watchmen was now only twenty yards away. Another trumpet blast sounded somewhere off to the right.

"Fran?" Cyrus whispered.

She reached out and took his hand. "Let's slip away while—"

Yet another trumpet blast sounded; this time it was three quick notes, the signal for a lycanthrope sighting. A chorus of distant shouting filled the night.

Cyrus turned and saw two of the lofting kites flying in the direction of the trumpet blast.

"This way and fast," Nicodemus said somewhere in the darkness.

A rough kobold hand landed on Cyrus's shoulder. They ran parallel to the line of watchmen, away from where the horn blast had come. After maybe fifty yards, the kobolds turned and led them straight for the torch-bearers.

Cyrus swallowed and looked for an escape. Perhaps he could dash away? No good. They were flanked on either side by dark figures.

A man appeared before them, standing atop a rubble pile and facing away. He was bare to the waist, tawny skinned, with long black hair tied into a ponytail. A man in a green and white cloak stood not twenty paces away, staring at the strange man. Ahead of them was a break in the line of watchmen.

Cyrus frowned beneath his veil. Farther away another three-note horn blast sounded. Lofting kites circled above the spot. The kobolds led the group forward through the break in the line. "That was Nicodemus?" Cyrus whispered.

"You thought it was the Queen of Spires?" she asked dryly. "I'd have guessed the lack of breasts would have been a giveaway."

"Fran, I'm just trying to figure out what's happening. Nicodemus has Canic allies among the watchmen who are letting us slip through the line?"

"I think so. He made it sound as if they've done this before. But I'm not—"

"Did you see that?" Cyrus interrupted.

"See what?"

"I . . . I'm not certain," he said. He thought he had seen a flash of blue in the sky above them. But it had appeared and then dropped so quickly it couldn't be a patrolling kite.

"Something's wrong," Nicodemus said beside them. Cyrus turned to look at him. "Not enough kites are flying to the false alarm our man sounded."

"What do we do?" Francesca asked.

"Nothing else to do at this point but run forward," Nicodemus answered.

They left the ash and rubble and entered an alley between rows of houses. "What do you think—" Nicodemus started to say when glass shattered behind them.

Cyrus turned back to see two men holding poles atop which shone the brilliant blue light. "Lucerin lanterns," Francesca whispered.

Before the lantern bearers stood two men armed with spears and large rectangular shields.

Breaking glass now sounded behind them. Cyrus turned to the other end of the alley and saw two more men with similar poles. A swordsman stood between them, dressed in bright scale armor and hefting a massive Lornish greatsword as if the weapon were as light as a dried palm frond.

No, Cyrus corrected himself, not a swordsman, a swordswoman with long black hair.

The kobolds hissed and leapt into action, cocking their arms back to hurl missiles of darkness at the brilliant blue-white lantern. But each kobold spell dissolved into nothing before it could reach and destroy the light source.

Nicodemus's figure appeared beside Cyrus. While barking orders, he flung his arm out in what seemed to be a backhand throw. Instantly, a blast tore through the night as the alley wall before the swordswoman exploded. Cyrus turned away just before a shockwave slammed into him and knocked him back a step.

When he looked down the alley, he saw the swordswoman had stepped back a few paces. A line of blood ran down the face of a lantern bearer, but neither of the bright blue lights had been damaged.

Nicodemus cocked his arm back as if to throw another spell, but then there came the sound of breaking glass from above. Cyrus looked up to see a green-robed hierophant crouched atop a roof, holding a blue light out on a pole so that it was directly above them.

The lucerin glare washed over Nicodemus and his kobolds, clearing the subtexts off of their skin the way rain might wash away wet paint. For the first time, Cyrus looked at the party.

There were five kobolds, their midnight skin and blond hair more alien in the strange light. All were armed with hatchets. Four of the monsters had formed a protective square around Cyrus, Francesca, and an old wizard with white dreadlocks and blank white eyes. The old man was cradling a blue parrot. A fifth kobold stood beside Nicodemus.

Cyrus pulled up his veil and saw that his breath was again filling his cloth with sentences. The lucerin light had disspelled whatever censoring text Nicodemus had cast on his mind.

Nicodemus spoke to his own party. "No one starts slashing until I say." He turned to face the woman carrying the greatsword. "Deirdre will want to talk for as long as she can slip the demon's control so we can get ready. Magistra DeVega, can I ask for your help?"

"You can ask," she said with her usual calmness, "but the clerics haven't developed a cure for death by idiotic leadership."

Nicodemus ignored this. "It's time to prove you're no demon worshiper. When the sharp objects start flying, destroy the lucerin lanterns, starting with the one above us. Don't shatter it or a rain of lucerin will cover our skins and censor us."

"As you so delicately pointed out earlier, I've no prose style for wartexts."

"Magister Shannon can write the appropriate spells," Nicodemus said calmly, "but he hasn't the strength to cast them."

"I'll do what I can," she muttered.

"Hierophant," Nicodemus said to Cyrus, "see what you can do to help."

Cyrus was about to point out that Nicodemus had disspelled all the text in his robes when the other man cupped his hands to his mouth and called, "According to Avel's ancient laws, I demand parlay."

The woman in scale armor with the giant sword called back, "Parlay is reserved for combatants at war, not for monsters and outlaws."

Francesca whispered to Cyrus, "That's Deirdre, the one I told you about."

Nicodemus called back. "The ancient Kobold Realm of the Pinnacle Mountains is reborn. We speak for its tribes who are at war with your master."

The old wizard, the one whom Nicodemus had named Shannon, murmured to Francesca, "Don't worry, Magistra; she'll talk. She wants to give us time to spellwrite. Now, look at this text in my right arm."

Deirdre called back. "The serene Canonist of Avel recognizes only the six human kingdoms."

"I am human," Nicodemus called back. "And I seek to preserve the peace. The city's ancient law gives me the right to parlay. Will your canonist deny her city's own law?"

Cyrus frowned at this exchange. It seemed scripted, as if they had previously performed this act. Perhaps they had.

Deirdre began to tremble. For a moment, it seemed as if she would fall forward. But then she stood up straight and handed her greatsword to the soldier bearing the lucerin lantern next to her.

The man grunted when he took the weapon; he had to sink its point into the mud to keep from dropping it.

"We parlay," Deirdre called out. "Send out your captain."

Nicodemus stepped a few paces forward and waited for her.

As Deirdre approached, she stumbled as if drunk. "Hide her!" Deirdre whispered harshly as she drew near. She brought the back of her hand to her brow, covering her eyes. "Hide her! I can't keep her image from Typhon. I can't—"

"Cyrus, stand between us and the cleric," Nicodemus commanded. "Whatever happens, don't let Deirdre see her."

Cyrus stepped in front of Francesca and drew a few sentences from his veil and into his shoulders. By rewriting them to long and stiff paragraphs, he turned his robe into a screen.

"You can look at me now, Deirdre," Nicodemus said in a softer tone.

She didn't move.

"Deirdre," Nicodemus half-whispered.

As the woman lowered her hand, Cyrus saw that she was beautiful—dark olive skin that made her wide green eyes even more striking. She looked vaguely related to Nicodemus.

"Nico," Deirdre said. "Every time I see you, I expect the wide-eyed apprentice I knew in Starhaven. So strange that you've become . . ." She gestured to his bare chest and the kobolds.

"No longer game-piece Nicodemus."

"Something sad about that," she said. "But at least we haven't killed you yet."

"This time you might. Really, my friend, I'd give better odds to a peasant attacking a Lornish paladin with a toothpick."

"You said that last time." She quirked a half smile. "When you filled the sanctuary with that wretched tarlike darkness that slowed everyone down."

"And well I should have; you punched a broken chair leg through my left arm and knocked me off a five-story building."

She sniffed. "You're lucky that's all I did. That sticky darkness ruined my hair for days." She paused. "It is good to see that Shannon is still alive. I thought we had murdered him when we caught you in that Canic warehouse."

Cyrus found himself leaning closer, trying to better hear everything they said.

"How did you know to catch us in this alley?" Nicodemus asked.

Deirdre shivered. "After we found you with the rebellious militia, we figured a tree-worshiping watchman was letting you slip through our lycanthrope lines. So after forming this company, I placed these men just behind the only company with Canics."

Nicodemus grunted. "Is there any way you could be a shade dumber?"

"Was just about to ask you to be a shade smarter."

"If we somehow escape, I promise we'll recover the emerald and free you. I was so close today, before the Walker came. But why did you send me Fran—"

"Don't say her name," Deirdre interrupted with a sudden twitch. She covered her face and looked away. "Don't say her name or let me see her. Typhon is suspicious again. He looked, not very deeply, into my mind. But it's changed things; he is more aware of my mind now. If I see her or hear her name, it will be harder to hide her memory from Typhon."

"I will keep her hidden," Nicodemus said quickly. "What can you tell me?"

"Almost nothing or Typhon will see it in my mind. But I can tell you this: there are two Astrophell wizards, agents of your half sister, in the city. I'm not sure why."

He nodded. "We've avoided their kind before."

"This is different. They came straight into the sanctuary to treat with the canonist. They were . . . aggressive. I'm not sure why but Typhon has refused to kill them. He's . . . excited about one of them, the woman. I think she's an avatar. Likely her deity belongs to the Alliance of the Divine Heretics."

"Why do you say that?"

"I can't think of another reason why Typhon should not immediately eliminate her. I suspect he wants to capture her or imprison her the way he did Boann and Cala. Whatever the case, she poses a great threat to you and the . . ." She flinched. "The one I should not see."

Nicodemus nodded.

"But I do have one small triumph; I learned what the Silent Blight is." She quickly explained that Typhon was using the emerald to inhibit Language Prime's ability to misspell. When Nicodemus asked for more detail, she shook her head. "That's all I know, Nico . . . but regarding . . . the woman . . ." She paused as her head jerked.

"Don't say her name," he said quickly. "Regarding the one you sent to me, what must I do?"

"Keep her safe," Deirdre blurted. "With the Astrophell wizards now in the city, Typhon thinks he may not need her any more. She was to keep you alive when he captured you. But everything's changing so fast. Keep her with you. Listen to her. Typhon knows so much. He told me today that anyone who opposes him will become him. I don't know if he was talking about me or you . . . or maybe the dragon he claims is near completion. I don't know if that's the Walker or . . . or a second . . ." She twitched and drew her lips back. "My independence is slipping."

"Keep fighting him."

"Last thing," she said. "The Savanna Walker. I've learned his name. He calls himself Ja Ambher. If you think or speak that name it will reduce his influence on your mind. I'm not sure how Typhon made that so, but . . ." She twitched again.

Nicodemus took a step toward her. "Deirdre, we'll escape whatever the demon and the half dragon can throw at us. We'll never stop trying to free you."

She nodded stiffly.

"Deirdre, I think of you always."

Her pained expression slipped then, relaxing first into one of relief and then one of sorrow. "I won't give up, Nico." After another spastic arm jerk, she turned and marched back to the two watchmen who held up the lucerin lanterns.

The man who had been holding her sword tilted it toward her. She drew it from the mud and turned to face Nicodemus. Her expression had become blank, her arms and legs steady. "The parlay has failed," she declared. "Kill the monsters and the other spellwrights outright, save the half-naked man for questioning but do not let his bare skin touch yours."

With that, she leveled her greatsword at Nicodemus and advanced. A chorus of war cries sounded from the other end of the alley as the spear-men behind them charged.

Twenty-nine

Cyrus looked down at his robes. Only a thin network of pale blue text covered his chest, barely enough to manipulate the cloth, not enough for a protective spell.

"Now!" Shannon commanded.

Cyrus glanced up. Francesca cocked her hand back and threw something at the lucerin lantern the hierophant was holding above them.

But as she did so, a furl of the hierophant's sailcloth—bright with blue text—shot down the pole, wrapping around it and then encasing the lantern. For an instant, the party stood in relative darkness. Another blast, likely from Nicodemus's dark magic, rocked through the alleyway. The resulting shockwave nearly knocked Cyrus over.

But then the protective cloth on the lantern's pole partially unwound to reveal the lantern's dispelling light. Francesca's wartext must have dashed against the protective cloth and been disspelled.

"Good," Shannon yelled. "Nicodemus needs time in the dark. Quickly now, cast this." The old man was holding out something to Francesca. She took it.

A metallic clang made Cyrus look back down the alley. Nicodemus and three of his kobolds were facing Deirdre. As he watched, the woman thrust her massive sword at the nearest kobold. The creature leapt back while another jumped in and slammed both of his hatchets into her back. The axe blades chirped against Deirdre's scale armor and forced her to stumble forward.

Deirdre recovered her feet and swung at the attacking kobold. The monster leapt up, spraying mud as he sailed over her blade.

Meanwhile, the first kobold tried to dart around Deirdre to reach the lantern bearers. But she changed her swing into a thrust. The kobold danced away but slammed into the alley wall. The last inch or so of her blade sank into its left side. The beast bellowed.

Suddenly Nicodemus rushed at her. Unarmed, he reached with his bare hand for the exposed skin on her face. With a shriek, she stumbled back and brought her sword around.

Nicodemus jumped back. Compared with the kobold, he seemed agonizingly slow. But the wounded kobold brought both his axes down on Deirdre's arm, deflecting the swing. Even so, the blade missed opening Nicodemus's thigh by an inch.

"Now," Shannon said. Cyrus looked back and saw Francesca cast another spell with an overhand throw. Again the protective cloth wrapped around the overhead lantern and left them in dark. And again the hallway was filled with an earsplitting blast.

This time, the shockwave did knock Cyrus down. As he struggled to his feet, he saw that Deirdre was covered in mud, and a thin stream of blood ran down her face. Behind her, a lantern bearer had been knocked to his knees, but had held up his lantern on its pole.

Then the two kobolds renewed their attack on Deirdre—darting in and out as she swung at them with her massive sword.

Nicodemus barked a command and both kobolds jumped backward. With a rasping cry, one threw a hatchet. It whirled over Deirdre straight for a lucerin lantern.

The watchman jerked the lantern to his right, out of the axe's path. Cyrus didn't realize that the second kobold had also thrown an axe in anticipation of this move until the lantern shattered into a rain of glass and glowing liquid.

"Hurry!" Francesca yelled behind him. "We're losing ground."

Cyrus turned around. Francesca was glancing between Shannon and the two kobolds facing the spearmen. The fight here was going poorly. No matter how quickly the kobolds darted in to strike, they could not touch the two spearmen or reach the lantern bearers behind them.

One of the kobolds wielded a single hatchet, apparently having thrown the other. As Cyrus watched, the other monster threw his axe, but the watchman deftly pulled his lantern out of the weapon's trajectory. The spearmen advanced.

"Hurry!" Francesca cried.

"A moment," Shannon groaned. "We need a stronger disspell to get through that cloth."

Apparently, the hierophant crouching on the roof heard this since he began moving his hands. The cloth on his pole glowed more brightly.

Cyrus sucked in a breath as he recognized the hierophant's prose style as simple, almost childlike. The pilot was either incompetent or an apprentice. Cyrus stepped closer to Shannon. "Magister, those spells were written by a master hierophant but are being edited by a novice."

Shannon grimaced. "And?"

"Could you take a strip of my robe up to those spells?"

The old man frowned but then nodded. "Give me the strip."

Cyrus touched his chest and edited one sentence into a "draw" command. Instantaneously, all other sentences in his robes encircled the command. It formed a patch of vivid blue text no wider than his hand.

As quickly as he could, Cyrus composed a siphon spell—a text with draw commands powerful enough to steal the text out of a hostile sail. Pilots rarely used such texts; in the air, it was difficult to access the enemy's canopy. Worse, any experienced pilot could edit out a siphon attack.

But with no other options left, Cyrus cut his right sleeve into a long and neatly folded ribbon, the end of which he connected to the swatch that held the siphon.

"Cyrus," Francesca hissed, "hurry!"

"Here." Cyrus slapped the swatch into Shannon's open hand. The old wizard pushed a knobby index finger against the swatch and began moving both hands rapidly. The swatch hung in the air, suspended by wizardly sentences. "Magistra, take it."

Francesca grabbed the air above the swatch and flicked it up at the lantern. Cyrus watched as one end of his ribbon shot upward. But before Cyrus could see if the siphon worked, something knocked him into the mud.

He started to stand when a large blue foot—humanlike but for a black hind claw—splashed into the puddle next to him. He rolled over and saw an axe-wielding kobold standing over him. "Creator!" he swore and rolled away to stand.

The kobolds were in disorganized retreat as the spearmen attacked. The kobolds kept searching for a way past the spear points. But the watchmen were too skilled.

Just then one watchman thrust out and landed a glancing blow on a kobold's shoulder. The monster stumbled. Cyrus scrambled to get out of his way but then found himself staring at a blood-darkened spear point.

The watchman thrust at him. Cyrus jumped back but not fast enough; the tip of the weapon struck the folds of cloth at his waist. He cried out as the force of the blow turned him sideways. But he felt no steel sinking into this hip. He looked down and saw not only that the fold of sailcloth had stopped the spear point but also that the cloth shone with blue text.

He looked up. The ribbon Francesca had cast up now blazed with a torrent of blue light as it drained text from the sailcloth that had been protecting the lantern.

Looking down, Cyrus saw a spearman before him crouching as if to make a thrust. Cyrus stumbled backward, but the ribbon leading up to the siphon spell was nearly taut. He couldn't chance pulling it free and denying himself any more text. "Give me time! I nearly have him."

Faintly, he was aware of dark figures moving past him to attack the spearmen; he was too busy frantically forming new hostile commands in the hierophantic language. The old wizard yelled something, and a moment later one of the watchmen cried out. Cyrus looked over to see that one spearman's shield had been broken in half.

At last, Cyrus finished composing his textual attack. Using both his hands, he edited the siphon spell to stop it from drawing text. Then he began flicking hostile commands up the ribbon. Somebody backed into him, and he had to move quickly to keep from pulling his ribbon free of the cloth.

"Celeste, lend me your favor," Cyrus whispered. The enemy pilot moved his hands rapidly, trying to maintain control of his cloth. For a moment, Cyrus thought that his attack commands would fail. But in the next instant, the cloth reached down the pole and wrapped tight around its lucerin lantern, snuffing out its light.

Two large swatches of cloth cut themselves free of the furl. With a blast of wind, they flew at the lanterns held by the watchmen. The men saw them coming and tried to hoist their lanterns out of the way. But Cyrus's spells had been written to seek light; with serpentine undulations, the sheets changed course. In a few moments, they had reached the lanterns and wrapped around them.

Suddenly, the alleyway near Cyrus fell into darkness. The watchmen cried out. For a moment, Cyrus was blind in the dark. He heard two small blasts and then screams.

Cyrus's eyes adjusted. One spearman was lying facedown in the mud; the other had lost his shield and was bent over a hatchet planted in his belly. Behind them, the two lantern bearers were fleeing.

Suddenly Nicodemus was standing beside Cyrus. With a backhand flick he cast something at the two fleeing men. In the next instant both of them fell to the ground and disappeared into blackness. Then Nicodemus looked up. Cyrus followed his gaze to the hierophant who was still struggling to retake control of the cloth Cyrus had possessed.

Nicodemus made another backhanded flick. The young enemy hierophant never saw it coming. The text within his robes winked out, and darkness covered him.

The lucerin lantern, the pole it was attached to, and the sailcloth that had been protecting it fell to the ground. Cyrus ran to it, and with a few edits drew all of its text into his robes.

"You killed them?" Francesca asked.

"Only spellbound them," Nicodemus replied without looking at her. "They'll be freed in the morning when the light will burn my text away. But as for the spearmen . . ." He paused to frown at the motionless bodies in the mud. "Nothing we could have done."

"WHAT HAPPENED TO that swordswoman," Cyrus asked, "Deirdre?"

Nicodemus exhaled. "Fled when the lanterns went out. She looked relieved. But it won't be long before Typhon compels her to rejoin the lycanthrope hunt. We'd better move fast. Who's wounded?" The mud-splattered kobolds were gathering around him. One of the creatures pointed to a small laceration on his shoulder and said a few words in his language. He didn't seem concerned. Another kobold indicated a small wound on his left side and merely shrugged. No major wounds then.

Nicodemus nodded and then looked at Shannon. "Magister, how are you?"

"I wouldn't call myself spry," the old wizard said. "But I'll live."

"Then we run," Nicodemus replied. "Jasp, you take the rear. Vein and Slag, you're with Magister and the cleric. Dross and Cyrus, run with me in front." He turned and jogged down the alley.

Cyrus hurried to catch up with the man and was quickly joined by a kobold—Dross, Cyrus supposed, the one who had nearly opened his windpipe back in the temple. The monster and Nicodemus exchanged a few words. Then Nicodemus spoke to Cyrus: "Tell me if you see any hierophant in the sky or on the roofs."

Cyrus nodded.

"I saw how you spellbound those lucerin lanterns with the other pilot's sailcloth. Impressive."

"The pilot was incompetent, maybe a novice."

Nicodemus turned them into another alley. Their feet made splashing and sucking noises in the mud. "Typhon recruits among the youngest wind mages. Many are natives of Avel, excited about Cala supposedly wanting independence from monotheism."

Cyrus looked at him. "Cala doesn't?"

"It's not likely. Typhon can invest his soul into a deity's ark; that's how he took control of Deirdre and her goddess, Boann. He may have used the same tactic on the canonist."

Cyrus thought about this as they ran down one alley and then another.

"You'd do best by your city if you join us in opposing Typhon," Nicodemus said dispassionately.

Cyrus didn't reply.

They were now among the inhabited neighborhoods of the North Gate District, but the houses were dark and the streets empty. Word of a lycanthrope breach had spread through the district, and its people had fled to known houses that could be barricaded until the threat passed.

After a mile or so, Cyrus realized that Nicodemus was leading them north and east toward the city's outer wall.

Cyrus saw no pilots crouched on rooftops and only once spotted a distant lofting kite. The storm-washed sky was moonless, brilliant with stars. The empty city became surreal, almost dreamlike.

Then a kobold called out. Cyrus recognized the voice as belonging to the creature named Vein.

Nicodemus halted beside what appeared to be a store. Two kobolds approached; one had his arm around the other. Nicodemus examined the wounded monster. "Magistra," he called.

"I'm here," Francesca replied calmly. "The patient's name?"

"Vein."

"Tell me everything he said."

"Took a spear thrust to the left side. Painful but didn't penetrate too deeply. No more than a cupful of blood. But since we started to run, he can't breathe. His heart's racing. The spear wound still hurts, but it's the breathlessness that has him scared. It's getting worse."

Francesca made a thoughtful sound. "What do you know about kobold anatomy?"

"More muscle and the obvious superficial differences, but otherwise, as far as I know, it's identical to human anatomy."

"Have him lie down," Francesca ordered and flicked her wrist into the air. Several sparks began to flit above her head. Cyrus recognized them as flamefly spells. Their incandescence created floating globes.

Three of the kobolds hissed at the light, baring sharp black teeth.

"It won't hurt you," Francesca said in a clipped tone. "Tell him to stop acting like an overgrown cat." She looked at Nicodemus, who was also staring at the lights. "Nicodemus!"

The man started and then looked at her.

"You going to hiss too? Want a giant scratching post? Maybe a massive saucer of milk? Would that get you to translate for me?"

Nicodemus spoke in the kobolds' language, and Vein lay down on a drier patch of street. Cyrus noticed the kobold seemed older than the others and had a thin white scar running down his cheek. Vein uttered a few short words. Nicodemus translated. "He says it's harder to breathe lying down."

After getting onto her knees, Francesca held her ear to Vein's chest, first the right side then the left. She listened just above the wound.

"Hierophant," Nicodemus asked, "do you see anything aloft?"

Cyrus scanned the sky. "No, nothing. I'll keep a lookout."

Francesca spoke. "Order two of your men . . . kobolds . . . whatever to hold him down."

"What's the matter with—" Nicodemus started to ask.

"Now!" she snapped.

Cyrus found himself looking down from the sky to watch the drama.

Nicodemus issued commands, and the four healthy kobolds jumped to obey, each one pinning down one of Vein's arms or legs.

Now even Cyrus could tell that Vein's breathing was shallow. The muscles along his neck jumped out into cords every time he inhaled. Francesca took his hand. "You're going to be all right," she said. "It's going to be just fine."

She looked back at his chest. "Nicodemus, back in the temple, what was it you said about my jeopardizing those who follow me?"

"What does that have to do—"

"You implied," she interrupted as her hands moved over the kobold's chest, "that I am careless, sloppy, that I led Cyrus into danger."

Cyrus looked at her. Had she worried for him?

Nicodemus was frowning at Francesca. "Maybe we could discuss this—"

"I take my calling seriously and am never cavalier with the lives of others. I sought you out only because Deirdre gave me no other choice. But what I want to know now, Nicodemus blasted Weal, is what you are? I'd wager every coin ever to drop into my purse that you're a cold-minded killer. What you did to those watchmen back there, you're not even disturbed by it."

Nicodemus cleared his throat. "Magistra, can you save Vein and demean me at the same time? Because if you can't, I could gag you with a few sentences."

"I'm so bloody infuriated right now I don't think I could save him without God-of-gods damn demeaning you!"

"Then insult me quick; he doesn't look good, and I have an urge to threaten violence unless you take his health more seriously."

"I still see no kites," Cyrus said in a low tone, "but if you two can't quiet down, the lycanthrope hunt will hear us from half a mile away."

Francesca seemed to ignore him. Her hands were still moving fast across Vein's chest. The kobold holding down Vein's right leg said something. Nicodemus replied curtly.

Francesca suddenly spoke: "You know, Nicodemus Weal, the fact that you would even think of threatening violence against a healer makes me need to belittle the tiny, wrinkled, frozen organ you call a human heart."

Nicodemus glanced at her: "Magistra, if you save my student, I don't care a snap what you say about my heart."

She snorted. "Typical of a man, caring only when an external organ is belittled."

Nicodemus frowned in confusion and then let out a single, humorless laugh. "What an extraordinary reaction you have to crisis."

"Your student's one mistake away from death and your expression is as bland as a loaf of wet bread. So tell me, whose reaction is the extraordinary one?"

"Holy sky!" Cyrus whispered. "Why don't the two of you just start yelling about where we are so the hunt can find—"

"Shut up!" both Francesca and Nicodemus said in near unison.

Cyrus threw his hands in the air and wondered how he'd fallen in with a pair of lunatics.

Francesca glared at Nicodemus and then pointed at the narrow slit on the left side of Vein's ribs. "The spearhead slipped between his ribs and punctured his left lung in such a way as to make a flap. It's letting air out of his lung but not back in."

Nicodemus frowned. "A one-way valve?"

"A miracle! You understand a basic principle. Every time he inhales, air passes out of the lung laceration into the chest. But the wound between the ribs is too thin and tight to let the air out. So pressure is building up in his chest cavity. Why would that be dangerous?"

"Dangerous . . . I . . . shouldn't you be doing something?"

"I am," she snapped and nodded at her hands. "Can't you see the texts I'm writing in Magnus and Numinous?"

"Yes, but they're . . . I mean, I don't . . ."

"So why would increasing chest pressure be dangerous?"

"It might compress the organs in the chest?" Nicodemus said hesitantly.

"What organs?"

"Lung?"

"Good, the left lung's collapsed. He's breathing only with his right. What other organs are in jeopardy? Here's a God-of-gods damned hint, you don't seem to care about this organ."

"The heart?"

"Amazing. What else?"

"Windpipe?"

"Yes," she gestured to the kobold's neck. "See how the trachea has deviated away from the wound?"

Cyrus leaned closer but could see only that the creature's catlike eyes were wide with fear. Apparently, Francesca noticed the same thing. "Tell him he's going to be all right."

Nicodemus murmured kobold words that sounded gentle despite all their harsh sounds. Francesca focused on her hands. "So what should we do for our patient?"

"Burning heaven, cleric! Why in Los's name should I—"

"I've treated types like you before—soldiers and criminals. You want me to save a life you endangered? You want me to heal a creature who just killed a watchman of my city? Fine. I've treated murderers and rapists. But once, just this blasted once, I'm going to make a killer like you answer my damned questions."

Cyrus studied Francesca's face. Even in the heat of their old lovers' arguments, he had never seen her this upset.

She moved her hand from a point two inches below the middle of her patient's left collarbone to a nearby puddle. She looked up at Nicodemus, anger burning in her dark brown eyes. "So what do you want to do for your student, Nicodemus Weal?"

"G-get the extra air out of his chest?"

"Tell them to hold Vein down," she said while keeping her eyes locked on Nicodemus. He said a few words and the kobolds at Vein's arms and legs tensed.

Francesca slapped her patient's chest. The creature shrieked. The broad muscles of his arms and legs flexed and bunched, but his companions held him down.

Slowly he relaxed, and Francesca looked down at her patient. She peered at his neck, pressed her ear to one side of his chest, then the other.

Bubbles appeared in the puddle next to Francesca. "What under holy heaven?" Cyrus asked. One of the kobolds pointed and said something in his language. The bubbling seemed to be occurring in time to Vein's breathing, as if Francesca had magically transferred his breath into the water.

Francesca didn't seem to hear him. "You see my medical prose?" she asked Nicodemus.

"I do."

"With the interlocking Numinous sentences, I've defined the surface of his collapsed lung here." With her index finger, she traced a tiny circle on her patient's chest. "With the noninterlocking sentences, I've defined the surface of the lung cavity. The space between those two is the air that's collapsing his lung."

Nicodemus gathered his long black hair and leaned closer. Cyrus leaned closer as well.

She continued. "I wrote a long tube in Magnus and punched it into his chest here." She pointed to a small bleeding flap below the kobold's left nipple. "I could have wasted time writing a valve subspell that would allow air out but not in. Instead, I extended the tube and stuck its end into this puddle."

She pointed to the puddle that had been bubbling, and to his surprise Cyrus saw a thin cylinder of muddy water rising up out of the surface. Then the water dropped into the puddle and bubbles began to come up.

"The water acts as a valve. When our patient breathes in, the negative pressure in his chest can suck the water up less than an inch." She pointed from the cylinder of floating water back to the patient. "But when he breathes out, the positive pressure forces the air out the tube and into the puddle."

The kobold exhaled and the cylinder of levitating water sank and bubbled.

"Holy canon!" Cyrus swore.

She gestured back to the patient's chest. "With every breath he is pushing more air out of his chest and reinflating his lung."

Nicodemus stared at the puddle with wonder. "You created a shunt to compete with his lung laceration."

Cyrus felt as impressed as Nicodemus sounded. He had never seen Francesca in action as a physician.

She nodded curtly and then looked up at him. "Effectively."

Nicodemus spoke rapidly to the four healthy kobolds, who all looked at Francesca with catlike eyes wide with surprise.

Meanwhile, Nicodemus looked back at Vein. He and the kobold spoke briefly; then Nicodemus stepped even closer, his eyes darting from the kobold's chest to the puddle. "Magistra," he said softly, "your prose is . . ." He lifted his hand as if to touch some sentence on the kobold's chest but then stopped. He looked at her, his eyes darting across her face as if seeing her for the first time. "Your prose is beautiful."

Heat flushed across Cyrus, and he felt his hands ball into fists.

Thirty

The bluemoon hung as a bright shard among the skeins of stars. Francesca, so rarely abroad in the night, studied it from the party's resting place against the northern parameter wall. Soon the whitemoon's crescent—three times longer but half as bright—would climb after her brilliant sister. The kobold Vein had improved; however, as they had run, more air had accumulated in his chest. So they stopped by a puddle below the wall and Francesca had shunted his chest again.

When they had first arrived, Nicodemus had exchanged hand signals with a watchman, who afterward ignored the party as he patrolled the walls. Behind the party stretched a maze of dark shacks and deserted streets. The Canics had yet to emerge from their barricaded houses.

Francesca took her patient's rough hand and inspected his throat, making sure that his neck veins collapsed during inhalation—a sign that nothing was putting pressure on his heart.

Francesca's own throat tightened as she remembered Deirdre's distended neck veins as she had lain dying. The poison of self-disappointment filled Francesca. She had trained so hard—the memorization, the abuse from superiors and patients, the sleepless nights, so many sleepless nights—in hopes of becoming something extraordinary. But her failure to save Deirdre had illustrated that she was only a competent physician, nothing more.

Realizing that she was pitying herself, Francesca took a deep breath and studied the kobold's neck; the veins collapsed with each inhalation. "You're doing fine," she whispered and squeezed his hand. His retracted claws rested between the metacarpal bones of his palm; she could feel them. Vein looked at her with golden eyes, beautiful. Mud had darkened his blond hair. He nodded.

She squeezed his hand again, and he squeezed back. In that moment, she could see his body in alternate futures, all healthy in the short term. The greatest danger had passed. This strange talent for prognosis was the one thing that distinguished her among physicians. At least she could take comfort in that.

"Hold tight," she whispered and then stood. The four other kobolds were crouched against the wall. All of them were watching her with wide yellow eyes. She couldn't read their expressions. Interest maybe? Apprehension? She nodded to them and then walked away to be alone.

A black cloud was tumbling across the sky, changing shape with dreamlike fluidity. The brisk air bore a poststorm scent, clean and invigorating.

"Magistra."

Only with great effort did she keep from jumping. "Pleasant as it is to be accosted in darkness by a man I distrust, could you perhaps drop the subtext when approaching me, hmmm?"

The darkness beside her unfolded to reveal Nicodemus. "Apologies."

She studied him. His dark green eyes were fixed on hers. "What do you want?"

"How is Vein?"

"He could tell you better than I could."

"Thank you for saving him," Nicodemus said. "He is dear to us."

Francesca could feel her expression soften a bit. She nodded. "I think he understands me well enough, but he doesn't speak to me."

"All of the kobolds understand our speech, but they will not speak to you. Please don't misunderstand. They are grateful for what you did for Vein, but they instinctively distrust humans."

"I can't read their expressions."

"They do not wish them to be read. Their ancient civilization was destroyed by the legions of the Neosolar Empire. We are their demons."

"But not you? You're the good demon to them."

"They would find your phrasing amusing." He smiled humorously. "It has to do with their prophecies. Please forgive their secrecy. But now, tell me, may we safely take Vein over the wall?"

"If it's not too jarring. He's recovering faster than any human. If we continue shunting the air from his chest, his body may heal the lung laceration on its own. But to be certain it closes, I want to use a specialized text to sew the lung laceration shut."

"Can you do that now?"

She shook her head. "Ideally, I'd take him to the infirmary, but if—"

"No, Deirdre is still abroad."

"—if I retrieve some texts from the infirmary's library," she continued, "I can manage it out here."

Nicodemus looked at Vein. "How long will that take?"

"Most of the day. But I'll show Magister Shannon how to work the shunting spell until I can return here in the evening."

Nicodemus looked back at her. "We won't be here."

"Then where will you be?"

"Elsewhere."

"You've really committed yourself to this whole air of mystery, haven't you?"

"You think I should trust you with where we hide outside the city?"

She nodded.

"Magistra, can you tell me more of who you are?"

She folded her arms. "You know everything: born in the Burnt Hills, trained in Astrophell, then Port Mercy, now here."

"Nothing you left out?"

"Oh . . . you know . . . you're right," she said with exaggerated enthusiasm. "I forgot to mention that under a full moon I turn into an eight-foot-tall, fire-breathing, God-of-gods damned potato."

His face was blank. "Unfortunate. You're a half-baked monster. Or do you breathe on yourself?"

She scowled at him. "That was in poor taste."

"The pun or the half-baked potato?"

"Stop trying to mash things up."

At last he laughed. "Well said. Seems we have the same sense of humor. Perhaps we can understand each other after all."

"A shared appreciation of bad jests would foster a wonderful friendship, true. So don't give up; I'm sure you'll eventually find someone else with your sense of humor."

He laughed. "So rough with everyone else and yet so gentle with patients."

"I wouldn't know; I've never seen you care for one."

"I meant you."

"Oh, did you?"

He paused. "Magistra, there's something wrong with you."

"What a charming way you have with women."

"Forgive me. But . . . you appear more alive than anyone I've ever met. Too alive."

She fanned her face. "Stop, you're making me blush."

"I'm not saying it well . . ." He frowned. "Magistra, do you know what Language Prime is?"

"It's blasphemy."

"So you were taught. But we've discovered it's real. Language Prime is the first language, the language from which all living things are made. I've learned the four runes that make up its sentences. I see them glowing in all living things."

"Lovely," Francesca muttered. "You really are a few biscuits short of breakfast."

His eyebrows furrowed in confusion.

"You're a few colors shy of a rainbow?" she offered. "Not pulling a full wagon? Knitting with only one needle? All foam and no beer? Your cheese slid off the cracker? You couldn't pour water out of a boot with instructions on the heel?"

"All right. I get it."

"So," she said cheerfully, "you truly believe you're the Halcyon, the savior who will deliver us from the demonic hoards?"

Nicodemus shook his head. "Prophecy isn't about humans and demons or even good and evil; it's about two competing conceptions of how language might exist."

"Hmmm. I was wrong about the water and the boot. I think a better description of you would be . . . oh, I don't know . . . fell out of the crazy tree and hit every branch on the way down."

"You heard what Deirdre said about Typhon stopping Language Prime from misspelling. The demons want to alter life itself."

She sighed. "And you can restore order to the demonic chaos?"

"You've got it backwards. Right now, I'm a force for chaos. Typhon stole my ability to spell when I was an infant. He's keeping it in the Emerald of Aarahest. Now I'm the Storm Petrel of counter-prophecy. Only when I recover the emerald will I become a force for order." Passion was making his eyes wider, his breath faster.

Francesca nodded slowly. "Riiight."

"Here, write a Numinous spell resistant to misspelling. It doesn't have to be functional."

"An apprentice could write a nonfunctional spell that even the Lord Chancellor couldn't disspell."

"Do it."

She wrote several Numinous sentences in her biceps, folded them back on each other, and interlocked all words. It was a luminous, useless half foot of golden language. Nicodemus eyed the text. "Cast it between us."

"Unless you chew on the damn thing, you won't be able to disspell it."

"Just cast it."

With a shrug, she dropped the golden spell. The incandescent words floated down through the dark. Nicodemus gently touched the spell with his index finger, and the prose blasted into a thousand fragments.

Francesca jerked back and covered her face.

"You can look now."

Slowly she lowered her arms. Nothing of the spell remained. "Creator!" She looked at Nicodemus, expecting a smug expression. But he gazed at her with haunted eyes. She'd seen that look before on so many sick and dying patients that she felt a pang of sympathy. Here was a man acutely aware of his own frailty.

"Your cacography?"

He nodded. "I can focus it on a text and it just . . . disintegrates or explodes or warps."

"But the spells you and the kobolds cast? The subtexts and the blasting spells?"

"I'm not disabled in their languages. But they function only in darkness and take a toll on the skin." He tapped his chest.

At first Francesca saw nothing peculiar about his skin. But when she leaned closer, she realized that his chest was scored with hundreds of tiny welts. They were hard to see in the darkness. "And how does your cacography affect Language Prime?" she asked and realized she was using her soothing physician's voice.

"I distort Language Prime as I do wizardly languages." He looked around. "If there were an insect or a plant at hand, I could show you. I could . . ." His voice trailed off, seemingly looking over her shoulder.

She turned around to follow his gaze. She saw nothing but dark shacks. "What is it? Do you see someone coming?"

"Magistra, do you see that cat on that roof?" He pointed.

She followed his finger to what seemed a grayer patch of a dark roof. "No."

"There's something not . . . I'm not sure . . ." He looked at her. "Have you noticed a gray cat around you?"

"The city's full of strays."

"But one cat repeatedly."

"No. Where are you going with this?"

His mouth pressed into a thin line. "Maybe I'm wrong."

"Wrong about what?"

"Never mind. But about Language Prime, perhaps I'll touch one of the kobolds. Dross will let me do it. Kobolds are resistant to what my touch creates. They can rip them out. It's a . . . disturbing sight."

"But when you touch creatures that aren't kobolds, it harms them?"

"Kills them. Distorts the Language Prime texts so as to give them cankers, large, blisterlike, dark with death. There's a term the clerics use that means dead tissue within living tissue . . ."

"Necrosis."

He was looking away from her. "Yes, necrotic, the cankers become necrotic."

Francesca took a sharp breath as her mind made a sudden connection. "Magister Shannon has cankers."

He looked at her, his green eyes even more haunted. "How did you know?"

"His gaunt face and thin body. His weakness. It's a state of muscle wasting a body enters when fighting cankers. We call it cachexia."

Nicodemus closed his eyes, and his mouth bent slightly, the thin smile of agony; Francesca had seen it a thousand times. "Did you accidently touch Magister Shannon?" she gently asked. "Is that what caused his cankers?"

"No, a creature from the ancient continent, called itself Fellwroth, used the Emerald of Aarahest to canker curse Magister. When I have the emerald again, I can cure him." He looked away to the distant sanctuary. "It's another reason why we will stop at nothing to retrieve the gem." He looked at her and blinked, no longer haunted, no longer betraying any awareness of his frailty.

Francesca felt her spine straighten. This man was not her patient. "So what does this have to do with Deirdre's message about two dragons?"

He looked away to the sanctuary. "Typhon is using the emerald to create dragons. Ten years ago, one attacked Trillinon. But dragons aren't what you suppose. It's difficult to explain exactly what—"

Francesca rolled her eyes. "Yeah, yeah. Deirdre laid it down: dragons are not giant reptile pyromaniacs but unbound incarnations of all things dangerous and partially incomprehensible who can alter the way people near them think. Witness the Savanna Walker and aphasia."

Nicodemus smiled. "That about sums it up. When Typhon stole the emerald back from me, we knew it had enough power to create half of a dragon. When we arrived in Avel, we expected to encounter such a beast. But the Walker is far more powerful than expected."

She pursed her lips. "You're saying the Savanna Walker predated Typhon's arrival in Avel?"

Nicodemus nodded. "From what the Canics tell us, the Savanna Walker is ancient. For hundreds of years, he's been known to drive men mad. But until Typhon arrived ten years ago the Walker was never known to cause aphasia."

"Typhon arrived, possessed Canonist Cala, and transformed the Savanna Walker into a half dragon?"

"So we believe." He paused. "Some aspects of the Walker are quite ordinary, pitifully so in some cases. But because he started as an insanity-inducing monster, the partial draconic transformation made his mind into a grotesque power of nonperception and incomprehension."

"Oh, is that all?" Francesca said casually and made a slight "huh" sound, as if he just explained the price of bread had gone up. "And now, Nicodemus, you know that there are two dragons out there. Well . . . you know that, if you trust me."

Nicodemus met her eyes. "I trust Deirdre. Your message comes from her."

"Do you love her?"

"Of course."

"You say that the way a man might order a shank of meat."

He shifted his weight. "Deirdre saved my life. Her old lover, a druid named Kyran, sacrificed himself to keep me alive. I owe her my love."

Francesca was unimpressed. "How heartwarming."

"Outside the city, we dwell with Boann—the river goddess who once made Deirdre an avatar. It's Deirdre and Boann who share the brilliant love I believe you want to hear about."

"Do you envy Boann's connection with Deirdre?"

"No. I see how separation hurts them both. You are suddenly nosy."

A gust of wind made Francesca pull her black robes more tightly around her. "I can't take your measure, Nicodemus Weal."

"No measure is needed. I'm working at great hopes with few resources and little ability." He studied her face. "Are you sure you've never met a Lornish woman named April? She was a tutor in the northeast of Spires."

"I've already told you that I haven't. Why do you ask?"

He looked her body up and down. "She was my tutor when I was a boy. She looked like you: long brown hair, fine features."

Francesca fought the sudden urge to step away from his uncomfortable gaze. "Why is this important?"

"I suppose it's not. It just seems odd."

Francesca exhaled. "In any case, I'm going to take a chance and trust you with some information." She described her evacuation to the garden tower and how a warship had docked there after her landing.

"The Kestrel we saw flying over the city?"

She nodded. "The *Queen's Lance*. She carried two passengers who were wizards. It seems a strange coincidence they should arrive—"

"It's no coincidence. Who were they?"

"One was named Vivian Niyol; she wore the robes of a Deputy Vice-Chancellor. Tall, olive skin, long white hair, blank white eyes, spry for however many millions of years she's lived, formidable with words."

"Coming from you, that's a compliment."

Francesca frowned but continued. "The other black-robe was a grand wizard, younger, very handsome, dark skin, long dreadlocks, wore a white-lined hood of a linguist. His name was—"

"Lotannu Akoma," Nicodemus finished for her. "Damn."

"You know him?"

"Know of him. Magister Akoma is an expert in quaternary cognition. He was one of Shannon's brightest students back in Astrophell. In the last few years, he's made breakthroughs with spells that can detect quaternary cognition."

She held up her hands. "Wait, wait, waiiit. If you're sneaking around Avel, how can you know what's happening in the academy?"

"We have an agent hidden in Astrophell."

"You're trusting me with this information?"

He shrugged. "My half sister already suspects it. She's been hampering our communication for years now. Fortunately, we just received word from our agent that my sister is in Ogun, meeting with envoys from Starhaven and Starfall Keep. So at least we know she's nowhere near Avel at the—"

"So it's time to stop talking about that," Francesca interrupted, "because this is the part of the conversation when you tell me who in the burning hells your half sister is."

One side of Nicodemus's mouth turned up in a smile. "You really have no idea what you've been pushed into."

"None whatsoever, which is why, God-of-gods damn it, you're going to tell me."

"My half sister has been cloistered in Astrophell. I've never met her, never heard her description or her name because she is the Halcyon."

"The what?" Francesca nearly sputtered.

Nicodemus smiled. "Well, more like the Halcyon-in-waiting. The counter-prophecy faction in conjunction with several ancient deities called The Alliance of Divine Heretics have sworn allegiance to her as the Halcyon."

"Why has the world not heard of this?"

"Academic, political in-fighting. My half sister will also be fluent in Language Prime, and most believe Language Prime is blasphemy. She must be careful when revealing her true nature."

Francesca thought about this. "And because of the counter-prophecy, your sister believes you are the Storm Petrel, the demon's champion?"

"And the one most likely to kill her," he said with a solemn nod. "Hence the agents who sweep the land looking for me. But I'm not the biggest threat to my half sister; Hakeem is."

"Nicodemus, you're not making sense. Hakeem is the patron god of wizards. The Halcyon will be his champion."

Nicodemus grinned. "That's the rub. The Alliance of Divine Heretics isn't part of the wizardly academy. If Hakeem suspects her deities are infiltrating his order, he'd destroy my sister, prophecy or no. So she and her allies have to prove she's the Halcyon. Of course, she can't prove she's destined to slay demons if she can't find a demon."

Francesca shut her eyes. "Well, at least your hallucinations make sense. Your half sister's forces are prowling for Typhon so they can pick a fight and, by drawing him into the open, proclaim their leader the Halcyon of prophecy."

"Exactly. But it seems that she's been amassing power too quickly for those in Starfall Keep. That's why she's in Ogun meeting with southern wizards."

"How do you figure?"

"According to our agent, the opposition to the counter-prophecy leadership in Astrophell has gathered in Starfall and is now seeking allies in the south. The most inflammatory rumors speak about the formation of a separatist faction who want to unite Starfall and Starhaven in the League of Starfall and split the southern wizards away from Astrophell."

Francesca pressed the heel of her hand to her forehead. "So why send Vivian Niyol and Lotannu Akoma to Avel?"

"I'm guessing they're dragon hunting, hence their airship showing up just when the Savanna Walker tore through the sanctuary."

"They told me they were here for you."

He shrugged. "They suspect me of creating, or helping to create, the half dragon. They would expect me to be near the wyrm."

Francesca still didn't like the idea. "But how could they have known? How could they have gotten here that fast?"

"I'd guess Magister Akoma has written some quaternary cognition surveillance, textual constructs perhaps who alerted him via the colaboris station in Avel."

A sudden thought popped into Francesca's mind and she smiled. "I just solved your problem regarding the second dragon."

"How's that?"

"If Lotannu can see quaternary thoughts and dragons induce quaternary thoughts, then he should be able to see both the Savanna Walker and this second dragon."

Nicodemus was silent for a while. Then he said, "You want to ask Vivian and Lotannu for help finding the second dragon?"

She nodded.

A growing breeze blew a lock of Nicodemus's black hair into his face. "Deirdre said you'd help me avoid the second dragon."

"Guess you better listen to me then."

He chewed his lip.

"I'll give you another piece of information. Maybe you'll trust me more then. Someone has been paying desperate Canics to smuggle sheets of steel charged with highsmith runes into Avel." She produced the sheet of metal from her belt purse.

"Ohhh hell," Nicodemus whispered, staring at the metal. Faintly Francesca could hear in his tone the frightened boy he had once been.

She frowned. "I had hoped you'd solve this little puzzle for me. But right now your expression is kicking those hopes in the crotch. Do you have any idea who's running Lornish steel into Avel?"

He still hadn't taken his eyes off the metal sheet. "Not a clue under the burning heaven."

"Lovely."

He looked up at her. "If Lorn is involved, then things are even worse than we suspected. We have to act fast."

"You're saying this to talk yourself into letting me go back and see what I can learn from Lotannu, right?"

He scowled at her.

"Don't forget I need to get the texts to close the laceration in Vein's lung."

"You do," he agreed. "I suppose Magister and I can tell you where to meet us in this district tomorrow night. We'll take you over the wall. But you must come alone without any followers, otherwise—"

"You'll disappear," she said dramatically while holding up a fist and then splaying her fingers, "like smoke into the wind. I can slip Vivian's surveillance; I did it before."

He looked at the kobolds, who were now all crouched around Vein, then back at her. "Now, will you tell me what you really are?"

She threw her hands in the air. "Holy heaven aflame, this again? You know everything about who I am and where I've come from."

"No, I don't," he said while studying her face with intense interest. "And unless you're an unsurpassed liar, neither do you."

"Did you take a special class at Starhaven in sounding arrogant, because you have this ability to make me feel—"

"Magistra," he interrupted, "to my eyes, all living creatures glow with Language Prime texts. That is why I keep asking who and what you are. It is how I know that there is something wrong with you."

"What do you mean?"

"You shine too brightly."

"I don't understand."

"Your Language Prime texts, the magical language that make up your being, shine brighter than those of any living creature I've ever seen."

"What does that mean?"

"I'm not sure." His dark green eyes flicked up and down her body. "Magistra, you are simply too much alive."

"I bet you say that to all the girls."

He opened his mouth as if to object but then stopped. He narrowed his eyes and leaned forward, staring over her shoulder.

She turned. "Are you staring at the gray cat again?"

"I don't think it's a cat. Look." He pointed.

This time she could see it skulking between two shacks. "So if it's not a cat, it's taking some marvelous fashion tips about how to wear a cat's body."

"It looks like a cat," Nicodemus agreed. "Moves like one as well. I'd be willing to guess it's been following us, or perhaps just you." He paused. "Magistra, go back toward the sanctuary after we go over the walls. Find out who is watching us."

"You going to explain that?" she asked. "Or should I consult a mystic about the enigma that is Nicodemus Weal."

"There's one peculiar thing about that catlike creature," he answered flatly; "it's not alive."

Thirty-one

"What under the holy sky do you mean we're being watched by a cat that's not alive?" Cyrus asked.

Francesca was crouching next to him a few feet away from the kobolds still huddled around Vein. Farther away, Nicodemus was speaking to Shannon. The cat-that-perhaps-was-not-a-cat had slunk into the shadows. Francesca kept her voice level. "Just tell me, do you see any hierophantic spells among the shacks?"

"No," Cyrus answered curtly. "It's completely black."

"Not even subtextualized?"

"Not even subtextualized. You think the cat's made out of cloth? A hierophantic construct, like an intricate warkite?"

She kneaded her temples. "Not if you can't see its text."

"How does Nicodemus know it isn't alive?"

"He can't see Language Prime glowing in the creature."

"That's insane. Language Prime is blasphemy."

"He said he'd prove Language Prime is real by touching one of the kobolds."

"Maybe the thing out there is a wizardly gargoyle."

She shook her head. "Then Shannon would be able to see its prose; losing mundane vision has made his textual vision more acute."

"So if it's neither a gargoyle nor alive, what is it?"

She exhaled. "How much text is in your robes?"

"I stole a fair amount from the pilot with the lucerin lantern," he said. "Enough to loft me fifty feet. Why?"

She looked into his eyes. "I have a plan."

A HALF HOUR later, after leaving Nicodemus's party, Francesca and Cyrus were walking back toward the sanctuary, looking for a place to spend the night. A cold wind had picked up, and above them the crescent moons illuminated a shifting river of clouds. Another storm was coming.

"You're talking about a man who thinks he's prophesized to save the world and runs around half-naked with blue-skinned monsters," Cyrus said as they went. "You can't trust anything he says."

"You saw what his touch did to the kobold's arm, the canker it formed." Francesca shuddered at the memory of the deformed tissue that had bulged out of the kobold's skin and the meaty sound it had made when the kobold tore it off.

Cyrus exhaled and his veil bulged out. "That was troubling. But it hardly means we should trust Nicodemus." They navigated around larger puddles, splashed through smaller ones. A few ravens flew overhead.

He sniffed. "I mean, truly: 'You shine too brightly?' 'You're more alive than anyone else?' Who outside a knightly romance speaks such honeyed drivel? Did he say your eyes shine like stars?"

"Don't be foolish."

"Then at least he compared your smile to the brightness of the sun?"

"Nor that. Nor did he compare my breasts to the white- and blue-moons, which was kind because though no woman's breasts are perfectly symmetric, I'd like to think my celestial bodies are more equal than those two." She nodded at the sky. "Besides, what's wrong with knightly romances? They're the best thing that comes out of Lorn. You bought me one once."

"*The Silver Shield*, by Isabella Gawan," Cyrus replied. "You loved it. Read it in two days, I believe."

"But you didn't. Did you ever finish?"

"Not for lack of trying. All the invented names and countries just seemed a bit . . . silly."

"But Gawan is brilliant. I should have given you *Sword of Flame*, by Robert DeRigby, that's more what a man would like."

"You did. Couldn't finish that one either."

"Pity," she said and changed subjects. "But you're being a ninny about Nicodemus. He's all frozen on the inside; whether or not the bit about prophecy is true, he believes it is. It's made him into a killer. He's also a delusional, self-absorbed, arrogant bastard."

"That's your official diagnosis, cleric?"

She sighed. "Suppose you're right. Suppose it's easier for me to see the pathology and not the person."

"Even with me?"

She looked over and found his brown eyes searching hers. A twinge of guilt moved through her. "No. Not with you." She touched his arm lightly. "I am sorry for dragging you into this mess. Can you forgive me, old friend?"

He looked away and laughed dryly. "Just as soon as we survive this little bit of intrigue and I make captain."

She took her hand back. "Fair enough," she said and then paused. "I do wish I had told you I had disspelled that sentence in your chest."

He looked at her, his eyes softer. She remembered that look from years before. He seemed about to say something. His veil moved. Or perhaps it was the wind. He looked away. They continued walking.

A moment later, Cyrus said, "But surely you don't believe Nicodemus's claim that there's something wrong with you, that your Language Prime text shines too brightly."

She looked at the bulging dark clouds. "I don't know, Cyrus. We know some kind of unknown text was cast on me with the anklet. And if the demon had the emerald, as Nicodemus claims, he could have cast some Language Prime curse on me. Perhaps Nico is seeing the double glow of my body and the curse. Or was it something to do with the Savanna Walker's aphasia curse getting so close to me?"

"You're speculating about a problem you don't even know exists."

There were more ravens flying above them now, some hovering in the wind. Francesca studied them and said, "I guess I should worry about the problems we know exist."

"Like what to do about Vivian and Lotannu?"

"Not really; they'll be expecting us later tonight, but when they learn about the lycanthrope hunt, they'll suppose we got stuck in a districtwide lockdown."

"They might wonder why I lacked enough text to loft us over a few district walls."

She shrugged. "So we tell her the truth. You cast all your text when things got dangerous. Honestly, why shouldn't we tell her about Nicodemus?"

"But she might force our hand. Make us take her to Nicodemus or imprison us."

Francesca laughed. "She's an academic, Cyrus. Even if she's skipping out on Astrophell politics now, she'll have to go back. She can't abuse an appointed physician without infuriating the clerical order or dispose of the air warden of Avel without worsening relations between the black-robes and green-robes."

He sniffed. "In a storm, all sails become dispensable."

"You want to hide that we met Nicodemus?"

He seemed to think about this. "If we tell Vivian, she'll never let us out of her sight again."

"After we slipped her last spy, she'll do that no matter what. At least if we tell her, we're holding a bargaining piece."

A light rain began to fall. At last Cyrus said, "You mean to flirt with both sides until we know which one to bed?"

"Something like that. At least we're sure we don't want to get in bed with the demon, should he exist. So, do we tell Vivian what we know before or after I go back to treat Vein?"

He looked at her. "Don't you have to close the tear in his lungs?"

"No. After a few days of Shannon working the shunting spell, the lung will close on its own."

"You didn't tell Nicodemus that."

"We need bargaining power with him too."

"For a physician, you're ruthless."

"Cyrus, my dear, my honey, my turtle dove of unsullied and slightly nauseating innocence, all practicing physicians are ruthless. A ruthless game requires a ruthless player. I'll do what I must, say what I must to end the game with the fewest possible corpses. Cyrus, are you listening to me?"

They had just turned onto an empty street. He pointed to a spot on the road. "How about here for your hare-brained plan?"

"But it's so wet."

"Everywhere's wet."

She sighed. "Here it is then." She let herself fall forward, hitting the cold street with a muddy splat. A moment later she heard and felt Cyrus hit the ground next to her. They lay still. Francesca tried to slow her heartbeat and breathing. Despite the waterproofing text Cyrus had cast into her robes, cold water was seeping through an opening near her neckline. She felt the skin on her chest and stomach thrill into goose bumps.

The rain fell harder. Above them several ravens croaked as if in surprise. Francesca fought the urge to frown. What had gotten them excited? But the birds soon quieted down. The rain surged, beating hard upon her back and making such a liquid racket that she couldn't hear anything else.

The water had now seeped down her sternum and, agonizingly, was pooling around her left breast. It took every dram of her restraint not to push herself up.

"NOW!" Cyrus bellowed, grabbing his left sleeve and casting it away.

Francesca sat up. A spray of raindrops struck her face as the cloth shot forward.

Cyrus was already on his feet. She struggled to join him. The rain was letting up, and the night was filled with a tortured yowling. About ten paces away, Cyrus's cloth had wrapped itself into a small bag that was rolling through a puddle.

As she drew closer, Francesca could see small claws tearing through the cloth. But no sooner did the claws cut fabric than the threads wove themselves back together. "You got it!" she laughed. "You got it!"

"Whatever it is," Cyrus grumbled and then reached for the bag. His left arm and shoulder were now bare to the rain. The instant his fingers touched cloth, the bag became still and silent. He looked up at her.

"What?"

"I just activated a disspell in the cloth."

She looked at the still bag. "So it was a construct?"

"Give me some light," he muttered while reaching for the cloth again.

Francesca extemporized several flamefly paragraphs. The rain had dwindled to a fine drizzle, which slowly pushed the incandescent sentences down.

Cyrus touched the bag, and it split itself open to reveal a motionless gray cat. "What under heaven?" Cyrus said as he bent closer. Tentatively he poked the cat's side. "It's stiff and . . . hard. Like it's made out of stone under its fur." He rolled it over and its petrified legs stuck straight up. "It's heavy."

"But how could it be a gargoyle and avoid my eyes or Magister Shannon's eyes?" Francesca had forgotten about the cold water running down her robes. Now she wrapped her arms around herself, trying to hug warmth back into her aching left breast.

The cloth around Cyrus's hand split itself into fine, sharp strips that cut into the cat.

"Oh Creator, not on a cat! Don't—" She had to look away even though she had used sharp words to open thousands of human bodies.

"It's not alive," he grumbled.

Still, she looked away to a nearby shack where several ravens had perched. Something was strange about the birds . . . but before she could figure out what it was, Cyrus made a low, thoughtful sound. She looked down. Cyrus had taken the skin off the feline construct as if it were an orange peel. Now, reflecting the incandescence of her flamefly paragraphs was a quicksilver-smooth body. As he turned it over in his hands, she could see that it had only one eye—the right eye, which was made of polished brass.

A realization flashed through Francesca's mind. "Los in hell!"

Cyrus stood. "What? What is it?"

The thoughts were coming too fast to articulate. "Of course, he was such a damned . . . snot! And he had all those questions for me. The bastard was pumping me for information!"

"What in Celeste's name are you talking about?"

"Cyrus, we've seen this thing before, we just didn't think . . . I didn't think . . ." her voice trailed off.

Cyrus's veil moved as if he were frowning. He bent back down to pick up the bag. As he did so, the cloth leapt to life, wrapped around his arm, and reformed his sleeve. "Can you explain a little better what—" He paused and then pointed. "Fran, look."

He was pointing up to the ravens on the shack. With a sudden thrill of surprise, Francesca realized what had bothered her about them before. There must have been twenty of them, all perched on the gutters, all their heads tilted to the exact same angle. Twenty or so corvid eyes, bright as black jewels, stared back at her. "What are they doing?" she asked.

Suddenly all the dark birds took flight and, with a flutter of wings, were gone. Save for dripping gutters, the night was dead silent.

"Well, that wasn't a vaguely threatening and frighteningly indecipherable phenomenon," Francesca said flatly. "Or anything."

Cyrus was still holding the metal cat. He tucked it under his arm. "I saw something like that once on a merchant galley bound for Warth. We broke company when the galley reached the Dralish port, but for a while we docked the airship on their deck. When in Dralish waters, schools of seals would swim up beside the ship. They weren't natural. They swam as if of one mind. They all studied us, counted us on the ship. I swear you could see them reading the ship's name off her hull."

"You think somewhere in the city there's a druid?"

"Or several," he said and then added, "though I suppose it could be a shaman down from Verdant."

Suddenly Francesca remembered the cat. She looked back down at its brass eye, and the glorious flight of ideas tore through her brain once again. "No, it's druids."

"The cat told you that?"

"Yes, and if we're going to catch him, we'll need a lot more hierophantic text. When's the earliest you can get more charged sailcloth and some coins? Our only chance will be when he's in the market. We'll need silver to catch him."

"Catch whom? What are you talking about?"

She shook her head. "Just tell me, how soon can we get more cloth?"

"If we can catch a morning patrol, I could get to the sanctuary and back an hour before dawn. But, Fran, for what? The night market? Just what in the burning hells did this cat tell you?"

She pointed at the lifeless brass eye. "It just told me who's been smuggling Lornish steel into Avel."

Thirty-two

The wind picked up as Nicodemus took his students over the wall.

It was an involved procedure, requiring several complex hoisting spells written in the Chthonic languages. But the kobolds threw their minds and muscle into the task, and their allies in the city watch pretended not to notice. All told, it took maybe a quarter hour.

Then they were hurrying into the safety of the grass ocean. The savanna grass grew to seven feet and consisted of thick bamboolike shafts. The Silent Blight had killed about one in twenty stalks, their shallow shafts becoming brittle in death; even so, the grass would have stopped any party not led by a lycanthrope or a kobold. The powerful wind was making the tops of the grass dip and sway in a loud rush.

With textually augmented machetes, Jasp and Dross took the lead. The party moved quickly, having cut the path when sneaking into the city.

Over the sound of the wind in the grass, Nicodemus could hear a few guttural voices. He could feel the ground vibrated by heavy footfalls. The lycanthropes had arrived, summoned by the scent of open wounds. But the wolves also recognized the smell of kobolds. They would come no closer.

To Nicodemus's eyes all living things glowed softly cyan. But surrounded as he was by the grassland, his Language Prime vision penetrated only twenty paces or so into the stalks before everything seemed an indistinct glow. During the dry season, when the stalks dried to golden yellow, he could see for miles and make out individual birds and reptiles and insects. But in the late wet season, peering into the grassland was like peering into murky water. He could make out the lycanthropes only as massive, sleek shapes.

The wolves' throaty voices sent Nicodemus's memory back to when he'd left the Heaven Tree Valley with fifteen of his best students. Collaborating with Magistra Amadi Okeke—their agent within Astrophell—they had discovered that Typhon had made Avel his new stronghold. The journey took them nearly forty days of trekking through the Savanna, suffering heat by day and lycanthropes by night. Five of his students died during the journey. Then had come the delicate task of infiltrating the city, befriending the Canics, beginning the secret war against Typhon.

Nicodemus's thoughts returned to the present when they emerged onto a short, muddy bank. Before them stretched a small cove of the reservoir. The wind had blown its surface into miles of half-reflected starlight. To the west, clouds were gathering.

The kobolds jogged along the bank to find the two skiffs they had hidden in the grass. Dross, Slag, and Flint loaded Vein in one boat. Jasp carried Magister Shannon into the second boat and took up the forward seat. Nicodemus pushed the second boat into the water and then hopped in and assumed the aft seat. He and Jasp placed their long oars in their locks.

In moments, both boats were lauched and rowing windward. No other vessels could be seen. The lake towns had migrated far up the narrows to fish among the shallows. In half an hour, they were out on the main water of the reservoir.

For Nicodemus, rowing a lake skiff with a kobold was a tricky proposition. With his greater height and longer limbs, Nicodemus could produce a longer stroke. But a muscular kobold could exert inhuman torque. It had taken weeks of practice before Nicodemus and his students could avoid sending the skiff in circles. Worse, once at speed, dropping the oar became a dangerous mistake; the boat's momentum would push the oar blade aft, the handle fore, and in the process evict the rower into the lake.

Though the kobolds believed in Nicodemus, they were still kobold warriors. A mistake at the oars would diminish their respect. So Nicodemus paid special care to his technique: release, feather the oar, recovery sweep, right the oar, catch, drive, repeat. Repeat. Repeat. Over and over.

Shannon was sitting in the stern, bundled up in a cloak and holding Azure in his lap. When it began to rain hard, Nicodemus halted long enough to write the old man a canopy of Chthonic language. Once rowing again, he told Shannon of Francesca's report about Vivian and Lotannu. He also explained about Francesca's Language Prime text shining unnaturally brightly.

"You're sure it's her Language Prime?" Shannon asked.

"And when I'm close to her, I feel my face getting hot, like I'm having a synesthesic reaction."

"You mean you blush."

"It's different. I can't put my finger on it."

Shannon seemed to think for a moment. "Whatever Francesca is, Deirdre sent her to us. It suggests that Deirdre has a plan."

"I hope so."

"Because you don't have a plan," Shannon said coldly.

Nicodemus grimaced but said nothing.

Shannon shifted in his seat. "And Typhon has let my ghost free, meaning he's set a plan in motion as well."

"Magister, the ghost . . . I didn't mean to say—"

"It's nothing."

"Once we've recovered the emerald and I can cure you, you'll be able to write a new ghost that—"

"We've been over this," Shannon interrupted and then cleared his throat. "Your half sister's agents—Lotannu and Vivian—they are aware of the Savanna Walker?"

"It seems so. It won't take them long to find him, or vice versa. We're running out of time."

"We've run out of the time we gave ourselves when we left the Heaven Tree Valley."

A flush of anxiety moved through Nicodemus, but he forced his voice to remain steady. "Magister, we didn't leave the valley too soon. I couldn't watch you die."

The old man was quiet for a moment and then said, "Now you're going to watch me die anyway."

"Magister! When we have the emerald—"

"We won't have this argument again. The question is what to do now."

Nicodemus readjusted his grip on the oars. "What else can we do but sleep at camp and return to the city in the evening to meet with Francesca?"

Shannon scowled. "To follow whatever Deirdre's plan is? To try to discover this second dragon?"

"Unless you have a better scheme." The rain was letting up.

"But what is Deirdre thinking?"

"We could ask Boann," Nicodemus suggested.

"We will. I wish we knew something for certain about Francesca other than her Language Prime text shines too brightly."

"We know she's got a tongue sour enough to curdle milk by talking to it."

Shannon sniffed with amusement. "Yes, we know that."

"It's because she's so pretty and tall. She's probably used to rebuffing advances despite keeping her hair in that tight braid and wearing a haughty expression. If only she'd had less sourness and more knowledge about the second dragon."

"How could we have fought Typhon for the past three years and not have encountered this second dragon?"

"Whatever it is, Francesca's bright Language Prime gives me hope that Deirdre knows what she's doing. It truly is amazing how brightly she shines."

"You think it's something to do with her ability to fight off the second dragon?"

"I don't know what to make of it."

They fell silent. Nicodemus focused on his rowing. They had entered one of the narrows. Redwood-covered hills rose on either side of them, silent and dark.

Shannon spoke again, "Where is your half sister again?"

"Amadi's last report puts her in Ogun meeting with envoys from Starfall and Starhaven."

"Attempting to prevent the League of Starfall from forming?"

"So it seems."

"But she's sent Lotannu and Vivian Niyol," Shannon mused. "I understand why she let Lotannu go; he's special talents. But Vivian?"

"What do you know about her?"

The old man shrugged. "Not much. She was at Starfall Keep most of her career. Never heard her name until I was shipped down to Starhaven. Her fame was rising as mine was falling. I think she was one of the first in Astrophell to support the counter-prophecy faction."

Nicodemus pulled his oar. "Should we try to scare Vivian off? Buy a little time?"

"Not until we know more about what Deirdre is planning," Shannon said, rubbing his eyes with a bony hand.

Though he had seen the thin appendage so many times before, Nicodemus felt his stomach tighten. Shannon seemed to be growing frailer by the day. "Magister, what was it like to see your ghost?"

The old man's expression contracted into one of pain. "It's almost worse that he still exists . . . and that he is longing for me. It makes me feel . . . almost dead already."

"We're going to recover the emerald. Then I'll cure your cankers—"

"And I'll have time to write another ghost. I know, I know, Nicodemus. I hope so too." He sounded exhausted.

Nicodemus fought the urge to stop rowing and take Shannon's hand. But touching the old man would only give his mentor more cankers. "Magister, you can't give up."

The old man paused. "I won't, my boy."

Nicodemus forced himself to ignore the empty feeling in his chest. Instead he visualized the emerald. If he could only end his disability, if he only had the emerald. He had to redouble his resolve. "There's much to live for," Nicodemus said awkwardly and then refocused on his rowing. All he could do now was sweep and dip and drive, sweep and dip and drive.

Shannon adjusted his blankets. "Yes," he said weakly. "Much to live for."

They rowed on in silence for a moment. And then Shannon sniffed as if amused. "You know," he said, "I don't think the remarkable thing about Francesca is her Language Prime."

"No?"

"No, she's remarkable because of something that she just made you say." He paused. "I never heard you say something like that."

Nicodemus frowned at his oar stroke. "Something like what?"

"That you think she's pretty."

Nicodemus dropped his oar.

WOLF'S CREEK WAS a slender extension of the narrows that snaked into the Auburn Mountains. Here, unlike elsewhere on the reservoir, water lay beneath sheer stone banks. The fisherfolk avoided the place for fear that the lycanthropes might leap down on them from the forest. But for the past two years, the creatures stalking the banks were not lycanthropes. The kobolds' camp—a collection of cabins built amid a dense redwood grove— lay a half mile west of the creek.

Nicodemus, wrapped in a thick wool blanket, sat on a stone bank watching his students fish. Jasp had gotten Shannon to write a few flamefly paragraphs onto a stalk of savanna grass. One held the flylike lights over the dark water while Vein and Flint lay flat against stone ledges.

Nicodemus could see into the life of the reservoir. Tiny floating plants gave the water its deep greenness; as such, the water shone with dilute Language Prime. Through this wan glow he saw the brighter shapes of fish circling the dangling flameflies.

"It is strange fish are drawn to brightness," a soft, singsong voice said above and behind him. "It does them no good."

"Goddess," Nicodemus said in greeting to Boann, the Highland deity who had made Deirdre into an avatar. Since Typhon had nearly destroyed her ark, Boann had become little more than a ghost. She was a young deity with bright lapis eyes and hair that looked like a miniature rushing river. Her green robes floated as if suspended in water.

Around them, the forest was quiet save for the dripping of rainwater from branches. The rain had stopped and the winds were calming.

"Shannon told me of your daylight misadventure," Boann said. "I've thought about Deirdre's plan, but I have no deeper insight into what it might be."

Nicodemus nodded.

Boann sat next to him. "You took a bit of a swim on the way home."

"Shannon told you?"

"I felt it."

Nicodemus nodded; she was a water goddess after all.

"Shannon said you dropped your oar because you were thinking of a pretty girl."

Nicodemus groaned. "I feared the kobolds would think less of me for it. But while I was clambering back into the boat, Shannon explained I was distracted by thoughts of Francesca. I think Vein understood, but most of them were confused. They have trouble distinguishing male humans from female humans. But once they understood, they couldn't stop laughing. Dross and Jasp especially. I doubt either of those two will shut up about this for years."

Boann smiled.

"I pity any nearby fishermen; guffawing kobolds sound like echoes escaping from the burning hells."

"You were distracted by Francesca?"

"Her Language Prime text shines brightly."

"You are fascinated."

He paused before admitting that he was. He paused a moment longer before saying. "But am I fascinated like a boy admiring a pretty girl or like one of those fish?" He nodded toward the silhouettes circling around Jasp's fishing light. "In either case, I shouldn't think about her; I should focus on the emerald."

"You can still sense the gem?"

"It is still pushing against the spells tattooed around my scar." He rubbed the back of his neck and found himself thinking again of James Berr, his murderous cacographic relative who had lived three centuries ago. No one knew if Typhon had made Berr a cacographer or if Berr had been born that way. Nicodemus looked at the goddess and changed the subject. "How do you think Magister is holding up?"

"After seeing his ghost again? He's heartbroken."

Nicodemus closed his eyes. "We must help him keep fighting. Deirdre has a plan." He looked at Boann. She was staring down at the kobolds. "Goddess, if you don't mind my asking, what has it been like to miss Deirdre for so long? To spend all these years circling around her but never recovering her . . ."

"The worst moments are when I blame myself for being jealous of Kyran, for pushing her away. There are days I can barely stand to be myself."

Nicodemus nodded.

Boann pointed. "They should strike now. The fish are as close as they're going to get."

The kobolds remained stone still.

"Nicodemus, something occurs to me now," the goddess said gently. "If you are mesmerized as those fish are, it may not be by Francesca." She stood. "It may be by the emerald."

Just then Jasp yanked the light away from the water to where Flint smothered it in a leather bag. With the redwood canopy blocking out moon and starlight, the lake surface became complete black. Vein cast a net of coruscating indigo prose into the water, where it tied itself into a tight bundle.

Whooping delight, the kobolds hauled a tangle of luminous sentences and flopping fish out of the reservoir. Nicodemus called out his approval. Dinner was caught.

But then, as often happened when he contemplated fresh food, Nicodemus's elation subsided. His stomach was empty, but he'd have to wait hours before eating any fish. If he put food too fresh into his mouth, his lips would misspell its still-viable Language Prime and distort the tissue into tumor.

Thirty-three

Shortly after dawn, the rain clouds rolled away from Avel and left the sky a pale, limpid blue. For the first time since the rains began, the winds had calmed to breezes. Even with the sun only an hour into its climb, the morning was warmer than so many of the previous.

This late in the rainy season, it was possible the storms were over, that from now on the year would be a succession of burnished days with the city gardens flourishing and the walled fields below the dam growing chickpeas, wheat, and lentils.

The fine weather had brought buyers out of their houses and into the South Market. The weather was pleasant, but talk was tense and nervous. Craftsmen whispered to cooks and housewives about the lycanthrope incursion in North Gate or trouble within the sanctuary.

Through the warm air and whispers, Magister Robert DeGarn walked. People eyed his black robes and afforded him space, which he acknowledged with a smile and a nod. He went to two different spice stalls. Neither time did he seem to find what he was looking for. Smile gone, DeGarn approached the third spice stall. In clipped words he explained that he wanted to buy mint for the day's tea but that someone else was buying up all of the herb in the market.

The stall's owner, a young man with a sparse black beard, looked nervously between DeGarn and the man beside him. Short and dressed in a too-heavy white cloak, the newcomer grabbed DeGarn's sleeve. A puff of wind blew the wizard's red-lined hood over his head.

"Wh—" DeGarn spoke the single surprised syllable before a strip of his hood cut itself free and then wrapped around his mouth.

Francesca stepped from the crowd and slid her right hand under DeGarn's left arm. The cloth of his robes had become as hard as steel. With her free arm, she tossed two silver coins to the spice seller. "As we agreed, you saw two ordinary citizens greet Magister DeGarn and walk away with him. Keep to that story, and I'll be back with twice your payment."

The young man nodded.

Francesca secured her grip on DeGarn's arm. "Cyrus, relax the skirt of his robes a little more. Otherwise he can't walk."

By pulling on DeGarn's arm, Francesca led them out of the market, down an alley, and into a courtyard. The place belonged to the tavern that surrounded it, and Francesca had paid a heavy purse to ensure they wouldn't be disturbed.

The courtyard's white walls were covered by thorny clouds of bougainvillea vines, their crinkled-paper flowers of purple and yellow just beginning to open. Four dwarf orange trees grew among the court's terracotta tiles, their waxy leaves glinting with retained raindrops. In the courtyard's center stood a small raised reflecting pool. Francesca and Cyrus sat their captive on the pool's brightly tiled edge. DeGarn's robes allowed him to sit but then tightened around his body.

Fran stood next to Cyrus, in front of the older wizard. Cyrus pulled back the man's hood to reveal an enraged expression bound by a tight headband—containing Cyrus's censoring spell—and a cloth gag. DeGarn's fierce brown eyes glared at Francesca.

She met his gaze and then pulled from her satchel the metallic cat they'd caught the previous night.

DeGarn's eyes fixed on the object. His jaw muscles flexed and his pupils dilated. Genuine surprise.

Francesca dropped the cat. It struck the tiles with a clang. Then Francesca dropped the sheet of Lornish steel. DeGarn looked at the new object and then back up to her.

"You know how these got into Avel?"

He shook his head.

"Don't try to lie. Your bald head is going pink with embarrassment." It wasn't, but judging by the way DeGarn's eyes widened, he didn't know that. "You've got two of these constructs"—she kicked the metal cat—"sitting on the war-weight gargoyles that guard the inner door to your colaboris station. One of them was missing its left eye. I thought they were decorations when I saw them. But they're not. They're safeguards for your guests . . . your Lornish guests."

He narrowed his eyes.

"You're hiding highsmiths in your station," she said flatly. "One was dressed up like a servant and served us mint tea. I saw his tray indent around his fingers. At the time, I thought the tray was thin or old. But that wasn't it, was it? There was text in the tray, warping its metal, because the man holding it was a highsmith."

Again she kicked the metal cat. "You've let these constructs sit on your gargoyles as proof you wouldn't use the brutes against the metal mages. And you let the druids fly their raven familiars all over your station and your city."

DeGarn didn't move.

"And that's why you were so damn . . ." she searched for the right word ". . . smarmy about Starfall being a miserable nothing and Astrophell being exultant. You wanted to see if I'd declare my allegiance to the North. You're a Starfall agent, aren't you? You're out here fighting to form the League of Starfall so that Starfall can break away from Astrophell?"

DeGarn still didn't move.

"Well then," she said, "that begs three questions. First, why are you sheltering highsmiths and druids in a colaboris station? Second, how in the Creator's name have you managed to stop them from tearing each other's hearts out? And finally, how were you so completely, incredibly, brainblisteringly stupid enough to walk out into the market by yourself after we disspelled the metal cat?"

She nodded at Cyrus, who tapped DeGarn's shoulder. His gag fell away.

DeGarn frowned but said nothing.

Francesca waited a few moments and then said, "Let's play a game: I'll tell you what I think is happening, and you'll sit there dumb as a bag of mush until I say something wrong. Fair?"

He glowered at her in silence.

"You've already got the hang of it!" She smiled. "So, I learned about the League of Starfall from a man who believed that Starfall was looking to join forces with Starhaven against Astrophell. But seeing a highsmith construct working with druidic familiars got me wondering if Starfall has stopped looking for allies within the wizardly academy. Up north, the counterprophecy faction has a young woman they're going to dub the Halcyon. I'm guessing Starfall got wind of this and became desperate enough to do the unthinkable and look for allies outside of the academy. How close am I?"

DeGarn looked away from her.

"Well done, Magister! You have this game down pat." She smiled. "So, who would join Starfall to oppose Northern power? The two ancient enemies, Lorn and Dral? Might not seem likely candidates until one considers that the only thing ever to get druids and highsmiths in bed together was the war to break free of the Neosolar Empire . . . which was, unless I've forgotten my history, ruled from Trillinon."

Finally, DeGarn spoke: "You're spinning this loose assemblage of . . . conjecture out of one metal feline statue and a few blackbirds."

"Don't forget about your being a consummate snot," she quipped happily. "That was a big tip-off."

"I don't have to take this abuse."

She made a show of looking around the courtyard. "Hmmm, maybe you mean that these are druidic orange-tree constructs? That they're going to pelt Cyrus and me with unripe fruit until we let you go?" She looked expectantly at the trees for a moment. "Oh, wait, they're not. Pity. Because now I'm really God-of-gods damned certain that, actually, you do have to take this abuse."

"Cleric," DeGarn said with all the dignified loathing of a Lornish courtier, "you are a rude and vulgar woman."

"And you're a blooming idiot," she said brightly. "Truly, what made you dumb enough to stroll around the market after we'd disspelled the cat? The ravens saw us do it and flew away."

Cyrus grunted. "Unless the druids and the highsmiths didn't tell you what their spies saw."

DeGarn glowered at him.

"Huh," Francesca said. "There's a thought. Now why would they not tell you—"

"You found Nicodemus Weal," DeGarn said.

Francesca found that it was her turn to be struck dumb.

"It's the only thing they would hide from me," DeGarn said, his keen brown eyes fixed on Francesca's. "You found Nicodemus Weal."

Francesca looked at Cyrus, but it was too late; her reaction was as good as an admission.

"Cleric, you have an extraordinary opportunity to shape history," De-Garn said, now in earnest. "Starfall must be free. Lorn and Dral will not submit to Northern rule. The woman who would be Halcyon cannot be convinced of this. We have tried diplomacy, but she believes she is prophesied to rule the entire continent. Unless she realizes that the South will not kneel, there will be long, bloody war."

Cyrus grunted. "And Nicodemus is simply going to . . . induce the soon-to-be Halcyon to abandon her ambitions?"

"No," Francesca heard herself say. "Starfall wants something to make Astrophell nervous; it wants its own Halcyon."

DeGarn shifted under the robes that had become his restraints. "Rude and vulgar, Magistra, you are certainly that. But you are also irritatingly perceptive."

Francesca bowed. "I'm rather fond of you too, Magister. Especially your flouncy Western Lornish way of speaking. It reminds me of the Lornish romances I like to read."

DeGarn rolled his eyes. "Spare me your poor literary taste."

She laughed. "Magister you are in a rare and truly miserable position.

You've got Vivian and Lotannu in the city, Northern agents who are also searching for Nicodemus. What do you mean to do with them, assassinate them?"

"The League of Starfall wants independence, not carnage. Listen, you must take us, or at least our message, to Nicodemus. The Astrophell spies are here to destroy him; they think he is the one of counter-prophecy."

"What if he is the one of counter-prophecy?" Cyrus asked.

"The counter-prophecy is rubbish. Besides, if he can keep us free, we don't care if he is Los's child and sprouts antlers from his head while—"

"He's rediscovered Language Prime, you know," Francesca casually interrupted.

DeGarn held motionless for a long moment. "What did you say?"

Francesca explained how Nicodemus had learned the magical language that composed the basic elements of life, how his touch could distort flesh into a bulging necrotic tumor, how he had known the metal cat at her feet was not alive by looking at it. "Still sound like a fellow you want to lead your bid for independence?"

DeGarn grunted. "Assuming you're telling the truth, the whole thing will fit quite well. Both the tree lovers and metal mages have . . . shall we say . . . peculiar prophecies. The highsmiths believe in a savior they call the Oriflamme, who will create living metal, with which they will fight off the demons during the War of Disjunction. Understanding the language that creates life would greatly impress them . . . once . . ."

"Once they got past the whole blaspheming against the Creator part of things?" Francesca suggested helpfully.

"As you say," DeGarn replied uncomfortably. "Meanwhile, the druids are aflutter about the Silent Blight, which as far as I can tell involves dying trees. Around the highsmiths, they embark on intensely poetic descriptions of nature being unbalanced."

"How many of each are you hiding?" Cyrus asked.

"Five druids, seven highsmiths."

"And the metal you're smuggling into the city?"

DeGarn scowled. "The highsmiths are doing that against my orders. They're nervous because the druids have snuck so much wood charged with their runes into the city."

"Los in hell!" Francesca swore. "Magister, how much linguistic weaponry do you have in this city?"

"Enough to protect Nicodemus from almost any action," he answered with a note of pride, "if Nicodemus accepts our invitation to join the League of Starfall."

Francesca sniffed in disbelief. "Or enough to eliminate him if he doesn't?"

"We are not as bloody-minded as you suppose," DeGarn insisted.

"Then why are the druids and the highsmiths withholding information from you?"

"They desire first access to Nicodemus. If he does become our champion, and if one group should catch his ear first . . ."

Francesca nodded. "I see."

DeGarn looked between her and Cyrus. "Come with me to the station to talk about the League. We shall discuss how—"

"I'd rather beat my face with a hot brick," Francesca interrupted. "I can't think of a single earthly reason why I should trust you."

DeGarn started. "I've just recalled something. A neophyte delivered your clinical journal to us before dusk last night."

"My clinical journal? Who sent my clinical journal?"

"You did, of course. It has your Numinous locator paragraph inscribed on the delivery notice."

Francesca looked at Cyrus. "I didn't send that book to anyone, let alone myself."

Above his veil, Cyrus's eyes narrowed. "Magister, can you tell if there's any malignant text in the book?"

"There is none. Any manuscript we receive is scrutinized before we admit it into the station. Let me fetch the book for you, as a sign of appreciation for taking our message to Nicodemus."

Francesca exchanged looks with Cyrus. He nodded. "You may fetch the book," she said. "But before we agree to play messenger for you, we'll need your assistance."

"How so?"

"First off, get your God-of-gods damned faction under control! This city is near to blasting itself into pieces without druidic familiars flapping about and highsmiths smuggling Lornish metal into it. I want to deal with you only, not a gaggle of squabbling steelskins and branch-wavers."

DeGarn's mouth hardened into a thin line. "I plan to make my displeasure very clear to my allies. And though I'm appalled by your uncivil treatment, by insisting to treat with me only, you've handed me a way to consolidate my authority."

Francesca nodded. "Good. I also require a small purse of silver, say two hundred pieces."

"Hakeem!" DeGarn swore. "Do you also want our war-weight gargoyles? The robes off our backs?"

"Don't be dramatic, Magister. You can fetch the purse while you're getting my clinical journal."

He looked from her to Cyrus and then back again. "I don't like it."

"You don't have to like it," she said airily. "You just have to do it."

"How do I know you will keep your end of the bargain?"

She met his eyes. "I swear on the Creator's name that I will bring your message to Nicodemus and return with his reply."

DeGarn studied her for a moment and then nodded. "I'll get what you ask for."

Cyrus looked at her. She nodded, and he touched the band of cloth wrapped around DeGarn's head. It fell away and his robes went slack. With a courtier's dignity, the old wizard stood and walked from the courtyard.

Cyrus cleared his throat. "You're sure we can trust him not to come back with his druids and highsmiths?"

"And lose access to Nicodemus?" Francesca asked. "Not likely. He's right, you know; by insisting we talk only to him, we've handed him control of his faction."

"That was your intention?"

She bowed.

"Fran, he's right. You are perceptive at political games. Where did you learn it?"

She sighed and sat by the reflecting pool. "I suppose the infirmary is filled with politics, in a petty way at least. But really, it . . . just . . . comes naturally."

"It's more than that. It's like you're more fully alive than you ever were back in the infirmary."

She frowned. "I wish it was the other way around. That medicine brought me more to life. Perhaps I missed my true calling of being a fast-talking political manipulator."

Cyrus sat beside her. "Fran, you're brilliant with patients. They love you." He lifted his hand as if he was going to adjust his veil, but then he reached out and took her hand.

The gesture surprised Francesca a little. It also felt comforting and . . . familiar. She looked down at his hand but did not take hers away.

A moment later she heard herself say, "Deirdre died on my table. A master physician would have saved her."

"You are a master physician."

She fought the urge to deny his words; he knew nothing of medicine, so what did his words mean? But that wasn't his fault. "You're kind. But I'm truly not. I've won an appointment out here in Avel. Had I been impressive, I would have been placed in Bearselton, Tota, or . . . Chandralu." This last she mentioned in a softer voice. The Infirmary of Chandralu was the most prestigious outside Port Mercy. She'd once had great ambitions.

"Nonsense," Cyrus murmured and again squeezed her hand.

They sat in silence for a while. The day was growing warmer. In the new silence, they could hear calls of merchants hawking their goods in the nearby market. "You do have enough charged cloth to lift us out of here if DeGarn does come back hostile, yes?" she found herself asking.

"More than enough."

They fell silent again.

A squeak from the gate's hinges made them both stand. DeGarn appeared alone, holding a small bag. He approached, a broad smile on his face. "Magistra, Hierophant, here's your purse." He tossed a small bag to Cyrus. It clinked when he caught it. "And here is your journal." He held out the black moleskin book. A loose sheet of paper was tied to it with a single silvery Magnus sentence.

Francesca took the codex and looked at the paper. It did indeed contain her own locator paragraphs. Above them, someone had written, in faint black ink "To Station."

She frowned. Who would bother to send her journal? No doubt the other clerics were hopping mad she'd disappeared from infirmary duty. But they wouldn't send her a book—a furious message perhaps, but not her own clinical journal. Unless perhaps a note were written within the journal?

She tucked the codex under her arm and found DeGarn smiling. "I want to thank both of you again for agreeing to carry our message—"

"There's no need, Magister," Cyrus interrupted while looking up at the roof surrounding the courtyard. "Your allies can see we will treat only with you."

Francesca looked up and felt a small thrill to see thirty or so ravens perched on the gutters. All their heads were pointed at the same angle and moving in unison.

DeGarn nodded. "As you say, Hierophant. Please know that if either you or Nicodemus should require assistance or protection, we will provide it."

"Thank you, Magister," Francesca said. "We shall return with his reply. For now, you will leave us in private and not assign any followers . . ." she looked at the ravens, ". . . of any kind."

"Of course," DeGarn said before bowing first to her and then Cyrus. At last, the old wizard turned and walked from the courtyard. The instant he opened the gate, all the ravens took wing and flew away over the roof.

Francesca waited until it was quiet enough to hear the calls of vendors in the market. "That went rather well."

Cyrus looked at her, and she wondered if he would take her hand again. "Who do you think sent you the book?"

She looked down at the codex. "I'm not sure."

"Aren't you going to open it?"

"I suppose I must." She grabbed hold of the sentence that bound the paper to the journal and was about to break it but her hand paused.

Something seemed . . . off.

"What's wrong?" Cyrus asked.

"I'm not sure. It just . . ."

"Do you want me to open it?"

"No, no." Suddenly she felt foolish. "It's probably nothing." With a pull, she broke the Magnus sentence.

The book flew open and a large, transparent head covered with silvery dreadlocks emerged from the pages. With a shout, Francesca dropped the codex and jumped backward. The book hit ground, its pages flipping past as an ethereal neck, then chest, and then arms spilled out of the book.

Suddenly, Francesca was surrounded by a wall of protective cloth. Cyrus was yelling and all around her wind blasted.

Then she realized that the frayed textual being—now lying on the terracotta tiles and blinking in the sunlight—was Shannon's ghost.

Thirty-four

Deirdre chewed her lip while looking at the loose pages and candle stubs strewn across her desk. Her buildings stood on the eastern side of the sanctuary complex. The rooms were simple but spacious—white walls, Lornish chairs and tables, a four-post feather bed. Outside her door, morning sunlight was drying the night's rain off a few young palms and the gravel path that led toward the dome.

Deirdre's stomach made a croaking protest. She hadn't eaten or slept in far too long. After encountering Nicodemus, she'd spent most of the night mucking around the North Gate District, doing her best to ensure that the watchmen wouldn't find their query. Toward dawn, she'd returned to the sanctuary and reported her failure to Typhon. The demon had listened and then dismissed her. She had asked what his plans were regarding the two academic wizards. Rather than answer, the demon had ordered her not to investigate the matters and sent her away to attend to her duties as his Regent of Spies.

She couldn't disobey the demon directly, not without killing herself again. But she could review reports from her agents in hopes of learning more about the two Astrophell spies. But after a sleepless night at her desk, she had learned little. If a Kestrel had carried black-robes to Avel, then Astrophell and the Spirish Crown had brokered an alliance despite a century of animosity. No doubt Nicodemus's half sister, the Halcyon-in-waiting, was involved. But exactly how was unclear. All reports put her in Ogun, treating with representatives from Starhaven and Starfall Keep, not Spires.

Deirdre was mulling over the situation when the sound of boots on gravel made her look up. Amal Jaen, the clerk, was hurrying toward her. She jumped to her feet and ran to him. "What is it?"

"I-in . . ." he stuttered. "I-i-in . . . h-h-hall . . ." His eyes were wide and bloodshot. She'd never seen him so frightened.

"Is something happening in the Hall of Ambassadors?"

"G-go-governors."

"In the Hall of Governors? It's happening now?"

He nodded and tried to reply. Rather than wait for an answer, Deirdre took off at a dead run. The priests and servants working on the grounds stopped their tasks to watch her dash through courtyards and down walkways.

At last she reached the reflecting pool that stood before the Hall of Governors. She could not yet see anyone but forced herself to a walk. Quickly, she ran her hands through her black hair, attempting to appear appropriate for a diplomatic encounter.

But as she hurried along a path that ran beside the myrtle bushes, she still could not see anyone in the hall. Was she too late? Had the black-robes come and gone? Had Francesca or Nicodemus been captured?

The morning was silent. No voices rang out across the courtyard.

Deirdre ran the last steps into the hall. It seemed empty. The rug, cushions, and braziers had all been removed. She peered into the deep corners to see if someone was talking in the shadows but saw nothing but darkness.

Her breath coming faster, she looked back out onto the courtyard but saw only the reflecting pool. She licked her lips and tried to think clearly. Perhaps Amal hadn't meant the Hall of Governors. Should she run back to find him? Or perhaps she should find Typhon and . . .

She stumbled to her left.

She struggled to keep her balance and found it difficult until she looked at the floor.

Suddenly she understood, and terror bloomed in her mind. Amal had not been stuttering; he had been made into a devotee. When she had looked into the back of the hall, she hadn't seen nothing but shadows. She hadn't seen at all.

She tried to yell or even simply think the creature's true name, but in the next instant her skin went numb, her eyes blind.

CYRUS UNWOUND HIS turban and rubbed his temples. He and Francesca had taken a private room in the tavern. Presently, Francesca was sitting next to him on a cushion and staring at something he could not see.

Francesca had explained that the invisible something was Shannon's ghost, who had woken in a hierophantic library and found a note claiming his author had been murdered. She had described the other aspects of the ghost's story between bouts of arguing with him.

"You're sure the note read 'our memories are in her' and nothing else?" Francesca asked. She held out her hand, reading a sentence from the ghost. "Yes, but how could memories be stored in me?" Another pause. "I know the other note told you to find me. You told me that already." Pause. She read another sentence. "No!" Pause. "As I said, Nicodemus only said that my Language Prime shines brighter. How could Language Prime hold your memories?" She read another sentence. "Of course I'm sure I don't have any of your memories. God-of-gods! Memories of being a blind, parrot-loving, cranky old man isn't something I'd forget! Burning hells, peeing while standing up would be memorable enough—"

"Francesca," Cyrus tried to interrupt. She ignored him.

From what Cyrus had heard, the ghost was dim and fraying around the edges. Apparently the poor construct was almost frantic to reunite with his author and his insistent tone was agitating Francesca. Again Cyrus tried to calmly interrupt, "Francesca, Shannon."

She ignored him. "No, I think you're right about that," she said to the ghost. "I agree: 'our memories are in her' is probably incomplete. Sure. The blood could have obscured a letter to make it, 'Your memories are in her,' but that still doesn't make a snap of sense. What else can you tell me about—"

"Francesca!" Cyrus said loud enough to interrupt. He looked at her and then where he guessed the ghost to be. "Shannon." He paused. "You've been at this for an hour, and it's going nowhere."

Francesca looked at him for a moment. Then she plucked something out of the air. "No, not always. But he gets fussy when people aren't paying attention to him."

"So will you pay attention to me now?" Cyrus growled.

"I'm listening." She read another sentence. "We're listening." She smiled innocently.

Cyrus exhaled. "We're not going to discover who separated ghost from wizard here and now. We don't have any proof. However, the ghost might be a form of proof by himself."

Francesca lowered her eyebrows. "Proof of what?"

"That some force within the sanctuary is hostile to Shannon and Nicodemus. Someone who can see the ghost might be convinced that the sanctuary and Nicodemus are not allies but enemies."

Francesca wrinkled her short nose. "Cyrus, who in all the hells would care about th . . ." Her voice died off. "Oh . . . right," she said while looking at the empty cushion next to her. "Them."

BLIND, NUMB, AND deaf, Deirdre tried to yell or simply remember the Savanna Walker's true name, but the beast must have muffled her voice and damaged her memory. She tried to thrash, but without sensation she couldn't know if her blows were landing or even if her limbs were moving. Perhaps the beast was killing her.

Moving a limb was nothing Deirdre had ever had to think about. Now it was all she could think about. She focused her every desire on resisting, on escaping the nothingness in which the Savanna Walker had trapped her. But her sense of time was gone. How long had she been struggling? Moments or hours?

Fear closed around her mind. Again and again she reached out for perception—the lightest touch, the faintest smell—but there was nothing. Her mind was floating in . . . absence. It was the most horrible of prison-houses.

She searched again for sensation. Nothing.

Searched again. Nothing.

Nothing.

Nothing.

Time passed. Or maybe it did not.

She couldn't tell.

Perhaps the beast had killed her. Perhaps this was one of the flameless hells that housed the less wicked souls. Was this a punishment, to be for-ever alone with her memories and regrets?

She thought of her life long ago in Highland, the husband her family had chosen for her and whom she had left to serve Boann. She thought of her two sons. She had never known them. They would be old and gray by now, possibly dead. She wondered if she had grandchildren or even great grandchildren. She remembered Kyran, her old lover, with whom she had betrayed Boann's trust, and whom she had led to his death in Starhaven.

Perhaps this was a flameless hell.

Something flashed before her, blurry, blue, vaguely round. Then it was gone.

It took her a moment to realize that she'd just seen a glimpse of sky through a horseshoe arch.

She wasn't dead. She thought about the present situation. The Savanna Walker had corrupted Amal's mind, made him into a devotee. She had mistaken his aphasia for a simple stutter and run into a trap. The Walker's cunning wasn't surprising, but his power was. After she had thrown him from the dome, the beast should have been weak. Typhon should have limited the beast's freedom so that it could not attack her.

The vision of blurry blue returned and this time did not fade. Slowly the image came into focus. She was indeed looking up through an arch at sky streaked with thin, wispy clouds. There was no sound, smell, touch, temperature.

She tried to sit up but could barely lift her head. The Walker had nearly paralyzed her. Her head fell back.

Only Typhon could have enabled the Savanna Walker to move this fast and this freely. But why? Had the demon discovered that she'd been deceiving him?

That didn't seem likely. If the demon knew she had been dissembling, she would now be dead. No, this had to be the Savanna Walker's doing. The beast couldn't kill her. Or rather, if he did, he'd be compelled to recapture her once the demon's soul revitalized her.

Deirdre tried to sit up again. This time her arms moved. It was a bizarre sensation since she could feel neither texture nor warmth nor coolness. She rolled over and looked out on the reflecting pool and myrtle bushes.

Why would Typhon give the Savanna Walker so much strength without warning her? She pushed herself up, but her legs still flopped uselessly.

Then, suddenly, she realized why the demon had empowered the Savanna Walker. Typhon always used the best tool at hand. And now in Avel, there were two hostile authors possessing special powers. What better tool to eliminate them than aphasia?

But why had the beast struck first against Deirdre? She had no objections to the beast's eliminating the foreign authors. Deirdre would have interfered only if the Walker were going to attack . . .

Deirdre's arms faltered and her face struck the floor. She felt no pain, only a jolt of motion. But fear was throbbing through her body. She knew why the Savanna Walker had left her paralyzed, and she had to stop him. But how could she stop the creature when she couldn't even stand? What was more, Typhon had compelled her not to interfere; even if she could go charging after the beast, she would suffer a fit of spasms the moment she attacked.

Perhaps one of her agents could act for her. She tried to call out. Though deaf, she could feel her voice in her throat. She yelled and yelled, but no one came. She was being foolish. The beast was not stupid. If he had planned her paralysis, he would have ensured no one would come near this hall.

She looked around the courtyard for a way to stop the beast. But there was only sunlight on green leaves and still water.

Deirdre tried to turn herself around to see if there was something within the hall that might help her. But as she began to roll over, she stopped and looked back at the reflecting pool.

Realizing what she had to do, Deirdre began to drag herself forward.

Thirty-five

"I believe everything you said," Francesca said to Vivian, "except for the things you lied about. Those things I don't believe at all."

Vivian smiled tightly. "Francesca, I can't discern if you're a brilliant negotiator or a blathering idiot."

"Huh," Francesca answered thoughtfully. "Those statements might not be mutually exclusive."

Both women were sitting on cushions in a private room on the third story of a Holy District tavern known as the Silver Palm. Vivian and Lotannu had rented rooms on the floor below. Bright sunlight poured through the wide, open windows. Somewhere nearby a priest with a powerful voice was singing devotions to Cala.

Cyrus sat at Francesca's right. His green veil was up, his turban tightly wound, and a packed lofting kite was strapped to his back. He had insisted on carrying a good deal of cloth into this meeting.

Beside Vivian, Lotannu sat dressed in his fine Verdantine clothes and wearing an expression of calm focus.

Francesca continued. "It's the lies of omission that make you seem both manipulative and academic. But I repeat myself."

Vivian sighed, her white eyes looking down toward the floor. "And what did I omit?"

"The Halcyon, the Storm Petrel, the demon, and—oh yes—the League of Starfall and the impending schism of the bloody Numinous Order of Civil blasted Wizardry."

Vivian's usually imperturbable expression tensed. Lotannu shifted. Francesca couldn't help but smile. She glanced over at Cyrus, but he was frowning out the window.

"The separatists are in Avel?" Vivian asked.

Francesca nodded. "And they are rather keen on speaking to Nicodemus, which is interesting because we had a bit of a run-in with the cacographic fruitcake last night. Strangest thing, he wouldn't shut up about a God-of-gods damned demon he thinks has usurped this city. Which, if you had known to be true, is perhaps something you should have mentioned before setting us loose in this city."

"You spoke to Nicodemus?" Vivian asked.

"We did."

"And he trusts you?"

"As much as one might after a first impression involving hatchets."

"Magistra," Vivian said. "You are in a position to prevent bloodshed if you help Astrophell keep the rebels from—"

"Let's forgo the how-to-help-your-faction-continue-to-rule-the-inhabited-world section of this conversation," Francesca interrupted, "and go back to the blasted demon usurping Avel."

Lotannu touched Vivian's arm. "The contingency plan is still—"

Vivian held up a thin hand to stop him. "Francesca, I might now accuse you of omission. Let's have your complete story."

"All right," Francesca said and readjusted her backside on the cushion. She described almost everything that had happened to her, starting with Deirdre dying on her table. She obscured only where she was to meet Nicodemus and anything that might implicate DeGarn as the agent of the League of Starfall. Despite this, Vivian asked a few pointed questions about the wizards of the colaboris station. Francesca sidestepped the questions and continued her story.

When Francesca finished, Lotannu folded his hands in his lap and calmly asked, "And you believe Nicodemus Weal, the boy who killed all those wizards back in Starhaven? How do you know he isn't aligned with the demon?"

Cyrus answered: "We have a text that might convince you otherwise."

Francesca picked up her clinical journal from the floor. "Don't be alarmed," she said before opening the book. As before, the covers sprung open with a flutter of pages. Shannon's one-armed ghost fell onto the floor. The construct was less frayed than before but still very dim. Francesca guessed he could exist outside a book for only one more day before he deconstructed.

Pale as the ghost was, Vivian's all-white eyes, able to see Numinous text, locked onto him. She jumped to her feet like a woman a quarter of her age. A profusion of gold and silver sentences burst from her arms and legs. The resulting blaze was so bright Francesca had to look away. "Fiery blasted heaven!" Francesca swore. "He's not hostile, damn it!"

When she peered back, Vivian was still on her feet and shining so luminously that Francesca could still not look directly at her. It was as if a small star were standing on the cushion a few feet away from her. Cyrus moaned.

His synesthesic reaction was nausea; around this much wizardly text, the poor man might vomit.

"Vivian!" Francesca said, "Los damn it, but knock it off with the war-texts."

The painful incandescence dimmed, and Francesca looked back to see the ancient woman standing, a few sentences still twining around her arms. She was staring sternly at Shannon's ghost. The dim text himself stared back at her, his ghostly dreadlocks pulled back, his expression composed and dignified.

Francesca felt her cheeks flush as she realized how foolish she must have looked when flinching. This embarrassment faded but was followed by a pang of envy. Judging by how much text Vivian had just extemporized, she was the most prolific spellwright Francesca had ever seen. Indeed, Francesca hadn't known that a body could produce so much text. The ancient woman was more talented that Francesca would ever be.

As before, Francesca's sudden surge of envy felt strangely foreign, as if they were someone else's emotions she were feeling.

In the next moment, Francesca chastised herself for indulging in such envy and self-pity. She had to be more secure. She was a physician, perhaps not a master physician, but comparing herself with other women this way was childish.

She looked at Vivian. "This is the ghost of Magister Agwu Shannon, Nicodemus . . ." Her voice trailed off. Vivian had wasted no time speaking to the ghost but had cast to him a thick golden passage. With inhuman speed, the ghost read the message and cast an equally thick response. Vivian caught and read the spell faster than Francesca had thought possible.

Then ghost and old woman were engaged in a rapid correspondence. Mostly the words moved too fast for Francesca to read, but she caught enough to know the ghost was explaining to Vivian everything he had explained to her.

Another pang of envy filled Francesca's heart. Perhaps if she had talent like Vivian, she wouldn't have been placed for medical training in the backwater of Avel. Then, for a second time, she told herself that such a comparison was childish, but . . .

She bit her lip.

There was an emptiness in her chest. It had been there since she had first come to Avel. The needs of patients were so great, and her talents so limited. Compared with the physician she wanted to be, she was . . . insufficient.

She looked at Cyrus, who was again staring out the window. Cyrus had never understood about her hollowness. He'd always been comfortable with his successes. He pursued his dream of becoming an airship captain, not to quell any insecurity, but simply because of a love of soaring. She envied him that, even though it sometimes made him seem complacent. Cyrus was the steadier of the two of them. Perhaps that was why, at some level, Francesca felt that he never understood her.

Just then Cyrus stood and walked over to the window. Both Vivian and Lotannu were too engaged with the ghost to notice. Francesca went to Cyrus. "What's the matter?" she whispered.

His eyes were scanning the sky. "I saw a pilot flying patrol when we came in here. That's to be expected after last night. But just now, I thought . . . I'm not sure, but I think I saw a warkite overhead."

"One of your military constructs?"

"Since the Civil War, 'military' isn't the right word for them. They're more like aerial guards against hierophantic attack. Mostly they're written to shred the canopies of hostile pilots."

Francesca found herself leaning closer to Cyrus. Only an hour or so ago, he'd taken her hand. In a way, she didn't want him to do so again. But . . .

She touched his elbow. "Why would a warkite fly here?"

He looked at her—wide, light brown eyes between folds of green cloth. Francesca took her hand away, suddenly regretting the touch.

"I'm not sure," he said. "I'm not even sure it was a warkite."

"Magistra," Vivian said behind them. Francesca turned around. "The ghost thinks his memories are stored in you."

She rolled her eyes. "Yes, he found a note that read 'our memories are in her' and so thinks I'm somehow hiding some part of his mind."

"Hiding it in your Language Prime text, nonetheless," Vivian added. "Quite a blasphemy."

"I don't have his blasted memories," Francesca said.

The ghost began to write something, but then Vivian held up her hand. "Why did you bring him to me?"

Francesca adjusted her long braid so it hung behind her. "I'd hoped he'd provide some evidence that Nicodemus and the demon are not aligned."

"He's convinced you of this?"

She studied the older woman's face. Her blind eyes were directed somewhere to the right of Francesca. "In combination with my encounters with Nicodemus and Deirdre, yes he has. Tonight, I will meet with Nicodemus. I want to offer him your alliance against the demon."

Vivian became still. Lotannu looked at her. "In light of . . ." Vivian started to say. Lotannu leaned in as if to whisper, but she continued speaking. "In light of what we have discovered, I will come with you to meet Nicodemus."

Francesca shook her head. "He won't appear if you're with me." She spoke slowly; she hadn't expected Vivian to agree so quickly. Something was wrong.

Now Lotannu did lean in, but instead of whispering, he placed a paragraph in Vivian's hand. She read it and handed another paragraph back. "Francesca, I cannot let you go."

"I'm sorry?" Francesca asked.

"The ghost may unwittingly be Typhon's agent. If he has convinced you, then he may have made you the demon's agent as well."

With a quick backhand motion, the ghost cast a spell that broke into three sentences: one floated to Vivian, another to Lotannu, the last to Francesca. She translated it, *"I might not know who edited me, but I am no servant of the Disjunction."*

Vivian's expression softened. "Ghost, you don't know what you are. To win my trust, we must retrieve your memories."

"For the last time," Francesca exclaimed, "I do not have his memories hidden in—"

"Magistra," Vivian interrupted, "the memories are not in you or any woman."

Everyone looked at Vivian. Then Shannon cast out three copies of a question: *"They're not?"*

Vivian turned to the ghost. "The note you read, it had the words 'our memories are in her' flanked by bloodstains?"

The ghost nodded.

"And because there was no capitalization or punctuation, you assumed some mark was obscured?"

Again the ghost nodded.

Francesca spoke. "He guessed the first letter was obscured so it should have read 'Your memories are in her.'"

Vivian seemed to ignore this. "And this note was on a book?"

The ghost nodded for a third time.

"Then we have to go into the sanctuary and find that library."

"But the demon is in there."

Vivian shrugged. "It doesn't matter."

Francesca turned to Lotannu and said, "So you know she's out of her mind, right?"

Vivian spoke louder. "The ghost's memories are written in the book that the note was resting on."

"And how the blasted hell do you know that?" Francesca asked.

"You were so preoccupied with the obscured first letter that you forgot about the last."

Francesca frowned until she realized what she meant. "It's not 'your memories are in her' but 'your memories are in here.'"

The ghost wrote a quick sentence. *"But who would keep my memories in a book but cast me?"*

Suddenly it made complete sense to Francesca. "Someone who isn't a spellwright," she said. "Deirdre told me, when we were in the kite and she was fighting off a seizure, that she'd sent someone to help but that she wasn't sure if it had worked. It hadn't made any sense at the time."

Lotannu was frowning at her. "But how could Deirdre have gotten to the library?"

"She'd been brought in from the lycanthrope attack bleeding and with the curse on her lungs. She wasn't in a dangerous condition until I tried to disspell that curse and it moved to her heart. With the curse only on her lungs, she could have slipped away to the hierophantic library. She would have been short of breath and bleeding, but she could have done it. She must have known which books you and your memories had been stored in but not how to cast them into you."

Vivian was adjusting her long white hair. "Whatever the case, we must get back into that library and—"

"Everyone get back!" Cyrus cried as he jumped away from the window. Automatically, Lotannu and Vivian obeyed, but Francesca only frowned at the man until he grabbed her arm and yanked her farther into the room.

"What?" she whispered.

"Three lofting kites circling above the building. They're in formation. They'd only be doing that if they were about to strike."

"Ghost, get back into the book," Vivian ordered. "The rest of you protect yourselves. Lotannu and I can handle any attack."

Shannon's ghost wasted no time jumping into the journal that lay open on the floor. Cyrus pulled Francesca toward the door that led to the hallway. She started to protest but then stopped. She'd heard something strange. "Quiet!" she barked. If only because of her sharp tone, everyone obeyed.

In the silence she could hear it more clearly, the distant priest singing; his devotional song had become unintelligible gibberish.

"Aphasia," Francesca whispered. "We have to go now!"

"No, we stay," Vivian calmly said while picking up the journal. "You are referring to Typhon's half dragon?"

Francesca shook her head. "You don't understand what a dragon can be! That creature would destroy your capacity for language."

Vivian only smiled. "Lotannu, please construct whatever texts you need to see quaternary thoughts."

"Vivian, I can't seem to . . . It's just that . . . only . . ." Lotannu answered while staring at his hands. "There's a word that means . . . means . . ."

Francesca grabbed Cyrus with one hand and opened the door with the other. "Run!" she commanded while pulling him into the hallway. Lotannu yelled something; she didn't care what.

The hallway was a narrow space, sandstone walls leaning close on either side. Beside her Cyrus tried to speak but produced only meaningless sounds.

"God-of-gods, save us!" Francesca swore. The floor shook and orange flecks swam through Francesca's vision. She ran down the hall, trying each door they passed. All were locked.

Suddenly, Cyrus grunted. She looked back to see him kick open one door. Peering inside the room, Francesca saw a plain carpet and sleeping pallet, white walls, and a wide rectangular window. The ground shook again.

Francesca ran though the room and climbed into the window. Her vision was clearing, so she saw with perfect clarity a swirling white cloth and flashing steel talons. "Creator!"

The warkite was flying not twenty feet from the window, moving back and forth like a serpent about to strike.

Francesca tried to back out of the window, but Cyrus's hands stopped her. "Kite!" she blurted.

"It's not . . . closer for . . . a reason," he said with effort and then pointed down. Six feet or so below them hung a roof to the stables. "Jump."

"It's too steep. I won't be able to—"

Cyrus pushed her out the window.

Screaming, she fell the six feet to land awkwardly on her feet and then onto her side. As she had feared, she began to slide down the redwood shingles. A crash sounded behind her. A hand grabbed her arm, and her robes stiffened. She screamed louder as she and Cyrus slid over the roof's edge.

Then they were in the open air, the muddy alleyway rushing up toward them. All around her blasted a violent torrent of wind. Then she was falling upward. Above her spread the green expanse of a billowing jumpchute.

Her black robes had woven themselves into Cyrus's green ones. A radial web of suspension lines rose up to the chute. One side of the chute went limp, and they lurched toward the inn.

Swearing, Cyrus worked his hands along the lines. An instant later the chute reshaped itself to pull them away from the tavern. "The text misspells near the Walker," Cyrus yelled. "That's why the warkite is staying back. When we enfold the construct, keep away from its talons."

"When we do what?"

Just then the warkite struck their chute. Cyrus cast some spell, and the suspension lines began to coil around themselves. Above them the warkite's talons cut through the canopy with loud ripping. The coiling suspension lines pulled Cyrus and Francesca up toward the construct.

Francesca had just enough time to scream again before they struck the chaos of cloth and steel. She tried to cover her face, but her sleeves had become stiff while the cloth around her legs flowed like silk.

The world seemed made of sailcloth until a part in the folds revealed the ground. They were again falling toward the stable roof. Something hard and sharp pressed against Francesca's thigh. Cyrus shouted and the brutal cloth vanished. They were dangling in midair. A green canopy now containing strips of white cloth billowed above them.

Cyrus hung beside her, his left shoulder dark with blood, both his hands working fast on the suspension lines.

Within moments they had flown high enough to see across the wide city. They were heading northeast, with the wind and out toward the Palm District

"The enfoldment cut much of my text," Cyrus yelled. "We're going to have to race them to Spillwind's Hope."

Francesca remembered Spillwind's Hope was the ridge lift, but otherwise his words made no sense. "Race whom?"

"The wing behind us."

Francesca turned and saw three kites, two yellow and one black, rising up from the city and heading straight for them. Then she saw the snaking motion of two white warkites. The streamerlike constructs were rising with shocking speed. "Cyrus, can we outfly a warkite?"

He glanced back. "Hell! We might have to make a crash landing in one of the . . ." His voice died as it became apparent one of the warkites was going to reach them in only a few moments. With a flurry of movement, Cyrus worked on the suspension lines.

The jumpchute changed shape and stooped into a dive. Below them stretched the maze of sandstone buildings that made up the Palm District. The thick perimeter wall was less than a mile away. Green savanna lay beyond.

Cyrus looked back. When Francesca also did, she sucked in a sharp breath. The warkite flew only tens of feet away. They banked hard right and then rose into a climb.

The warkite shot past Francesca and snaked up to the canopy. Cyrus again coiled the suspension lines, and again Francesca found herself flying up into a canopy that was being attacked by a warkite. This time she curled into a ball before they struck. Again she was battered by the folds of cloth. Again they began to fall. But this time, Cyrus did not call out. She felt a flash of fear and then a strange sense of detachment. They had been falling too long and were going to smash against some tiled courtyard any moment now.

At last the cloth left her and a reformed canopy spread above them, pulling hard up. They were only twenty feet or so above a watchtower on the perimeter wall. Francesca could make out several men in chain mail staring up at them.

Their rig was rising again. "Are we going to make it?" she yelled, looking over at Cyrus.

His turban and veil had been torn free, and his black curls fluttered in the wind. Before he could respond, another warkite struck the canopy and set the world spinning.

Cyrus moved his hands, and the suspension ropes twisted, but this time they shortened only slowly. Cyrus wasn't going to reach the warkite before the construct tore the canopy into fluttering rags.

Francesca looked down and saw to her horror that they had drifted over the wall and were now falling toward the savanna. As the chute spun, her view swung around so that she looked out over the grass sea. Maybe half a mile away and moving fast were two dozen waves of grass. Running lycanthropes made such waves. The beasts were headed straight for where she and Cyrus were about to crash.

Just before they struck the grass, Cyrus did something that made the ruined canopy exert the last of its wind. Their descent slowed, and the grass stalk that stabbed Francesca in the hip sent mere pain—rather than its stiff shaft—lancing through her abdomen.

Then Cyrus and Francesca fell the last five or so feet among the stalks to hit the moist ground. Impact knocked the wits out of Francesca. For a moment she lay, looking up at the slivers of blue sky amid the waving grass.

Cyrus was standing above her, yelling something about lycanthropes. Then she was on her feet, grasping his hand and trying to follow him as he struggled against the grass. "We have to get back to the wall before they come!" he called.

But the grass was pressing hard against Francesca, and she could not find stable footing.

She fell.

Cyrus was above her again, pulling her back onto her feet. But in doing so, he fell.

Something massive moved through the grass near them. Cyrus somehow stood. A guttural, inhuman voice called out.

"Cyrus!" Francesca yelled as he tried to pull her forward. Her ankle turned and she fell again.

"Cyrus!" she called out, but then something exploded through the grass. The air was filled with splintered stalks and clods of dirt.

Then the sky shone above her, first painfully bright, then completely black.

Vivian's palms went cold as she listened to Lotannu try to speak. "Can't . . . the words."

She moved toward his voice. "Come here. I can't get these texts off my eyes fast enough. Let me look through yours."

Vivian soon encountered Lotannu's hand. After initiating the textual protocol, she was looking through his sharp eyes. For the first time, she saw the private dining room—an ornate white-and-black rug, a nest of embroidered pillows.

Lotannu tried to speak again but produced only a slew of syllables. He squeezed her hand. She squeezed it back. "It's all right, my friend. I've trained all my life for this."

Francesca and Cyrus must have fled. Likely they would be caught by the half dragon. Or perhaps they would escape. Either way, once Vivian dealt with the wyrm, they would return more interested in joining her cause.

The floor shook. A moment later, chaotic wailing sounded, followed by footsteps. Someone cried out. Francesca had mentioned that the Savanna Walker attacked with his devotees. Vivian supposed that a few of these were now at hand.

Sure enough, the door burst open to reveal two men in ragged Spirish longvests. Each held two short swords in the dual-wielding Spirish style. Vivian was as gentle as possible, casting a net of Numinous around each man's head. They fell unconscious to the floor.

But to Vivian's surprise the prose she had cast began to decay, an effect of the half dragon. Soon the spells would deconstruct, and the men would awaken.

Vivian frowned. She had thought her prose was cogent enough to resist the half dragon. She refreshed the stunning spell and added Magnus bindings to the devotees' hands and feet.

Another yelling devotee appeared in the doorway, this one with a spear. She hit him with both restricting and stunning spells, and he went down.

The floor shook harder now. It wouldn't be long. Lotannu relaxed his grip on her hand and looked at her. For the first time in what felt like ages, Vivian saw herself. It was disorienting. Her snowy hair and all-white eyes made her seem impossibly old.

The ground shook hard enough to make Lotannu stagger. He looked at the doorway. What Vivian saw shocked her so much that she accidentally jerked her hand away from Lotannu's and was dropped back into her all-but-textual blindness. Lotannu gasped. She grabbed his hand and again saw the seething, amorphous mass of gray skin and limbs. Among these was a human face with bright green eyes that looked exactly like her dead mother's eyes.

Suddenly Vivian felt a surreal certainty that these eyes did not merely look like her mother's eyes; they were her mother's eyes. Her heart began to flutter; the half dragon was a creature beyond anything she had yet imagined. It took every bit of her self-discipline to force down the growing panic. Lotannu started to look away, but she gripped his hand. "Look straight at him."

". . . can't . . . blind . . ." Lotannu answered between meaningless syllables. "Dizzy."

"I can see him," she answered. "Look straight at him."

The half dragon was staring at them with her mother's green eyes. With every ounce of her strength, Vivian forged powerful Numinous and Magnus paragraphs. In a heartbeat, she wove the two languages into a hybrid wartext, a tirade of razor-sharp language.

With a quick backhand throw, she cast the spell at the beast. It shot forward like a lightning bolt of incandescent silver and gold. In a gray blur of speed, the beast withdrew into the hallway like some sea creature retracting into its shell.

The light dimmed. Vivian turned her head toward the window but with her blind eyes saw no text. "Lotannu, the window." He turned and her breath caught.

Bulging arachnoid appendages of gray flesh crisscrossed the window like a nightmare. Vivian's head swam with confusion. How had the half dragon gotten outside a third-story window so quickly?

She cast a second blast at the many-jointed limbs. Her lightning-like sentences cut through several appendages, leaving them squirming on the floor. But then Lotannu looked back at the doorway and saw the phantasmagoria of gray skin and limbs oozing back into the room.

A whirl of vertigo wrapped around Vivian as she realized that the half dragon wasn't moving between the window and the door; it was in both places. The creature's size was staggering; it enveloped half the building.

She cast another spell at the flesh sliding into the doorway. But when her text struck it, the sentences misspelled and fell to pieces. The monster's face amid the gray limbs was chanting something, but Vivian couldn't hear what. Then, with growing terror, she realized that she couldn't hear anything at all.

She'd gone deaf.

Vivian had made a grave error—this creature negated her power in a way she had not thought possible. In her pride, she had outmatched herself.

The room darkened as the limbs with impossibly many joints filled the windows. Vivian tried to scream, but part of the beast shot from the door. She barely had time to turn away before the gray flesh knocked her to the floor.

She lost hold of Lotannu's hand and was blind again. Some unbearable force pushed her down. Pain and terror exploded through her mind. She had the sensation that something was about to be torn out of her.

But then the force stopped moving. Everything became still. Suddenly the weight vanished and she was gasping. Tears streamed down her face.

A hand found hers, and she was looking through Lotannu's eyes at herself bawling like a child. The room was full of light. A breeze whispered at the window. She and Lotannu struggled to their feet.

"I'm sorry," she blurted between sobs. "I'm sorry. I'm sorry. I was wrong. I didn't know what it was."

Lotannu shook his head. "The . . . thing . . ." he said. "It left . . . not . . . made it do that . . ."

But it didn't matter what had compelled the creature to spare them. All that mattered was that they were still breathing.

Lotannu picked up the book that held Shannon's ghost, and they ran down the stairs of the inn. They stepped over men who had been crushed to death and hurried out into a street filled with hot afternoon sunshine.

DEIRDRE CONVULSED BACK into life in the still green water. She had never drowned herself before; with the restrictions Typhon had placed on her mind, she never would have been able to stay underwater long enough to die. It was only the partial paralysis that allowed her to do so this time.

Reflexively she tried to inhale and discovered her chest was full of water. The reflecting pool was only four feet deep, so she stood and began coughing water out of her lungs.

Sunlight poured down out of the blue sky, but Deirdre shivered as she waded to the pool's edge and climbed onto the garden's path.

Somewhere in the city, the Savanna Walker would be compelled to turn away from whatever he was doing and come to repossess her for Typhon.

The demon must have sent the Savanna Walker to kill the Astrophell wizards. He had not wanted her to interfere and so gave the Walker the power to paralyze her. Deirdre couldn't have cared less about the Astrophell spies; she had drowned herself to stop the Walker from hunting down Francesca after he dealt with the wizards.

But now Deirdre had played her last move. After this suicide, Typhon would search all her memories and discover how she had liberated Francesca and Shannon's ghost.

A breeze picked up and chilled her skin even further.

Deirdre turned and looked back at the reflecting pool. On its glassy surface she could see a mirror image of the sanctuary's dome, the tall slender palm trees, the limpid Spirish sky. So strange that this is where she should find an end. She thought of her native highlands, the long verdant glens, the constant gray skies, flowers in spring, winter mountains dusted with snow.

Now, between her revival and repossession, she was free. For a brief period, she was again mortal. She could die, and Typhon could not retrieve her.

She thought again of her lost sons and her unknown grandchildren. She thought of Nicodemus and Shannon and Francesca, all of them striving with quests and grand ideas. Deirdre had never been like them; she had only loved her goddess, her one true love. Her Boann.

She remembered her deity, the way Boann would touch her cheek, how childish the river goddess could be, how some nights the young goddess had taken her out in the highlands, how they had slept beside fern-lined waterfalls, how the young goddess had nearly curled up in her arms.

Deirdre was shivering. Her last moments in the sun and she was shivering. The wind picked up, and she could hear it rushing through a nearby palm.

Boann was a river goddess. Her home was among the secluded creeks and falls, so far away now. In this savanna city there were only reservoirs and pools.

Deirdre had to protect Boann, had to keep the memories of Francesca and Shannon's ghost away from Typhon. She stepped back into the pool. No time to delay, no time to admire this world. The Walker would come soon. She lowered herself. The wind calmed. It was silent again.

Deirdre took one last look at the world of burnished light and blue sky. Then she sank into the dark green water, the last thing she would know.

NICODEMUS WOKE TO screaming.

He was lying under a wool blanket, staring at the slanted cabin ceiling. It took a moment to remember he was in the redwood camp with his students.

The screaming came again, high and ragged. He rushed for the door. Jasp, who had been sleeping on a nearby cot, was struggling to his feet.

Outside, Nicodemus looked around his camp: seven cabins beneath the forest's tallest trees. Here the shade was so complete that, even at midday, Chthonic spells could briefly function. The ground under Nicodemus's toes was wet from rain and ruddy from centuries of decaying redwood bark. The air had a sweet, fermented scent.

Nicodemus scanned the surroundings but discovered only trunks, branches, and a few bushes. Using his ability to see Language Prime, he could make out a pine martin scrambling through the nearby branches. Through the cabin walls, he could see his students rousing from sleep. But nowhere did he see the massive, sleek shapes of the lycanthropes. Nor did he see any of the Walker's many forms.

He saw no threat at all.

Then she stumbled in front of him and fell onto her side. The long frothing currents of her hair were splayed into a ragged white corona. Her face was twisted into a sharp, inhuman mask of pain. As he watched, her eyes melted and trickled down her face. Her dark green robes had broken into seaweed strips. Her body, once an idealization of youth, was now slack. The skin on her ribs sagged to reveal the rows of bones. Her breasts hung flat against her concave belly.

Shocked, Nicodemus could only stare—unable to look away. Finally he whispered, "Boann?"

The goddess snapped back into the beautiful youth she had been and ran to Nicodemus. Wailing, she looked up into his face like a child who had hurt herself so badly that she could not stop the tears or the instinctive panic that follows a first intimation of mortality. It was an expression so earnest, so human that Nicodemus forgot she was a deity and opened his arms as if she were a child.

She ran to him, and he tried to gather her up into an embrace. But her waist became viscous. Nightmarelike, she oozed out of his arms and fell to the ground in two pieces. Her hair dissolved. Her eyes melted out of her sockets. "Dead!" her mouth moaned. "She's dead for all time!" Then she jammed her fingers into the soil. Her shoulders broke apart. Her head wrinkled like a winter apple and then melted. Slowly the rest of her seeped into the dirt.

"Fiery heaven!" Nicodemus whispered in shock and stepped back. "Creator save us!"

The goddess was gone.

"It's Deirdre," someone said.

Nicodemus looked up and saw Magister Shannon. He and all the kobolds had emerged from their cabins. Suddenly Nicodemus understood. "Deirdre has died?"

Shannon put his hand up to touch Azure on his shoulder. "Nothing else would have done this to Boann."

Nicodemus looked at the ground. "Is she . . . is Boann dead as well then?"

Shannon walked to Nicodemus. "Her ark seemed unchanged." He gestured to the unremarkable rock sitting in the middle of the camp. "But I don't know."

Nicodemus looked at his teacher's gaunt face. The contours of his skull had become prominent around the temples. "Deirdre's dead," Nicodemus heard himself say. He was suddenly, absurdly terrified that Shannon was going to die. It was a hard and strange pain, almost like nausea. Shannon might not die in a day or even a year. But his mentor was going to die far too soon, and far too soon Nicodemus would join him.

Then something in Nicodemus seemed to fracture or split. He felt first embarrassed and then almost numb. He ordered Dross, Slag, and Flint to search around the camp and then sent Jasp up a nearby promontory where he could look out onto the reservoir and the city beyond. Vein he ordered back to bed.

Shannon invited Nicodemus into his cabin. The old man had a fire going and set to boiling water. Nicodemus sat on his sleeping cot and watched the flames. Neither of them spoke. A quarter hour later the cries of Jasp made both men hurry outside. The young kobold came running down from the promontory yelling about lofting kites flying over the city. One kite had crashed into the savanna, where the lycanthropes had been waiting.

Thirty-seven

Before anything else, Francesca became aware of the hot, musty air. It pressed down on her skin and dragged in her throat and lungs. She opened her eyes and found it difficult to understand what she was seeing. A faint light shone from far away. Something massive moved near her. Above her loomed a face, snouted and furry, with eyes like black plums.

She stared at it without comprehension. The creature drew in a sniff so voluminous it made her loose hair dance. She put her head back down. The ground spun. She remembered running through the grass and then some kind of explosion.

The creature sniffed her again and then withdrew into the dark. Francesca closed her eyes. Somewhere a man was talking. The voice seemed familiar. The ground continued to spin . . .

Flickering dreams: swimming in Port Mercy Harbor, the stink of a gangrenous foot, suturing an eyebrow laceration, the thrum of distant guitar music . . .

"Well, isn't this just a heartwarming little scene?"

Francesca woke. "What happened? What patient?" she asked automatically.

Someone laughed. "You and Windbag, I guess. You're cuddling cute as puppies in a basket while the city's in chaos, thanks to you. But never you mind about people dying. You want me to get a blanket? Pillows maybe, hmmm?"

"Luro?" she asked, recognizing the voice. She sat up. "What's happened? Where are we?" She could make out the old man's diminutive form. "And, Los in hell, but why are you here?"

"Not because I want to be. Trust me; I'd hoped never to have to return to this homestead. But you made a hot hash out of that."

Francesca tried to forge a flamefly spell but found that no golden text formed in her arms. "I'm censored," she realized with shock. "I can't—" she started to touch her head to search for a censoring text. But as she did so, the massive unseen creature moved beside her.

"Don't," Luro commanded. "No mumbo jumbo. It was enough of a pain to keep them from eating you when you were as floppy as dead fish. Toss around some magic and you'll get intimate with a lycanthrope belly."

Francesca lowered her hand. "We're in a lycanthrope den?"

"Something like that."

"And you talk with the beasts?" She asked. "Or are you a lycanthrope?" She laughed. "You got enough hair growing out of your ears to be at least part lupine."

The old man cleared his throat.

"YOU'RE A GOD-OF-GODS DAMNED LYCANTHROPE?"

The unseen creature growled so low that it made Francesca's chest vibrate as if it were the skin of a drum. Beside her a man moaned. It sounded like Cyrus.

"All right, physician, calm down," Luro grumbled. "No, I'm not a proper lycanthrope. I never fully changed the second time."

"When did you change the first God-of-gods damned time?"

Cyrus grabbed her hand. "Fran, where are—"

"We're safe," she interrupted and squeezed his hand. "I think."

"You are safe," Luro confirmed. "For now at least. But it's time to be on your feet."

On tremulous legs, Francesca stood while explaining to Cyrus what she knew. Luro spoke to the unseen creature. It responded in a language that sounded like growling and yipping had been put into a bag and then kicked until they acquired grammar and syntax.

Luro told Francesca and Cyrus to follow the sound of his voice. As they did, the massive creature moved behind them. Francesca looked warily in the thing's direction but distinguished little more than a massive silhouette. After a while, they reached the tunnel's mouth and emerged onto a brief plateau that looked out on what Francesca initially mistook for an amphitheater.

It was, in fact, an embankment that ran a wide circle and was crowned by crenellated walls. The interior of the earthworks had been leveled into concentric rings of tiled plateaus connected by cobbled ramps. Into the vertical walls of each plateau stood arched entryways leading into tunnels. At every level stood thick redwood spars that rose high above the embankments to suspend a mesh of woven grass, above which shone a clear sky dimming into evening.

"We're in a lycanthrope warren," Cyrus said.

"Homestead, Windbag," Luro snapped from the tunnel mouth.

Cyrus ignored this. "That grass screen is to protect their water. Without it, our pilots would drop poison into it." He gestured down to the embankment's center. Francesca started as she realized that the dark, smooth surface at the bottom of the embankment was a small reservoir.

"Don't talk too loudly about how windbags kill our people," Luro growled from behind Francesca. "Bad for your health."

Francesca turned, expecting to see the old man standing in front of a massive wolf. She saw only the old Canic with the dark tunnel behind him. Something was moving in there. One large creature and several smaller ones.

Cyrus, his green robes torn and his turban and veil missing, was studying Luro. "So the Canics formed an alliance with the lycanthropes?"

"Don't be stupid," Luro grumbled while walking toward them. "Standing here, you should figure it out."

Francesca noticed more movement in the tunnel. Again the single large creature and several smaller ones. For an instant one of the lesser creatures ventured close enough for Francesca to glimpse a . . .

She frowned and narrowed her eyes. Perhaps she had been mistaken. But then it came again: a large but otherwise normal dog. In fact, it was one of the same breed that the Canics kept in the North Gate District.

"You keep the same dogs here as you do in the city?" she asked.

Luro sniffed. "Not dogs."

"Oh," Francesca said in a flash of understanding. "They're your children!"

Luro nudged Cyrus. "How's it feel being the stupid one of the pair, eh?"

Cyrus was massaging his temples. "Grand. But it'd feel a lot grander if consorting with her didn't require consorting with idiots like you."

Luro looked at Francesca. "Touchy, isn't he?"

She ignored the men and pointed at the tunnel opening. "The dogs are the same ones we saw all over North Gate."

Cyrus looked at her. "Fran, what are you talking about?"

"You noticed the Canics have an abundance of children and elderly with hardly any souls between. That's because all the Canics in the middle years aren't in the city; they're out here in the savanna."

Luro looked as if he were tasting something sour. "Not all of us change the second time."

"You're born as humanoids and become lupine?" she asked.

"Other way around. We're born on the savanna as pups and then spend childhood in the city or one of the towns. Some of the Deep Savanna tribes keep their two-legs home, but most of us prefer to live in a human settlement. Comfortable. Plus, we keep an eye on your tribe. We come back to our homesteads sometimes, do things the four-legs can't: building walls, raising spars, mending nets, that stuff."

Francesca felt a pang for Luro. "But you didn't change?"

"Maybe one in eight of us don't. So we go back to the city and become the adult Canics."

"But the lycanthropes run amuck in the North Gate," Cyrus exclaimed. "How could you . . . I mean, are they killing their own kind?"

"No Canic ever died in those 'attacks,' as you call them. Mostly they're attempts to bring the outer wall down so we can move freely between the city and the savanna."

Cyrus shook his head. "But there are reports of the wolves going wild and devouring whole families."

"Reports don't mean truth, Windbag. Yeah, whole families disappear, but they're not eaten; they're moved out here. Easiest way to disappear before the children make their second change."

Francesca spoke up. "So the story you told me earlier about the Savanna Walker and the lycanthropes attacking your caravan?"

"All true. Human clans feud, so do our clans. We were being harassed by some northern wolves with no love for my family. So we weren't so broken up when the Walker tore them to strips."

"When was that?" Francesca asked.

"Maybe thirty years ago. Why do you ask?"

"I'm trying to imagine what the Walker could be."

"Well, imagine it somewhere else. You've managed to get yourself into a hot mess, and my brother has pulled me out here to deal with it. If you'd like to live to the next midnight, I need you to answer one key question, and answer it fully and honestly."

"Wait," Cyrus said. "Your brother?"

"The male in the breeding pair for this homestead. Don't ask what all that means. Just think of him as the wolf most likely to gnash your head into something resembling sausage filling if you screw this up any more than you already have." The old man began walking up a ramp.

Francesca followed. "I'm a little curious why we're not sausage filling already."

"It's got to do with my question," Luro grunted. "No one has seen a windbag chase another into the savanna since the Civil War. They want to know if there's to be another one of those. Some are always planning how to knock down the walls. They think a war will help them with that. If you ask me, another civil war would go poorly for us in the city. When food gets rationed, my people starve first. The hotheads need to cool. But enough of my fussing. You still have to answer the question."

Francesca cleared her throat. "Luro, what question?"

"Is there gonna be a blasted Second Civil War?" he nearly shouted.

Cyrus replied hotly: "We'll have nothing to do with helping lycan-thropes know—"

"There might be," Francesca interrupted. "And you're right, Luro, the Canics in Avel would be the first to suffer. So help us prevent that war. Stopping hostilities will depend on several things, one of which involves Lornish metal being smuggled into Avel."

The old man raised his eyebrows. "Solved that one already, eh?"

"Lornish highsmiths are in Avel, among other foreign spellwrights. They've come to find Nicodemus Weal, whom we found despite your little diversion back in the North District."

He scowled. "Tried to protect you from that. But nooo, you had to go and bring a whole lycanthrope hunt down on the district. Every Canic knew there wasn't a four-legs in the city. Consequently, the next morning, I went around asking if anyone had seen you. I wouldn't wander around the North Gate anytime soon. People have become suspicious of your name."

"Helpful, Luro, very helpful," Francesca muttered. "We had nothing to do with the hunt . . . or at least, nothing directly. But unless you get us out of here via something other than a lycanthrope digestive tract, the high-smiths will keep using Canics to smuggle Lornish steel. You want the city finding out your people are helping a foreign power threaten their sover-eignty?"

"All right," Luro groused. "I take your point. Now stop trying to talk my ear off." He turned and started back up the embankment.

Cyrus scowled at Francesca, no doubt upset she had admitted that a Second Civil War was possible. Not meeting his gaze, she hurried after Luro.

"What's going to happen to us?" Francesca asked.

"If I get my way, we sell you off. If I don't, they eat you. Either way, I get back to the city before breakfast."

"You're going to sell us?" Francesca squawked. "Luro, you owe us for dis-covering the steel smuggling, not to mention my work in the North District as a physician. We can help stop this war from—"

"Ha! Back in the city, you said you wouldn't start trouble when trying to find Nicodemus. Admirable job you did there."

"To whom are you going to sell us?" Cyrus asked. "Another lycanthrope tribe?"

He chuckled. "Something like that."

Just then they crested the embankment and discovered a horizontal world of deep green and dark blue. The grass ocean stretched out before them in long, rolling waves. Far off in the distance, a herd of white-furred and long-necked creatures was moving steadily through the grass.

When Francesca had traveled in a caravan from Dar to Avel, a guard who had been flirting with her let her climb atop a wagon to see a distant herd of katabeasts: they had seemed like small islands of thick gray hide without head, neck, or tail. The guard had explained to her that a family of birds lived on the back of each beast.

She had never heard of such pale long-necked creatures as she now saw, but she knew there were many types of beasts that migrated through the Deep Savanna during the rainy season. They avoided Avel, fearful of being hunted by hierophants; their hides and meat fetched high prices in the city's markets.

Just then Cyrus reached the embankment's crest. "Celeste!" he swore.

Francesca glanced at her old lover. He was looking down the embankment to where it met the savanna. When Francesca followed his gaze, she too swore: "Hell!"

There were four lycanthropes. Two of them stood on all fours on the embankment. They were as large as any horse Francesca had ever seen. Their bodies were as sleek with golden brown fur, their limbs muscular and tense. These two were facing away from the embankment, so she could not see their faces.

The two other lycanthropes were a few feet into the grass. Apparently they were standing on their hind legs because amid the waving grass, she could see their poised forepaws, their powerful necks, and their snarling maws.

Lycanthrope faces were strikingly human despite their muzzles and perked ears. Their wide all-black eyes shone with intelligence even as their lips pulled back in a snarl.

More specifically the lycanthropes were snarling at a huddle of four humanoids, dark blue of skin, blond of hair, and armed with hatchets. At their head stood a man with long black hair. He was staring at her with dispassionate green eyes.

"If you're planning on selling us to him, Luro, forget it," she said dryly. "I'd rather be chewed into sausage filling."

SHANNON'S GHOST FOUND himself falling from a book onto roof tiles. Above him stretched a sky going deeper blue with evening; only two bright stars shone. He sat up with a jerk. Last thing he had remembered, the Savanna Walker had been closing in on them. His chest was still heaving, his every sense painfully alert.

A bewildering moment passed in which the ghost looked out on Avel's serene Holy District, the red-tiled dome of the sanctuary rising from its center. Apparently, he was sitting atop a building somewhere at the district's edge. Somehow they had escaped the Savanna Walker.

Slowly, the ghost's sense of danger passed and in its wake came the now familiar sorrow of being separated from his author.

He looked around and was not surprised to see Magister Lotannu Akoma sitting on the roof tiles beside him. A complex spell had been cast upon Lotannu's head, the fine sentences running in and out of his skull. Two cylindrical passages grew out from his eyes to form lenses wide as a man's hand. It made him look like a giant gold-leafed insect. Lotannu had been one of Shannon's most accomplished students in Astrophell.

"Magister," Lotannu said with a respectful nod.

On the ghost's other side sat Magistra Vivian Niyol. Her long, silky white hair was tossing in the wind. She'd wrapped herself and was studying him with all-white eyes.

"Magister, you are disturbingly dim," she said gently. "You've lost a great deal of text, so you must use as few runes as possible when communicating with me. Then we'd better get you back in here." She nodded down at the book she was holding.

The ghost extracted one of the sentences from his shoulder and translated it to *"What happened?"* and cast it to her.

"We barely avoided the half dragon," Magistra Niyol replied. "It was my fault. I hadn't anticipated a creature able to so profoundly affect the nature of language. I will never again underestimate what a dragon might become."

"What of Francesca and Cyrus?" he asked quickly. Francesca was still his best hope of finding his author and convincing him they should reunite.

"I believe and hope they escaped. But now we need you to tell us about the library in which you awoke." She nodded to some place two or three miles north of the sanctuary.

The ghost frowned until he remembered that she was blind to the mundane world, as he had been in life. *"You still want to go after my memories?"*

She nodded.

"But the half-dragon."

"That spell around Lotannu's head allows him to see quaternary thoughts. He can locate the Savanna Walker. Presently the beast is in the sanctuary, but we are betting that with Nicodemus loose, it will soon leave."

"But Typhon is in there."

Vivian smiled. "The demon will not be a threat as long as I am there. On that point at least, I am correct. My mistake was failing to imagine the Savanna Walker's nature."

"Who are you that you do not fear a demon?"

"You do not need to know."

"An avatar?"

"Magister, you won't get an answer; don't waste your words asking."

"*A goddess?*"

She smiled. "Clearly the goddess of youthful beauty, no?" She indicated her blind eyes and knobby, spotted hands. "Magister, please, tell us where we might find this library."

The ghost frowned. "*Why aren't you sending word to Astrophell and demanding an army in support?*"

She nodded. "A fair question. A force in Lurrikara waits to assist us. However, getting word to them has proved difficult. Francesca informed us that League of Starhaven separatists have infiltrated Avel. Our suspicions fell on Magister DeGarn and those under his command in the relay station. Lotannu interrogated several of the gargoyles surrounding the station and confirmed our suspicions. Therefore, we cannot cast a colaboris spell to Lurrikara until we travel over the mountain to Coldlock Harbor. From there, I will extemporize a colaboris and cast it from the lighthouse."

"*Extemporize a colaboris spell?*"

Vivian only smiled.

"*Magistra, you must tell me who you are!*"

"I am much more interested in learning who you are."

"*You mean recovering my memories?*"

"You too might want to know if the demon edited your prose. I suspect your author would also be curious about that fact."

The ghost felt his chest tighten. The hope of reunion was almost too much to bear. He looked at Lotannu and then back to Vivian. "*I will tell you. When will we sneak in?*"

Vivian nodded toward Lotannu. "As soon as that nightmare half dragon moves."

Thirty-eight

On their trek through the savanna, Francesca thought about snide things to say to Nicodemus.

It was tough going. Two kobolds were far ahead, widening the path they had made when traveling to the lycanthrope homestead. Even so, Francesca found it difficult to keep her balance on the wet ground strewn with slick grass stalks.

Behind her, Nicodemus walked barefoot on the tangle. Whenever she glanced back, she found him gazing out into the grass sea. He would notice her watching, meet her gaze, and then look away. Ahead, Cyrus was having as much trouble as she staying upright. Every half mile or so, the hierophant would compound his troubles by attempting to wrap a strip of his ruined robes into a makeshift turban and veil. It never went well.

Though Francesca had to focus on the path, she glanced up into the grass sea. She had always supposed that the savanna was composed of a single species of grass and nothing else, that it was uniformly composed the way the reservoir was uniformly water. In fact, the savanna was exuberantly diverse.

Some species of grass grew as thin as bootlaces, reaching only five feet and bending in any wind so as to lash her neck and shoulders. Elsewhere the grass grew as thick as a man's hand and stretched up to nine feet, reminding her of the bamboo forests around Port Mercy. In the groves of such grass grew an understory of vines and shade flowers. In one tall grove they discovered a flock of black and lavender birds that produced warbling cries. With a flutter so loud as to sound like fire, they took wing to become a cloud of dark feathers.

There were many rabbitlike creatures, their fur as gray as shadow, which she only glimpsed before they fled. Once something large and feathered bounded away through the grass. With joyful cries, two of the kobolds hurled hatchets after it. Francesca was relieved neither weapon hit its mark. Once, Nicodemus knelt and placed his palm to the ground. Curious, Francesca did the same and felt it vibrating to a steady beat. "What is it?" she asked.

Nicodemus answered, "Something heavy and with feet."

She sighed. "Ask a stupid question . . ." Slowly, the vibrations lessened and disappeared.

On they went through endless variations of grass and green. When the sky began to darken, Francesca walked close to Cyrus. "Do you think Vivian survived the Walker attack?" he asked.

Francesca snorted. "God-of-gods but that woman has almost as high an opinion of her abilities as our cacographic crackers-for-brains does." She looked back at Nicodemus. He was peering into the grass but then turned to her. Green eyes in a dark face.

"But who knows," she said, turning back to Cyrus, "maybe Vivian killed the Savanna Walker. She certainly acted like she could."

"I think she's dead," Cyrus said grimly. "I think we should talk cracker-brains into taking me to the wind garden so I can warn the marshal of polytheistic insurrection in Avel."

"Why don't you ask cracker-head then?"

"Because he's not making eyes at me . . ."

"Is there some fundamental aspect of male nature that compels you people to say something obnoxious every hour, or do you train to be regular with your idiocy?"

"Look back at him and he'll look you in the eye and then look away."

"I'm right in front of him. Of course he'll notice when I look back. Anyone walking behind someone who isn't a thickskull would—"

"Just do it."

She didn't answer. But in a few moments, the path veered to the west. She turned as if to look in their new direction but then glanced at Nicodemus.

He had turned his head to one side and was frowning. One of the kobolds behind him seemed to be talking. Francesca was about to tell Cyrus that he understood human emotion as well as a brain-damaged goat. But then Nicodemus looked at her. His expression was as blank as ever, but his eyes lingered on her face a moment too long. Francesca looked away with the abruptness that universally communicates to interested males the sentiment "piss off" without requiring the woman to say it aloud.

"Is this when I say 'I told you so'?" Cyrus asked.

Francesca ignored him.

"Go convince him to take me to the wind marshal."

"You talk to him. I don't know anything about wind marshals or polytheistic rebellions."

Cyrus looked back at her. "But I'm not a six-foot-tall brunette with dimples and an obnoxious wit. Besides, don't you like his attention?"

"Would you like the attention of a half-naked, arrogant killer who thinks part of his mind has been stolen and put into a bauble? It's not exactly flattering. He'd stare at anything with breasts."

Cyrus nodded. "He's still more likely to listen to you. Go on, find out what his plans are and then get him to take me to the wind garden."

Francesca said nothing for a long moment. Then she felt foolish about her reluctance. So what if it was going to be awkward? She slowed her pace until Cyrus was far ahead.

"Are you all right, Magistra?" Nicodemus asked in his flat tone. "Are you having trouble balancing?"

"Only when I'm walking," she said airily and then pretended to slip.

Nicodemus didn't laugh at her gag; rather, he stopped abruptly and backed away.

Francesca wondered why he did this until she remembered the canker his touch had created on the kobold's forearm. She shivered thinking about what would have happened if he had bumped into her. She hurried forward.

"How long until we reach your camp?" she asked.

"At this speed, maybe two hours."

"What happens then?"

He was silent for a long time and then said, "Deirdre is dead."

Francesca looked back to see if he was serious. His face was blank. The man was as cold as a construct. She looked away in disgust. "I'm sorry to hear it."

Nicodemus emotionlessly described Boann's misery and dissolution. When finished, he said, "We had been trying to follow whatever plan Deirdre had in play. For so long, we've hoped to free her. It's unclear what should be done next."

"You're voice is so flat it sounds like you could be talking about the weather."

"I don't understand."

"Never mind," she quickly said. "I am very sorry to hear about Deirdre."

He made a low noise, maybe a grunt of annoyance, maybe a sound of gratitude.

She didn't care. "After we saw you last, Cyrus and I caught the cat that wasn't alive." She related everything that had happened to her.

"I don't trust the ghost," Nicodemus said when she finished describing the textual spirit. "If it got out of its book, Typhon wanted it to get out."

Francesca explained how she thought that Deirdre had inexpertly cast the ghost and gotten blood on the note that had read, "Your memories are in here."

"And Vivian wants to fetch the book out of the sanctuary?" Nicodemus asked.

"If the Savanna Walker didn't drive her mad, I'm guessing she'll attempt it. She thinks almost as highly of her talents as you think of yours."

"I'm only a cacographer," he replied automatically. "I work hard and have been fortunate in my teachers and students."

"A fine sentiment of humility," she said, trying to keep her tone free of irony—well, mostly free. "We might find aid from DeGarn and the League of Starfall."

"Without the emerald, I'm no Halcyon. If anything, I'm the Storm Petrel. They're more likely to kill me than support me. And I've no doubt that Vivian came to Avel with my half sister's orders to assassinate me."

Francesca smiled. She had thought he would react this way. "Cyrus has another suggestion. If you take him to the wind garden, he can convince the marshal that the rising polytheistic sentiment is a threat to Celeste. I don't know if he'll mention the demon. That is a large bite to chew, but—"

"No good," Nicodemus interrupted. "If a Kestrel flew Vivian into Avel, then the Celestial Court must be aligned with Astrophell. They'll want me dead."

"This seems a theme in your life."

"I'm hoping it won't be the final theme."

"In any case, Cyrus needn't mention you in his report. You don't even need to be here. We might smuggle you and your students away from here. Think about it. Let Celeste, a high goddess, deal with Typhon. She'll tear him to divine pieces."

Nicodemus said nothing. She waited, expecting him to pipe up with any of several objections she anticipated. But still, he was silent.

She looked back. He was, as before, gazing into the grass ocean. His expression was passive, but now there was a hint of something else about his eyes that made him seem exhausted. Or was it sadness? "What?" she asked.

He didn't look at her. "Let me talk it over with Magister Shannon."

"You have doubts."

"Avel is home to many people."

"Nearly forty thousand."

"I worry Typhon may go to ground before Celeste can act. And I worry Celeste might blast the city to ruins to eliminate him."

"Oh, yes, I forgot. Once you get your emerald, you're going to become the Creator-made-flesh. Then you'll poke both the demon's eyes out using only your nose."

Nicodemus cleared his throat. "What happens if you don't make your metaphors overly emphatic? Does your head explode or something?"

She smiled slightly. "I've never dared try."

"My students are quite fond of you now that you've saved Vein. They'd be willing to hold your head together while you experiment with restrained language."

"No. I don't think you'd respect me afterwards."

He sniffed with amusement.

"And furthermore, forget restrained language, if you can't be exuberant about life, or at least emphatic, why go on living?"

"Perhaps philosophy and not medicine was your true calling."

"Philosophy is far too barren. Come up with an idea, and you have an idea. But mend a girl's broken leg and she might live long enough to become a grandmother."

"I supposed that in philosophy one idea might inspire another, that two ideas might become a greater idea. In my conception, philosophy is prolific."

"You can't have a conception."

"And why not?"

"You're a man."

"So why can't a man have a conception."

"You don't have the anatomy for it."

He chuckled. "What kind of anatomy, other than a brain, does one need to conceive?"

"I'll tell you when you're older."

"I'm thirty-five."

"Someone really should have told you by now."

He chuckled. "Don't baby me."

"That statement is pregnant with meaning."

"Twinned meaning?"

"Oh, no, not me. I avoid double meanings, give them a wide berth."

He chuckled again. "It's a relief to talk to someone who goes in for wordplay. With Magister so sick, he's not inclined to it. And my students, well, puns usually incite violence in kobold culture."

Francesca sighed. "Cyrus gets rather worked up if I go on too much."

"If that's the worst of your problems, you two don't have many problems."

She glanced back and saw that Nicodemus was smiling at her. She looked away. "So, you'll consider taking Cyrus to the garden tower?"

"I will talk to Magister."

She looked back again and saw he was still smiling, but now the expression seemed like a remnant of an older emotion. "Is there another reason you hesitate to take Cyrus to the wind marshal?"

He didn't speak for a few steps but then said: "Perhaps no good reason."

"What's your bad reason?"

"Just . . . the emerald. If you call in Celeste, I'll never recover it."

"Right, the emerald, the missing part of yourself. The piece that would have made you complete and a mighty savior."

"Yes, that piece," he said in an exhausted tone. "The piece that could have defeated Typhon, or at least freed Deirdre before she died. The piece that could cure Magister before he dies."

For some reason, his tone annoyed Francesca. "What if someone else can defeat Typhon and cure Shannon?"

"I would be overjoyed."

"But would you still want the emerald?"

He was silent for a moment. "I don't see why I wouldn't. As long as I don't have it, I'm disabled."

"But what if your disability weren't important?"

"What do you want me to say, Magistra?" For the first time anger heated his voice. "That I'd give up the emerald for a chance to see Typhon dead and Shannon cured! Of course I would."

"Of course," she said quickly, worried she pushed him too far. "I was only curious about who you would be if you weren't obsessed with the emerald."

He didn't answer.

"I'm sorry, don't mind me. I was only playing philosopher and wondering about the things we imagine will make us feel complete." She was, in fact, thinking of her disappointment at having been appointed a physician in Avel's less-than-prestigious infirmary. And she was thinking about the strange pangs of jealousy she felt when encountering accomplished women like Vivian.

Nicodemus said, "I find it difficult to think about anything other than keeping both the war against Typhon and Magister Shannon alive."

"Perhaps there is something I can do, as a physician, for Magister."

"Perhaps. But I saw what the canker curse spread across his gut. It's nothing you could cut out of him without cutting him into nothing."

"You don't know how well I can cut."

He didn't reply.

A wave of irritation washed over Francesca. She found Nicodemus too cold, too obsessed with his own lack of power. She had to fight the urge to walk faster and far enough away that they couldn't talk.

But she'd come back here to convince him to take Cyrus to the wind garden. So she said, "Tell me about the lycanthropes. How did you come to deal with them, through an ancient alliance between them and the kobolds?"

Nicodemus grunted. "The opposite. They were once bitter rivals. Both creatures came from the same group of immigrants from the ancient continent."

"When humanity fled the demons during the Exodus?"

"Before." He went on to explain how, back in Starhaven, he had sent his mind into a tome known as the Bestiary and within it found a fragment of what had been the ancient goddess Chimera. Long ago, she had fled the Ancient Continent with her devotees to settle this land. She had then used Language Prime to modify her followers. Some became kobolds or goblins or other types of humanoid. To populate the savannas and woods, Chimera had combined the Language Prime of wolves with those of her devotees to create lycanthropes.

"For a time, Chimera had governed all her children. But then the kobold mountain kingdoms sought to expand their influence to the plains. Wars raged between kobolds and lycanthropes for centuries. Then the demons forced humanity across the ocean to this land. Divided, the Chimerical peoples could not repel the landfall kingdoms. Later, when the kingdoms were unified under the Neosolar Empire, humanity began to eradicate the Chimerical kingdoms.

"But the people we now call the Canics were sly. When the empire reached this savanna, the Canics used their Bestiary to change their Language Prime so they appeared human for large portions of their lives. They built towns and even a small city around the base of their Heaven Tree."

"Like the Heaven Tree you mentioned earlier, the one you and Shannon inhabited after you fled Starhaven?"

"Much like it, but it was a redwood of almost unimaginable height. In any case, their scheme worked; the empire incorporated them even while destroying the other lycanthropic peoples."

Francesca made a thoughtful noise. "So when the empire fell, Spires destroyed their Heaven Tree and Bestiary?"

"Exactly. So they acquired a cynical philosophy. They see themselves as a fallen people, exiled from control of Language Prime."

Francesca frowned. "But none of us can control our Language Prime. It's not natural to control Language Prime."

"It's not natural for humans, but they're not human."

Francesca looked at Nicodemus. "Can you alter your own Language Prime?"

"No. Only that of others."

"I find that reassuring, but I'm not sure why."

"It is a bit odd, thinking about what it would be like if I could rewrite myself."

"What would you change?"

"I'd edit out my disability," he said automatically. "Prompt whatever part of my brain was altered by the curse to regrow."

This bothered Francesca, but she didn't say so.

"How would you rewrite yourself?" he asked.

"I'd make myself smarter. I suppose."

"Smarter?" he asked with a laugh. "You're a wizard and a cleric. What else do you want to become? The goddess of the academy? Give Hakeem a push out the door?"

"Don't be so dramatic!" she said with more heat than she intended. "I'd simply like to be a better physician."

"You saved Vein; that was almost miraculous."

"I also killed Deirdre," she answered flatly, and then instantly regretted her words. "I'm sorry. I didn't think—"

"I know what you meant," he said in a low voice. "I know what it's like to lack ability."

Silence fell as they continued to walk. Francesca again wanted to walk faster, but she felt as if there was something more to be said. Suddenly Nicodemus spoke: "How hard is it when your patients die?"

"It depends on the patient," she said. "Sometimes it doesn't affect you much at all. Sometimes there's too much to do for it to affect you." She paused. "But some patients break your heart."

Twilight was fast progressing toward night. Behind her, Nicodemus made a soft noise that she took to mean, "Go on."

"When I first earned my physician's stole in Port Mercy," she found herself saying, "I cared for this crabby old man who had started seeing double. He put on a show of being sullen around others, but when we were alone he would talk and talk and talk. He liked me because when he got sassy, I'd sass back. One of his grandsons would walk into the city to see the old man. After two days, his double vision worsened and he developed a pounding headache. That night he began to vomit. None of our drugs or spells could stop it. It went on for two days. Between the heaves he would cry a little. Not a word of complaint, just tears. The vomiting got worse. He was very dehydrated. There are certain texts that allow us to restore water to a patient—ingenious spells, they push fluids into a shinbone and the body redistributes it."

"Into the bone?" Nicodemus asked.

"Yes. The phrase 'dry as a bone' turns out to be horse crap. They're wet organs, filled with marrow and blood vessels."

"Huh."

"In any case, we were preparing to push such a text into the old man's shin, but he fell into a seizure. When it stopped, he didn't know where he was. He kept begging for water and asking when his grandson would arrive. One eye was now completely blind. The other clerics feared that giving him fluids wouldn't help the cause of his vision changes and seizures. They worried that spiking him would only increase his pain before he died."

She paused to let out a long breath. "But he kept asking for his grandson. Hearing him . . . I felt that if I could keep him alive until his grandson returned, it would make a difference. So I explained about the spell and the shin. He seemed to understand, but when I pushed the text he screamed. God-of-gods, did he scream. However, the fluid we returned to his body took him out of mortal danger."

She paused to swallow. "The seizures came back that evening. They made him confused and frightened. I stayed with him all that night and much of the next day. Once his confusion passed, he cried quietly and was still . . . so still that I worried he'd stopped breathing. I've never seen anyone cry like that again. I . . . had to keep him alive until his grandson came. But the boy didn't come that day. A storm had turned most of the mountain roads to mud. The next morning the old man had his worst seizure yet. I thought it would kill him. Somehow it didn't. He was so disoriented afterwards it was like he was drunk. After making sure he was stable, I moved on to my other patients. I wasn't in the room when the grandson showed up. The boy was only fourteen, and apparently the old man was so strange after his seizure that the boy ran out. Someone caught him and browbeat him into staying in the hospital.

"By the time another physician fetched me, the boy was ready to jump out a window. I pleaded with him to stay, promising that his grandfather's mind would clear. He waited in the hallway. I went in to see the old man, and he was more lucid. When I said his grandson had come, the old man smiled for the first time in days. I went out into the hallway to tell the boy to go in, but . . . you never saw a child so frightened . . . he wouldn't look me in the eye, kept staring up at the ceiling and blinking to stop himself from crying. The boy hadn't seen his grandfather; he'd seen senility and frailty replace his grandfather. I suddenly felt weak. I couldn't push the boy anymore, so he left the infirmary. When I told the old man what had happened, he didn't make a sound. The next night, he entered a seizure that did not stop until he died.

"I felt nothing but hollow. I had to work straight through that night. Then in the morning, when I was heading to my bed, I saw the boy standing in the hallway with his father. I knew he had come back with his dad to see his grandfather. I don't know what expression I had on my face. I still wonder if it was surprise or grief. Whatever it was, the boy knew. He turned and ran. I brought the father in to see the body, but I never saw the grandson again."

When Francesca finished, the sky above them had become deep violet and the darkness seemed to be rising up from the ground and into the grass as if it were mist.

She peered behind her and found Nicodemus looking at her. In the dark, she couldn't see his face, but he nodded as if to indicate she still had his full attention.

"I didn't cry much at all," she said and turned her eyes back to the path. "Maybe a little before I fell asleep. But when I woke up, everything felt empty for days." Again she fell silent. Nicodemus made his soft sound again but said nothing. They walked in silence, and Francesca began to hear the nocturnal savanna: wind whispering through the grass, the fibrous stalks creaking and clicking against one another. Ahead of them came the footfalls of the kobolds, their heavy breaths.

"What was it that killed the old man?" Nicodemus asked.

"Autopsy found a brain tumor."

When Nicodemus spoke again, it was in an even softer voice: "I worry about that happening to Magister."

Francesca sucked in a sharp breath. "Oh! Nicodemus, I'm so sorry. I didn't think . . . I mean, I had forgotten." She remembered Shannon's frail face. "It's so blasted stupid of me. How could I be so retarded?"

He laughed. "I don't think using the word retarded around me is going to make you feel any better."

Heat flushed across her face. "Oh, God-of-gods damn me. I did it again. And I'm a physician, for crying out loud. I've spent a lifetime trying to learn how not to say heartless things. Dear sweet heaven, I'm never going to open my mouth again."

He laughed again. "Now it's my turn to tell you to stop being so dramatic."

She didn't speak . . . for a few moments at least. "I'm not saying anything," she announced. "That might sound like I'm saying something, but really I'm not talking right now."

He laughed softly.

She wanted him to speak, but he didn't. So she said, "I'm embarrassed I didn't think of Magister Shannon."

He exhaled. "Deirdre suffered from seizures as well," he said. "It's odd how much I miss her. We spent so little time in each other's presence. In a way, it was the idea of her I loved. The idea of her escaping possession and of returning to Boann. None of it will happen now."

Francesca tripped. It wasn't until she regained her balance that she realized she had been tripping less and less. She was learning how to walk on the grass, but now in the rising dark she could make out little of the ground. She wrote several flamefly paragraphs so they would circle around her knees. The instant the Numinous spells began to incandesce, the night exploded into a chorus of hissing. She jumped and looked about for the creatures making the sound.

"It's Dross and Jasp," Nicodemus said calmly. "The light will deconstruct any spells they might cast."

"Well then, they can bloody well carry my nonnocturnal butt all the way back to your camp," she snapped.

Nicodemus laughed. "They'd approve of that sentiment if I translated it, especially Dross. But go, share your light with Cyrus. He's been looking back at you to see how you're doing at pumping me for information."

"I wasn't pumping you for information! Why would I be so foolish as to assume you have any useful information to pump out? I might have been trying to manipulate you into taking Cyrus to the garden tower. Manipulation, fine. But information pumping? Leave a woman some pride."

"Well then, cleric, why don't you take your pride up to Cyrus? He seems more than a little concerned about how friendly you're getting with the man who's crazy enough to worry about becoming the anti-Halcyon."

"Oh, Nicodemus, you shouldn't say such harsh things!" she said in a voice laden with sympathy. "You and I are not at all friendly."

"Then why don't you take your flameflies away from me so you don't disspell any text I'd like to cast."

"All right," she said with a sniff. But then she added, "I'm sorry for telling that story without thinking about Magister Shannon."

Nicodemus was silent for a moment. "No," he said and then paused. "I'm glad you told it. I'm anxious to see him now."

She looked back. "I'll go talk with Cyrus then."

He smiled. "Go."

She cast a few more flameflies and increased her pace. But as she approached Cyrus, insects swarmed around her knees. Some of them—the betel-like ones with iridescent blue carapaces—struck her legs with palpable force. "Stop that," she said in her sweetest voice. "Stop that, you disgusting little abominations of the natural world."

"Making new friends?" Cyrus asked.

"Imagine having a brain so primitive that the image of something attractive could drive you to hurl yourself at that image. Oh, but I forget, you are male. You can sympathize."

He sighed. "So, will Nicodemus take me to the wind garden?"

"He wants to discuss it with Magister Shannon, but I think I made a convincing case."

"You two were laughing a great deal."

"Weren't you the one who sent me back there to charm him?"

"I did. And you do deserve to enjoy the admiration of others."

"Stop playing the courteous man. It gives me unpleasant feelings of respect for you."

"Yes, Magistra, I will straightaway become an egotistical bastard who displays just enough vulnerability to excite your displaced motherly desire to heal."

"Are you accusing me of wanting to take my work home with me?"

"Home, Fran? You have lived in the infirmary for the last ten years. You never wanted to take the wounded home. You wanted a home with the wounded."

"Give me a moment, and I'll come up with a scintillating retort for that."

"Maybe if I had figured how to be admitted to the infirmary, I could have held on to you."

"You . . ." Francesca's voice died. It was an awkward situation, but she felt no great embarrassment. "Cyrus, it's late. We've just escaped lycanthrope captivity. I just had to manipulate a cacographic fruitcake. And now we're marching through a deadly wilderness in the dark. Maybe we could rehash our affair—"

"You're right. I shouldn't have brought it up."

She looked up into the tangle of stars. The thin crescents of the blue- and blackmoons were high overhead. From somewhere in the nearby grass came a chorus of chirping and clicks, perhaps from some sort of cricket.

"At least it's a lovely night for a long walk," Francesca said to try to change the mood. "Except maybe for the demon-controlled city somewhere out there and the potentially violent lycanthropes everywhere else."

"Long walk indeed," grumbled Cyrus. "When are we to reach Nicodemus's camp?"

"Nicodemus," Francesca called out, "when will we reach your camp?"

From the dark behind them, he called back. "At the rate you two are stumbling along, about an hour more."

Cyrus was frowning at her.

"What?" she asked.

He turned back to the path. "It's a long walk," he said and quickened his pace.

Francesca tried to match his speed and tripped. Though he was more than twenty paces behind her, she could hear Nicodemus clomp to a halt as if he were afraid of running into her. Again she thought about what his touch would do to her flesh. She shuddered. Out in the grass sea, something that sounded like a hawk screeched.

Francesca struggled to her feet and hurried on, acutely aware of the man stalking behind and the man hurrying ahead.

A long walk indeed.

VIVIAN WOKE TO someone shaking her shoulder. "Who is it?"

"Me," Lotannu rumbled in his low voice.

"What time?"

"Near midnight."

Vivian sat up and felt hard tiles under her backside. It took a moment to remember that they were camped on a rooftop so Lotannu could watch the sanctuary. She felt around until she located Francesca's clinical journal, in which she'd stored Shannon's ghost.

"Did you see something?"

"The Savanna Walker has left the city."

"In which direction?" She pulled her cloak tight. The wind, though gentle, was cold.

"Out the North Gate. He's disappeared into the savanna."

Vivian struggled to her feet. "Well then, let's see how hard it is to break into a demon-controlled sanctuary."

Thirty-nine

Francesca supposed that it was an hour or two after midnight when the party reached Nicodemus's camp. The towering redwoods blocked out moon and stars, leaving the understory as dark as a cave, which she guessed was why the kobolds favored the place.

The blond humanoids began laughing and calling out to one another. When the scent of cooking reached Francesca, she understood why. Her belly complained and her feet ached.

The party hurried the last hundred yards to discover Shannon stoking the fire and tending to a pot of boiling lentils. Beside him lay a stack of fried fish. Hooting and laughing, the four kobolds fell upon the fish and started to gulp it down.

Nicodemus barked sharp words and looked as if he might fling a wartext at the kobolds. They cringed and hissed but did not stop wolfing down the fish. But when Nicodemus took a threatening step forward, they jumped into a line before Magister Shannon. One by one, they took his hand and bowed over it, muttering something. When finished, the kobolds ladled out bowls of lentils, giving the first two helpings to Francesca and Cyrus. The lentils were bland but hot and filling.

Nicodemus sat near Shannon but left two feet of space between them. Francesca watched them speak in low tones. The old man looked exhausted, frail, irritable. She would have thought Nicodemus's flat mouth and unexpressive eyes were signs of coldness if she had not, only two hours ago, told him the story of the grandfather with the brain tumor. Now she could see the fear within Nicodemus's guarded expression.

Cyrus offered her half his lentils, but she was already full and ended up giving him the rest of her bowl. She was always amazed by how much hierophants ate and how slim they remained, no doubt a consequence of forging text with every heartbeat.

"Are we safe here tonight?" Cyrus asked between mouthfuls.

"Nicodemus, are we safe here tonight?" she asked loudly.

The cacographer undid his ponytail and let his hair fall into a black curtain across his olive shoulders. It made Francesca wonder about her own hair and if there was a comb in the camp.

"Typhon hasn't ever found us here," Nicodemus answered. "Given how dark it is and how many skinmages we have, I wouldn't worry about anything short of the demon flooding the forest full of lucerin."

"Well there you are," she said to Nicodemus and looked at Cyrus. "Well there you are."

After they finished eating, she asked where Vein was. Shannon explained the recuperating kobold was asleep in his cabin. Francesca woke her patient to examine him. Once satisfied he was recovering, she left his cabin and went in search of Magister Shannon. The old wizard was in the smallest cabin talking to Nicodemus. Shannon's parrot-familiar was perched on a bedpost, her feathers puffed out and her eyes closed.

Francesca ordered the younger man out and then turned to Shannon. The wizard tried to refuse examination, but she patiently ignored his protests and plied him with questions until she understood the history of his disease. She then examined him, listening to his heart, lungs, gurgling stomach. She percussed along his back, chest, and stomach.

In the process, Francesca felt his resistance dissolve, his embarrassment fade. Her gift for seeing a body move through time took effect. She could peer forward into his potential physiological futures—none of them long—and backward, past the gaunt cheeks and wrinkled features, to the dark and handsome youth he had been.

When the exam was nearly over, he suddenly said, "They've never seen how frail I've become. Nicodemus and the other boys haven't." He paused. "Not that I want them to see, but . . . they haven't."

She motioned for him to sit on his bed while she sat on a stool. "I am glad I did. Your canker curse does not seem to be impinging any organ presently, but you display many of the signs of advanced disease."

"Prognosis?"

"You are in no immediate danger. But I worry for you longer term. I'd like a physician to see you once every sixty days."

The old wizard laughed. "Creator send that I have access to any physician sometime between now and my death."

Francesca fought the urge to volunteer to be his physician.

"Might I try to ghostwrite again?" the old man asked.

"No," she said gently and then winced internally as she saw his pained expression. "It would place too great a burden on your body."

Shannon sighed. "Nicodemus believes he will recover the emerald. But with Deirdre gone . . . It is horrible to lose her."

"You and Nicodemus were arguing about this?"

The blind old man shook his head. "Not truly. There wasn't anything to argue about. I've become a sour old man in my illness. I snap at him for dragging me to this forsaken wilderness. I have to slowly die in a cabin while he lurks around in the city without a word of the wizardly languages I spent so long teaching him."

She nodded. "It bothers you he has abandoned the wizardly languages?"

"Maybe it shouldn't. But it was the only legacy I had to give him."

"He might disagree."

"He would . . . But if we had just stayed in the Heaven Tree a little longer, I'm sure we could have made progress."

Francesca remained silent.

"You're not nocturnal like we are in this camp," Shannon said while rubbing his beard. "Sleep is more important than listening to an old soul grumble."

"I'm not accustomed to sleeping regular hours."

"Then maybe I just want to be alone now. Or maybe I'll wake up Azure." He gestured toward the puffed-out parrot.

"Goodnight, Magister," Francesca said and made for the door.

"Magistra," Shannon said when her hand was on the door, "I don't know if it is appropriate for an old man to say so, but . . ."

She waited patiently.

"But it was good to be examined, to be seen, and be . . ."

She knew he was struggling to say "be touched." But because she was a younger woman, it was not something he could say. So she spoke for him, "I'm glad I could examine you. I feel much more comfortable about your health now."

He nodded.

She stepped outside. The wet smell of the redwood understory swept around her. Though her eyes stung with exhaustion and her feet throbbed, she felt more complete than she had since leaving the hospital.

She found Cyrus and Nicodemus sitting by the fire. None of the kobolds seemed to be about. When Nicodemus heard her footsteps, he stood and looked at Shannon's cabin. Francesca cleared her throat. "He's asked to be alone for a while. My exam revealed signs of advanced disease without acute threat."

Nicodemus looked at her and then back at the cabin.

"But perhaps you should talk to him about wizardly languages again."

Nicodemus exhaled. "That fight again."

She waited a moment before saying, "Discussing it might lead to other difficult matters."

He looked at her and she again saw his fear of losing Shannon. Or perhaps it was anger at the old man. It didn't really matter. She rubbed her stinging eyes. "Lovely as the company is tonight, I should leave this social affair and sleep."

Nicodemus started. "Oh yes. You and Cyrus should use my cabin." He pointed. "The blankets are clean, and I'll be out until morning hunting with my students. Ask Magister if there's anything else you need."

They said their goodnights, and Francesca and Cyrus went to his cabin and cast a few flamefly paragraphs. It was a narrow place but clean and furnished with two sturdy beds. Something like a writing desk was propped up along the far wall. One of the legs had broken. A large book was wedged under the broken leg to keep the desk level. Curious, Francesca took a closer look at the book and then swore.

"What is it?" Cyrus asked.

"The Index!"

"The what?"

"A priceless artifact that can access any text within Starhaven's walls. I heard Nicodemus destroyed it years ago. But he didn't destroy it; he's using it to hold up a God-of-gods damn broken desk!"

Cyrus laughed. "If he can't use wizardly text, it's useless to him."

Francesca shook her head. "And here I was thinking he's half-sane. The blasted bloody Index."

"He'd be glad you're impressed. He'd be sure to keep making eyes at you."

"Don't start with that again. He put both of us into the same cabin."

Suddenly Cyrus's hands were on her shoulders. He began to massage her neck. She let him for a while. Neither of them spoke. She thought about how Shannon had thanked her for examining him, for truly seeing him. She wanted to be seen in that way, to be touched in that way. Not amorously, not even romantically, but carefully and almost objectively.

She patted Cyrus's hands and then stepped out of his reach. She looked at him, wanting and not wanting him to reach out to her.

He sat on the cot and motioned for her to sit beside him. "You've just made yourself a physician to a band of outlaw humanoids. So who's going to be physician to you?"

She sat next to him, but not too close. "I'm exhausted."

He looked at her, his light brown eyes searching her face. Slowly, he leaned in to kiss her cheek.

She didn't move or say anything and it was difficult to know how she felt other than suddenly warm. Cyrus brought his hand up and touched her cheek. She turned her head into his fingers. "Cyrus, we're only going to sleep."

He gently pulled her into an embrace. She sat unmoving for a long moment then let her mind go blank with exhaustion. He gave her a squeeze, and she felt safe. This was how she wanted to be touched. They lay back onto their sides, fitting together like two left shoes placed side by side.

Francesca felt herself falling fast into sleep. Cyrus kissed the back of her neck, just below the hairline. She woke a little more, but when she didn't move, his breathing became slow and regular. She felt herself fall asleep.

SHANNON'S GHOST FOUND himself, once again, pouring out of a book. Now he was standing in the same library he had woken in not two days ago. The circular room was dark save for a sparse cloud of flameflies wandering around the ceiling.

Behind him, Magister Akoma stood holding the opened book from which he had come. Beside him was ancient Magistra Niyol, her all-white eyes bright in the flameflies' incandescence.

At their feet lay two bodies wrapped in green cloaks. One had the golden stunning spell coiled around his mind. The other's neck was bent at an impossible angle. The ghost drew in an unnecessary breath and looked at Magistra Niyol. She looked back with a grim expression. "We tripped some kind of alarm coming in here," she said in a cool voice. "The result is regrettable."

The ghost glanced at the wind mage with a broken neck and then cast, *"And the demon?"*

"No sign of him or the canonist. I fear he's fled."

The ghost resisted the urge again to ask who or what she was. Instead he wrote, *"The book with my memories?"*

She pointed behind him. He turned around and saw the same book he had discovered two days ago. Someone had removed the note, but there were dark stains spangled across the cover. Shannon held his remaining hand toward the book but then paused, unsure if he could open it.

"Let me, Magister," Magister Akoma said and turned the cover.

The ghost looked at the young wizard, his handsome face and intelligent eyes. Shannon had taught Lotannu before he could grow a beard. He had never been close to Lotannu as he had to other students, but he had always liked him. Now the ghost nodded and wrote, *"Thank you, Magister."*

The other man bowed his head.

The ghost looked down at the opened book. Its pages glowed with Numinous prose. He had no idea how one separated a memory from a ghost, or how that ghost might put that memory back into his head. So, experimentally, he put his hand on the page.

Nothing happened.

He pinched the first paragraph and pulled. The sentences spun around his hand and formed a golden, swirling nimbus. The page flipped over, and more language joined the cloud around his hand. The pages flipped faster and faster, and the cloud around his hand shone so brightly that he had to look away. There was a sudden flash, but when he looked down he saw nothing but his own transparent hand and a blank book.

"Did it work?" Magistra Niyol asked.

"*I don't think so,*" he cast to her but then wrote, "*Wait.*" When he tried to recall leaving the Heaven Tree Valley, the image of Nicodemus's scowling face came to mind. He remembered the feast the kobolds organized the night before they left, the drinking, the singing. He remembered the long journey across the savanna, their first skirmishes with the lycanthropes, a whole year building contacts in the city of Avel.

"Can you remember how Typhon got a hold of you?" Magistra Niyol asked.

He frowned. "*There was an attack on a warehouse where we were hiding. My author and I were still one . . . but some kind of warkite surprised us. I remember seeing myself bleeding on the ground and thinking I'd died.*"

Magistra Niyol nodded as she read this. "Then what?"

"*They took me into the sanctuary, to rooms near the top of the dome. I was fighting as hard as I could, so I couldn't see things clearly. Deirdre was there. And a pale demon, Typhon I suppose. But there was a woman . . . or what I thought was a woman.*"

"She wasn't a woman?" Magistra Niyol asked.

"*Give me a moment,*" he wrote while wracking his memory. "*I think she was a ghost. She did something to my mind. I think it was she who took out my memories. That would make sense. Deirdre wouldn't have known what was happening to me. She wouldn't have been able to see me or this other woman. Perhaps the demon told her, but she simply thought it was part of Shannon's murder. That would explain why she left the note for me to find my murderer. Especially given the fact that I didn't recognize that ghost at the time, but I think she was the ghost of someone I've since seen.*"

Magistra Niyol narrowed her white eyes at Shannon after reading this. "Typhon took you to the ghost of someone who's still alive?"

The ghost nodded. "*This might sound mad, but now I'm certain about whose ghost removed my memories.*" He paused before writing, "*It was Francesca's.*"

LATE AT NIGHT, Francesca woke when Cyrus got out of bed. She heard his feet clap on the floorboards, the door open. He was going to pee. Her own bladder felt distended. When Cyrus came back, she got up and was surprised to see a kobold in the other bed. Dross maybe? Except for Vein, she couldn't identify any of the kobolds.

Outside the sky was lightening with dawn. The air was cold, so after squatting behind a nearby fern, she hurried back into the cabin. Inside, it remained dark. The kobolds would have built it to be so.

Once by their bed, Cyrus lifted the blankets for her to climb back into their warmth. As she did so, she saw his head against the sheets: his black curls on white cloth, his mouth covered by a veil. Though her mind was still slow with sleep, she had a sudden lucid awareness of her progress through life, not yet old but well away from youth. She'd lived half a spellwright's life already. It had seemed to go by so fast, and yet there was so much more she wanted to do.

Settling into bed next to an old lover, his lungs drawing even breath, his heart softly kicking, Francesca felt as if life was a spinning firework of night and day too soon exhausted. She wondered what it would be like when the whirling exchange of sun and stars ended for her. She wondered if death would seem strange, or if it would be a return to what she had known before birth.

Pulling the covers more tightly around her shoulders, she felt a dreamlike conviction that death would be a state she had already experienced.

SHANNON'S GHOST WAS the first into Typhon's private study. Like the rest of the quarters atop the dome, it was deserted. Magistra Niyol was certain the demon had fled. Her ancient face had tightened when she announced that the hunt for the demon would have to start over when he resurfaced in another city.

Typhon had left in haste. Chairs lay overturned. Books and scrolls lay strewn across a table and floor. Magister Akoma stood frowning over the loose manuscripts. "It's some kind of research," he mumbled while moving a few sheets around. "Not like anything I've seen."

Meanwhile, Magistra Niyol and the ghost searched the shelved books. After only a moment, Vivian pulled a book from the shelves. "This one," she said and undid the clasp. The ghost walked over to her. Magister Akoma didn't look up from the pages spread before him.

Vivian leafed through the book and then, with fingers surprisingly dexterous for their age, plucked free a page of golden prose and tossed it into the air. A stream of text followed in a glowing eruption. The pages of the book flipped until they reached the back cover.

The resulting golden cloud condensed into the transparent figure of a tall woman with freckled skin and a braid of dark hair streaked with white. She was without doubt Francesca's ghost . . . only she seemed twice as old as the living Francesca.

Magistra Niyol cleared her throat. "Francesca?"

The female ghost turned, a confused look on her face. Then she closed her eyes and lowered her head as if falling asleep.

"Francesca?" the living woman repeated.

The female ghost's eyes snapped open and she looked around.

This somnolent state must have been what Shannon's ghost had been in when Deirdre had freed him from a book. *"Ask her to write a note to herself,"* Shannon wrote.

Magistra Niyol frowned at the request but then asked Francesca's ghost to write in Numinous the date of her author's birth. The ghost obeyed. Magistra Niyol stepped closer and plucked the golden sentence from the ghost's hands. "She thinks her author was born more than three hundred years ago."

Shannon's ghost frowned. *"Ask her to write down when her author died."*

Magistra Niyol did, and when she took the sentence from Francesca's ghost, she shook her head. "The ghost thinks her author has been dead for a hundred years."

"I don't understand," Shannon replied.

"Nor do I."

"How long will it take before she becomes lucid enough to correspond with us?"

Magistra Niyol seemed to consider the question. "I can't say. But we shouldn't dally. Even if Typhon has fled, the many rebellious hierophants could make things bloody." She looked at the ghost. "Let's put both you and her in this journal. We can pull you out in a safer location."

"Where would we go?"

"Tonight, we'll have to find a room in a tavern. Then we find a caravan out to Coldlock Harbor so I can cast a colaboris spell to Lurrikara."

"But what of my author? And Nicodemus and Francesca?"

Vivian nodded. "After the colaboris is off, we can focus on finding Nicodemus."

"He's not the anti-Halcyon."

"I will make my own judgment about that when we find him. And when I do, no doubt he won't be far from your author."

The ghost rubbed his chin and then nodded.

"Vivian," Magister Akoma said.

Ghostly Shannon turned to see the man still standing over the table covered with open books and research.

"I think it's a metaspell," he said. "Something that can change the nature of language within a large area. It seems to take some linguistic aspect of the caster and imbue that area with the rules inherent to that aspect."

Magistra Niyol let out a long breath. "My friend, could you say that in a way that makes sense?"

He looked at her. "If a demon cast this spell, it would make all languages in the area more demonic, which I think would mean that language would become more chaotic . . . maybe more intuitive as well. I'm guessing it's meant to help the demonic legions gain a foothold on this continent."

"We should destroy it," Shannon cast to both of the wizards.

Magister Akoma shook his head. "But consider what would happen if the Halcyon cast this spell: she could make all languages more logical. She could make the nature of language itself antidemonic."

Vivian paused and then said, "Gather up all the manuscripts. When there's time tonight, make a copy of your findings in here." She held up Francesca's clinical journal.

"One thing more," Magister Akoma said softly. "The Halcyon could cast this spell, but so could the Storm Petrel."

Magistra Niyol went stiff. "Then we had better put it someplace safe and try to discover who Nicodemus truly is." She glanced at the ghost. "While we're at it, let's find out what kind of creature is walking around in a living body calling herself Francesca."

FRANCESCA WOKE AGAIN when her bed rocked. She looked up and saw Cyrus stumbling onto his feet. He didn't say anything, so she turned away and closed her eyes. A hand grabbed her hip.

"What?" she groaned as she rolled over. Or rather, tried to groan. For some reason, her voice didn't seem to work. She swallowed. Cyrus was swaying above her, his lips were moving but his voice was also gone. She sat up and tried to say "Cyrus?" but heard nothing. The light slipping through the few chinks in the boards began to fade. The cabin grew darker.

Cyrus was moving more frantically now. "Cyrus, what's happened?" This time she could feel voice vibrating in her throat, but she couldn't hear that voice. In fact, she could not hear anything. She had gone deaf. She tried to run for the door, but the light had disappeared. It was then she knew the cabin wasn't growing darker; she was going blind.

CHAPTER

forty

Francesca burst from the cabin into sunlight and chaos. Uprooted redwoods lay all around. One had crushed a cabin. A kobold head and severed torso protruded from the wreckage. Something massive had torn deep gashes into the dirt. All through this scene twisted tendrils of blindness.

Francesca yelled to Cyrus but could not hear her own voice. For a moment she went completely blind. Panic coursed through her, and then she was running. Vision returned with a giant, toppled redwood trunk. She jumped onto the giant tree. The bark jabbed into her chest and stomach, but she ignored the pain and climbed over the tree and fell into a bank of ferns.

In the shade her vision improved, but she still could not hear. She tried to run farther into the forest, but suddenly the ferns around her burned with direct sunlight. She turned to watch a redwood come crashing down to soundlessly slap the forest floor. The gigantic tree slowly wobbled as it rebounded.

She looked toward the tree's roots and saw a ball of blindness. The nothing grew larger in her vision, as if it were moving toward her.

She turned to run but veins of blindness twisted around her. Dark figures, kobolds maybe, sprinted past. Something struck her back, and the visible world vanished. She sensed acceleration. Agony flying up one arm. Then all pain, all touch, all orientation in space vanished.

She had died.

She was dead.

She was pretty sure she was dead.

What else could this be?

She searched for something to move, for her body. Nothing. She tried again. Still nothing. This was death?

A quarter hour passed.

Maybe.

A day passed.

Maybe.

Perhaps no time had passed. Was death a mind isolated in void? She had always assumed death would be either as the priests claimed or be nothing at all. But the priests seemed to have it all wrong. There was no spirit hurtling through the universe to an eternity-deciding judgment by the Creator. Then again, she had not returned to the nothingness she had been before birth.

She was still herself.

And she was still capable of irritation. If this was the afterlife, then it was bloody pathetic. To have thought but not perception, it was God-of-gods damned anticlimactic. It was evidence of a poorly constructed moral underpinning of the universe.

She wondered if, sometime during eternity, she'd get to speak to the God-of-gods. If so, she had some bloody choice things to say. A soul should be judged, transformed, or evaporated. It should not, under any blasted circumstances, be suspended in nothingness the way a cucumber might be suspended in brine to make a pickle. That smacked of a Creator who had gotten halfway through imbuing moral value into the universe and then said, "Screw it, let's get a drink."

The list of snide, enraged, and blasphemous things she'd like to scream at the God-of-gods flared through her isolated mind.

But then . . .

The blurry image of a redwood canopy flashed before her. A pale sky high above. Slowly her eyes focused on individual branches. Something moved above her. A massive creature. She could see the backs of its legs, its buttocks, its skin a deep gray, in places glassy, in others covered with mollusklike parasites that dug their shells into its skin and extended feathery organs into the air where they fluttered in the wind.

The creature took a step backward, and the ground shook. Then her hands tingled and she felt an invisible wall slam down on her. It took a moment to realize that it must have been the shockwave from an explosion.

The nightmare creature vanished.

Shakily, she stood and looked around the empty forest. A kobold was by her side. It wasn't Vein. One of the others. He took her arm and led her away. When she fell, he carried her in his arms as easily as if she were a child.

The kobold ran into the forest, eventually reaching a tight ring of trees with a pit in their center. Francesca had heard of such "fairy rings," created by young saplings that grew up from the roots of an ancient, dying tree. Magister Shannon, Azure, Vein, two other kobolds, and Cyrus were crouched at one end.

Cyrus ran to her and took her in his arms. She embraced him and discovered that tears were streaming down her face. Cyrus was speaking to her. But she couldn't hear. "I can't hear," she said. He winced as if she had just yelled. Maybe she had yelled. She couldn't tell how loud her voice was. "I've gone deaf," she said.

Cyrus seemed to talk to Shannon. An arc of golden prose was flowing between the old wizard's brow and that of Azure. The familiar was studying Francesca.

Cyrus's arms were still around her, but her legs were shaking. "I'm going to sit," she announced and sank to the ground. The forest floor felt cool on her backside.

Her breathing was becoming ragged, so she closed her eyes and dug her fingers into the soil, soft and dark. Moments ago she had thought she was dead, and her first reaction had been to critique the Creator. Now that her mind was again possessed by a body, she felt panicked that she might yet die.

The world was ineffably beautiful—dirt in her fingernails, the fragrance of rot and growth. Cyrus's hands were on her shoulders. She looked into his face. His eyes were opened as if they couldn't open wide enough. She looked at his sharp black beard, his light brown skin.

He was beautiful. It made her cry harder.

The world was beautiful and she had almost left it. Her chest began to shake. She felt like a child. One type of shock seemed to be wearing off and another was setting in. She closed her eyes again, and Cyrus's arms closed around her. Thoughts of death made her weep. After a time, he began to rock her. She let herself be rocked until her chest stopped shaking. She wiped mucus from her nose and felt the strange peace that only a half hour of abject sobbing can bestow.

She opened her eyes and again saw Cyrus's face. With his rough thumbs, he wiped the tears on her cheeks. She took his hand. It was so warm, so real. He kissed her cheek. She wrapped her arms around him and held on.

She noticed Nicodemus sitting on a massive root, his hair splayed out across his shoulders. Sweat glistened across his chest and stomach. His olive-brown skin was covered with red welts. He must have been pulling tattooed Chthonic spells from his skin.

A two-inch laceration on his chest was weeping blood. His neck and beardless face were splattered with something that looked like black paint. Her clerical mind analyzed and categorized him as "minor wounds, nonemergency." Three kobolds were crouched at Nicodemus's feet while Shannon stood to one side. Everyone was talking.

"Cyrus, what happened?" she asked in what she hoped was a soft voice. She looked at him. His lips were moving. "I can't hear you," she whispered. "I'm deaf."

Cyrus turned toward Nicodemus. Suddenly everyone was looking at her. Shannon walked over and held out a golden sentence. She took it and translated it into: *"Are you hurt?"*

"No," she said.

He handed her a paragraph. *"The Savanna Walker got a hold of you. Nicodemus saw something flash between you two before he could reach you. We're worried that the beast did something."*

"I'm fine," she said. "Except for this temporary deafness."

Shannon grimaced.

"What?"

He paused and then held out another sentence: *"We're not sure it's temporary."*

She sat up straighter. "Why?"

"Everyone but Nicodemus went deaf when the Walker neared, but we've already regained hearing. Can you tell me if anything else might be wrong?"

"Nothing's wrong," she wrote back and then struggled to her feet. "Nothing's wrong," she said aloud.

Now Nicodemus was standing before her, something like sympathy or pity on his face.

Irritation flashed through her. "I said I'm fine."

Nicodemus and Cyrus winced. She must have spoken too loudly.

Cyrus was standing beside her now. They were closing in on her, looking at her as they might a wounded dog. "Just . . ." she tried to say more calmly, "leave me alone."

Cyrus and Shannon only stepped closer. They were talking to each other. But Nicodemus's eyes went to hers. He seemed to be searching for something. She begged him with her eyes. He understood and turned away. First Shannon and then Cyrus looked at him. They seemed to be arguing. Shannon turned away from her and went to Nicodemus. But Cyrus touched her cheek. He was speaking rapidly. "I can't hear you," she repeated with irritation and was surprised when her eyes started to tear.

He looked at her quizzically. Cyrus had learned only the hierophantic magical language; therefore, lacking fluency in the wizardly languages and the common magical languages, he could not communicate with her textually. He seemed to be talking aloud again. He tried to take her hand, but she pulled away. "Damn it, I can't hear you!" she snapped and went to the opposite side of the fairy ring. Blessedly, he didn't follow.

Safely away from their pitying stares, Francesca prayed that she had never made a patient feel the way the men had just made her feel. For a moment, her mind filled with graphic ways to tell these men, or all men in general, that they lacked the sense the God-of-gods had given to a large pot of heated glue.

But then the tears came faster and her hands began to tremble. She focused on keeping quiet her ragged breaths and sudden, involuntary inhalations. It frightened and shamed her that she could not tell if the men could hear her. Gradually her breathing slowed, and she focused on her hearing . . . or lack of it.

She strained, trying to detect even a whisper. Nothing. Not silence, nothing. She snapped her fingers next to her ears. Again nothing. She thumped her fingers against the bony protuberance behind each ear. She could feel each finger strike but could not hear the vibrations moving through her skull.

She took a deep breath and tried to remember the last thing she had heard. It must have been the previous night. Or perhaps when she had woken up to pee. But she couldn't remember having heard any sound then. She had spoken to Cyrus before falling asleep, so she had heard his voice. But no matter how hard she tried, she could not remember the sound of his voice. She could recall every word she had said, but she could not remember the sounds of those words. When she recalled them, she recalled an image of the written words.

Her hands began to tremble more violently, and she realized that she could not remember the sound attached to any word. She knew her name was Francesca, but not what Francesca sounded like. "Cyrus," she tried to say. "Nicodemus."

The two men almost ran to her. Shannon followed more slowly.

"I can't remember sound," she tried to say and realized as she did that she remembered the movements of the mouth, tongue, lips, larynx that produced a word, but not the tone, pitch, or timbre those movements would produce.

As Shannon moved to stand by Cyrus, he cast a golden sentence. She translated it into, *"What does that mean?"*

She cleared her throat and spoke. "It means that whatever the Savanna Walker did involves more than my ears. Or perhaps doesn't involve my ears at all. He has altered the part of my mind that perceives and processes sound."

The men were looking at her and one another in confusion.

"It's the only explanation why I can't remember or imagine any sound that—"

Shannon interrupted her by casting another sentence. *"I am sorry, Magistra, but we cannot understand you."*

She frowned at the message until she understood: unable to regulate her voice, she must have produced a mash of sound. She folded into a ball and began to rock. Cyrus's arms surrounded her. They stayed like that for a long time. When she looked up, she saw Nicodemus crouched a safe distance away. She had again reached the calmness that comes after weeping, and from this calmness she recognized Nicodemus's sympathetic expression. She was now disabled like he was.

She wrote an explanation as to how she knew that her mind's ability to perceive, recall, and imagine sound had been extinguished. She cast the resulting spell to Nicodemus. But the man jumped away from her spell. An instant later, a thin silvery sentence wrapped around her paragraph and yanked it to Shannon's waiting hand. The old wizard seemed to read the passage aloud.

The other two men looked at her—Cyrus's expression full of pity, Nicodemus's pained as if the agony of his own disability had worsened. The men talked for a while. Then Shannon wrote a response and cast it to her. "We think the Savanna Walker might have taken a portion of your mind the way Typhon took Nicodemus's ability to spell. We might get it back once we chase after the beast."

"Chase after?"

"Nicodemus wounded the Walker. Using the beast's name allowed Nicodemus to escape the Walker's influence; however, Nico could combat it only in the forest shade, and the beast escaped into the sunlight. We are not sure why, but he did not flee back into the city. He ran north into the savanna."

She frowned at this. "How could we find him? The savanna is vast, even to the north."

When Shannon read this aloud, Cyrus took her hand and said something. She looked at Shannon who wrote: "Jasp and Flint are to take Cyrus to the wind marshal to try to enlist her help."

She shook her head. "We can't go to such lengths just to recover my hearing."

Shannon replied. "It's not just your hearing that's been lost. The Walker killed Dross and Slag. They were brothers. The beast cut Dross down, and Slag charged."

Francesca brought her hands to her mouth. She had been so terrified that she'd forgotten about the dead kobolds she'd seen.

Shannon held out another sentence. "Also, Boann's ark is gone. The beast might have taken it. We're not sure how the beast found us, but we think it has something to do with Deirdre's death and the residual bond her body had with the ark. And the beast is now wounded. If Nicodemus can catch him at night, he could deprive Typhon of one of his dragons."

Francesca grimaced. She had forgotten that she was supposed to somehow confound the trap the demon was setting with the still-hidden second dragon. Given that she could no longer even hear, it seemed impossible that she could do anything useful, much less help Nicodemus escape a creature like the Savanna Walker.

But she looked at Cyrus and nodded. He spoke for a while. Shannon translated for her: *"He doesn't want you to worry. He promises we will get your hearing back."*

She shook her head. *"Tell him I'm fine. Tell him to be careful."*

Shannon spoke to Cyrus and then wrote to her: *"He promises."* Once she had read this, Cyrus took her hands and kissed her cheek. She nodded and squeezed his hand. After a few words with Nicodemus and Shannon, Cyrus hiked off into the forest with Jasp and Flint.

Feeling more collected, Francesca stood and found Vein. Little air had spilled into his chest. She shunted the air out and gave his shoulder a pat she hoped would reassure him.

That done, she went back to the camp. Nicodemus and Shannon were searching through the ruins. Two kobold bodies, Dross and Slag, had been laid in the shade and covered with blankets. Francesca stood at their feet and said a short prayer to the Creator for them. Halfway through, she wondered if they also prayed to the Creator.

When finished, she turned back to Nicodemus and Shannon, who were picking through the remains of what had been the storehouse. Azure rode on the old man's shoulder to help him see. Both men wore hardened expressions; the Savanna Walker had killed their comrades before. This was only one battle in their ongoing war.

As she walked toward them, Francesca passed a ruined cabin and spotted on the ground a tortoiseshell comb.

She picked it up. One of its fine teeth had been broken, but the others were strong and smooth.

By patting around her head, Francesca discovered that much of her hair had come loose from her braid. She hadn't had a chance to brush it since . . . God-of-gods, the night before Deirdre had died on her table. That had been only two days ago, but it felt like a lifetime.

She sat down on a log and pulled her braid over her shoulder. She remembered that she had often sung to herself, a rustic song about a widow waiting for the long Northern Spirish dry season to end. She could remember all the words to the song, but none of its sounds or notes. She felt hollow as she realized that music had become something she understood only in the abstract.

She began to comb out her braid. Her hair was her only vanity. It was comforting now to watch it slowly spill down around her shoulders in loose curls that shone like darkly polished oak. She'd learned that if she wore it loose like this it would distract her male patients.

When finished, she held the comb and traced the broken tooth. As she did so, she realized something strange.

She knew that such combs came only from the Ixonian Archipelago, that Port Mercy was among those islands, and that she had spent nearly a decade there learning to become a cleric. And yet she could not recall seeing a single tortoiseshell comb there. She frowned as she realized that she could not picture the city of Port Mercy or the clerical academy.

She thought about her mother's combing song. She knew the words; she knew her mother had sung it; but she had no memories of a comb moving through her childhood hair, of her mother's face, or . . . anything to do with her home. It was as if she had read a biography about her own life but not lived it.

She jumped as the shock of realization moved through her.

She looked up toward the ruined storehouse and found Nicodemus looking at her while he dragged away a beam. The instant he saw her looking at him, he turned back to the beam.

She paused as she realized that he'd been staring at her, likely at her hair. It almost made her smile before she remembered her discovery. "Nicodemus," she called, hopefully understandably. "Shannon."

When the men came to her she looked between them and then handed Shannon a sentence. When the old man read it aloud, she saw the pain on Nicodemus's face increase.

It read: *"Every memory I had of my life before I came to Avel is gone; the Savanna Walker stole them."*

forty-one

Cyrus had been in the wind marshal's quarters only once before, years ago. Marshal Oria had called him in and offered to promote him if he joined the Sharptree expedition. One of Cyrus's old shipmates—a young and pretty pilot named Sylvia—was stationed on that expedition. The marshal had given Cyrus a day to decide.

He hadn't seen Francesca until late that night, when she returned to their quarters exhausted. She had only four hours to sleep before starting another shift. When he mentioned his possible promotion, they quarreled for an hour. Almost frantic that she would now get only three hours of sleep, Francesca had threatened to find an empty cot in the infirmary. He relented.

The next morning, Cyrus accepted the promotion. After writing a brief farewell letter to Francesca, he flew out to Coldlock Harbor and shipped out on the evening tide.

And now Francesca had come crashing back into his life. Or perhaps it was the other way around. He had been the one who left, and now he had returned. He liked to think that he lived as he flew, with practiced precision and taking only calculated risks. But Francesca had been like a powerful ridge lift, at once unpredictable and turbulent but also uplifting. Perhaps things between them had failed because they had been too young, too volatile.

Now they were older, wiser. She was a physician; he of sufficient rank to one day make captain. Provided they survived the current crisis, he would still need to wait a year at least for an airship. Perhaps here in Avel they could start again. Then after he made captain . . . well . . . she had always wanted to practice in a larger eastern city, and he would be able to fly her anywhere. It was an attractive daydream. But it was only a daydream.

First he had to confront the growing potential for violence in Avel and track down the beast that had stolen Francesca's ability to hear.

Cyrus looked around the rooms. They were large for hierophants' quarters: colorful rugs, cushions, ornate screens, several plants that looked related to Ixonian banana trees. It was more or less the same as it had been all those years ago. Except for the man he had just censored and bound in sailcloth. He was new.

Voices sounded down the hall. A moment later the door opened and Marshal Oria and Captain Izem stepped inside. They stopped when they saw Cyrus and his prisoner. With a flurry of motion, the newcomers set blazing blue paragraphs flying across their robes. Their cloth billowed up, ready to strike.

Cyrus removed his veil.

"Cyrus?" Izem asked.

"Captain," he said with a bow and then faced Oria. "Marshal, apologies for violating protocol."

Izem shut the door and locked it while Oria walked toward the bound man. "Who?"

"A young pilot unfortunate enough to rescue me when I came stumbling out of the forest. Unsuspecting, he wove me into his rig, trying to get away from the lycanthropes."

Izem turned to Oria. "If I can fight our way to the drop deck, I can get the *Queen's Lance* aloft in an hour."

She shook her head and looked at Cyrus. "Talk fast. You may have just touched off the Second Civil War."

Cyrus reported everything he had discovered in Avel, including his encounters with Nicodemus Weal, the man's suspicion of a demon in Cala's court, the hierophants who had attacked Nicodemus's party, and finally the disastrous encounter with the Savanna Walker.

"Did anyone see you come in here?" Oria asked.

Cyrus shook his head. "I had my veil up and controlled my prisoner through his robes. Also, you should know he admitted to supporting Cala's independence, though he denies any knowledge of a demon."

Oria lowered her own veil to grimace. Then she turned to Izem. "Captain, have this prisoner assigned to your ship. Explain his disappearance however you can. Then have him discretely flown to Coldlock Harbor. No dramatics like last time."

He bowed. "Yes, my lady."

"Marshal," Cyrus blurted, "permission to suggest a plan of action."

"What do you want, Warden?"

"Captain Izem's assistance searching the Northern Savanna for the Walker."

She stared at him. "Maybe you don't understand the importance of the situation. Izem couldn't tell me until we were in private, but Celeste has ordered the entire western fleet to Lurrikara. They're ready to cross over to Avel. Those two black-robes, Vivian and Lotannu, are on some mission to

defuse the situation. Something to do with this supposed demon and finding Nicodemus Weal. Given what you said, it seems they'll fail. That being
so, I cannot spare Izem to chase after some strange creature."

Cyrus thought fast. His first instinct was to explain how desperately he
needed to recover Francesca's ability to hear. But that would mean nothing
to the marshal. So he found himself saying, "My lady, if the wizards are
here to apprehend Nicodemus, then might I assume that it is also our Celeste's desire that we apprehend Nicodemus?"

Oria pursed her lips and looked at Izem. "Do you remember the wording
of the orders?"

"I do," he said. "And I believe that the warden's interpretation is correct.
If we can bring Nicodemus into our custody, we must."

Cyrus cleared his throat. "Let me fly Nicodemus out to hunt this creature. If Nicodemus dies, that will be the end of that. If he kills the Walker,
surely that will weaken whatever power is ruling Avel. Perhaps more important, Nicodemus will be in our custody."

Oria kept her lips pursed. "I don't like the idea of Izem being away." She
drew a breath in through her nose. "I have spent the last few days bringing
those pilots faithful to Celeste into the garden tower and sending the rest
to Avel. If violence breaks out, the wind garden must survive."

Cyrus resisted the urge to renew his argument.

"However," she said slowly, "sending Izem's warship away would reduce
the tension between tower and city." She looked at the captain. "How fast
can you make a run to Dar, out to Lurrikara, and back here?"

"A day with full sails. But we'd have to find the creature before we could
begin the run."

Oria nodded. "But you might take my report to Dar and the fleet. Very
well, Captain, your orders are to search for this beast for a day. If you do not
find it, begin your run."

He bowed. "As you command."

Oria turned to Cyrus. "Warden, you've just talked yourself aboard a
warship."

Francesca helped Nicodemus and Shannon salvage what they could
from the wrecked storehouse. Afterward, they trekked farther into the forest and made new camp in dark shade. In brief golden paragraphs, Shannon explained why the coming night might be a soggy one: redwood pine
needles condensed moisture in the air to make it rain on their roots. This
happened most when cold fog came in from the sea. Though there was no
rain in the dry season, the fog rolled in each night and burned off each
midmorning.

As they worked, Nicodemus and Shannon bickered. Francesca tried to follow along, casting requests for translations. Shannon complied when he could, but the argument often absorbed all his attention.

Francesca grew tired of this and sat down to brush her hair again. This seemed to give Shannon an unfair advantage as Nicodemus glanced at her every few moments. Francesca felt a little guilty for handicapping the younger man, but only a little. After what had happened to her, she deserved a small indulgence.

Once finished with her hair, she tried to rejoin the conversation by casting sentences to both Shannon and Nicodemus. But the younger man jumped away as if the spells might burn him. The old man replied only briefly.

So Francesca asked if she could head out for a walk. The old man reassured her that the forest lycanthropes wouldn't come near a kobold camp. She wandered at first, heading toward the nearest finger of the narrows. Though she'd spent years gazing at the redwoods from one infirmary window or another, she'd never been among them.

The giant trees grew to impressive height, their branches forming dense canopies, the spaces between which were filled with dark, flitting birds. The little sunlight that slipped through the branches glided down in slender beams. The forest floor was green with arching ferns and smaller, tilted laurel trees.

Wandering farther, Francesca began to feel as if the whole world was made of solemn groves and sunlight. But then she saw a black-headed blue jay, its beak open and its tiny feathered chest contracting. She couldn't hear if the bird was singing or squawking.

She walked with purpose toward the narrows. There were a few fern banks she had to fight through and a steep ravine to traverse, but then she came across bushes growing among gray boulders. Picking her way through these, she found herself standing in the sunlight.

After the forest's darkness at noon, the brightness was dazzling. The narrow before her was perhaps twenty feet wide, its glassy surface a green mirror for the sky. Slow, circular ripples expanded across the water from a point somewhere to her right. Francesca looked down just in time to see the shell and languid hind legs of a turtle disappearing into the deeper green.

She stood and looked around. Everything was still.

Slowly, she tied her hair into a ponytail and pulled off her stole and robe, then her boots and underclothes. Naked, she crept to the waterline so she could dunk her clothes. She cast a few frothy white runes into the cloth before washing out the soapy texts. Then she hung the clothes on the bushes to dry.

She had begun to sweat and so dipped her ankles into the water and found it surprisingly warm. She paused and looked down at her body. It was strange how often she examined the bodies of others but how rarely she examined her own. Usually bathing was a hurried ritual, racing through the motions so she could get to her patients. Now she truly looked at herself: her tall frame; pale skin, solar white in the sunlight; long legs that had always been too muscular for her liking; her waist, no longer as narrow as it had been; her breasts still too small. She ran a hand down her stomach. Fortunately it was still flat . . . well, flat enough that her iliac bones were visible on either side of her pelvis. Her navel had a bit more padding around it now. She noted a few red dots, cherry angioma. She sighed again. Cherry angiomata were a normal sign of aging skin.

She wasn't young anymore.

And now she was deaf and had lost the most personal memories of her life. Could she still be a physician? Had she retained enough knowledge? How could she listen to her patients—their stories, their hearts, their lungs, the gurgling of their guts? She crouched, wrapped her arms around her legs, expected to cry. But she didn't.

The sun became hot on her shoulders. She sat back and felt the warm rock on her backside. A breeze picked up. She stretched her legs out into the water. Using her hands, she scooted farther and farther into the water until she slid off the rock.

Though the sun had heated the upper layers of water, the deeper green was startlingly cold. She launched herself into a crawl. She knew that in Port Mercy she and her classmates had snuck away from the university to splash in the warm Ixonian Sea. And yet she had no specific memories of swimming. Again she had the feeling that she had read her own biography but not lived it.

She crossed the water and swam back. The exercise warmed her, and she stroked along the bank until she found a small gravelly beach. Crouched in a warm pocket of shallow water, she took handfuls of the fine gravel and scrubbed her face and back.

Suddenly worried someone would steal her clothes, she swam back to her rock. But her things were untouched. She pulled herself onto the rock and lay out to dry.

At first she shivered, but the sun above and the rock below were warm. At some point, she must have fallen asleep because she woke with trembling hands and began to cry for her lost hearing and memories. At first she fought the tears, but then she curled into a ball. She wept until she felt calmer, almost numb.

She rose, washed her face, and dressed. The shadows were longer now, and she supposed she had slept for an hour. Shannon and Nicodemus had likely finished arguing. She could return to camp without being ignored. But she wanted to be alone for a little while longer. So she wandered down the bank, frightening frogs and turtles into the water as she went. It was often tough going; bushes grew densely by the water, and they forced her to take detours into the forest. The farther she went, the higher the bank rose, until she was walking along a ledge that dropped ten feet to the water. Here the redwoods grew up to the edge and left the bank in dark shadow.

As she walked, Francesca tried to decide how she was feeling. Mostly numb, she supposed, but there was fear below the surface, along with shock and agony . . . and hope of recovering her hearing and memories.

A boulder required Francesca to walk into the forest a ways. As she did so, she realized that she hadn't seen a single dead tree near the camp. Everywhere else the forest was strewn with them. The Silent Blight seemed to be less severe here.

She had just returned to the bank when something dark rose out of the water. Reflexively, she dropped into a crouch. Her heart began to hammer. She looked back for a sign of danger. But the forest held nothing but ferns and sunlight.

She turned back to the water, expecting to see a strange species of aquatic lycanthrope or some grotesque, living fragment of the Savanna Walker. She saw only Nicodemus, his wet hair pasted down his shoulders, his broad back facing her. As she watched, he waded onto what must have been a sandbank. He sank down and then came up with a fist of sand, with which he started to scrub his armpit.

As he worked, Francesca could see in perfect detail the muscular anatomy of his back—his shoulder's deltoid bunched up as he lifted one arm, the wing of his scapula bone moving smoothly under his olive skin, the broad latissimus muscle that give him a triangle shape.

Francesca stepped closer.

He bent forward to scrub his face. Up out of the water came his lower back, water running down the gentle grove of his spine, the V of his pelvic girdle narrowing to the elevation of his gluteus medius and gluteus maximus muscles that, one stretching over the other, proceeded down under green water to form his buttocks.

He sank down, disappearing under the water. Unexpectedly, she felt no rush of desire, no sudden embarrassment or heightened sexual curiosity.

He was a young healthy male, a study in anatomy, beautiful to her physician's soul the way a bright star was beautiful, beautiful the way the interlocking currents of a river were beautiful.

He came up out of the water and pushed himself into a side stroke. His long left leg rose through the green to demonstrate the parallel design of the quadriceps muscles. "Nicodemus," she called out.

The man became a thrash of white water that propelled itself to the opposite bank.

"Nicodemus, it's just me!"

He was now standing in a recess of deep shade, one hand on his chest, ready to pull free some Chthonic wartext and, light permitting, blast her into pulp.

Ignoring this, she picked her way down to the water. When she looked up again, Nicodemus had pressed one hand to his face in exasperation. His lips were moving. She doubted he was saying anything complimentary about her.

His pants were spread across a nearby boulder. She looked up at him and motioned for him to come closer.

He frowned but sank into the water and made a creditable breast stroke to her. She forged a sentence that would read, *"Could you bear to correspond with me for a moment?"* She grinned, wondering if he'd catch the play on "bare."

But as the golden sentence floated away from her, Nicodemus waded to his right so it wouldn't touch him. The spell floated halfway across the water before sinking below the surface and disappearing into the green. Francesca looked at him. He shook his head. She wrote and cast, *"What's the matter?"* But again, he sidestepped the question.

"Nicodemus!" she scolded. "Please?"

He looked at her and shook his head.

She met his eyes. "I'm deaf."

His expression softened. His shoulders rose and fell. He waved toward himself in a gesture that might mean "come here" or "let me have it."

She wrote out. *"Why are you so afraid of corresponding?"* and sent it floating to him.

He plucked the sentence from the air. Instantly, the runes began rearranging. He wasn't even trying to translate it. Rather, he looked at her with a face that might have been ashamed but was perhaps only pained. He held the now nonsensical sentence out to her: "This is why," he was saying in the language of gesture. Abruptly the golden sentence tore itself into nothing.

His cacography. He could make it powerfully disruptive or slow it down. But he could not stop it.

"Try!" she said out loud.

He shook his head.

"Please. Try," she said. "I'm deaf."

He held out both his hands, palms up.

"G'ahh!" she groaned. "Try!" she repeated and then looked around for anything that could force his hand.

Her eyes fell on his pants.

She looked back at him just as he looked back at her.

She grinned. He moved his lips, clearly saying, "Don't—"

But she was off, bounding over the rocks until she scooped up his pants.

He was only a few strokes away, but he could not grab her foot or pull her into the water without giving her a canker curse. So she nimbly climbed up the shady ledge, giggling.

Nicodemus was still waist deep in lake water. His lips were moving fast, and she would have paid a year's wages to know what he was saying. She managed to stop laughing long enough to yell out, "Try!" He looked to still be swearing, so she yelled again, "Try!"

He only looked at her.

"Try, or come and get these." She shook his pants.

He glared.

Only with supreme control could she keep from laughing.

He glared for a while longer but then wrote a small golden spell and threw it up to her.

Gleefully, she translated it to "*I hate yu*" and then exploded into laughter.

She replied: "*Bet you say that to all the girls who leave you naked in a lake.*"

After catching the reply, he had to rush to translate it before it misspelled. Even with his full concentration, the text crumbled into golden dust. At last he tossed up an answer: "*I tryed. Give my close back.*"

She smiled at the misspellings but knew better than to mock them . . . yet. She wrote to him: "*This isn't so bad, is it?*"

"*Yehs, it is!*"

"*Promise me you'll keep corresponding.*"

"*NO!*"

"*Otherwise, you won't get your pants.*"

"*I hate yu.*"

She giggled again and was about to reply when Nicodemus looked up at the sky. She followed his gaze and saw what she at first mistook for a giant white seagull. Then the long, slim lines declared the object to be the *Queen's Lance*. It shot overhead, flying straight for their old camp. She looked down to see Nicodemus climbing up out of the water.

Francesca was a physician, and she was also a curious woman. Had Nicodemus been any other man, she would have looked, perhaps only for a discreet moment, at his penis. But, because of the tribulations she had already put him through, she averted her eyes. Given that he had just been standing in cold water, doing so was probably denying herself a source of teasing that would have lasted her for the next hundred years.

When Nicodemus reached the ledge, she began to offer his pants to him.

But he peeled some skinspell off his left arm and cast it with a backhand motion. She tried to jump away but found herself already spellbound. Apparently, the deep shadow was dark enough for his skinspells to function.

The pants flew from her hands to Nicodemus's. He never even looked at her. After hopping into his pants, he jogged off toward the camp. A moment later, Francesca's bonds dissolved. Still laughing, she ran after.

Forty-two

Francesca had always thought of airships as flying boats. She had imagined hierophants dashing around like sailors on cloth hulls, hoisting halyards or adjusting sails or doing whatever it was pilots did. This belief had been reinforced by the few airships she had seen docking, their crews climbing over their vessels, preparing to collapse their giant constructs into stacks of cloth.

However when, using Magister Shannon to translate her Numinous sentences, she told Cyrus about her conception of airships, he laughed. "Once at altitude," he said, "the *Queen's Lance* will be very different." Francesca watched as he cast hierophantic spells into her robes that caused them to weave their cotton threads into the airship's silk. While tying a turban and veil onto her, Cyrus explained via Shannon that, unless a warship flew slowly, its pilots didn't walk on the vessel; they wore it like a garment.

Francesca didn't understand. The *Queen's Lance* looked as she always had: a hexagonal hull with bladelike wings. Francesca was now sewn into that hull as tight as a button, but that didn't make the ship a garment.

Then they set sail and Francesca discovered—while trying to scream her lungs inside out—that the airship could fold around her like a massive, demon-possessed bedsheet and yank her through the air with such velocity that she felt like her major internal organs had been mashed into paste.

Fortunately, once the *Queen's Lance* rose high enough that she could see the ocean to the west, the warship changed its conformation to become a single wing that was wider than any two market squares. Francesca, no longer screaming, was now woven into the ship in a facedown ordination. Looking up, she found an open space had been left so she could raise her head above the upper surface. Amazingly, the entire warship had become as thin as a sheet of paper.

She lowered her head to the underside. Below her stretched five thousand feet of liquid air and then the rolling savanna. She had been holding her arms against her chest, but now she let them hang in the wind.

She looked forward for Cyrus and the other pilots and saw their cloth-wrapped forms moving within the wing. The pilots were now suspended in their magical language. It allowed them to swim through woven threads like fish through water.

Looking to her right, she was surprised to see a tremendously fat hierophant not two feet from her. Then, realizing who this was, she laughed.

Getting Nicodemus aboard the warship had proved more difficult than anticipated. As soon as his skin had touched the airship, the nearby text had misspelled and fallen out of the silk. If this happened when aloft, the crew would spend the rest of their lives experimenting with screaming as a method of preventing death by high-velocity impact with the ground. Experimentation would have been brief, the results disheartening.

To prevent this scenario with some textual insulation, Cyrus and Izem had wrapped Nicodemus with so much cloth that he resembled a giant baby swaddled by an overly zealous goddess of motherhood. Francesca wrote Nicodemus a message: *"I know you were uncomfortable when I saw you naked, but this is overdoing it with the cloths just a bit, don't you think?"*

Cyrus had left the fingers of Nicodemus's right hand unbound so he could free himself in an emergency. He used the exposed digits to take Francesca's sentence and translated it. After a moment, he handed it back to her. Wondering if he had written a new message, she reached out. But the text misspelled and blasted itself into sentence fragments. Francesca jerked back, crying out in alarm.

When she looked back, Nicodemus had tilted his head forward so that he could look up at her. Even though she could see only his eyes, she recognized the expression as one of exasperation.

She wrote a sentence, translated it, and held it out to him. Being translated, it could not leave her hand without falling apart. It read: *"You're childish and irksome!"*

He gently touched it with an outstretched finger. The "c," "*ildish,*" and "*irk*" misspelled and then fell out of the sentence. The line contracted, and she was left holding *"You're handsome!"*

Snorting, she flicked the sentence away.

Nicodemus held out another sentence. *"Stop, your making me blush."*

Rolling her eyes, she replied: *"You've a high opinion of yourself."*

"You rote it."

"You misspelled what I wrote."

"I just removed the leters you accidently put in."

"Don't be retarded."

"That's like asking you not to be superselious."

"That's supercilious."

"Now its ironic."

"What's ironic?"

"You were just being superselious."

"Supercilious!"

"I'm pretty sure its irony because you don't now your being superselious."

"FLAMING HEAVEN, it's super-ci-lious!"

"That same sound could be made by 'se.'"

"Sound doesn't exist for me anymore."

"Then why under heaven are you correcting me?"

"It can't be spelled that way."

"It can be pronounced that way."

"Words aren't their sounds. I understand words, but I don't understand sound."

"Word's aren't there spelling. I understand words but I don't understand spellings."

He seemed to be searching her eyes. She wrote a reply: "You think you're handsome."

After reading this, his head bobbed and his chest shook, the very vision of laughter. She rolled her eyes, but he didn't notice. At last, he handed her a reply. She took it and read: "Hansom to whom, a bunch of kobolds? I don't know if you've resaerched their females, but I'm exactly for breasts shy of qualiffying as a looker to any of my students."

"!" she flicked back. "4?"

He shrugged.

Under her veil, she chewed her lip for a moment then replied: "Some people are born with third nipples, which are always on the same vertical line as the two expected nipples. Sometimes there is even breast tissue under the accessory nipple. In fact, any mole or dark spot you find on the same vertical line as your nipples—all the way down to your pelvis—is probably an uncompleted third nipple."

Nicodemus took the paragraph and translated it, but it fell apart before he could finish. He looked at her with eyes that seemed ashamed.

Francesca felt a little foolish. Physiological trivia was hardly important to their task. Was there anything in that last sentence that he really needed to know? Damn sure there was. She handed him one sentence: "Any mole you find directly below your nipples is probably an uncompleted third nipple."

He patted his chest and abdomen with exaggerated movements.

She smiled.

He handed her a sentence: "We're suposed to be looking for the Svanna Walker."

She looked down at the grassland rolling out to the horizon. She handed a sentence back to him: "You said the monster would run to an oasis."

He shrugged. *"All living things in the savanna must find watter."* A moment later he added, *"I don't like coresponding with you."*

She was taken aback. *"Why not?"*

"I don't like youre seeing my misspellings."

Only with great effort did she refrain from commenting on how he spelled "youre." *"You don't misspell all that badly."*

"It's not niece to lie to the retarded."

"All right! All right! I'm sorry! I won't use the word 'retarded' anymore, okay?"

"It's embarasing to misspel in front of a pretty woman."

"It's not nice to lie to plain looking women."

"I'm not lying."

"How would you know, you've spent the last decade with kobolds?"

"So you don't have 4 breasts?"

She sighed in exasperation, even though she was smiling. *"You're being childish and irksome again."*

He reached out, likely trying to again misspell her sentence into a compliment. Laughing, she jerked her hand back. But as he reached farther, a shiver moved through her as she imagined what would happen if he accidently touched her. She dropped the sentence, and it tumbled away in the wind.

Seeming to sense her fear, he withdrew his hand and looked back to the savanna. She did as well and saw amid the grass a dark circle. An oasis? Broad, squat oak trees grew around it. Nicodemus held out a sentence: *"The Walker passed thought their."*

"How can you tell?"

He pointed at something. *"The katabeast body on the bank."*

Francesca squinted. She could indeed see something ragged on the water's edge. Then, grimacing, she realized that the water around that something was tinged red.

Nicodemus handed her another sentence. *"That sould be covered with gorging lycanthropes. Or at least smaller preditors."*

"The Walker is keeping them away?"

"Kept them away but nocking out every beest's ability to smell for miles."

"How do you know he's not still down there?"

"Do you see nothing down their?"

She frowned at him before replying. *"If you're going to start with the puns again, cut me free so I won't have to endure the pain."*

"Do you see nothing? As in do you see a blind spot?"

Then Francesca understood. If the monster were down there, some part of the oasis would appear as nothing. Francesca had never looked for a blind spot before and wondered if it was even possible to "see" blindness.

But after moving her gaze across every square foot of the oasis and the surrounding grass, she realized that she had just looked for blindness. She
handed Nicodemus a sentence: *"You're right. The monster's not down there."*

"He's heding for the Greenwater." After handing her this, Nicodemus
looked forward, and his head bobbed as if he were yelling. One of the hierophants moved toward them.

"Greenwater?" Francesca asked.

*"A spirng-fed oases north of here. Once the trianing ground for lycanthrope
spellrights. The empire destroyed it. There are still metespells moving throu the
place."*

Just then, Francesca realized that the pilot coming toward them was
Cyrus. He was upside down relative to her—his belly pressed against the
airship. He was moving across the silk by reaching forward and sinking his
fingers into the fabric and then pulling himself along. He stopped a few feet
before Nicodemus. The two men seemed to yell back and forth. Nicodemus
pointed to the oasis and the dead katabeast. After a while, Cyrus pulled
himself back toward the ship's nose. The ship turned north.

Francesca handed Nicodemus a question: *"Are you able to see the Savanna
Walker?"*

*"I can. His texts misspell when they touch my skin, so they have little affect
win they reach my brain. Best he can do is make his image blurry. But now wen
I spek his name, even that fails."*

"What does he look like?"

Nicodemus shrugged. *"Like a man."*

She threw *"Lies!"* at him so fast he dropped it and it went tumbling into
the air. She was about to describe the nightmare monster she had seen
when Nicodemus held out a paragraph. *"Thou he looks like a man to me, he's
still draconic, still an incomprehensibel mosnter. He can incorperate other bodies into his own. Make himself half-horse and then grafts human arms onto that
horse. Or when he wants wait, he'll put himself into a katabeast's body and add
the torsos of his devotees. Whatever he comes up with, it's always grewsome and
he makes them seam more so by distorting your parceptions. But underneath all
that, his own body is just that of an old man with blotchy skin and missing
teeth."*

Francesca thought about this. *"Who was he before he became this thing?
And, is he still a man if he's also half a dragon?"*

Nicodemus shrugged.

"Does he talk to you?"

*"Insesently! He raerely makes sense. All the words come out in a sing-song
mash."*

Francesca lowered her eyebrows. *"When does all this talking happen?"*

"We've clashed over the years. The advnatage goes to him in brigther enve-ronments and in the city where he can make those nearby into devotees. Away from the city and in the dark, I have the advatnage."

Francesca studied Nicodemus's eyes for a while. They seemed cold again. This was the person he wanted to be—detached, calculating, ag-gressively focused on one goal.

She looked back toward the savanna. He didn't write anything more. After a while, she began to think about her own desire to become a master physician. Suddenly she found herself asking: "Could you ever read for en-joyment?"

"I was nevar fast, but I injoyed it, yes. Right up to when I fled Starhaven, I always had a book under my bed."

"What kind of books?"

He took longer to reply. "Nothing speciel."

"You're embarrassed!" she gleefully wrote.

"I am not."

"What were they, erotic Ixonian poems?"

"Knightly romances, mostly from Lorn. But a few by Spirish autors."

"I love knightly romances!"

"What did I tell you about mocking the retarded?"

"No! I read them every chance I get, which isn't often. Whom do you read?"

He stared at her for a moment and then wrote, "Robert DeRibgy."

"I love DeRigby! Though at times he can be a bit overwritten and . . . cli-chéd. What do you like about him?"

"That he's a bit overwritten and . . . clichéd."

"You're being ironic."

"I'm trying to be supercelious."

"You're not going to let that one go, huh?"

Nicodemus was looking at her differently. He held out another sen-tence. "Do you read any Isabella Gawan?"

"She's my FAVORITE!"

He seemed to laugh when he read this. "Even thouh she can get slow and . . . prechy."

"Especially when she's slow and . . . preachy!"

"Are you sure you never met a woman named April in Northern Spires?"

"Your tutor when you were young? You already asked me. No. I'm certain. Why?"

He shook his head. "Gawan was her favorite as well. It's just odd. And your long hair. But never mind."

Francesca did not know how to respond to this so she looked down to the bright savanna. Maybe a quarter hour passed. Then, suddenly, she found herself writing, *"What if we can't recover my hearing?"*

Nicodemus studied her for a long time. *"You would adjust."*

"But I wouldn't be able to speak to my patients, or listen to them. I couldn't be a physician."

Again he studied her for a long time but wrote nothing.

"It's a disability that would destroy me."

His eyes were sympathetic. *"You don't want me to lie to you and tell you it would be easy."*

"LIKE HELL I DON'T! Tell me we'll end my disability and that life'll be cream and honey and beautiful young men giving me foot massages."

His veil moved as if he were smiling. *"I'm sure your right."*

"There you go again, lying about how everything's going to be fine."

He seemed to laugh again but looked at her with a curious intensity. *"Disability might destroy part of you, but some part will remane. There is strenght in what remains."*

Francesca read this and then looked at Nicodemus. There was something beautiful in the strength he had found, something horrible as well. He was, after all, a killer. She looked back down to the grasslands and wondered what she would do to recover her hearing and her memories.

Below them the savanna was beginning to rise. Looking ahead, Francesca saw low stony hills near the horizon. She pointed.

Nicodemus handed her a sentence. *"The Greenwater is within that rang. It won't be long now."*

She didn't reply but watched the hills draw closer. Twice Cyrus came back and he and Nicodemus shouted to each other and pointed. The airship became narrower and then dropped into a dive that made the air rush past more quickly.

Maybe a quarter hour later, they flew over a hill and looked out on a wide valley, at the bottom of which lay the Greenwater—a long, narrow lake that glinted with the late afternoon sunlight. Its bank was surrounded by trees that looked like oaks but possessed trunks nearly twenty meters in diameter. Beyond the oaks stretched a valley floor covered by short grass that was interrupted by stretches of sand.

Suddenly Francesca jumped.

Nicodemus looked at her. *"What do you see?"*

She pointed at it and held out the word, *"Nothing!"*

forty-three

Nicodemus tried to sleep as they waited for darkness.

The hierophants had anchored the *Queen's Lance* to a boulder atop a rocky hill and then split the airship. Half of the cloth and all the crew landed on the hill while the other half remained aloft, kitelike. Should the crew be threatened, they could cast a spell up the tether, and the flying half would burn enough text to pull everyone aloft.

The crew, still connected to the ship by silk cords, set up a basic camp. They used the ship's silk to fashion short two-person tents and then served a meal of flatbread, cheese, and water.

When the sun set, Francesca sat beside Nicodemus and handed him a sentence. He translated it quickly but still introduced a few misspellings. *"You'd beter come back or their be won't anyone to rite me agravatengly misspelled messeges."*

He handed her a sentence that read *"a'!Djnr'WeO9WC;EsrioN"* and then, *"was that enuff misspelling to tide you over untill I get back?"*

Laughing, she threw his own words back into his face. He pretended she'd just put one of his eyes out. It wasn't terribly funny, but he laughed loudly, nervously. Her laughter was a disconcerting monotone. She couldn't hear herself.

She handed him, *"What if it's a trap? The trap with the second dragon?"*

"Youll save me from it."

"How do I do that?"

He shrugged. *"Youll think of soemthing."*

She rolled her eyes.

Neither of them wrote for a moment. The horizon was darkening. She made ready to stand and leaned in slightly. He recognized this as the action of someone about to lend a comforting touch—a hand on the shoulder, a pat on his back.

He quickly leaned away.

Hurt registered on her pale face and in her very dark brown eyes.

Hot panic knotted itself up inside his chest as if he'd just broken something valuable.

But then her face relaxed as she remembered what his touch would do to her. She held out a sentence: *"Be careful!"*

After he nodded, she walked away. He thought about her as she went: her height, her long brown hair, her very dark eyes.

The evening crept on. When the sun sank behind the horizon, Cyrus appeared beside him. "When will you go?" he asked curtly.

Nicodemus didn't stand. "Soon."

"We anchor here until midmorning tomorrow. Then Izem must start the run for Dar and Lurrikara."

Nicodemus nodded. "I will be back before dawn, or I won't be back at all."

"Bring back her hearing."

Nicodemus looked up. Fierce brown eyes between veil and turban stared back at him. "I will do all I can."

"May I come with you?" Cyrus asked.

"You'd just get in the way. He would infect you with aphasia."

Cyrus said nothing for a while. He moved as if he was going to walk away, but then he stopped and said, "In a way that's hard to explain, I worry for her. I never stopped worrying for her, and I want her to be happy."

Nicodemus nodded, understanding that the other man had just made the closest thing to a declaration of love as he could. "I can see why," Nicodemus said.

"Good. Bring back her hearing." Cyrus met his gaze and then went away.

A quarter hour later, the black sky was bright with stars. They shone with a precision that Nicodemus had only ever known on savanna nights. Though the day had been warm, the temperature was dropping fast.

As Nicodemus set off for the Greenwater, the crescent blackmoon rose over the hills. With his ability to see Language Prime, Nicodemus could make out every fold in the dark land by the faint glow of moss on the rocks or short grass on the soil. Bats—flares of life against the crystalline sky—fluttered about catching insects, which were specks of life so faint that they disappeared when he looked directly at them.

When he topped the last hill and looked out upon the valley of the Greenwater, Nicodemus stopped to check his skinspells. He had covered his every inch with sharp Chthonic language.

As he walked down into the valley, he had no doubt he was walking into a trap; of whose design—the Savanna Walker's or Typhon's—he did not know or particularly care. The demon, or the half-dragon, might have a surprise waiting for him, but he was carrying a surprise to them.

He left the long sheets of stone that covered the hilltops and stepped onto sandy soil, still warm from the sunlight. Compared with the lush savanna, alive with birds and rodents and large animals, the valley was barren; only the grass and the squat oak trees glowed with Language Prime.

A year ago, a lycanthropic spellwright had told him that the trees were ancient creations of Chimera—hybrids of plants and animals, and as such could create the runes of the lycanthropic magical languages. It was from these trees, deranged by the attack of the ancient Neosolar legion, came the area's feared metaspells.

Nicodemus suspected that the Savanna Walker would be lurking among the trees. But just in case, he began to walk a wide circuit around the Greenwater.

About halfway around, something unseen clamped down hard on his left shoulder. Reflexively, he peeled a short cutting spell from his right hip and punched it into his attacker. Ten thousand razor-wire sentences sprang out to coil around an eight-foot-tall figure that leapt away and fell on its back.

The thing thrashed. The only sound was that of grass and sand shifting. Then the creature began to jerk and twitch as if it were made of stiff metal limbs and springs.

Nicodemus stepped closer and saw that his many lacerating sentences had coiled themselves around a snouted head. He could see in the shape that its maw was open, its lips peeled back in agony.

A lycanthropic ghost.

Nicodemus's cutting spell contracted, and the ghost crumbled. Nicodemus remembered the clamplike sensation on his shoulder and realized that the ghost must have tried to bite him. Contact with his skin had begun to misspell the construct and then allowed his cutting text to crush the ghost.

Nicodemus didn't feel much of anything, except perhaps a touch of solemnity: a textual intelligence that must have been written before the Neosolar legions marched down the peninsula was no more. Hopefully the other ghosts haunting the valley had seen the spell die and would know not to attack him.

A voice called out in the night, low and slowly forming words, and then came a guttural grinding tone. Nicodemus looked up to the row of wide oaks and the water beyond. They were moving between the trunks, some on all fours, some standing on their hind legs. Even in the pale starlight, their large black eyes glinted like mirrors. Twelve of them, he counted.

They fell silent. One among them was larger than the rest. His legs bowed out and he moved awkwardly as if bearing weight. To Nicodemus the creature appeared blurry, as if he were looking at the creature underwater.

The Walker.

The dozen creatures around him were lycanthropes. Or, rather, they had been lycanthropes before he infected them with aphasia and then rotted their minds until they were his devotees. He must have caught them when he ditched the katabeast corpse and then used the carcass as bait.

Cold determination filled Nicodemus. The lycanthropes would be dangerous, but it was a one-moon night; in the resulting darkness, he could wield all his skill in the Chthonic languages. His first instinct was to attack, but there was the issue of Francesca's memories and hearing.

The Walker's singsong ravings carried across the chill night air. Nicodemus folded his arms and waited. The raving got louder ". . . misspelled the spook spoke . . . retardation, end of creation, retardation . . . Nicoco, such a stupid boy, such a cripple cripple. Crinkle cripple!"

The usual nonsense. There was no point in responding. He waited.

The aphasic lycanthropes joined in the ranting, growling and barking nothing words to accompany the Walker.

"Mmmother to me. The different one. Different one. She's here for you. Moother to me. Crack your creekers, cripple, suck out the slippery marrow."

This was new: the Walker had never spoken of a mother before. Nicodemus was growing cold and impatient.

"Break your bones, suck out your bloodmakers," the Walker raved. The lycanthropes moved in slow, twitchy movements around him. "Cracker your creekers. Crack your creatures. Suck it out, hot and slippery."

A wave of disgust moved through Nicodemus. If the beast had a trap, he should get on with springing it.

"It's retardation, end the creation. Nicocococreaker."

Nicodemus peeled from his forearm a paragraph of tightly packed Chthonic runes. He held it between his thumb and first two fingers as he might a writing quill. Carefully, he pointed the paragraph at one of the lycanthropes and disengaged its restraining sentence. The compressed paragraph sprang open, launching its functional end forward. Bright as a sunbeam, the sentence shot through the night and, with needlelike phrases, bit into a lycanthrope's hind leg. Perhaps the creature felt a sting akin to an insect bite. But judging by how little the lycanthrope reacted, Nicodemus guessed it hadn't noticed.

He'd never known the Walker or any of his devotees to use one of the Chthonic languages, so Nicodemus was certain that his spells were invisible to his enemies.

Aside from the Walker in the wolf's body, there were eleven lycanthropes. Nicodemus pulled four more condensed paragraphs from his forearm and cast them on the four lycanthropes farthest from the Savanna Walker. Should his targets touch the Walker, his sentences would be disspelled.

But he wasn't worried.

Quickly, he peeled from his lower back five tattooed blasting texts. Each of these he attached to one of his targeting sentences. He chose one and, with a wrist flick, cast it away. The blasting text flew along the targeting sentence for ten feet and then a small after-paragraph detonated with a crack and sent the bulk of the text flying down its sentence to strike its target. With a blossom of molten prose, the text tore the lycanthrope into a hundred pieces no bigger than a bread loaf. A moment later the auditory report echoed through the valley.

The lycanthropes cringed but then looked around, confused as to what had just happened. Nicodemus cast another blasting text. As the first did, the spell shot away and then blasted a beast into pieces.

This time the lycanthropes bolted for the cover of the trees. The Savanna Walker snarled and snapped at them but then made the same retreat.

Nicodemus grabbed hold of the three remaining targeting sentences floating before him and watched them dance as fishing lines taut with live catch might.

In a moment, the lines stopped moving, which he took to mean that the lycanthropes had found what they considered to be cover.

He cast the three remaining blast spells, the second a few moments after the first, the third a much longer time after the second. He wanted to demonstrate that he was in no particular hurry.

It worked.

Three of the creatures emerged from the trees in a dead sprint away from him.

Of those that remained, one seemed to have gone mad, snarling and snapping as something unseen knocked it over again and again.

Nicodemus grimaced. The beast was being attacked by a ghost. Without cacographic ability to misspell the ghost, the lycanthrope was being bled to death by invisible jaws.

A moment later, the other lycanthrope seemed beset by a similar attacker. The third bolted into a frantic retreat.

Nicodemus looked at the Savanna Walker's blurry image. The monster had run to the aid of his devotee, somehow clearing away the ghosts. But the wolf, confused and terrified, bit the Savanna Walker. The larger monster landed a claw swipe on the creature's head with enough force to make the night resound with the crack of its skull.

The last remaining lycanthrope fled.

That left only Nicodemus and the Walker. The monster was beginning to rant again. Nicodemus called out, "Ja Ambher."

Instantly the monster's image became sharper. Now Nicodemus saw how the lycanthrope body had become bloated about the chest and belly with the Walker's parasitic human body.

The creature let out a low, forlorn moan: "Ja Ambher. Jaaa Ambher. Ja . . . Jaaaambher."

Nicodemus waited.

"Catch me with your iron language. He has, he has. Burned me with my name. Burned. Bhurrrned." It turned toward Nicodemus: "You want to talk the iron talk, speaking the steel speak. Dirty foul, Nicodemus. Cruel. Talk your iron talk and rub your chin with feces."

Nicodemus didn't know what any of this meant. He didn't care: "Ja Ambher," he called again.

"Jaaaambher," the creature wailed as if compelled to do so. The monster's shoulders slumped. It seemed to crumple as if exhausted, defeated.

Then its head bobbed as if sniffing. The bloated lycanthrope body pawed over to one of its fallen comrades. The animated body opened its jaws wide, and a sleek head and shoulders emerged from the maw. The man was covered in a thick glistening liquid, saliva perhaps. "Always in all ways hungry. So hungry." A slick arm emerged from the mouth to pull the carcass closer so that it could take noisy bites of flesh.

"Ja Ambher!" Nicodemus called.

Like a long giant tongue, the man's body slipped back into the lycanthrope's mouth. The monster reared up on its hind legs. "Scatter rat!" he bellowed. "Scatter rat and bother me no more, no more with your iron talk, your almost diamond mind. Cram your eyes full of filth. Cram your—"

Nicodemus peeled off and cast a target sentence onto the cadaver next to the walker. With a single smooth motion, he cast a blasting spell. The corpse exploded into a shockwave of blood and bone that knocked the monster onto its side.

"Ja Ambher, now!" Nicodemus yelled. The Walker scrambled to his feet and sprinted at him. Nicodemus reached a hand behind his head and let it rest on his most powerful wartext. But the Savanna Walker stopped ten feet away and hunkered down. "There was a woman in my camp," Nicodemus said, "a wizard and a physician. You stole her memories and ability to hear."

The creature shook his head. "Nononono!"

"You did."

"She didn't have the memzies to steal. And nonono sound of the ear to hear. She had no—"

"Shut it."

The Walker cowered.

"What did you do to her?"

"Was supposed to catch you in daylight, bring you back to make the emerald shine and complete the diamond mind. But I wanted to know her, to feel her, to feeeel what she was. But it shocked, it burned like ice. She has it. She has all of it."

"Has all of what?"

"Diamond Mind. Diaaamond Miiiind."

Nicodemus took a threatening step forward, and the monster cringed. "Make sense damn it! What does she have?"

The Walker was shaking. "The demon didn't know I could catch her. She didn't have memzies to steal, she didn't hearing to have."

Nicodemus took a deep breath. "Does this have to do with her Language Prime shining so bright?"

He nodded. "And the second one has come into the city now, straight from mother. Mother of us. She is what mother wanted."

"The second dragon?"

The creature shuddered and backed away. "Worse than you know, so much so much worse. They have minds not filthy not like you and I do. Me do. I do. They have minds that are crystalline. Crys-ta-line-mind."

"Who does?"

"Demons do. Dragons." He shook his head. "Demonic minds like diamonds."

"Make blasted sense!"

"They have minds not fertile, not filthy, not fecund."

A surge of anger heated Nicodemus. "Can you restore Francesca's memories or her hearing?"

"Nonono. Not ever. They never were there."

"And how did you find our camp in the redwoods after we had remained hidden for so long?"

The lycanthropic jaw opened and the slick face of the man became visible underneath. "Typhon gave me Deedee to feed the hunger. Always in all ways so hungry and we had her in the gullet and knew where the ark was."

Nicodemus felt his gorge rise. "You ate Deirdre's body?"

The monster shivered, but this time in undeniable pleasure.

Nicodemus's hands began to shake. "And Boann's ark, what have you done to it?"

"Cracked it open and sucked out the diamond mind within. So sharp a sensation in the gut."

"You murdered Boann?"

"A sharp sensation sliding down." The monster paused and then opened the lycanthropic mouth so that his human head could extend. After blinking the saliva out of his eyes, the man named Ja Ambher looked Nicodemus up and down. His ancient face was wrinkled and blotchy, the hair brittle and short, but his eyes . . .

His eyes were bright green.

"They want their diamond minds," Ja Ambher said slowly. "The emerald to put to you and make me into the diamond-minded dragon." His voice has become level, calm. "I have the fertile mind, the fetid mind, the filthy filthy mind. They want that always to end, no more misspellings."

"Who?"

"Demons and Los the first demon. They want no more for there to be misspelling in Language Prime. They want the Silent Blight to become all."

"Tell me about the Silent Blight."

The monster nodded. "It is the iron talk come to Language Prime—no more nonsense, no more error in language. Make no more. They make you speak by rules. Only . . . language like ice."

Nicodemus shook his head in confusion.

The monster continued. "I wanted you to have in my belly the slow pain, so I could leech the language from your mind. But then I found that woman with no memzies. I knew Typhon would make my mind crys-talline, like hers. It was what they wanted in Starhaven."

Nicodemus blinked. "Starhaven?"

The still-glistening face nodded. "Ssstarhaven, where they write like iron, where I was like you before you were like me."

"I'm nothing like you."

"The purple prose, the violate violence. Your tattoos, if I didn't know the lie of iron, I could have them too. I learned the Chthonic ghost words. They wanted me to stay, to stay, but I broke away and learned and went away. Born long before you; I am your cosang, consanguinity, cacographer cousin." The monster paused and spoke as clearly as any sane man. "I know Language Prime. I know what a cacographer truly is."

Nicodemus took a step back as his mind made a sudden connection. "Ja Ambher," he whispered. "That's not how your name used to be said."

"Jaaaambher," the creature crooned. "Jamber. Jams Bherr."

"James Berr," Nicodemus said.

"James Berr," he repeated. "Once, long ago once, James Berr."

"History's most hated cacographer," Nicodemus whispered as he met the green eyes. "You didn't die three centuries ago when you fled into the savanna."

James Berr shook his head. "I mished and I mashed Language Prime. I made life into Jibberish. I learned to slip in and slip out of the beasts, to mix them. I learned to drive men mad with Jibberish."

"Jibberish is your dialect of Language Prime."

"And languages made filthy."

"All these hundreds of years, you've been the Savanna Walker."

"Until diamond-minded Typhon made me tame, made me a city dweller, forced into my mind the iron language. He's made half a dragon of me, so I can knock out language in others." The monster shuddered. "Words, words, words! Must and lust and unpacking my heart with words, words, words, like a whore." His voice shifted if impersonating someone else. "We take it from you, James, we take it from you! We break you, Nicodemus. Your mind must be icelike or not at all. They jammed their language into me, and I made all profit on it to curse them in their own language, curse their mechanical minds."

Nicodemus swallowed. "All those years ago, when you were a student at Starhaven, and all those wizards died of misspells, was that an accident? Your mistake?"

Sharp laughter. "All misted take, no mistake. The red plague of misspells. My curses burned them into boils. Always they should suffer and die for forcing my mind."

"You are a monster," Nicodemus whispered.

Berr smiled at him, imperial green eyes shining bright. "You're just like me, cosang. We have the filthy minds. We rot their rules. Rot their rules. Rotrotrot—"

"I am nothing like you!"

Berr smiled and stepped closer. He began to croon: "Cousin, cosang, coooousin. Hatred is for the iron language, the diamond minds. You must free me from Typhon."

"Free you? You are his half dragon!"

Berr grimaced. "His slave. If we get that emerald to touch you, he will crystallize my brain, make it think latticewise. He will make me unable to misspell, unable to err. You must set me free before the demon figures to make me catch the second. Once I am diamond minded, I will cross the ocean, and the demons will cross. The Disjunction will make it impossible for anyone to misspell."

Nicodemus took a step back. "I thought the Disjunction would make language meaningless by making language chaos."

Berr shook his massive wolf's head. "Backwards cacographer." He laughed. "Language is meaningless without error, without fetid rotting chaos. Perfect order makes it de-script-ive, slave to nature. Fecund chaos makes it pre-script-ive, creating nature. When all language is perfect, feces-loving life will expire and only the diamond minds will remain. Language Prime needs the slippery mind, the error, the monsters, the war. Obscene words to find the fittest, fattest word."

Nicodemus took a step back. "You are telling the truth?"

Berr nodded his lycanthropic head and then looked down at his massive body. "This wolf flesh, your touch would turn it to necro canker. Were I to set upon you with this flesh, you would rot it away." The lycanthropic body gagged and then vomited out Berr's slick human body.

As the naked man rose to his feet, the lycanthropic body fell over and convulsed once before dying.

Nicodemus pulled his most powerful wartext from his back. The violate and indigo runes leapt off of his skin into sharp paragraphs that interlocked to form a long sword, pointed with dancing flamelike spikes.

Nicodemus leveled the blade at Berr.

The grotesque man only smiled. In a calm tone he said, "I am the older cacographer. Anything you write will misspell on my skin."

Nicodemus took a step back. "I killed your devotees without your misspelling my texts."

Berr's smile broadened. "I meant you to. How else would you come so close? Why else would I tell you so much?" He took a step forward. "You must free me before I am diamond minded. You must become like me, powerful in your filthy, fecund mind. You must do this now to stop the demon."

Nicodemus took another step back. "I'd sooner burn on every level of hell."

"They are forcing you into the iron talk. If you fight the demon, you will become the demon. You think you want the emerald, the crystalline mind. But you must be original as monsters are original. Now I have freed you. You must free me. Free me!"

"Take another step, and I'll free your head from your neck."

Berr walked straight for him.

Nicodemus thrust the textual sword at his chest, but the instant it touched the Savanna Walker, the textual blade dissolved. Nicodemus started to peel a tattooed blasting spell from his forearm, but Berr grabbed him and the text broke itself into nothing.

Like streams of water, all the spells written across Nicodemus's body fell to the ground and splashed into nothing.

"I am the older cacographer," Berr said in a singsong tone. "You must come with me now. You cannot fight the demon without becoming the demon. The filthy mind is life's only hope of escaping the diamond minded, of escaping the Disjunction."

Nicodemus froze and stared into the eyes that were the same shade of green as his own. Berr was holding his arm. He was the first human in ten years to touch him without withering with disease.

Berr nodded slowly. "You understand it all now. I will show you how. We shall be free. We shall not become the demons. We shall escape the Silent Blight and the Disjunction."

Nicodemus searched the eyes of his ancient cousin. Hot panic and cold certainty swept through his body like the fever and chill of an illness. He felt as if he might vomit. He felt relieved; this was his fate, no denying it.

"I am the older cacographer," Berr said softly, revealing the jagged teeth that had eaten Deirdre.

Terror and frantic rage burned so hotly through Nicodemus that the world became unworldly. With all his strength and fury, Nicodemus slammed his fist into the old man's mouth.

Berr's head snapped back.

Nicodemus grabbed his shoulders and pulled him in to drive his knee into his cousin's stomach.

James coughed out air and fell over.

"I am the younger cacographer!" Nicodemus snarled. He was strong, faster, more alive with hatred.

Nicodemus fell on the man, pinning him down with one knee as he slammed long, looping punches into his cousin's mouth.

James fought back for the first twenty blows or so. Then blood was splattered across his face and his nose was broken one way. His arms and legs moved in feeble random motions. Nicodemus was screaming, long wordless wails, rising and falling like a chant. His vision blurred with tears. His arms kept swinging, battering Berr's face first right then left, right then left.

Nicodemus picked up a rock and hammered it hard onto his cousin's face. He felt a tooth break under the blow. He struck again and felt more snap. He slammed the rock into the ridge above his cousin's eye, shattering the bone beneath.

Nicodemus couldn't see anymore; the tears and blood had transformed the visible world into a stinging blur. But he struck with the rock again and again, missing his cousin's head and hitting throat, chest, shoulder, breaking one collarbone. He howled and howled until he had no more breath left and the world spun.

He fell over onto his hands and knees, gagged, tried to vomit. He couldn't. Desperate for breath, he sucked in short gasps of air. Gagged again. Came up with a mouthful of stomach acid. Spat it out.

Crying. Crying, bawling like a baby. Nicodemus fell onto his elbows, face pressed against the ground, sandy soil sticking to the tears and blood and sweat on his cheek, sucking in long breaths with bits of grass and sand. Crying. Crying . . . long gasps of breath . . . breath slowing.

At last the world stopped spinning. He used his arm to wipe the blood and tears from his eyes and saw James Berr, face broken into a nightmare of tissue and bone. One eyeball torn open in its broken socket.

But James Berr was still breathing.

Without feeling, Nicodemus dropped the rock and then put his knee on the half dragon's windpipe. When he used his weight to mash Berr's windpipe shut, the man did not struggle.

Only a little while to wait for death.

But then a shudder ran through Nicodemus. He had killed many times during his years in Avel, often snuffing out hierophants for committing no greater crime than unknowingly serving a demon.

Now Nicodemus removed his knee from the throat of a murderer, a savage subhuman. The older cacographer would not have to teach Nicodemus how to become a monster. Nicodemus already knew how. Slowly, he stood. Beneath him, Berr continued to breathe.

Maybe the old man would drown in his own blood. Maybe a savanna predator would devour him. That would be fitting. Maybe he would survive. Did it matter?

Though Nicodemus was standing above his foe with a thundering heart and heaving chest, part of him lay dying on the valley floor.

Or perhaps it had died long ago.

It didn't matter. Nicodemus felt too sharply the course of Berr's life: the violent rage of a disabled child, an exile from home and later from humanity, enslavement by Typhon. Berr had made his life into savage pain; others had transformed him into a creature of agony. It was disgusting. It was pitiful. And Nicodemus clung to this shred of pity. It was, he thought, the last thing protecting him from what the Savanna Walker truly was. On the ground, James Berr moaned.

Nicodemus turned away. He couldn't bring himself to kill his cousin. Slowly, he walked out of the valley.

forty-four

Francesca couldn't sleep. Cyrus lay next to her in the white silk tent. He was wrapped tight against the chill, his eyes peaceful, his breath puffing out his veil. She rolled over. It was too hot under the sheets. She sat up and crawled outside. Around her she found other dark tents and the tether rising into the night to connect to the still-flying half of the airship.

The blackmoon had set, and the sky was awash with stars. Francesca looked up and bit her lip. The cold air felt good on her face. She sighed and then jumped when two dark figures faced her.

The first she recognized by his short stature and turban as Captain Izem. But it took a moment to realize that the second man was Nicodemus.

She ran to him and cast a golden question before even coming to a stop: *"What happened?"* By the light of her words, she saw his blood-splattered face and chest. He caught the question with a hand he had been cleaning with a bloody rag. His knuckles were a motley of lacerations. *"Are you in pain? Are you aware of any major wound?"*

He began wiping the blood from his arms and cast a reply: *"I'm not hert. There's no need to worry."*

"Well then, WHAT IN THE BURNING HELLS HAPPENED?"

His hands trembled as he cast the response. *"I'm vary cold and hungry. Give me a moment, plaese."*

Francesca's head spun as she realized that he was delaying; he didn't want to tell her the bad news. She sat down hard. Suddenly Nicodemus was squatting next to her. His lips were moving and then he cast a sentence: *"I'm sory. Im so sorry."*

Francesca knew then that she would remain deaf. Never again would she remember her mother's voice or listen to a heart's beat. Never again would she hear music. Nicodemus hovered above her, making awkward motions as if starting to comfort her but then realizing he couldn't touch her. He turned and called to someone behind her.

Suddenly Izem appeared and dropped what seemed to be twenty pounds of silk onto Nicodemus, covering every inch of his skin. Nicodemus put his arms around Francesca. He pulled her gently in. It felt like being comforted by a pillow. But Francesca didn't care; she turned into his embrace and cried into the silk.

He rocked her for a while, but then a pair of hands pulled her up onto her feet. She turned and saw Cyrus's worried eyes. She must have woken him with her crying. He embraced her and stroked her hair.

When she was calmer, Nicodemus wrote an outline of what had happened: the revelation that the Savanna Walker was James Berr, the Walker's belief that Francesca had never had memories or the ability to hear and that her mind was similar to a demon's. None of it made a snap of sense.

Numbly, Francesca let Cyrus lead her back to their tent. He held her, and she laid her head on his chest. She could feel his voice buzzing inside his chest, like a bee buzzing within a large flower. She wondered what he was saying to her, or if he was singing to her.

She fell asleep and woke up on her side of the tent. Cyrus seemed to be sleeping, so she crawled outside. Under the stars, she felt slightly intoxicated, as if the arrival of anticipated bad news had freed some part of her. By the light of flameflies, she found Nicodemus's small tent and climbed inside.

He woke with a jerk and tried to crab-walk away.

"*Don't be dumb,*" she wrote to him.

He stared at her as if she had just caught fire.

She wrote a small cloud of flameflies that lit the tent with soft incandescence. "*If I never had memories, if I never could hear, than what am I? Some kind of construct?*"

He blinked. His long raven hair spilled across his dark shoulders. He wrote: "*Your made of Languag Prime.*"

"*A Language Prime construct then?*"

He frowned. "*All living things are Langauge Prime constructs.*"

"*But my Language Prime shines too brightly. Maybe Typhon did something to me? Stole something from me?*"

He studied her face. "*It's posible.*"

"*Maybe we can still get my memories and my hearing back.*"

His expression softened.

"*What?*" she flicked it at him. "*You're looking at me as if I were a puppy caught under a wagon wheel.*"

He wrote a golden sentence but then deconstructed it. He wrote another, but then he began to edit it and the thing misspelled into nothing. Then he just frowned down at his hands.

"*NICO!*" she shouted at him with a flick of her wrist. "*What under heaven are you thinking?*"

He disspelled another sentence and then looked at her helplessly.

"*What?*" she repeated.

Tentatively he held out, "*It's not so bad.*"

"*What's not?*"

"*Living without part of yourself.*"

"*I don't know who the God-of-gods damned hell I am!*" She laughed bitterly and then wrote another sentence, "*I don't even know what I am!*"

He wrote, "*To the city, your phisician. To the sick, you're a healer.*" He seemed to think about this and then added, "*To everyone eles, you're a pain in the ass.*"

She laughed but then grew somber. "*But can I be a physician if I can't hear?*"

He pressed his lips together. "*I know nothing about the practice of medieince, but surely there must be a way.*"

"*But patients won't be able to tell me their symptoms. I won't be able to hear the coughs or wheezes, their heart sounds.*"

He leaned forward. "*You can't be who you were.*"

The truth of his statement jolted through her. In the resulting shock, she wanted to cry for what she'd lost and laugh hard at the unfairness and absurdity of it all.

Nicodemus was holding out another sentence: "*But with the strenghts and tallents of what remains, you can do much.*"

She pressed both her hands to her cheeks. She'd never felt so strange in her life, as if she wasn't really herself. She laughed and wrote, "*Is this what it's like to be you?*"

He smiled. "*Yes, but with fewer handsome heirophants in love with me.*"

She laughed, probably louder than she should. "*That's because you don't play hard to get.*"

"*Then I'll make Izem jealus tomorow by talking only to Cyrus.*"

She smiled. "*Will you go back to Avel and keep trying to recover the emerald?*"

He nodded. "*I will talk to Shannon first.*"

"*You will let me come with you to see if the demon stole my memories?*"

He nodded and seemed to be studying her face as if it were the most fascinating thing he had ever seen. "*What?*" she wrote.

He sat back, wrote a sentence, and then discarded it. He glanced up at her before writing a second one, which he held out. "*It's odd to see somoene else wonting to recover something lost.*" He paused. "*I both want to help you recover it and stop you from feeling incompleate without it.*" Then he quickly added. "*I'm sorry. I don't know if any of that makes sense. It's is strang for me to see this.*"

"*Strange for us both,*" she wrote. She wanted to add that their situations were entirely different. Nicodemus had been a cacographer since birth, and she had only just lost her hearing. Didn't that make them completely different? But some nagging doubt stopped her. In any case, what mattered now was what they had to do next. *"When we go back to Avel, will you let me go to Vivian and DeGarn and try to enlist their help?"*

He frowned.

"Heaven aflame, let me at least try! We're getting short on allies, if you hadn't noticed."

He took a moment to reply. *"Let's discuss it with Shannon."*

"Are you sure you shouldn't go kill the Savanna Walker?"

He looked at her with the gaze that had first revealed to her the frightened boy he had once been. Pity moved through Francesca. Suddenly she had the illogical feeling that if only she could change his pained expression, somehow everything would be all right.

Slowly Nicodemus wrote, *"I can't kill him."*

"Tell me."

So he wrote about the Walker's nonsensical words, their possible meanings. He wrote of the monster's hatred for those who wanted to make him speak and write logically and how he had killed wizards with misspells in Starhaven. Then Nicodemus explained how he had attacked the Savanna Walker, struck him over and over. He wrote about what it had felt like to put his knee on his cousin's throat and realize that some part of himself had already died.

All of this he wrote in jumbled, misspelled sentences. At first, Francesca was confused by many of his ambiguous words, but then she let it wash over her.

At last Nicodemus sighed. *"May be I shouldve gone with the Walker, let him teech me. Maybe that was my only cance to stop the Disjunction."*

She scowled.

He went on, *"Or mabye I should go back to him. Try to heel him, see if he'll join us against Typhon."*

"Ridiculous!" she wrote and felt herself make a vocalization of disgust. *"That monster deserves whatever Typhon does to him. If you want to stop Typhon, then you had better not become him."*

Nicodemus's face tensed. *"The Walker said fighting the demon would meen becoming the demon. Deirdre said something similar."*

She thought about this. *"There is a difference between fighting and opposing."* She gave him a wry look and then smiled. *"You don't always have to tear your opponent into pieces, Nicodemus I'm-a-warrior-of-the-night Weal."*

"That sounds very wise," he wrote and frowned. *"Why didn't you start out writing wize things? Or can you wright wise things only after being a pain in the ass?"*

"*If I were always wise and sympathetic, you'd find me uninteresting.*"

He grinned. But when trying to hand a reply to her, he dropped it and with clumsy hands picked it up and cast it to her: "*I'd never find you uninteresting.*"

She chuckled at his awkwardness. Her giddiness returned, twice as strong. She felt almost drunk. She wrote, "*Don't be clumsy; you shouldn't be so nervous about flirting with me.*

"*I wasn't flirting with you,*" he tossed back.

"*Not very well you weren't.*"

"*Magistra, I was only trying to . . .*" she didn't read the rest of the sentence but tossed it away. She made him meet her eyes and then rolled them. Then she wrote, "*If it wouldn't have given me a horrible, incurable disease, I would have taken your hand when you were writing about the Savanna Walker.*"

He replied with a sentence, the first word of which was going to translate as "*Magistra.*" So she slapped it into fragments and wrote, "*Let me teach you something about flirting: relax. Call me Francesca or Fran.*"

He was once again staring at her as if she had just caught on fire.

She sighed and shifted uncomfortably in her seat. Perhaps she should go. Maybe she was only being foolish, trying to distract herself. She began to write an apology. But just before she was about to cast him the resulting paragraph, one of his golden words floated into her lap.

"*Stay.*"

She looked up at him. His expression was intent, his green eyes darting all about her face. Suddenly she felt a little frightened. "*All night?*"

"*As long as you can.*"

"*What if you roll into me when you're asleep?*"

"*I'll wrap up in my robes, and when the fireflies burn out, I'll write a wall of Chthonic text.*"

She smiled at his earnestness. "*Being too eager frightens a woman off. You're not very good at flirting.*"

"*I have a horrible teacher.*"

She laughed. "*Now you're getting the hang of it.*"

"*Cyrus loves you.*"

She threw her hands in the air. "*Just had to prove me wrong, didn't you?*"

"*He does, and I can see why.*"

"*You don't know who I really am.*"

He smiled easily. "*You don't know either.*"

She rolled her eyes at him but couldn't help smiling.

"*Do you love Cyrus?*"

Her smile wilted. "*Once I did.*"

"And now?"

She looked away. *"He is kind to me. I like his affection. I have told him it wasn't working."* She looked at him, but then added, *"He'd be jealous if he knew I came to talk to you."*

"Don't go."

"I wasn't planning to."

"He can't be too jealous. He gets to share a tent with you. He may touch your hand or face. All I want is for you to stay."

"I said I'll stay."

He grinned like a boy. "Maybe I just wanted you to admit that again."

Also grinning like an idiot, she shook her head. *"You're childish and irksome."* But as she cast this she realized that a twinge of guilt was moving through her. Cyrus would be hurt if he knew about this.

Nicodemus was leaning closer, leaning on his right arm. The flexion caused the smooth curves of his triceps to pronounce its lateral head and long head as they ran up to his shoulder.

He studied her studying him and he smiled—in the half-light his teeth seemed whiter, his skin darker. *"I thought you despised me."*

"I kind of do."

He laughed. *"I'm glad you stayed."*

"So am I."

"Will you do something for me?"

"Depends on what it is."

"It may seem a bit odd."

"Oh, don't ruin this now, Nico. I may be acting oddly, but a little flirtation has been the only pleasant thing to happen in what's otherwise been the worst night of my life."

"It's not that odd."

"What is it?"

"I think of you far too often. I've thought about you ever since I watched you save Vein."

"God-of-gods, just tell me what you want me to do."

He picked up something from the tent's corner and tossed it to her.

She caught it and was surprised by the sharp points she felt within her hand. But when she tilted it to catch the light, a smile spread across her face. The tortoiseshell comb.

Nicodemus lay back to rest on his elbows, accentuating his deltoid muscles. Francesca pulled her braid over her shoulder and untied the ribbon at the end. Gently, with short strokes, she untangled her wild hair. As it passed through the comb's fine teeth, her dark brown curls grew into their natural loose spirals and caught the luster of her incandescent prose.

After a hundred strokes, all her hair was free and flowing down to obscure her shoulders.

Nicodemus watched her with patient unwavering eyes until the last flamefly paragraph winked out and left them both in darkness.

Then Francesca lay down on her side of the tent and felt her curls all around her face and neck.

She dreamt that her body had become the wide earth and her hair the vibrant grass sea—green with the rains, golden under the sun, and rolling forever away into the horizon.

forty-five

Francesca woke in a tent lightening with dawn. It took her a moment to realize the man sleeping beside her was Nicodemus. Guilt washed over her, and she hurried out of the tent.

Outside the chill air visualized her breath into pale wisps. A thousand feet above her, half the *Queen's Lance* flew from its tether. Up that high, the sunlight was already shining and so illuminated the silk, brilliant white against the still-brightening sky. Normally Francesca would have been captivated by the sight; now she didn't spare it a second glance.

She crawled into the tent she had shared with Cyrus, only to find it empty. Her stomach tightened. He must have noticed her absence when he woke. She turned to leave but found him crouching in front of the tent, turban wrapped, veil up.

She froze.

His light brown eyes searched hers for a moment; then he climbed into the silk tent and sat beside her.

"Cyrus," she said softly, hoping her voice was intelligible. "I sorry I—"

He held up his right hand to stop her and then produced a small black vial with his left. She had a moment to frown before he poured the vial's contents onto the silk between them. The liquid stained the cloth so darkly that it could only be one substance. "Ink?" she asked.

Nodding, Cyrus pressed his index finger onto the stain. Instantly the blackness came alive, sliding through the silk to form flowing letters. He was using hierophantic spells to move the pigment through the cloth. The fluid ink formed a sentence: *"I've thought all night about how my words could reach you."*

She looked at him and said aloud, "I'm sorry I left."

He gestured to the ink, which had flowed into another sentence: *"You can write."*

Tentatively, she put her finger to the stain. A small patch of ink magically pooled around her touch. She wrote out the letter "*I.*" The strokes her fingers made were thick, messy; however, at the last stroke, the ink reformed into a beautiful, thin-limbed "I." Cyrus had written a surprising, delightful spell. She wrote on: *"I went to correspond with Nicodemus in Numinous."*

He looked at her and wrote: *"Could he help you?"*

Francesca bit her lip. *"He understands what's happened to me in a way that is hard to describe."*

Cyrus's hands moved more hesitantly. *"Could I understand as well?"*

She looked at him and then wrote, *"I can try to explain, but maybe not now. I feel . . ."* She picked her finger up to try to discern how exactly she did feel and then wrote, *"exhausted inside."*

"I am sorry, Fran. How can I help?"

"Your understanding helps. I am sorry I left last night to talk to Nico."

Cyrus hesitated. *"You trust him?"* Pause. *"He's clearly enamored of you."*

"Don't be jealous, Cyrus. I could never touch him. No one can ever touch him. The poor man. Honest, he was only making eyes at me, and I probably shouldn't encourage him as much as I have been. I just . . ." Pause. *". . . needed to talk to someone about disability."* Longer pause. *"Now I feel guilty."*

"You shouldn't. It's understandable." Cyrus moved closer. *"How do you feel now?"*

"Better. Tired. Still . . . a bit shaken by my deafness."

"You're not deaf."

She looked at him to see if he was joking.

But he looked back at her with an even gaze. He lowered his veil to show her his fine, black beard, and his mouth set in an earnest line. The ink under his fingers shifted again. *"We will find a way to restore your hearing."*

She looked from the sentence back to Cyrus's face. He hadn't looked away from her. *"You think so?"*

He nodded. *"If Nicodemus can recover his ability to spell, you can recover your hearing."*

"But what if I can't?"

He reached out and took her hand. After the night spent avoiding Nicodemus's touch, the warmth of his calloused hand was a shock. Cyrus placed his other hand on the ink. The stain flowed. *"We will find a way. It's going to be all right."*

Francesca felt as if something were collapsing inside of her. Gone was the fear and strange giddiness that had charged her encounter with Nicodemus. When she thought about how flirtatious she had been, it was like remembering a night spent drinking. And yet Nicodemus had fully acknowledged her new disability, which had both liberated her from her denial and shocked her with pain and loss.

Cyrus's insistence that she was not deaf—or would be deaf only briefly—
was pushing her back into denial, pushing her back into hope.

Francesca lowered her head, felt her shoulders sag. She didn't feel like
crying as much as lying down to sleep forever.

But then Cyrus leaned in and touched her cheek. She sat passivly in his
embrace. He kissed her forehead. Slowly, she leaned into his arms. She did
not know whose conception of disability—Nicodemus's or Cyrus's—was
more accurate. But when Cyrus pulled her closer and kissed her again, she
found the strength in his touch.

The part of her that was collapsing completed its decline. She was not
crying. She would not cry. But a weight now rested upon her soul with such
force that she put her arms around Cyrus's neck and hung on as if her life
depended on it. And, judging by the pain of her despair, it might.

NICODEMUS WOULD NOT have guessed it possible to fall asleep while flying through the sky on a giant magical sheet. But when something nudged
his shoulder, he found himself blinking while suspended above a mile of
limpid wind. Below lay a city he had never before seen.

Like Avel, this was a city built of sandstone and red tile roofs. But unlike Avel, this city was not surrounded by thick walls. There were defensive
barriers and gatehouses, but beyond each of these grew small outlying towns,
the buildings of which extended almost up to the barriers. Even without
the extramural population, the city was twice the size of Avel. Its sanctuary
stretched wider and boasted a gleaming white dome. This was the house of
Canonist Zayd—whose godspells cut the canals that channeled snowmelt
from mountains west of Roundtower all the way down to his city's crops.
Above Zayd's sanctuary soared a flock of colorful lofting kites. To the west
a natural harbor was spangled with sailing vessels. In all other directions
stretched patchwork fields of wheat and chickpeas. This was Dar, the heart
of Western Spires for hundreds of years.

Someone nudged Nicodemus's shoulder again. He turned to see Cyrus's
upside-down face. The hierophant's robes suspended him belly-up from the
ship. "Dar," the wind mage yelled. "I didn't want you to miss it."

Nicodemus nodded. He and the hierophant had spoken a fair bit early
in the flight. The conversation had clearly been an excuse to demonstrate
civility toward each other after the previous day's icy exchange. Speaking
to Cyrus had made Nicodemus feel less guilty about the time he had spent
with Francesca.

Mostly he and Cyrus had talked of different types of airships. Nicodemus, genuinely intrigued by the aerial constructs, had asked about the

many different types, their tactics, the historical battles, and such. Though Cyrus was clearly passionate about the subject, it was apparent that he would rather not have been speaking to the other man. Nicodemus had been relieved when Cyrus had turned his attention to piloting.

Presently Cyrus pointed north. "We'll soon land at a garden tower north of the city. You might be able to see Mount Spires." Nicodemus squinted at the horizon and could indeed make out a spike of blue darker than the rest of the horizon. Then Cyrus turned and pulled himself away from Nicodemus and to Francesca.

Izem had placed the cleric far enough away from Nicodemus that they could not hand off text, and any spell they cast would be caught by the wind. Izem had said he needed them so positioned to keep the airship balanced in its current sleek shape.

A cold knot formed in Nicodemus's gut as Cyrus took Francesca's hand. The wind mage pointed to the ground. Francesca nodded and made a few gestures in response. He kissed her hand. She didn't seem to object, and she didn't look back until Cyrus had returned to piloting.

Nicodemus kept his eyes on the city.

Perhaps the Walker was right and he would need to use his cacography to resist the Disjunction. But if he could recover the emerald, only for an hour, he could at least touch another human in kindness. And, should that day ever come, the person he chose to touch should not be Magistra DeVega.

Despite the intimacy he had shared with her last night—thoughts of which had filled his head until they were aloft—she had behaved no differently toward Cyrus, not seeking his affection but not avoiding it either.

The ship flew northward along the coast for another hour, gliding low over hills covered with grass that grew only to hip height. Here a pack of lycanthropes could be spotted and attacked by lofting kites or hunted down by Spirish lancers. There were no redwood forests this far north; rather, broad oaks dotted the inland hills while slender palm trees bowed in the coastal wind.

Flying at various points within the hills were small flocks of windcatchers. Though still massive constructs of white cloth, Dar's windcatchers were smaller than those of Avel. They were also spread farther apart. The wind here wasn't as strong or as consistent.

When a tall fin-shaped tower came into view, the *Queen's Lance* tore itself apart even while sewing itself into a new vessel with a hexagonal hull made from evenly spaced strips of cloth and flanked by an array of sails that made reflexive adjustments.

After alighting in a wide landing bay, Izem wound a green robe around Nicodemus and then ushered him through narrow hallways to a small room with two beds and a cloth-covered window that glowed with mid-morning sunlight. After instructing him not to leave the room, Izem hurried off.

Nicodemus lay on a bed and tried to clear his mind. The pilots would fly him back to Avel, and he would consult Shannon. Then they could decide if they should make another try for the emerald or retreat to continue the fight some other year, in whatever city Typhon reappeared. Suddenly Nicodemus thought of James Berr and flinched. When flying over the Greenwater Valley, he had spotted several half-eaten lycanthrope bodies but no sign of Berr.

No doubt the creature had escaped back into the savanna.

From outside came the sound of rushing ocean wind and scolding gulls. Somewhere, likely in the quarters next door, a door opened and then closed. A bed creaked. The wind grew stronger.

A sharp knock sounded from the door. He sat up, and Cyrus came in with one bowl of fried fish and another of lentils. Until that moment, Nicodemus hadn't realized how little he had eaten. Nicodemus thanked Cyrus and dug in. The fish tasted of olive oil and salt, the lentils of cumin.

Cyrus sat on the opposite bed and unwound his turban. When Nicodemus finished, Cyrus lowered his veil and said, "I sold you out."

Nicodemus blinked.

"I sold you out to Avel's wind marshal so that we could use the *Queen's Lance* to chase the Walker. I did it in case you could get Francesca's memories or hearing back." He paused. "Do you understand why I did it?"

"I do."

"I'm not proud of it, but I would do it again."

Nicodemus didn't reply.

"I've spoken to Izem. We've grounded the fifth crew member so that Izem and I can fly the ship alone to Lurrikara and then to Avel. I will drop you at Coldlock Harbor; from there you may return to your camp. When I report to the marshal, I will claim you misspelled part of the *Queen's Lance* outside Dar and escaped. If you are foolish enough to return to hierophantic custody, stick to that lie or I will be dropped without cloth from two thousand feet for treason."

Again, Nicodemus nodded.

Cyrus pressed his lips together and then said, "Francesca wants to go with you."

Nicodemus kept his face neutral.

"Help me convince her that we will be able to restore her hearing."

"I'm sorry?"

"She's crushed by her new deafness. You have to help me give her hope back."

Anger twisted through Nicodemus's gut. "How do you know that we will be able to restore her hearing?"

"She must have hope. We can't take away her hope."

Nicodemus felt his fists tighten as he remembered a childhood filled with assurances that he would outgrow or overcome his disability. "You don't know if it's possible. It's no kindness to give false hope."

"You of all people should understand," Cyrus replied hotly. "You've dedicated your life to the hope of ending your disability. How could you deny her that same hope?"

Suddenly it was all Nicodemus could do to keep from shouting or striking the hierophant. Yet in the depths of his boiling rage, he knew there was a core of truth in the other man's words. He'd used hope like firewood, set it constantly burning under him to heat his life. He placed his face in his hands and, as calmly as he could, said, "I will believe whatever Francesca chooses to believe about her lost hearing."

Cyrus was silent for a long moment. "One more thing. Help me convince Francesca not to go with you into Coldlock Harbor. She will be safer staying with the fleet."

Nicodemus snorted. "You think she'll listen to me?"

"I'm going to tell her that we both agree."

"I might not know her well, but I know her well enough not to argue if she has her mind set."

"I'm going to tell her we agree. If she insists on doing it her way, you must keep her safe."

"If Deirdre was correct, the opposite is more likely to happen."

Cyrus looked away to the cloth-covered window. "I don't hold anything against you." His words were filled with anger and yet seemed completely earnest.

"Nor I, you," Nicodemus said as evenly as he could.

"I'll be in an officer's quarters two doors down. Find me if you have a desperate need. Otherwise stay in here. We'll be aloft in two hours." He left.

Nicodemus lay back down and closed his eyes. The racket of two squalling gulls grew louder and then receded. Nicodemus felt his anger calm and then surge as he turned over Cyrus's denial of Francesca's new disability. Dimly he sensed that part of his rage was directed at himself. He hated the idea of giving Francesca false hope, and yet he had dedicated most of his adult life to recovering the emerald—a hope that at its core was a denial of his disability and his wholeness despite that disability.

Another pair of complaining gulls flew by and Nicodemus felt the last of his anger wash out of him. He wondered what it would be like to give up his hope of recovering the emerald. He thought about what it had been like to see Francesca so distressed at losing her hearing and yet seeing her as so completely whole and beautiful.

Then, slowly, Nicodemus felt himself falling asleep. Footsteps and the mumble of low conversation sounded in some nearby hallway. The droning voices echoed and altered musically as they do sometimes in half dreams.

He wasn't aware of time passing, but then he partly awoke. It took a moment to realize what had changed, but then he recognized that the droning voices had become staccato breaths punctuated by a few brief moans. Two hierophants locking lips or making love. Annoyed, Nicodemus rolled over and then pulled the sheets over his head. He fell back into sleep . . . sometime later he rolled over . . . sleep . . .

A door opened, and he sat up suddenly. Francesca closed the door behind her and glared at him. Some of her curls had escaped her braid. Her red physician's stole was curiously tucked into her collar.

She backhanded a paragraph at Nicodemus.

He caught it and translated, trying to introduce as few misspellings as possible. *"I'd say you had the inteligance of a drunkan tadpole, but I don't want to insult an ampfibian. Why under a flaming haeven gave you and Cyrus the NERVE to deside what I will do when we reach Coldlock Harbuor. I should . . ."*

Nicodemus stopped reading and let his cacography deconstruct the text.

He cast, *"Whatever Cyrus told you was exhagerated. I don't suffer under the illushion that you care what I think."*

As she read this, he frowned at her disheveled curls and how her stole was tucked into her collar until suddenly he made a connection. He felt cold and nauseated.

Francesca threw several paragraphs at him, but he let them strike his skin and misspell. He flicked *"Plaese go"* at her and then turned away to face the wall. He pulled the blankets up to his shoulders.

A shower of luminescent sentences began to fall on the bedsheet before him. He closed his eyes. A moment later, Francesca tried shaking his bed. He didn't move.

"Nicodemus!" she said in a monotonous voice. "Nicodemus, look at me!"

He didn't move.

Suddenly a hand landed on his leg. He reflexively jerked away and sat up. Francesca had touched the blanket over his leg, not his leg itself. Nevertheless, he wound the blanket around his hands and grabbed her wrist.

Ignoring her protests, he studied each of her fingers, ensuring she did not have a canker curse.

When he finished, he then pushed her hand away with the blanket. *"You cuold have killed yourslef!"* He was about to turn away when he saw her expression, her mouth parted, her eyes wide as if in shock.

"Why ar you acting this way?"

"You forgot to pull your stol back after Cyrus."

She read this and then looked at him as if he were soft in the head. He pointed to her collar. She looked down and pulled her stole back out. *"Cyrus had noting to do with it,"* she wrote. *"I was naping too rooms over."*

The nausea moved though Nicodemus again. *"You couldn't here the noise you too made. You couldn't hear yourself moaning."*

Francesca became perfectly still. Her face didn't change.

"Pleas go now," Nicodemus cast at her and turned back toward the wall.

He heard her take a step away from the bed, then another. "Nicodemus," she said.

For a moment he didn't move, but then he rolled over. She handed him, *"It wasn't wat you think."*

"It's none of my busness."

He started to turn away again, but she laid a hand on his leg. Even through the blankets the sensation of being touched was a shock. *"We didnt have sex,"* she wrote with a physician's frankness. *"I wuold have sent him away. But he was their and afectinate and everything's gone to hell and don't be so blasted upset. We were just locking lips and holding each other because we are GOD-OF-GODS DAMNED SCARED! It wasn't anytihng immportant."*

"It's none of my busnes."

She was pressing her lips together hard enough to blanch. *"And now I'm sorry about how I acted in the tent the other nite. I meant everything I said. You understood about dissability in a way no one else could. But eveyrthing is confused and I can't ever touch you."*

When he read these last few words, Nicodemus flinched. *"Your wright,"* he wrote. *"It's dangerus."*

She didn't move for a long moment. Then she held out, *"I'm sory."*

"Their's nothing to be sorry about," he wrote and rolled over.

He could hear her breath quaver. Then, blessedly, she walked out and closed the door. He lay there and tried to think about anything but her.

LURRIKARA ISLAND ROSE sharply from the sea. At some primordial time, the island's cliffs might have been dark gray, but millennia and millions of seagulls had painted them white with a paste of their droppings and feathers.

The hierophants were flying the *Queen's Lance* low as they approached the island. Nicodemus could now see the massive gray bodies of elephant seals gliding through the dark seawater.

As the *Queen's Lance* flew over the cliff, it changed from an arrowlike shape to that of a broad-winged bird. The air around Nicodemus grew violent as they cut a tight circle coming up off the coast.

As the vessel rewove itself, it moved Francesca beside him. For most of the flight, she had been forward of him and too far away to correspond. Now, if she chose, she could hand him a sentence.

He kept his eyes on the island. Beyond the cliff stretched craggy highlands covered with grass and a few palms trees. Small homesteads, clusters of round wooden houses, were spread across the landscape. Near these Nicodemus could discern small herds of goats, dirty white and shaggy brown. From the corner of his eye, Nicodemus saw Francesca look over at him. After a while she looked back down.

The *Queen's Lance* glided along the coast. At one point the cliff wall turned inland to form a wide bay of two or three miles. Inside the bay, the cliffs were broken, like a set of stairs, into increasingly larger plateaus.

On the flatlands stood small houses built of stone and covered with thatch. More impressively, into the sheer face of the cliffs were carved intricate façades, doors, windows, and even balconies. Broad switchback stairs had been carved from one plateau to the next. All across the bay were fishing boats interspersed with larger trading vessels.

This was the island city of Kara.

Above the plateaued city stood a single gray spike. This would be the sanctuary of the Canonist Sabir, whose affinity for stone had allowed him to carve the city out of the cliffs. In the early days of the Spirish realm, Sabir and Cala had been consorts. When their deities had argued, Avel and Kara had briefly gone to war, but for centuries now they had enjoyed close diplomatic and mercantile ties.

A few lofting kites were tethered above the sanctuary. As the *Queen's Lance* approached, a white kite with a golden sun on its canopy shot up from the city before flying beside the warship. It loosed a long trail of flags. The pilot seemed to be waving. Nicodemus looked aft and saw the *Queen's Lance* now trailed flags of her own. The kite broke company to glide back down to the sanctuary.

The *Queen's Lance* flew for a quarter hour more over highlands. Then, as they neared the island's southern tip, Francesca pointed out to sea.

When Nicodemus looked in that direction, he started. There were twenty of them arranged in a circle. Each was as tall and thin as a

Starhaven tower. Delicate, arching bridges connected each structure to its neighbors.

He'd heard of this place as a child. The ruins of a city built by the two ancient races: the aquatic Pelagiacs and another humanoid people who had once inhabited Lurrikara Island. The Neosolar Empire had driven both peoples off the island and far out into the open ocean.

The defeated humanoids had left behind this ring of interconnected sea towers. Apparently, from a boat sailing beneath them, one could look down into the murky water and see the towers extend down into an underwater city.

It made sense, Nicodemus thought, that the towers should resemble Starhaven's; the Pelagiacs and the lost people of Lurrikara were undoubtedly Chimerical peoples like the Chthonics who built Starhaven. They must have had similar architectural techniques.

As the *Queen's Lance* neared the structure, Nicodemus could make out long, plumelike windcatchers that had been tethered to every level of the towers. The Lurrikara wind garden.

When only a mile away from the towers, the *Queen's Lance* came around into the wind to approach a wide bridge.

Francesca pointed off toward the horizon, where there brooded clouds so massive they seemed to be a distant mountain range. Francesca offered Nicodemus a golden sentence. Grudgingly, he took it and translated: "*Incomming storm?*"

"I supose."

"*Cyrus had beter delivar his reports quickly or we'll have to weight out the storm here.*"

Nicodemus nodded at this but didn't reply.

As they made final approach to the towers, he noticed that not all the rigs tethered to the towers were windcatchers. Five of them were much larger than the others and lacked cylindrical hulls.

Nicodemus frowned at these larger cloth constructs until he realized they were warships. Three were narrow vessels with four or five wind mages scurrying about each. Cruisers, he supposed.

The two largest warships were different. Instead of being shaped like an arrow or a blade, these ships were rounded, almost spherical. At their tops bulged several lofting sails; below these hung layers of stiff cloth wings, each one suspended above the other to form an array. Sunlight glinted off small metallic squares sewn into the cloth.

A coldness filled Nicodemus's stomach, and suddenly he felt foolish for being so upset by a woman whom he would never be able to touch. Compared with the sheer magnitude of death this construct could inflict, his jealousy of Cyrus was a trifle.

Francesca was also looking at the massive warships. When she glanced at Nicodemus, he met her eyes. She handed him a sentence: *"What are thay?"*

"I've nevar seen one before, but juging by what Cyrus discribed to me, I'd guess they're cariers."

She read this and then looked back at the ship. *"They cary warkites?"*

"Thousands of them. They can be deployed while the carryer is in flight. Most often the constructs are directed against the canopes of enemy air flet. But every so often they are deployed against an army or evan a city."

"The Seige of Erram?"

He nodded. *"The polythesits droped all their warkites on the quarter of the city with the most monotheists. The constructs cut down thousands of citziens on that first drop and then swarmed about the city for ten days, killing anyone who leaft shelter."*

She looked back at the carrier.

The *Queen's Lance* was now hovering above a tower bridge. On the stones, several green-robes hurried about. Cyrus and Izem had dropped an anchor line, and the ground crew was tethering it to a giant mooring cleat.

Francesca held out a sentence: *"What are the metal sqaures that shine so?"*

"Talens," he replied grimly. *"What the kites use to cut enemy sails or fleash."*

"Would the kingdum deploy them against Avel? Agianst their own people?"

He just looked at her.

She exhaled and wrote, *"Right, dumb question."*

PROTECTED THOUGH IT was within an estuary, the lighthouse of Cold-lock Harbor was buffeted by winds. It was a serviceable, if not grand, three stories of solid sandstone. Lotannu and Vivian had bribed the keepers to let them up to the top.

Presently, Lotannu hugged his arms around his chest. The wind chilled his face and hands. Vivian did not seem bothered.

"How long do we wait for a reply?" he asked. She had just extemporized a colaboris spell and cast it to a relay station on the Lurrikara wind garden.

"A quarter hour," she replied.

Normally the stations in Avel and Kara received colaboris spells from Starhaven's Erasime Spire. Messages between Avel and Kara were relayed through Starhaven. As far as Lotannu knew, no colaboris extemporization had ever been attempted between two locations so distant. But if anyone could accomplish it, Vivian could.

"Maybe I should cast another," Vivian said. "It's possible I missed the towers and they—" A streak of gold appeared out at sea. In the next instant, it enveloped the lighthouse in a horizontal blast of text. Sentences flashed through Lotannu's mind and made the world spin. Grunting, he put his hand to a wall to keep from falling. When at last sure of his balance, he looked at Vivian, afraid the spell had shot past her too fast.

But Vivian was standing calmly, reading a sheet of golden prose with her all-white eyes. "There's a storm above Lurrikara," she said absently. "It's blowing so hard they've put both carriers in dock. They anticipate the storm will last till morning. As soon as the winds die down, they'll loft the fleet and commence with the planned action."

"And what should we do in the meantime?"

She turned toward him and held out her hand. He took it and began to lead her toward the stairs. "We keep low and make sure not to be surprised by the Savanna Walker."

THE *QUEEN'S LANCE* passed over ocean waves to the dark redwoods just as the sun sank to the west.

Francesca shifted in the robes, which were woven into the ship. Nicodemus was somewhere behind her. She had to suppress the urge to look aft. Additionally, she had to resist the urge to look forward at Cyrus. Self-scorn washed over her for getting into a hot mess between two men. What she needed was help coping with her new deafness, not the adoration of either man. She needed to keep better watch on her words and actions.

Slowly her rage burnt out, and she assumed her physician's mask of calm. The warships at Lurrikara had reminded her of what was at stake. She closed her eyes and cultivated cool concentration until she felt the *Queen's Lance* shift.

She opened her eyes to discover the ship had broadened and turned so it could face out to sea and into the wind. Izem was letting the wind blow them back inland. Looking down, Francesca saw that they flew above a long estuary that extended for a mile or so into the forest. During and just after the rainy season, a river flowed out of the mountains and into the sea. At the end of the estuary, the fortress town of Coldlock Harbor stood atop a promontory. The town was rectangular, perhaps two square miles, enclosed by sandstone walls. To the east stood a gatehouse that opened onto the road to Avel.

When the *Queen's Lance* hovered above the docks, Cyrus came crawling through the cloth. He was going to fly both Nicodemus and her down to the docks.

With a few deft motions, Cyrus cut her free and she swung down to hang by a harness. He shouted something unintelligible and then moved aft to cut Nicodemus into a similar swinging harness. Though the cacographer was wrapped in cloth, Francesca flinched as he swung next to her. She remembered the canker his touch had raised on the kobold's arm.

Suddenly they were all falling. Francesca cried out before something pulled up hard on her chest and thighs. Cyrus was above her, and above him spread the wide canvas of a jumpchute. He'd somehow woven them all into a three-person rig.

With impressive precision, Cyrus landed them on the docks. Francesca's boots struck wooden planks as lightly as if she'd just dismounted a horse. She stumbled away and found her black wizardly robes were no longer interwoven with Cyrus's rig. She turned and saw Nicodemus unwinding the cloth that had insulated him from the ship's text. When finished, he handed the ball of silk back to Cyrus.

A fierce wind buffeted them as Cyrus's chute blasted its text downward and sent the pilot flying back up toward the *Queen's Lance*. He waved to Francesca. She held up her hand and watched his rig weave itself into the warship's hull.

Then the *Queen's Lance* broadened its wings and cast such a blast of wind that it set several boats rocking. In the next instant, the airship shot away toward the wind garden.

Francesca took a moment to inspect the ships still bobbing in the water. Most were of the sleek, two-mast design favored by Spirish and Lornish sailors. There was one wide catamaran with two hulls; it must have sailed all the way from the Ixonian Archipelago.

A movement to her right made Francesca turn and study a neatly dressed Nicodemus. Previously she had seen him bare to the waist in imitation of a kobold warrior. Then she'd seen him swaddled like a baby. But now Nicodemus wore clothing of the Spirish style—pants, a loose shirt, and longvest, all cut from the *Queen's Lance*'s white silk. He had tied his long black hair back into a ponytail. He looked like a wealthy Spirishman.

In her forearm, Francesca started to forge a sarcastic comment, but then stopped and chastised herself for such a frivolous impulse.

He tossed a word to her: *"Hungery?"*

"Always," she answered.

He started down the dock toward the town. *"We have to eat qiuckly and then get into the woods before the gaets close for the nite."*

She walked beside him through gates that separated docks from the town. Two green-cloaked city watchmen nodded to them. They had seen the warship deposit them and so knew they were important to the hierophants.

Francesca wondered how much the watchmen knew about the rebellion brewing in Avel.

Coldlock Harbor was a cramped place, consisting almost entirely of two-story wooden buildings. The only stone structures she knew of were the barracks near the gate and the small infirmary in the center of town.

The settlement, having been destroyed by lycanthropes, had been repeatedly rebuilt, each time with a more defensible design. In its current incarnation, all buildings were arranged into a grid. The muddy streets were too narrow to be convenient, but not narrow or winding enough to possess the charm of Avel's alleyways. The sky was still bright, but most streets were in shadow. Francesca guessed there were about two hours until nightfall.

A surprising number of people walked the streets. Most were young men in Spirish dress. Some—judging by the short pants, thick wool shirts, and bare feet—were sailors on shore leave. Their captains and officers wore pants and longvests. The other men about the town were likely guards or wagon drivers for the caravans that made the daily run from Coldlock to Avel.

Setting out at first light, a fast caravan could reach the city by the end of a summer's day. When the days grew shorter, or when a caravan encountered trouble, they had to form a ring in one of the defensible clearings constructed along the road to Avel.

Francesca saw only a few people who looked like Coldlock natives: a woman hawking flatbreads, a few old shopkeepers sitting outside their stores and holding small steaming cups of mint tea between pinky and thumb. Coldlock had a significant number of salmon fishermen, but they lived in the southern half of the town. Mostly the fisherfolk kept to themselves.

Much to her relief, neither Nicodemus nor she attracted much attention. A few older men eyed her black robes uneasily. But other than that everyone seemed preoccupied by their own business.

Francesca had lived for two seasons in Coldlock, both times serving as a cleric in the town's infirmary. She'd learned that many of the town's buildings were dedicated inns and boarding houses. Feeding and sheltering the many transient sailors and caravan men was the only livelihood besides fishing to pursue in Coldlock.

A man dressed in a fine blue longvest, staggering slightly, bumped into Francesca. As the man's lips moved, she smelt a strong whiff of aniseed-flavored liquor. Suddenly Francesca realized how little she knew about living without hearing. The drunk man seemed to be yelling. It wasn't a concern; she could extemporize a stunning spell that would put him out cold. But suddenly Nicodemus was in front of her, staring into the other man's face.

The drunk stepped back but seemed to continue yelling. Nicodemus didn't move or speak.

"*Stop puffing your chest out like a rooster!*" she cast. But he let the sentence fall and continued to glare at the other man. The drunk seemed to say a few more things before backing down and wandering away.

Nicodemus turned, and they continued down the street. She wrote to him: "*That wasn't chivalrous or dashing.*"

"*I didn't meen for it to be either.*"

"*Did you mean for it to be a spectacular display of male idiocy?*"

"*You have me their. I'd hopped only for an impresive display of male idicocy. Sccoring a 'spectacular' is a treat.*"

Francesca snorted, "*What if he had touched you?*"

He nodded. "*Your right about that. I should buy some gloves. I ususally carry a pair. Do you have any coin?*"

She still had the purse she had negotiated out of DeGarn. "*Let's order a meal first.*"

They found the nearest inn, and Nicodemus bargained with the owner for a private room and fast service. Together they walked up stairs to a dining room: dirty walls, narrow windows, a frayed carpet covered with rag-stuffed pillows. Nicodemus took a few coins and trotted down the stairs to find a glover.

From the room's windows, Francesca watched him jog down the street. The shadows were deepening, and more sailors and caravan men were about in search of dinner or entertainment.

She turned and looked about the room. She didn't see any lamps and thought about asking the innkeeper for one. A rush of embarrassment washed over her as she considered trying to communicate with a stranger.

She sat down on the carpet. As a physician, she had sometimes wondered what it would be like to have certain medical conditions. She had seen enough pain and frustration to know how powerful disabilities could be. To some extent, she had understood her initial feelings of loss and anguish because she had previously imagined them. But what she had not imagined—what perhaps no able person could imagine—was the myriad everyday desires a disability impeded.

She rested her face in her hands and then began breathing long and slow, letting the air drag at the back of her throat so she could feel it. She didn't need to get a lamp. Flamefly paragraphs could provide enough light. Then she rose and stood in front of the window, letting her eyes go out of focus.

Now a throng of people moved about on the street. Two children seemed to be singing, a bowl on the ground before them. Someone had dropped in a few brass coins.

Suddenly Francesca stood up straight, nearly flinching. Something had just passed in front of her, but she couldn't say what. The street was more crowded than ever. Then her eyes found them. Both were dressed in common Spirish clothes, she with long white hair, he with black dreadlocks.

Francesca ran downstairs and into the street. "Vivian!" she called as best she could. "Lotannu!"

Vivian was the first to turn around, her face tense with surprise. Lotannu turned a moment after, a blaze of silver sentences leaping from his forearms. Unable to see the runes, the other pedestrians paid them no mind.

"It's Francesca," Francesca called and then cast two golden copies of a sentence that read, *"It's Francesca."*

Both of the wizards caught the spells and read. Lotannu was holding Vivian's hand. He let go to cast, *"Magistra, it is a surprise to see you here."*

"I can say the same. But quickly, come with me. We've a private room in this inn."

Lotannu exchanged a quick correspondence with Vivian and then cast, *"We?"*

"Nicodemus and I. You came to Avel with orders to hunt him down, but I can assure you he is opposed to the demonic forces in Avel. The Savanna Walker attacked you too. He is our mutual enemy. Now you have to see the only way we're going to survive is to form an alliance." After casting this to Lotannu, she copied it and cast one to Vivian.

The wizards exchanged a rapid correspondence.

Francesca interrupted. *"At least consider a temporary alliance."*

Vivian responded. *"Magistra, we have learned many things, some of which concern you."*

"I realize that you do not trust me, but give me a chance to explain," Francesca replied but then noticed the book Lotannu was holding. *"Is Shannon's ghost still in my journal?"*

Vivian nodded, and then asked: *"He is. But first, please tell me why we are corresponding in Numinous and not speaking."*

"I've lost my ability to hear. But we shouldn't be having this conversation here on the street. At least come with me into the inn. I can explain and you can consider my offer."

The wizards corresponded again, this time for longer. At last, Vivian replied to Francesca: *"Lead the way, Magistra. But at the first sign of treachery, I will personally snuff out your mind."*

———

ON HIS WAY to a glover's shop, Nicodemus passed a large caravan guard wearing old brown gauntlets. The idea didn't occur to Nicodemus until the other man was a hundred yards away.

He ran after the guard and flipped him a silver sovereign. Then he offered one more in exchange for his gloves. The guard wanted three more. They settled on two.

Smiling at his luck, Nicodemus hurried back to the inn. The gloves were a bit large and smelled of sweat, but they would do just fine. From the gatehouse, there came a sudden chorus of shouting as if one caravan had tried to enter town when another was leaving. Nicodemus hurried back to the inn. But when he got there, a strange sight brought him up short.

Francesca was on the street, hurrying toward the inn's door. Behind her walked a man and a woman both dressed in nondescript longvests. However, the woman shone with a blaze of Numinous so glorious she looked like a small walking star.

The prose that covered her was more elaborate than any Nicodemus had ever seen, and it was so bright that he could catch only glimpses of her Language Prime texts. Nicodemus could remember only one spell that came close to matching this luminosity: the tirade he had cast against Fellwroth all those years ago in the Spindle Bridge above Starhaven. He had been able to compose that spell only with the help of the emerald.

Francesca cast a short text to both of her followers and then stepped inside the inn. Both the man with long dreadlocks and the woman covered with glorious prose followed.

Nicodemus started as if waking from a trance. The chorus of shouting coming from the gatehouse was growing louder, rising as if the caravans were taking turns bellowing at each other.

Nicodemus shook his head. A strange sensation was moving through his body. There was something about the prose-covered woman that seemed . . . impressive, certainly, but there was something else. Did she seem . . . familiar? Was that it?

He ran to the inn's doorway. The starlike woman was halfway across a common room filled with men talking and drinking.

Nicodemus's feet seem to move on their own, carrying him across the room. His hands seemed like someone else's hands as he pulled off his gloves. But the closer he came to the brilliant woman, the more certain he became that he knew her. That she was someone he had known all his life.

Abruptly, the men in the common room fell silent. They turned to face toward the door. Perhaps they had heard the shouting from the gatehouse.

Nicodemus was too focused on the starlike woman to care. She had turned sidewise to slip passed two groups of men, and Nicodemus could see that every strand of her long silky hair was wrapped in ornate text. Even her eyes were covered by a film of opaque prose. She had written a spell to block out all mundane light from her eyes, to blind herself. She looked at him but did not see him. She slipped between the crowds. She was holding the hand of the man with the dreadlocks.

The men in the common room began to murmur in a slow, almost melodic way.

Nicodemus stepped through the crowds until he was a few feet away from the strange woman. They stood in the back of the common room now, just entering the stairs that led up to the second floor. In fact, Francesca was halfway up the stairs.

At last Nicodemus reached the contextualized woman, and with his bare hand he grabbed hers.

He looked down at her fingers. The intricate texts surrounding them bent the light so the knuckles seem knobby, the skin blotchy. But with his cacographic ability, Nicodemus sent a wave of misspelling through this prose so that it evaporated. This left behind the slim and smooth hand of a powerful spellwright barely into her thirties. The olive-brown hue of her skin was the exact same color of his skin.

No cankers grew from where he touched her, so he sent another wave of cacographic influence flying up her arm to her head. The spells that twined around each strand of her hair made them shine silvery white. Now they unwound and fell to the floor, leaving the woman with a long ponytail of glossy raven-black hair.

Then his cacography peeled off the mask she had written over her face, revealing smooth cheeks where once there had been wrinkled impersonations of age.

Finally, Nicodemus's cacography dissolved the blinding textual folds that had made her eyes as pale as milk. Now he looked into irises the same shade of bright green as the Savanna Walker's, the same shade as his own.

This woman . . . her father had given her a nose shorter than Nicodemus's and a forehead that was longer. But the shape of her face and her mouth, even the way she held her head . . . it was, Nicodemus realized, the closest he might ever come to seeing their mother.

In her eyes he saw a recognition that surely was reflected in his own. Slowly his lips parted. "Sister," he said in a slow, stunned whisper. "Halcyon."

The world slowed until it hung, suspended, on a single moment.

But then time leapt forward, and the Halcyon pulled her hand from Nicodemus's.

In that moment, the crowd of men around them erupted into undulating wails, their mouths forming nonsensical parts of words.

Nicodemus jumped backward as his half sister reached at his throat, her hand a silvery coruscation of lacerating words.

CHAPTER

forty-six

As Captain Izem brought the *Queen's Lance* around to approach the garden tower, Cyrus frowned at the pass. Half of the usual number of windcatchers were aloft despite the powerful wind.

Izem and he had edited the *Queen's Lance* into her battle conformation: hexagonal hull, piercing forward sails. As such, Cyrus could trot up the hull to grab Izem's arm. "Captain, the windcatchers."

"I saw. Maybe Oria brought them in case the storm reaches here?"

Cyrus shook his head. "She'd know from scouting kites that the storm will miss her by miles."

Izem looked back at him. "Let's try the docking lure. Ready the auxiliary aft sail."

"Yes, captain," Cyrus said and hurried aft.

As he edited a sail that could double their thrust, Cyrus watched the *Queen's Lance* hover over the tower's jumpdeck. In the marshal's pavilion stood a robed and turbaned hierophant. Not Marshal Oria; she went bareheaded when commanding. From the pavilion's crown unfurled the colored flags that signaled to commence docking.

Izem raised the *Queen's Lance* a few feet and then dipped back down to hover. This holding maneuver would be usual for a larger airship needing to adjust its rigging. But a Kestrel could dock in any conformation. The commander on deck would know this.

Cyrus finished editing the additional aft sail and scanned the skyline for hostile sails. Seeing nothing, he turned back to the deck. The on-tower commander was looking up at them, his posture tense. He must know that they were studying him.

Then the commander made a quick motion. With a cry, they came running out on deck. Maybe twenty pilots, all carrying folds of language-charged cloth.

The *Queen's Lance* could tear any airship to pieces, but against a swarm of kites it could defend itself only by means of a crew casting out sharp side sails. With five pilots aboard they could manage it; however, with only themselves, Izem and Cyrus did not stand a chance against the kites.

"Auxiliary sail!" Izem yelled.

Cyrus grabbed the sail's central passage and cast it into action. The stiff sail folded away from him and let out a blast of wind. The *Queen's Lance* leapt forward even as bright jumpchutes popped open from the deck.

"Midship for the slip!" Izem barked.

Cyrus dove forward. As soon as his belly touched floorboard, he edited the text around him to sew himself into the ship. All around him the *Queen's Lance* folded into a thin, stiff sheet. With the reduced resistance, the warship shot forward into the wind.

Cyrus looked back and saw the round enemy jumpchutes pulling slowly windward. Within moments, the *Queen's Lance* had outflown them and was over the ocean. Cyrus glanced back again and saw half of the kites break north, toward Coldlock Harbor.

Izem banked the *Queen's Lance* north and commanded that the auxiliary sail be taken in. By pulling himself through the cloth, Cyrus obeyed and then hurried forward to Izem.

"The polytheists have taken the garden tower," the captain said gravely. "Marshal Oria is dead."

"Or captive?" Cyrus asked hopefully.

"You think she'd let them take her alive?"

Cyrus grimaced under his veil. The first casualty of the Second Civil War was one of the authors he had admired most.

"They'll prevent us from landing at Coldlock," Izem said with a nod toward the wing of lofting kites flying parallel to them along the coast. "Francesca and Nicodemus are on their own."

Cyrus looked at the enemy pilots. "How much text do we have left?"

"Enough to return to Lurrikara. We'll join the fleet there."

As they flew past Coldlock Harbor, Cyrus looked out at the fortress town and prayed to Celeste and the Creator.

FRANCESCA STUMBLED AND had to press one hand against the wall of the stairway. She tried to look at her hand but saw nothing. With a thrill of fear, she realized that tendrils of blindness were moving through her visions.

She looked back to warn her comrades. Lotannu stood not two feet away from her, but he'd turned to look into the common room. Everyone in the crowd was swaying.

A sudden blaze drew Francesca's eyes to a young woman with long black hair; from her right fist extended a profusion of Magnus spells so bright that it had become a silver flare. The woman thrust the wartext at someone whom Francesca could not see. Abruptly, the woman's textual blades winked out and Nicodemus was holding her arm.

"Nico!" Francesca yelled.

Vivian seemed to have disappeared.

The woman who had attacked Nicodemus yanked her hand back. Numinous sentences sprang from every inch of her body and then coiled around her arms. She lunged forward . . . but her text winked out again.

Nicodemus had stepped forward and embraced the stranger, one hand around her waist, the other pressed flat against her forehead. The woman slammed a fist into his jaw hard enough to make him stumble backward.

Francesca caught a glimpse of the woman's face. Her smooth olive skin was as dark as Nicodemus's, her wide green eyes as bright, her long raven hair the same glossy black.

Golden light flashed before Francesca as Lotannu cast a blazing Numinous spell with an overhand throw. The text shot across the room to wrap around Nicodemus's head. Nicodemus stumbled as the netlike spell enfolded his mind, but it then misspelled into nothing.

Lotannu took off at a run.

"No!" Francesca shouted. "Damn it, no!" She ran after him. Tendrils of blindness twisted across her vision. The Savanna Walker was drawing nearer. "The Walker!"

Nicodemus and the woman were stumbling like dancing drunkards. She threw an elbow at his face, but he pulled her in tighter so she didn't have room to swing.

Then Lotannu reached them and cast a ball of Magnus into Nicodemus's right eye. Nicodemus stumbled backward but held onto the woman. Francesca realized that he was using his cacography to censor her. As soon as he let go, she could tear the room to pieces with her shocking textual strength.

Lotannu reached out again, his arms crackling with Magnus sentences, but Francesca leapt into action. With her left hand, she grabbed a fistful of his dreadlocks; with her right, she brought her own stunning text down on his head. Her golden sentences locked around his mind, and he fell backward, unconscious.

With a cry, Francesca tried to get away from Lotannu, but he fell onto her, and they crashed to the floor. As they fell, whatever text he had been casting detonated.

The blast knocked the breath out of Francesca. Complete blindness washed over her but then relented. She struggled to escape from under Lotannu but then saw Nicodemus. Lotannu's blast had knocked him off his feet. He still held onto the strange woman's hand and was struggling to stand. Then she was above him and pulling hard to escape his grasp.

All around, men had erupted into chaos. Most were rushing toward the door. Others were fighting with each other. Everyone seemed to be shouting; the Walker had made them aphasic and delirious.

"Stop!" Francesca cried, still struggling to escape Lotannu's weight. "Stop!" But the woman kicked Nicodemus's shoulder to free her hand from his. At last Francesca wriggled out from under Lotannu.

Nicodemus rose to his knees. The strange woman extemporized a Magnus ball and suspended it by a sentence. With both hands and turning her hips to use all the strength in her legs, she swung the textual flail around and smashed its ball into the side of Nicodemus's face.

Francesca leapt at her, but Nicodemus's head snapped to the right, and he collapsed. The woman raised the textual flail over her head, but before she could bring it down, Francesca crashed into her, wrapping her arms around the woman's shoulders and sending them both to the ground.

As Francesca sat up and tried to pin the other woman down, she noticed that the common room had emptied of all but a few men.

Suddenly she was being lifted into the air by a sheet of Magnus. The spell tossed her onto the ground next to Nicodemus and then wrapped around her arms and legs. With a cry, Francesca struggled but found herself hopelessly spellbound.

Nicodemus lay next to her, blood from his head wound flowing freely into his left eye. He was still breathing, and the blood was causing him to blink.

"Nicodemus!"

He turned toward her, his one clear eye trying to focus. His movements were confused. With great effort he sat up. But before him stood the young wizard, her body now gloriously filled with Numinous and Magnus.

Francesca waited for a killing blow to fall on Nicodemus. But it didn't come. She looked up at the blazing woman and realized that the woman was facing away, toward the common room's entrance. Large sections of her sunlike prose vanished.

Another wave of blindness swept over Francesca, followed by a terrifying sense of falling and then spinning. Flashes of the world appeared before her: the woman's beautiful prose, Nicodemus's bleeding face, an impossibly large body made from gray skin infested by burrowing parasitic insects that peered down at them with fleshy white eyes.

The woman's beautiful prose dissolved, and Francesca fell into absolute blindness.

The Savanna Walker had come.

FRANCESCA WOKE WRAPPED in hot and itchy cloth. She also was bent over and something large was jamming itself into her stomach. She tried to moan.

The world turned right side up, and her butt landed on hard ground.
The next moment, whatever had been wrapped around her vanished and
she was looking up at a slice of evening sky that was framed by two Coldlock Harbor buildings.

Nicodemus squatted next to her. A laceration curved above in front of
his left ear. Darkening blood covered his face and shoulders. "*Are yu okay?*"
he cast to her.

She looked at herself and patted herself down. "*I'm fine, I think. What
happened?*"

"Berr," Nicodemus replied before looking over his shoulder. "*He came
and took the Halcyon.*"

"*The Halcyon?*"

"*My half sisster. He must have been weighting until I destracted her. Can
you walk?*"

Francesca got to her feet. She was standing on a large wool blanket,
which she supposed was what Nicodemus had wrapped her in before carrying her out of the tavern.

"*There's choas at the gates,*" Nicodemus wrote and started off down an
alley. "*The watchmen are in a panic. They think the lcyacnthropes caused the
afasia. They're searching the town for wolves. But we can hide in the fishermen's quarter.*"

Francesca picked up the blanket and found her clinical journal in it.
Nicodemus must have taken it from Lotannu when he fled the tavern. She
hurried after Nicodemus and wrote, "*Go back to the Halcyon part.*"

"*It was Vivian. She covered herself with subbtexts more ornate than anything I've ever imageined. She even put laguage in her eyes to make herself blind
to the mundane world. An amazing disgise.*"

Francesca shook her head. "*But you said your half sister was in a convoca-
tion in Ogun.*"

"*Seams that was a trick. Our agent was fooled.*"

"*But why disguise herself?*"

"*Given that she naerly split my head open, I'm guesing she wanted to get
close enouf to me to kill me.*"

"*That would also explain why she didn't fear an encounter with Typhon. She
must have known she could defeat him. But how is it the Savanna Walker over-
powered her?*"

Nicodemus winced as he read this: "*My cacography could cencsor my
sister. Berr is also a cacographic Imperial, and he has the quatronary cognition
spells Typhon gave him while making him half dragon. Vivian could have defeated any opponent except for Berr.*"

"*Did Berr harm you?*"

He shook his head. *"He beged me too free him. He said his mind would soon be crystalin. I have no idea what he meent."*

Suddenly Francesca remembered the way Nicodemus's head had snapped back from the blow of Vivian's mace. *"I need to look at your wound,"* she flicked at him. *"Did you lose consciousness after the blow?"*

He kept moving. *"I did, breifly. Look at it when we're hidden."*

But she stopped and turned around. *"We should go to the infirmary. They will hide us from the watchmen."*

He frowned at her. *"Can we trust the claricks?"*

"Neither the hierophants nor the wizards have any sway over them. It will be safer than squatting behind some fisherman hut."

He seemed to think about this and then nodded. *"All right, but we'll weight until dark. That why I can use the Chthonic spells."*

She looked up at the sky and bit her lip. There was maybe half an hour of light left. *"This creature-of-the-night habit of yours is going to put a dent in your social life."*

He put a hand to his forehead. *"Fran, you know I love how witty you are, but not now."*

"Fine, let's walk toward the infirmary." She paused. *"Do you have a headache?"*

He gave her a wry look and pointed to the gash above his ear.

"Right, ask a dumb question . . ." she replied but stepped closer. He didn't seem to have any confusion or trouble balancing. He stepped back and, with a slight frown, looked at her hand, which she had unknowingly raised as if to touch his head. She lowered her hand.

"The infermary is that way." He pointed and then set off.

The streets were still wet from the rain. The ground gave under Francesca's boots.

They seemed to be at the town's edge, and few people were about. The lycanthrope scare had sent everyone indoors. As they neared the town's center, she spotted a few souls darting from building to building.

"Why did the Walker go after Vivian?" she asked.

Nicodemus had again put a hand to his head. He blinked a few times and then replied: *"I'm not sure. Back in the Greenwatter, he mentoined someone he called 'the second.' I thought he ment the second dragon, but I'm guesing now he meant a second Imperail."*

She replied: *"We still don't know anything about the second dragon, do we? Vivian mentioned that Typhon seems to have fled the city."*

Nicodemus shut his eyes and then opened them wide. *"No, you hadn't mentoned that. But I'd bet he hasn't fled. I'd bet he's with the second draggin."*

Francesca couldn't help laughing. *"The second draggin? Well, your sister didn't knock the cacography out of you."*

He sighed. *"Dragin?"*

"Now you're just draggin-g it out," she sent back at him and smiled the way she knew would show her dimples. *"You had it right before. It's spelled 'dragon.'"*

He shook his head but still smiled. He was, however, blinking rapidly.

"Do you feel all right?" she asked again.

"Other thn the hedake, I'm phine. Just exhosted."

She frowned at this last word; his spelling seemed to be getting even worse . . . if that was possible.

They continued on, crossing two more streets and passing a woman and boy who were hurrying in the opposite direction. Ahead ran the central street. Red and yellow light flickered from an unseen fire.

She gestured toward a side street. Nicodemus stepped into it and squatted against the wall. She stood for a while longer and watched the foot traffic. No one seemed rushed. *"What should we do when we escape Cold-lock, find Shannon?"* She wrote and turned to cast to Nicodemus, but to her shock he was leaning against the wall and vomiting.

"God-of-gods!" she swore and ran to him. *"Nicodemus, what's the matter?"*

He looked at the sentence but then doubled over again. He was too incapacitated to translate.

"Nicodemus," she said while casting a cloud of flamefly paragraphs above his head. "Look at me."

He turned toward her but then slipped, started to fall. He put his hand to the wall to catch himself. Francesca took a step closer. His legs buckled and he fell.

Acting quickly, Francesca wrapped her hands in the wool blanket. She wiped the vomit from his mouth and made sure his airway was clear. Then she pushed his head back so the light from the flameflies shone in his eyes.

"God-of-gods!" she hissed. His left pupil was dilated to a wide black disk, his right contracted to a small circle. Often that was a sign of something pressing on the left side of the brain.

She manipulated the blanket so that the first two fingers of each of her hands lay in his palms. "Squeeze my fingers," she said in what she hoped was a clear voice. "As hard as you can, squeeze them both."

His left hand clamped down on her fingers, but his right barely produced pressure.

Most likely something was pressing against the left side of Nicodemus's brain, causing his left pupil and the right arm to weaken.

"Nicodemus," she said while using the blanket to turn his head to one side, "we're going to the infirmary now!"

Vivian had struck him on the temporal bone, the weakest point in the skull. An artery that supplied the skull with blood ran just under that bone. If Vivian had fractured the bone and lacerated that artery, Nicodemus would have bled into his skull.

The blow had initially knocked him senseless, but he had recovered from the concussion. But then the blood had built up enough pressure to compress his brain. That's why he had been lucid for so long but was just now flagging.

"Stand up!" she commanded. "Stand."

He had precious little time before the pressure in his head would induce a coma. A short while after that, he would stop breathing.

She hoisted him to his feet, and, using the blanket to protect herself, draped his weak right arm over her shoulders. She half-dragged him toward the infirmary.

She had performed the necessary operation only once before. Seven years ago in Port Mercy, but then she had had the assistance of more experienced clerics. And back then she had been able to use her whole repertoire of Numinous and Magnus spells. Now any text she applied to Nicodemus's body would misspell.

But unless she relieved the pressure in his skull in the next half hour, he would surely die.

FRANCESCA DRAGGED NICODEMUS into the empty solarium and pulled him on top of the table. After a few deep breaths she filled the dark room with flamefly paragraphs.

Below her, the infirmary was in chaos. The Savanna Walker had left several men unconscious, two blind, and one raving mad. The infirmary's few clerics and apprentices were frantically trying to manage the crisis. Francesca had been worried they would try to stop her. In fact, she had trouble getting anyone to notice her at all.

At last she'd been able to textually communicate with a young physician. He had had no trouble believing the present crisis had robbed her of hearing. When asked for the use of a solarium, he'd told her to take any one she liked but not to expect assistance.

Now she used the blanket to haul Nicodemus's legs onto the table and push him onto his right side. He was still breathing on his own. But he moved his limbs and opened his eyes only when she pinched his fingertips. He no longer responded to her voice. His brain was being jammed into the bottom of his skull. If she didn't act fast, it was going to stay there forever.

Just then the door opened and the physician she had corresponded with
came into the room. He set a tray down next to the table and removed its
cloth to reveal a row of metal instruments. The physician hurried out of the
room.

Clerics were required to gain fundamental skills with mundane medical
implements, but they used them only when their spells would not suffice.
Having mastery of Magnus, Francesca had not used a scalpel since she had
been an apprentice. Now she looked at the set of gleaming steel with trepi-
dation.

The other physician returned with two buckets of water. He placed one
on the washstand and the other beside the table. He cast a sentence of
faint green runes. She translated the common language message into *"I
must go back down to the main hall. You're on your own."*

Francesca thanked the young man and watched him leave. Then she
looked down at Nicodemus. Only a few days earlier she had looked down
on Deirdre.

Francesca closed her eyes and let swirling doubt fill her. But then she
took a long breath and leapt into the safety of action.

She slipped her arms out of their sleeves and went to the washstand.
After dipping her arms down to the elbow in the water, she cast a flood of
tiny white runes in a common magical language. Then she scrubbed every
inch of her hands and forearms before washing them in the other bucket.
Once they were dry, she returned to the table. Though her hands were
clean, she would have to do her best not to touch her patient for her own
safety.

So she picked up a scalpel and extended the existing laceration on the
left side of Nicodemus's face toward the back of his head, encountering
some refreshed bleeding along the way. She clamped forceps to both skin
flaps and lay each away from the incision to keep her operating field clear.
Using the blunt edge of the scalpel she scraped the skull's outer membrane
off the bone and then picked up the hand drill.

She paused, took another breath. The doubt flooded through her once
again. She fought it down.

The drill tip caught the bone. She turned the crank and felt it grind
against the skull's hard outer layer. After a few minutes the grinding ceased,
and with every turn she felt as if the drill were being pulled down into the
head; she'd reached the soft middle layer of bone. She'd known this would
come but still found it alarming. Twice she stopped and withdrew the bit.
Nothing that looked like brains was stuck to the metal so she knew she
hadn't gone too far. At last the drill began to grind again, indicating she'd
reached the innermost, harder layer of bone.

Every two turns she withdrew the bit and looked inside. After finding a clean swab on the tray, she dabbed at the hole.

Two turns of the drill. Nothing. Two more turns. Dab. Nothing. Three more turns. Nothing. Two more turns. Dab. Nothing. Two more turns. Dab.

A drop of dark blood welled up from the bone.

She put the drill back on the tray and picked up a blunt probe and a scraping probe. With the blunt, she poked the growing blood drop and felt the firm bone beneath. She pushed harder, felt it chip. A dark rivulet ran down from skull to skin flap.

Encouraged, she used the scraping probe to reach into the opening and chip fragments of the bone out and down.

Each new advance brought another dark trickle. The total volume of blood was not great, maybe a quarter of a cup. But even a small volume expansion in the skull could compress the brain into dysfunction.

Nicodemus was now breathing at a normal rate and more deeply. "Nico, can you hear me?" she asked and discovered that she was breathing easier too. "Nico, don't move."

His legs twitched and his mouth moved.

"Don't move, Nico," she said and then laughed. "You're going to be okay." She laughed again and then shivered. She blinked to make sure she wouldn't cry. He was safe. She'd done it. She'd saved him. Elation flushed through her.

This is what it felt like to be a master physician. This was all she'd ever wanted to be.

Nicodemus lifted his right hand. "Don't move," she said again. He put his hand back down. "You'll be fine."

She inspected the hole and noticed a wafer of bone remained on the lower half. She reached in with the scraping probe and broke the chip out.

Suddenly the drilling hole filled with bright red blood.

Fear shot through her. Bright red blood meant a bleed from an artery. Either pulling out the last bone chip had lacerated a vessel below the point of fracture or the decreased pressure within the skull had allowed an unclosed artery to bleed. The blood filled up the view of the incision and then began to run down the side of Nicodemus's face.

She panicked.

She had to stop the bleed, but how? She looked around but saw nothing useful. Normally she would have extemporized a spell to find and tie off the bleeding artery. Barring that, she would have simply inserted her finger into the wound to clamp off the flow. She could not do that here without contracting a lethal canker curse. The blood continued to run. Its flow surged and ebbed in time with his heartbeat.

Her own heart kicked furiously. But she no longer felt as if she were herself; she felt as if she were a spirit floating a few feet above her head and staring down through the eyes of a panicking woman. She was going to kill another patient.

And from this point of elevated detachment, a choice shone clearly before her. Compress the bleeding artery or don't. Save the patient or herself.

She looked down.

Compress the bleeding artery or don't.

His eyes were still closed and his expression was blank, almost peaceful.

Compress the bleeding artery or don't.

She knew what she would do; she wasn't sure why or even if it was what she wanted to do. Just then, it didn't matter.

She placed her left hand on top of Nicodemus's head, and slid her smallest finger into Nicodemus's skull and pressed.

The canker curse would now be coursing through her hand, misspelling her Language Prime.

But Francesca kept her finger steady. She waited, in a strange state of calm, for her patient's bleeding to stop.

forty-seven

When the bleeding stopped, Francesca dabbed the blood from the operating field. Her finger hadn't bulged into a canker; likely her Language Prime text had been misspelled in another way. Perhaps the cankers were spreading to her lungs or stomach. She used the pair of narrow forceps to pull blood clots off of Nicodemus's brain and then stitched his wound shut. During the last few stitches, he seemed to groan. At least, she imagined that's what he did when his mouth opened.

She talked to him, telling him he was going to live, that everything was going to be all right, that he shouldn't move. A half hour later he was sitting up and blinking at her. Now that the pressure was off his brain, he was more or less healthy—the skull fracture and hole drilled down to his brain would not affect him unless he was again struck in the head.

Using Numinous, she told Nicodemus that she would be back and stepped out of the solarium in search of a private room. Finding several up on the third floor, she returned to Nicodemus and motioned for him to follow.

He got off the table and discovered he could stand without trouble. But he clearly mistrusted his legs and walked far behind her, no doubt worried about falling forward and touching her. She hadn't yet told him that cankers were already inside her. His concern tightened her throat.

They entered a simple room: a cot, a pillow, several folded cotton blankets, a washstand. A room fitting for a physician's death.

Francesca cast a few flamefly paragraphs to curve lazy circuits across the ceiling and wondered if they would be the last spells she ever wrote.

Nicodemus sat on the cot, removed his boots, and lay down. When she sat next to him, he scooted away and looked fearfully at their proximity. *"Nico, during the operation, you bled briskly,"* she wrote and then floated into his lap. *"I had to touch you for a long time."*

When he read this last sentence, he held perfectly still, as if all his muscles had contracted, paralyzing him in the moment before horror set it. Then, slowly, he looked at her. His lips parted, his breath coming fast.

She reached out to take his hand.

He pulled it back.

"Please," she said, and without warning the tears came. She was frightened. It was a simple fear, like a child alone in the dark.

Nicodemus leaned closer but pulled his hands farther away. His eyes were wide with confusion.

Softly crying, she put her hand on the cot.

He looked at her fingers as if they were scorpions. Tentatively, he moved his hands toward hers but then stopped. He looked her in the face.

"I'm afraid . . ." she tried to say ". . . of what will happen next." The visible world was blurred with tears. She shut her eyes.

A moment later his hand touched hers. She could feel the trembling in his arm, the barely suppressed reflex to snatch his hand back. She interlaced her fingers into his and squeezed. Slowly, he returned the squeeze.

Francesca let out a long, shuddering breath and felt the sharp boundary of her life—all that she had wanted to achieve but had not, the loneliness to which she had committed herself.

Suddenly Nicodemus jerked her hand up.

She opened her eyes and blinked away the tears to find him stooped over her hand. He turned it over, splayed her fingers, poured his eyes over every aspect of each digit. Then he looked up at her with narrowed eyes as if she had just told an egregious lie.

She leaned away from him. "What?"

He wrote a sentence and pressed it into her palm. She translated into "I'm not mispelling you."

"Not misspelling what?"

He grabbed her wrist and held her hand up as if it was the most obvious piece of evidence yet seen by human eyes. With his other hand he pointed to it as if to conclude his argument.

"Nico, I touched only a small part of your brain. I couldn't have destroyed all of your God-of-gods damned sense" she wrote, before adding, "as little of it as you have."

He grabbed her hand. He let it go. With both of his hands, he grabbed every part of her arm. Then he pulled both of his hands away, and gestured to her arm as if dramatically presenting a bar of solid gold. He wrote: "You're Langauge Prime text is not misspeling, otherwise yu'd have chankers wherever I touched you."

She looked at him with bewilderment. "Maybe you've sent the canker curses to another part of my body?"

He shook his head. "When I touch you, I seanse all your Langage Prim. Notthing is misspelled."

They stared at each other for a long moment. Then she asked. *"Maybe you're not cacographic anymore?"*

He read this, frowned, and then wrote a Numinous spell on his bicep and cast it away from the bed. Francesca couldn't tell what the text was intended to do, but it fell to the ground and shattered. They both watched the fragments writhe and spin into nothing.

Francesca wrote, *"I'm guessing that's a 'no.'"*

"Yeh," he replied while still looking at the pieces, *"maybe you shuold have mashed a deferent part of my brian."*

"The brain in question was too small to encourage experimentation."

He seemed to laugh at the remark but didn't reply, only looked back at her undiseased hand.

She looked at him. He looked at her. *"So, if you're still cacographic,"* she wrote, *"and you don't misspell my Language Prime, what does that mean?"*

They stared at each other in silence. At first Francesca's mind raced with complex and frightening ideas about her own unknown nature. But like grains of sand shifting through the waist of an hourglass, all her chaotic speculations narrowed to a simple procession of practical thoughts that were neither complex nor frightening.

Judging by the look on Nicodemus's face, his thoughts were running the same course.

She pressed herself on top of him, wrapping her hand around the back of his neck to pull his mouth up to hers; even as he sat up into her, sliding one arm around her waist to pull her closer. Their lips met with too much force, and they both reflexively pulled back to halt the mash of teeth to lips.

They separated. Paused. Became more fully aware of what they were doing. Tried again.

But once more they pushed too hard into each other, feeling the urgent warmth of tongues before pulling slightly away in a confused desire for both consummation and temperance, like drinking fine wine when dying of thirst. So great was the need to take deep, intoxicating gulps of each other that each gulp made them regret the loss of savoring.

He pulled her down onto the cot so they lay side by side, face-to-face, and with cautious trial and glorious error they taught themselves to take slow, soft-lipped sips of each other.

WHEN THEY HAD at last schooled themselves in patience, Francesca climbed on top of Nicodemus. She peeled off her robes until she was bare to the waist. After a moment's thought, she cast a Magnus spell on the door handle that bound it to an iron cleat on the frame, ensuring their privacy.

Nicodemus looked at her body, drinking her in with his eyes. Tentatively, as if still afraid his touch would hurt, he ran his right hand up her side, avoiding her breast, to gently hold her face.

She pressed her cheek against his palm and whispered that it would be okay, that he didn't have to worry. But when she unlaced his shirt, she found her own hands were trembling. He sat up and they peeled off his shirt. Then he lay down and she put her head on his chest, her right hand splayed across his broad pectoral muscle. Their hues marked each other out—his brown skin both darker and brighter in contrast to her fairness.

His muscle tensed beneath her fingers as it formed a golden sentence that floated up. She translated his prose on his skin: *"I've nevar had a lover."*

She sat on top of him and smiled in a way that she hoped would show him both of her dimples. To reassure him, she forged a sentence in her own right pectorals and brought his hand up to her breast to translate it: *"Just don't write anything too stupid and we'll fix that."*

For a moment he stared at her as if she were the only woman in creation. Then he wrote, *"What about concpetion? We must not get you with child."*

"We're both spellwrights," she reminded him. Spellwrights were generally sterile. Very rarely a spellwright and an illiterate could conceive a child, but no two spellwrights ever had.

After reading this, Nicodemus nodded, but then wrote, *"Is it safe? You just drilled through my skull."*

She nodded. *"As long as you don't strain yourself."*

Finally he stopped looking frightened and smiled. *"I was hoping to strain myself."*

"I was hoping you would too."

"Guess I'll have to strain you instead."

She laughed.

"Let your hair down?" he asked.

Smiling, she undid her braid and used her fingers to comb out her locks until they hung loose around them.

He brought her down into an embrace, and soon they wore no covers but each other.

LATER THE FLAMEFLY paragraphs began to snow down around them as glowing sentence fragments. She lay with her head on his chest, feeling his heart's two-beat kick. As she drifted down into a dream, she began to see the sound of his heart: the first beat a bright vivid purple, lub, the second a beat of dark blue fading into black, dub.

Lub dub . . . lub dub . . . lub dub . . .

Color and sound and the softness of his skin: all the sensations of the world swirling into one rhythm without end.

Lub dub . . . lub dub . . . lub dub . . . as the dream enfolded her into deeper sleep.

forty-eight

Sitting on a ruined crate, Lotannu pulled a blanket around his shoulders and glowered. Though dawn was at least an hour away, a crowd of caravan wagons, horses, and men clustered before the gate.

The Savanna Walker's romp through Coldlock had convinced many of the town's inhabitants that another attack was coming and that they would be safer in Avel. Sadly, given what would soon take wing for Avel, the frightened souls would be in even greater danger in the city.

Lotannu took in a deep breath and wondered once again if he should join the caravan. "There's no room on any of the wagons," a woman said behind him. He jumped to his feet and faced her. Like him she was bundled up in a wool blanket. She'd wrapped her head so that only her face was exposed to the chill morning air. "Praise the Creator!" he whispered.

She motioned for him to sit back down. "Don't draw attention," she said, sitting on a nearby crate. "I doubt anyone would recognize us here. But it's better to be safe."

"The thing didn't kill you?"

She grimaced. "At the moment, I wish that it had."

He looked into her bright green eyes. It was disorienting to see her this way.

She stared at the gate. "I woke behind that tavern," she murmured. "An unsavory-looking man was turning me over. I can't imagine his intentions were good. But when he touched my skin—" She paused. "When he touched my skin, his hands bulged out into pale cankers."

Lotannu felt as if he'd been punched in the gut. "You misspell Language Prime?"

"I misspell every language."

He closed his eyes and exhaled, trying to wrap his mind around all the implications.

"We remain in Coldlock," she said. "The fleet knows we sent a colaboris spell from the lighthouse. They will send an airship to find us."

He looked at her calm expression. "Your ability to spell has been taken?"

She nodded. "The Savanna Walker stole it."

"You are still the Halcyon of course."

"Until we hunt down that beast and recover my ability to spell, I will be like my half brother." She looked away. "I will be a second Storm Petrel."

FRANCESCA WOKE TO small bright-orange flashes moving across her vision.

She sat up. The flashes diminished and then vanished. For a moment, the world made no sense. At first she thought she was in the infirmary in Avel but then realized she was in Coldlock.

Dawn was breaking through the window. She recalled the strange new realities of her life: the flight from the infirmary, the city's fomenting conflict, her loss of memories and hearing, Nicodemus.

Fearfully, she looked down. But he was still there—broad torso, dark face, a black halo of splayed-out hair. Relief spread through her. He was the one memory she was happy to recover.

Again the shower of orange flashes spread across her vision. They seemed to have leapt out of Nicodemus's mouth. She jumped.

She was not seeing these flashes with her eyes. With her eyes she was looking at Nicodemus's peaceful expression. But at the same time, in a different visual field, she saw tiny orange flashes. It was as if she was seeing through another pair of eyes that were not her own.

Again the flashes diminished and then vanished.

This was not the glow of magical text. She knew that. When the lights returned she noticed they coincided with Nicodemus's breath: multiplying on inhalation, diminishing on exhalation.

She laid a hand on her lover's chest. He inhaled, and the orange flashes spread away from his face and across her strange new vision. She also felt a slight shuddering vibration in her hand; her lover was snoring.

She was seeing his snores?

She poked his ribs. The scattered orange dots coalesced over his mouth into a red flare and vanished. Nicodemus rolled toward her. Where there had been flashes of his snoring, now there was only pale light over his mouth that ebbed and flowed in time with the rise and fall of his chest.

She was looking at the noise of his breath. It was a white noise. This was strange synesthesia indeed. All spellwrights could perceive proximity to unknown magical language as a vague, nonvisual sensation. But this was wholly different. No magical text was involved. She was seeing sound.

Then she remembered: just before falling asleep, she had seen Nicodemus's heart sounds. Could she see only sounds he made?

"Francesca?" she whispered and jumped as her auditory sight registered a firework of lavender and white.

She snapped her fingers next to her left ear and saw to her left a flash of a glossy black surface, like polished onyx. She snapped another finger behind her head and saw, more faintly, the same bright black sound behind her.

Her ears still perceived sound. But now their nerves were connected not to an auditory portion of her brain, but to a visual one. She frowned down at Nicodemus. He muttered something blue in his sleep. Normally she would have found this adorable, possibly even poetic . . . a lover mutters blue. Now she found it obnoxious. Had he just misspelled the nerves to her brain? Was that even possible?

Two years ago, Francesca had treated a musician with perfect pitch who knew what note was played on a guitar because of "the color it made." Francesca had written a long entry about her in her clinical journal.

Casting two flamefly paragraphs above her, Francesca climbed out of bed and padded over to the door. The air was chilly, and she had nothing other than her long curls to cover herself. She found the journal underneath the rumpled wool blanket.

After casting more flameflies, Francesca sat on her heels and opened the book. Instantly, she jumped back as a ghostly head and shoulder popped out of the book. She'd forgotten that they had used the journal to store Shannon's ghost.

But the specter that was pouring onto the cold floor stones was not an august man with long white dreadlocks; it was a tall woman with fair skin, long brown hair, and a physician's red stole around her neck. Francesca froze, awash in confusion.

The ghost sat up and blinked as she looked around the room. When the ghost's eyes fell on Francesca, she smiled and began to stand. As Francesca rose, the world seemed to spin. The ghost's face was an older version of her own.

It made no sense; Francesca had never written a ghost, had never even started to ghostwrite. The construct's smile remained benign, dreamlike. The ghost held out a transparent hand, palm out. Slowly, Francesca mirrored the gesture, holding her hand up to the ghost's. They touched. Gentle warmth filled Francesca's hand and then spilled down her arm.

The ghost stepped forward so that more of their arms coincided. Warmth spread throughout Francesca. The ghost turned around so that they were facing the same direction. Francesca stepped forward, and they stood in the same place; they were the same being, text and body.

Then Francesca knew everything the ghost knew. She was everything the ghost was and was everything the ghost's author had been.

She had been born under a different name three hundred years ago in the Burnt Hills, studied wizardly languages in Astrophell, medicine in Port Mercy. She had taken up her first clerical appointment not in the backwater of Avel—as she somehow would do hundreds of years later—but in the prestigious Infirmary of Chandralu, winning recognition as a master physician.

The memories of these experiences tumbled through her mind to produce a sensation that was at once otherworldly and yet also manifestly true. This was her true self. Some small part of her had always known this.

After Chandralu she had taken an appointment in the Infirmary of Trillinon, where she had overseen the building of a second infirmary outside the city walls to serve the growing population.

Her infirmary had been a great success, and soon she was approached by a secret society who controlled much of the city's wealth and business. She had joined their ranks and over the years had been brought to understand that they were demon worshipers. She had met Typhon, who convinced her that the Disjunction had already begun and that demon ascendency need not be violent. With the assistance of his devotees, Typhon would usher in a new golden age. Should the War of Disjunction end in her time, Francesca would become his chief cleric. If she would expire beforehand, he should appoint her ghost to the same position.

She had pledged herself to Typhon.

As was necessary for a demon worshiper, she had worked out of public view and without celebrity, even within her own infirmary. But using her influence, she had won funds and political support. In the last third of her life, she'd built up the infirmary's facilities and reputation to rival that of its counterpart within the city walls. Under her guidance, the amount of charity care given to the city's poorest tripled.

She had recruited the sharpest clerics to the Disjunction. She had provided Disjunction agents with medical training and set up care facilities for cells performing military action. She had even provided medical advice for assassination of several spellwrights thought to be sympathetic to the Disjunction's enemies.

A hundred years ago, on Typhon's orders, she had undertaken a rigorous ghostwriting, producing a text far more robust than any other ghost then inhabiting Astrophell's necropolis. On the day of her death, she had inscribed herself on a large codex in a private library. Typhon planned to withdraw her from the book once the War of Disjunction began. But the plans had changed; Typhon had withdrawn her from the book ten years ago. He had needed to replicate some of her text.

That was all she remembered.

Francesca stood inhumanly still.

Some part of her was horrified. But more overwhelmingly she was caught in a sudden rush of understanding. So many things made sense now. Her persistent old-fashioned accent had come not from the hinterlands but the distant past. Her ambitions were her own, part of her nature, but she had always believed she was a failure because she hadn't become a master physician in Chandralu or Trillinon. This insecurity had come from the just-barely-perceived discrepancy between her own life course and that of her author.

In fact, when appreciating Vivian's talent and prestige, Francesca had experienced pangs of envy that had felt as if they came from someone else. And they had come from someone else. They had come from her author.

Slowly, Francesca looked at Nicodemus. Her heart ached for what they could have been together.

Now she understood that Nicodemus perceived her Language Prime as bright because Typhon had written her with the emerald and with his god-spell to withstand Nicodemus's cacographic touch. His synesthesic reaction was a flush of warmth across the cheeks, which would have felt like a blush caused by his attraction to her.

The Savanna Walker had tried to pull the memories from her brain but had failed because she did not have a human brain. The Walker had instead destroyed the part of her textual mind responsible for hearing. Later, when making love to Nicodemus, her mind had appropriated his cacography to rewrite itself so it could perceive sound.

She understood then that Nicodemus caused language near him to become not only more chaotic but also more intuitive. Francesca was a creature of intuitive language; therefore, Nicodemus's effect on her was transformative.

Her thoughts moved faster and faster. Her intellect was rapidly developing away from a human mind into something with a hyperacute perception of the past and a perception of the most probable futures. She was embarking into a powerful quaternary cognition.

This skill for perceiving time, she realized, had always been manifest in her ability to prognosticate, to look into time and see the possible future bodies of her patients.

Now, her perception of time extended beyond bodies and she could see the potential of entire cities and realms. She now perceived the future as a three-dimensional and eternally descending landscape. She had to travel down this landscape, forward through time. But there was room for lateral alteration.

Francesca could see how Typhon had set forces into a temporal ravine, trying to force her and all others into the Disjunction. Now she understood why the Savanna Walker had attacked Vivian and not Nicodemus. The nature of the second dragon became clear to her. Typhon had been more successful than he had ever imagined he could be.

Suddenly fear filled Francesca's stomach. Typhon had written her to perceive time as a landscape. He would have taken precautions to ensure that she would execute his designs despite, or even because of, her sensitivity.

She was predestined to initiate the Disjunction.

When her hands began to shake, she looked at them and saw that they glowed with the Numinous prose of her ghost. Suddenly her fear gave way to indignity. What kind of half-brained author wrote a woman's soul, full of desire for freedom, into a construct he then trapped into a predestined outcome? Typhon either delighted in torturing his own creations or was too damn dim to figure out what he was doing.

Francesca's rage at her author flared hot. Glaring at the ghostly prose in her arms, she vowed that she would not become a reincarnation of her ghost or her ghost's author. Though Typhon had written her from these women, she was not either of them any more than a vase was the clay from which it had been fired. And just as a vase was not the hands of the sculptor who shaped it, she was not Typhon.

Francesca went to the bed and sat beside Nicodemus. She watched the sound of his breath, now ebbing from bright white to dull gray.

She laid her hand on his bare shoulder. Instantly, a translucent golden replica of her arm rose out of her arm; her ghost was trying to escape her lover's cacographic touch. But Francesca forged barbed sentences within her every limb, trapping the ghost within her.

She placed her other hand on Nicodemus's shoulder and felt her ghost writhe. From her hand rose tendrils of sparklike Numinous fragments as the ghost's arm misspelled. A central passage gave way, and the visual world disappeared into a cloud of runes that floated about her for a moment like vaporized gold.

Francesca's ghost was no more; she had deconstructed the text from which she had been made.

Nicodemus stirred in his sleep. She brushed the hair back on the right side of his face and thought about what she had been written to do and what she and Nicodemus could no longer be.

She brushed his hair back again and then froze. Something strange happened to her perception of time when she touched her lover: the landscape of the future changed. Experimentally, she touched his shoulder. Once more the courses she might take into the future shifted. Suddenly she understood, and an idea flashed through her mind.

Holding onto Nicodemus's shoulder, she sent her augmented mind racing forward to assemble a last, desperate course of action.

WHEN FRANCESCA HAD finished devising her plan, she pressed her lips to Nicodemus's. Sleepily, he smiled like a man satisfied with himself and wrapped his arm around her, trying to pull her on top of him.

She kissed him while pressing his chest away. He hitched a playful half smile at her and pulled more insistently.

She shook her head. "Lover," she whispered and saw the word as two bright notes: *lov-* bright green, *-er* pale yellow. With enough time she would learn what colors corresponded to what notes, what shades to what timbres, what brightness to what loudness. In time she would learn to hear and speak again, after a fashion. But now she still needed to write. Into his hand she pressed a sentence: *"Lover, I need you to wake now."*

He held the text and blinked at it. When it started to misspell, she touched it, correcting the letters. He looked at her and sat up. *"Is something rong?"*

She took his hand. *"Something happened last night."*

He laughed bright red and began to write something.

She stopped him. *"Yes, that happened too. But something more, something about why my Language Prime text shines so brightly."*

She had his full attention now.

"I was written for you."

His face tensed. *"You're a consturct?"*

"In many ways, yes. That is why your touch does not give me a canker curse. It is also why I resemble your old governess."

"April?"

She nodded. *"Fellwroth saw an image of April when you struck him back in the Spindle Bridge. So did Typhon when you touched him? Knowing that image, Typhon chose my ghost as the one most resembling her, to seduce you."*

Nicodemus was shaking his head. *"You can't be a construct. You're made out of Langauge Prime; you're aliv."*

She squeezed his hand. *"I don't have all the answers for you now but I will soon. I must go before the first dragon can get away."*

"The first dragin? Fran, what's hapening? Do you serve the Disjunction?"

She kissed a sentence onto his hand. *"I was created by the Disjunction just as you were. But I have a plan. Will you trust me and do exactly as I say?"* She met his gaze.

Without looking away he wrote: *"Without hesitateion."*

She was about to continue when something struck her as odd. "Wait, what do you mean 'without hesitation?'" she flicked at him. "Don't turn into a romantic soft brain because you finally got my clothes off."

He made a wry face. "Weren't you written to seduse me?"

"Pftt," she said. A puffy white sound. "You can't seduce a man who looks at you like you're a side of meat."

He exhaled as if annoyed but then smiled. "Well, you've convinced me Typhon's writen you; I can't imagin what other than a demonic craetion could be so exasparating."

She kissed him, hard.

He smiled and then put his back against the wall, and she leaned into him.

"When I was in the solareium on the table," he wrote on the anterior portion of her forearm, "you thought I'd misspell you. You stopped my bleding thinking you would dye. Or have I misunderstood?"

She looked up at him. "You understood."

"Then I trust you."

"Even though I was written by Typhon?"

His green eyes studied hers for a long time. "What are yu goinng to do?"

"Use what I know about the second dragon to threaten Typhon's plan."

"The second dragan?"

She nodded. "I can't explain. For my plan to work, you must confront Typhon ignorant of what I will do. Typhon will search your thoughts before he gives you the emerald. You can't know what is going to happen."

"The demon will give me the emerald? Fran, what if you're rong?"

"We both become Typhon's slaves," she wrote. "We'll be together."

He made a wry face. "As much as I addmire you, and as wonderful as the sex was, isn't it a littel early to start talking about eternil bondage?"

She snickered. "I didn't mention marriage, only enslavement by a demon." Then she made her expression serious. "Mark carefully what I write next."

He nodded.

She wrote out a long paragraph in her forearm and then edited it briefly before handing it over.

"Take my clinical journal and the ghost within it to your camp. Reunite Shannon with his ghost, who was not edited by Typhon. Leave the journal with the kobolds and make sure they keep it safe; Lotannu made a copy of Typhon's research spell in the back of it. Then hurry to the colaboris station in Avel and find Magister DeGarn. Promise to pledge yourself to the League of Starfall if he places all of his authors—wizards, druids, and highsmiths—under your command. Order them to protect you. Then take them to the sanctuary. The doors will be open and a guard will be waiting for you. When you are brought *before Typhon, agree to ANYTHING he asks so long as he will give you the emerald."*

As Nicodemus read this, the words kept misspelling, and Francesca was obliged to touch the paragraph to reverse his cacographic influence.

When finished, Nicodemus looked up. *"Fran, I'm not going to join the Disjuncteion."*

She nodded vigorously. *"You are if you want to have a hope of escaping enslavement, not to mention freeing me from his bonds."*

"I cann't!"

"You can and you will. Typhon is going to say horrible things about me. He is going to accuse me of deceiving you. But after I touched you everything changed. I haven't told you everything. I can't tell you everything! But you must promise to trust me and you must promise to agree to anything—and I mean anything—Typhon asks you to do. Promise me!"

He looked from the paragraph up to her and shook his head. *"I can't pleadge myself to the Disjunction."*

"Gahhh!" she said in exasperation. Then she grabbed one of his hands and mashed into it the word *"GodofgodsDAMNITNICO!"*

When he looked up, she shook his shoulders and then—only a little more gently—pressed a run-on sentence into his hand: *"I'm so infatuated with you now and so intolerably happy that we made love that I am an inch away from absurdly, idiotically, gratuitously falling for you if I don't BLOODY KILL YOU FIRST because you want to commit suicide by refusing to lie to a GOD-OF-GODS DAMNED DEMON!"*

When he finished, she grabbed him and, using her tongue, kissed *"!!!"* into his mouth.

He took the exclamation points off of his lips and laughed red. Then he took her hand.

"Promise you'll do what I say," she wrote for him and gave him her most pleading look. *"Trust me."*

He closed his eyes and exhaled. *"I promis."*

She kissed him again. Then she dressed, gathering up her things, and ran out the door. In a few hours everything would change.

CYRUS WOKE IN the near dark of a barracks. It took him a moment to remember the previous night. He and Izem had flown the *Queen's Lance* all the way back to Lurrikara in the dark, running into a rainstorm a hundred miles away from the island.

Night landings were difficult in the best of times—pilots had to use the flags of linguistically charged cloth as markers—and in the blowing rain it had seemed like suicide. But with no option other than ditching the

Queen's Lance in the ocean, Izem and he had laboriously gone through the protocols and docked the warship just before midnight.

Near delirious with fatigue, he and Izem had collapsed into beds the moment they were dry. Cyrus had slept like a stone, but now he was sitting up and rubbing his eyes. The sun couldn't be all the way up yet.

"Time to be out of bed, pilot," Izem said from the door. "Word just came down from the jumpdeck. The storm has passed. The whole fleet is going aloft."

Cyrus pressed both hands to his face. "Wonderful," he said flatly. He thought of Francesca in Coldlock Harbor and hoped she was safe.

Izem grunted. "In an hour, we begin the Second Siege of Avel."

forty-nine

Midmorning sunlight slanted through the redwood forest as Nicodemus rode through ferns and into the makeshift camp his students had erected. Vein was the first to emerge from his tent, blinking sleepily in the daylight. Francesca's shunting spell had been removed from the kobold's chest. He appeared healthy but moved gingerly. Nicodemus dismounted and carefully embraced him. A few moments later, Flint and Jasp came out of their tents.

As Nicodemus greeted each student, his heart ached. Of the fifteen young kobolds he had led out of the Pinnacle Mountains, only these three were still alive.

Vein reported that little had happened in the camp: Shannon seemed weaker than ever, but the three survivors were healthy and eager to seek revenge against the Savanna Walker and Typhon. Nicodemus shook his head and said that he needed them to stay in the forest to protect Shannon and an invaluable book he had brought back.

Quickly Nicodemus described all that had happened since he had left on the *Queen's Lance*. The kobolds listened carefully. Jasp petitioned to accompany him into Avel, but Nicodemus refused.

"If I succeed in the city," he said in the kobolds' language, "I will return to you in a few days. If I do not . . . make Shannon comfortable until his time comes and then return to your families in the mountains knowing you fought the demon with bravery and honor."

Jasp looked as if he wanted to deny the possibility that Nicodemus might not return, but the two older kobolds nodded and agreed. Nicodemus removed one of the saddlebags from his horse and asked where Shannon was. Vein pointed to one of the tents.

Inside, Nicodemus found the old man lying on a blanket, his face slack and his mouth hanging open. "Magister!" Nicodemus said, suddenly afraid Shannon was dead.

The old man jerked and snorted. He opened his white eyes and blinked. Azure, who had been napping on a nearby perch, made a few plaintive squawks.

Nicodemus exhaled. "Creator! You scared me, Magister."

"Nicodemus?" the old man said as he struggled to sit up. "So you didn't die out on the savanna."

Nicodemus sat down beside the old man. "No, Magister," he said. "No, I didn't die, but it wasn't for lack of trying."

The old man rubbed his eyes. "I don't doubt it. So, was it worth it? Did you catch the Savanna Walker?"

"We recovered your ghost."

Shannon turned his head sharply. He didn't look at Nicodemus. He didn't blink. He didn't even seem to breathe. "What did you say?"

"We've recovered your ghost."

Shannon looked at the book Nicodemus was withdrawing from his bag. "In . . . there?"

"Yes. Here, let me open—"

"No," the old man said quickly. "No. No, not yet. Tell me." He licked his lips. "Tell me everything."

The story tumbled out of Nicodemus: the Savanna Walker as James Berr, Vivian Niyol as the Halcyon, Francesca DeVega as a mystery. He explained about his head wound and how she had touched him without suffering a canker curse. He described her revelation and discovery of Typhon's two hidden dragons.

"She is your lover," Shannon said in an objective tone.

It wasn't a question. Heat flushed across Nicodemus's face.

"It's your voice," Shannon said. "I can hear it. And I don't know what to tell you. But how do you know my ghost hasn't been rewritten by Typhon?"

"Francesca," was all Nicodemus could think to say. "She said it wasn't."

"She might be some new kind of golem, some kind of body animated by a textual consciousness and then imbued with Language Prime to fool you."

Nicodemus didn't reply.

"You can't trust her."

"When I was dying on her table, she sacrificed herself for me."

"Maybe she was written to do so. Maybe she doesn't have free will."

Nicodemus said nothing.

"Creator, save us," Shannon muttered in irritation. "You think you're in love with her."

"I'm not some glassy-eyed boy, Magister. Deirdre found evidence that Francesca could stop the second dragon."

"You don't truly know who she is. She doesn't know who she is."

Noticing that the old man hadn't taken his eyes off of the journal, Nicodemus raised the book. "So, do you want to be reunited with your ghost, or not?"

Shannon's eyes followed the book as a starving man's might follow a loaf of bread. "I do," he said in a near whisper. "Nico, since you left my health has worsened rapidly. When I try to . . ." He paused and looked toward Nicodemus. Clearly working up to something. "Maybe I can't say; it's too embarrassing. But . . . see how pale I've become?" He tapped a frail hand to his cheek, and Nicodemus saw he was indeed frighteningly wan.

"Magister, Francesca believes the demon will give me the emerald—"

"Even if you were holding the emerald in your hand this instant, I don't think you could give me much time. As it is, I might have a handful of days or only one."

Nicodemus tried to speak, but the old man held up his hand. "You are going to go running off again. Off to meet Francesca in the sanctuary?"

"Magister, Deirdre sent Francesca to us. I have to—"

"You must do what you must," the old man said, but then his tone softened. "The Creator knows I had to leave others behind in my life."

Nicodemus knew the old man was thinking of the wife and son he had been forced to leave in Astrophell years ago.

Shannon nodded. "If you must go, Nicodemus, you must. But leave me the journal. Whether the demon rewrote it or not, the ghost will be my solace at the end."

"Magister, I'm not abandoning you. I will return."

"Creator send that you are right, my boy. Please, Creator, may you be right."

Nicodemus started to say something but stopped. He tried again but stopped. At last, he put the journal down beside Shannon. "I will be thinking of you, Magister."

Blindly, Shannon reached out his hand. Nicodemus knew that the old man did not mean to touch him, could not touch him. Nicodemus held his own hand out, inches away from Shannon's. It wasn't much of a gesture, but it was the only one they had. "My thoughts will be with you too, my boy," the old man said.

Nicodemus stood and was about to go when Shannon spoke again. "Remember, you're not facing an opponent who wants to tear you to pieces as Fellwroth did. Typhon is far more subtle. He may not be trying to capture you as much as captivate you." Shannon looked at the journal. "With this ghost, he may be doing the same to me."

Nicodemus shifted his weight.

The old man was silent for a long moment before he said. "Nicodemus, we may have committed our lives by falling in love with fictions." He paused. "Be careful, my boy."

"I will be," Nicodemus said and turned away. As he left the tent, his mind raced with thoughts of Shannon and his ghost, Francesca and her demonic author.

FOR THE FIRST time, the ghost was aware he was about to be pulled out of the book. Only parts of his paginated intellect were connecting. It was happening slowly, as if someone were opening the cover hesitantly. A few more pages connected; he regained an intuitive knowledge of how to walk. A few more pages, and his ability to recognize and remember faces improved.

It made him impatient until it made him apprehensive. Who was opening the cover so slowly?

At last, his intellect gained enough interconnection that a textual instinct pulled him out of the book.

The ghost stood inside a canvas tent, a wash of sunlight was moving on the wall. What, he wondered, had happened to Magistra Niyol's plans that they should be reduced to camping? He turned to ask Magistra or Lotannu what had happened when he saw himself, his author.

The ghost's first reaction was terror. He stepped back, fearing that Shannon would hurl a disspell or that Nicodemus would come charging through the tent wall.

But there was only the sound of wind in redwoods.

His author was lying on a bedroll, his beard wiry, dreadlocks pulled back from a skeletal face. But his eyes . . . his blank white eyes were staring at him with anxiety and anticipation.

The ghost's fear dissolved and he looked down and realized that his textual body was dim as the light from a Dralish lightning bug. His right arm had been deconstructed, and the passages around its end were beginning to fray.

He looked back at his author, at himself. "Shannon," his author whispered, "how did we get so old?"

The ghost smiled wanly and held out his hand. With a fine tremble, his author reached out, and they coincided. A wave of golden runes rode up the ghost's arm and across his body. Slowly, he got on his knees and then lay down into his author.

Unlike their previous meeting in the sanctuary, the author did not withhold himself, and so the two came to know each other perfectly. They became each other, and in doing so learned more acutely of their frailty, of the growing cankers in their gut, of their steady blood loss into their intestines.

This far from a necropolis, neither spellwright nor ghost would survive much longer.

Outside, the wind grew stronger in the redwoods. The sound of foot-steps on forest floor. The now-distant voice of Nicodemus, their former student.

There was bittersweet comfort in it all. The two versions of Shannon—textual and physical, creator and created—were reunited; it made exis-tence a fine thing, the simple beauty of light and shadow playing on the tent canvas, their shared memories of the world beyond. It was a sharp feeling, knowing that soon they would have to leave it behind.

THE SUN REACHED its zenith as Francesca, her mind and body now fully realized, stepped into the sanctuary. She had made sure that none of the guards or clerks could see her as she walked to the Hall of Ambassadors.

She found Typhon's large alabaster body sitting on the redwood throne. To his left stood Canonist Cala. To the right crouched James Berr. The Savanna Walker had changed, perhaps for the last time. His present form, massive and sleek, was the body of a voyager, a killer, a terror. Berr's skin shone pearly white and was covered by wavy iridescent rainbows. He pulled back wide lips to reveal fangs long as knives.

Francesca ignored him and turned her attention to her author. He looked at her with a smile that seemed both pleased and sad. She wondered how far into the future the demon could construct the landscape of time.

Typhon stood and bowed. He wrote her a short golden passage and tossed it to her. *"Welcome back to us, daughter. Truly, we have a bounty of success that was unforeseen."*

She sniffed. *"That might be because you have all the foresight that the Cre-ator gave to muddy shoe leather,"* she wrote to Typhon before glaring at Berr. *"You will have to choose between your successes."*

Typhon looked at Berr and then at her. *"Nicodemus is yours now?"*

She nodded.

"Completely?"

"He will be here shortly."

The demon narrowed his onyx eyes. *"How far into time can you per-ceive?"*

She gave him her brashest grin. *"Far enough."*

He studied her. *"I never imagined it possible for both dragons to manifest."*

"It seems I have another cause to compare you to muddy shoe leather, this time concerning imagination." She looked at Berr, who bared his teeth. Her smile broadened, and she took a threatening step toward him. Berr flinched.

"Daughter," Typhon wrote, *"I cannot choose between my creations."*

"Then I'll choose for you."

Typhon stepped down from the throne and walked toward her.

She leaned forward. *"Don't."*

The demon stopped; his expression was earnest, almost pleading. *"Look far into the potential futures. You cannot predict what Los will be like. I can change that."*

"It would be lovely if you could signal when you're trying to be impressive or threatening, because as it is now I'm not getting it. Perhaps you could raise your hand?"

The demon brought a hand to his chest. *"Daughter, please, do not resist."*

Up to this point, Cala might have been a statue. But now she looked at Francesca with keen interest. The demigoddess seemed to be trying to say something with her eyes.

Francesca ignored her.

Typhon put himself between her and Berr. *"There can be coexistence."*

"Only if I want to coexist."

He folded his arms in what was supposed to be a stance that conveyed power. *"I will do anything to ensure both Disjunctions survive."*

"Could you stop me?"

"I would sacrifice anything."

"Anything?"

He studied her with eyes of blank onyx. *"What must I do to convince you?"*

She laughed. *"Oh, you don't need to convince me,"* she wrote and then leaned over her author. *"You need to convince my lover."*

NICODEMUS STOOD BEFORE the colabois station. The day was windy but bright and warm. Nicodemus considered the station's massive redwood doors and wondered once again if he was insane for trusting Francesca. From the square behind him came the market's chatter.

Nicodemus took a long breath. He had chosen to put his faith in Francesca. And at present, with Shannon dying and a civil war brewing, he had nothing to act on but faith.

It was time to pay a visit to Magister DeGarn. He eyed the large brass knocker hanging on the station's door. Working it would begin a long chain of protocol: introducing himself to DeGarn and then the representative druids and highsmiths, explaining the urgency of the situation, providing evidence of who he was, negotiating what they would want from him in return for their protection.

A smaller door had been hung within the two massive ones. Around its handle shone the silvery glow of a Magnus lock and tumbler spell. Nicodemus balled his hands into fists. It was time to skip straight to the evidence.

He grabbed the locking text and sent a jolt of cacographic force running through it. The text misspelled in such a way as to coil backward and disengage the bolt.

He pushed the door open and stepped into a courtyard filled with hanging plants and a reflecting pool. Charging around this serene body of water were two war-weight gargoyles, each possessing a man's muscular body and lion's head.

Nicodemus proceeded calmly. Within moments the two constructs were circling him, baring their fangs and snarling. On the rooftops, ravens sounded a cacophonous alarm. Human faces filled the courtyard windows.

Nicodemus was walking toward the station's main entrance when two massive stone arms wrapped around his shoulders. A leonine gargoyle had pounced on him from behind. Nicodemus grabbed the construct's hand and, by focusing his cacography, blasted all text out of the gargoyle's arms, freezing them into place.

The gargoyle jumped back, lifting Nicodemus. He groaned as the air was squeezed out of him. But then Nicodemus managed to slip his shoulders out of its grasp. He flopped onto the ground, grabbed one of the gargoyle's legs, and misspelled its text.

He rolled away and jumped to his feet. Now hobbled by one paralyzed leg, the snarling gargoyle limped away. Nicodemus turned to the other protective creature. It eyed him warily.

"Stop!" a thin voice cried.

Nicodemus turned to see a crowd of wizards emerging from the station's double doors. At their front stood a short wizard with a sparse white wreath of hair. His robes boasted badges worn by a dean—an honor bestowed on colaboris station commanders.

Nicodemus nodded to the man. "Magister DeGarn."

The grand wizard's eyes widened when he was named. He studied the partially misspelled gargoyle intently, then looked back. "Nicodemus Weal?"

Nicodemus bowed.

DeGarn cast Numinous spells to each of the leonine gargoyles, both of which became still as statues.

A young woman and two older men dressed as servants emerged from a side door. The woman held a metal tray. Nicodemus nodded to her. She nodded back with more confidence than he would have expected from a servant. They had to be highsmiths.

"Magister Nicodemus Weal!" DeGarn cried. "A year spent searching for you, and now you have found us."

Nicodemus studied the academics and silently prayed Francesca was right about their political motivations. If she wasn't, this would be his end.

"Magister, I didn't want to be found by spellwrights whose prophecies might label me a demon worshiper."

DeGarn studied Nicodemus with intelligent eyes. "And the Cleric Francesca has told you that we do not consider you the Storm Petrel? That Starfall does not hold with the counter-prophecy?"

Nicodemus nodded, but just then noticed two men and a woman all dressed in druid white standing along the far wall. He nodded to them. They returned the gesture.

Nicodemus looked back to DeGarn. "She told me of the League of Starfall, who wish to keep the south free from a newly forming northern empire."

DeGarn spread his arms. "And that is what we are."

"I have come seeking your protection."

The grand wizard smiled. "And so you shall have it."

"And what would you have me do in return?"

"Pledge to be the league's Halcyon as we prepare to withstand the Disjunction."

"I am not a Halcyon now, and I might never be."

The grand wizard looked uneasy. "Perhaps you can explain?"

Nicodemus held his gaze. "If we are to come to an agreement, we must be honest with each other." He looked at the druids and the highsmiths. "I am descended from the ancient imperial family that ruled the Solar Empire. I am no master of ordered language. At present, my heritage manifests itself as an ability to misspell almost any text. As you just saw." He nodded to the misspelled gargoyle.

No one answered him.

"My half sister is Astrophell's Halcyon-in-waiting," he continued. "And she can write spells of a complexity beyond your ability to imagine. I saw her disguised in her own prose yesterday. She is here in Avel, and she gave me this." He gestured to the wound on the right side of his head.

The druids whispered to one another, and the wizards shifted uncomfortably.

"My half sister is poised to become an empress, but I want none of that life. I will be neither your political toy nor your ruler. I will pledge myself to your independence from my half sister's rule, but no academy or kingdom will control me, and I shall not control them. Do we understand each other?"

DeGarn coughed. "We have agreed that you should come to Starfall Island, which is to be neither Lorn nor Dral but neutral. And I may confidently say that many Ixonians do not cherish the idea of a dominant force in Trillinon. Judging from my latest intelligence, most of the Ixonian

Archipelago will soon join us . . . should we obtain a champion against the Disjunction."

Nicodemus nodded. "In a short time, a Spirish fleet will lay siege to this city to reclaim it from the demon who has come to rule it. It seems the hierophants and the Spirish crown will soon align themselves with my sister."

DeGarn replied. "Then all the greater is our need for a League of Starfall." He gave Nicodemus a meaningful look and then looked at the druids and highsmiths.

Nicodemus paused, unsure what he should say next.

DeGarn nodded encouragingly.

"Today, you have an opportunity . . ." Nicodemus began uncertainly, ". . . to strike at a demon before my sister's forces do so. To win my pledge, you must follow me today in this task."

No one spoke. DeGarn frowned at him. "What do you mean?" asked the young woman among the highsmiths.

"I'm going into the sanctuary after Typhon," he replied, looking around the courtyard. "And if the spellwrights of your League of Starfall can bring me out alive, then you can have me."

fifty

When marching into battle, druids wore plates of wooden armor, trading sober white robes for lacquered green, black, and gold. Not to be outdone, highsmiths donned armor of metal plates so polished they shone like mirrors.

Druid and highsmith had not marched together since the Dialect Wars, when the Neosolar Empire had crumbled and the ancient landfall kingdoms had regained their autonomy. The first rebellions against the empire had erupted in the South, with the Pact of Branch and Blade against the legions. But no sooner had the imperialists been driven up the peninsula than the southlanders had been at each other's throats, bitter enemies ever since.

Now, as Nicodemus strode through the streets of the Holy District, he was flanked by five druids, seven highsmiths, and four wizards, all glancing uneasily at him and one another.

During the hour it had taken the party to ready itself, an alarm had sounded through the city. The hierophants had spotted an air fleet approaching from the ocean. Outside the station, the market bustled as citizens bought up all the food and supplies they could before rushing home.

When Nicodemus's party had emerged, they found the streets empty save for bands of watchmen dashing about on hurried errands. Small formations of lofting kites crisscrossed the sky.

They turned a corner and beheld the sanctuary. Nicodemus grunted in surprise. Flying above the massive dome were three airships, each larger than the *Queen's Lance* and kept aloft by huge lofting sails. Hierophants crawled all over the ships, adjusting cloth and tending to the long lines that tethered them to the dome.

It wouldn't be long now.

At the gates to the sanctuary complex, Nicodemus found a regiment of guards. Their captain called out to him by name, claiming that he was expected.

Wearily, Nicodemus led his party behind a knot of guards, through a series of hallways, and then up a flight of stairs and into a massive space with a vaulted ceiling of finely carved redwood. Nicodemus believed this place was known as the Hall of Ambassadors. Rows of pillars stretched out before him like trees in an orderly stone forest.

He turned to regard the sanctuary guards, but they had turned their backs to prevent anyone else from entering the hall. Nicodemus looked around the glorious room. The spellwrights around him did likewise.

Nothing happened.

So Nicodemus walked farther into the Hall. About halfway across the floor, he saw a tall wooden throne standing before a massive screen that formed the hall's back wall. He stopped.

All of his spellwrights collapsed and lay motionless.

His heart kicking, Nicodemus spun around but saw only rows of pillars and slanting late afternoon sunlight.

"They are unharmed," said a low, rumbling voice.

Nicodemus turned around and saw Typhon's massive alabaster body. The demon's all-black eyes studied Nicodemus keenly. His expression seemed somber. "Your cousin, Ja Ambher has deprived them of sensation and movement. I have determined that the League of Starfall should support you, so they will be restored when the siege begins." Here the demon nodded toward the distant Auburn Mountains. What looked to be tiny billowing clouds were rising above the dark skyline. It took Nicodemus a moment to realize that these were warships. Nicodemus looked back to Typhon. "Where is Francesca?"

"This way," the demon said and walked toward the throne.

Nicodemus watched him but did not move.

Typhon stopped and looked back, his expression seemed exhausted, almost sad. "Nicodemus, my son, I have precious little time to show you why Deirdre sacrificed herself and why Francesca is now so devoted to you."

Ten years ago Nicodemus had confronted Typhon, and the demon had spoken with the same concerned tone. Back then it had confused Nicodemus. Now it terrified him.

"You must understand the truth about the Disjunction," Typhon said before turning back toward the throne. "You are about to become the Disjunction."

Tentatively, Nicodemus followed.

"The religions of your era teach that Los rebelled against humanity because of some human sin," Typhon rumbled. "The truth is that Los rebelled against humanity because he came to believe that the Creator didn't exist."

Nicodemus lowered his brows. "Los was a god before he was a demon. How could a deity be an atheist?"

Typhon sniffed. "Trust me, the irony was not lost on Los or any of his disciples. But we could not refute his arguments. We, the oldest deities, knew where we had come from. So when he began to perfect language, we pledged ourselves to his quest. When your ancestors discovered this, the war between deities and demons began."

"Demon," Nicodemus interrupted, "where is Francesca?"

Typhon reached the dais before the throne. "She is with you now."

Nicodemus looked around but saw nothing but pillars.

Typhon climbed the dais and stood in front of the throne. "You can't perceive her yet because you do not understand what she has fully become."

"And what is that?"

The demon sat in his throne. "A derivative of a ghost and a portion of my godspell. She is also a summation of all the choices and experiences she gained since I let Deirdre set her free."

"You knew of Deirdre's plan?"

Typhon nodded. "Deirdre was not capable of betraying me, though she tried. I limited that part of her soul long ago." His voice sounded flat. "My son, you must understand what a deity is, what a demon is. It may sound like blasphemy."

Nicodemus said nothing.

The demon nodded and then continued: "The first gods were nothing more than constructs. During the Dawn Age, humanity did not yet realize that they could create magical runes. But they did so unknowingly when creating their religious texts. Life was so primitive that those first authors lived in terror of natural disasters: floods, fires, droughts, earthquakes. They invented fictions—gods and goddesses who could control these disasters. The goddess who brings the rains, the god who stops the earthquakes—you understand.

"Over centuries, humanity's religious writings created powerful spells, and the action of its prayers forged magical runes that gave these young constructs power. Drawing on the strength of their worshipers, these religious spells grew until they became the first deities. To this day, all deities require many worshipers to provide them with text unknowingly generated through prayer. In return, the deities provide a service for their worshipers. Cala, for example, reinforced this sandstone to keep the lycanthropes out of the city and the water in the reservoir."

Typhon paused to nod toward the distant dam. Then he leaned forward. "You are the first human on this continent to learn the truth: deities are merely intellects written by humans. It may disappoint you, but the truth of the matter is that you created us, not the other way around."

Nicodemus met the demon's eyes. "It does sound blasphemous. All religions will tell you that deities are embodiments of the Creator, that the divine race was made first."

Typhon smiled. "Humanity lost the truth during the Exodus across the ocean."

"I don't see what this has to do with Francesca or even with the Disjunction."

Typhon leaned back in his throne. "Los didn't attack humanity. Los created a metaspell that made it impossible to err in language."

"As you are doing now to Language Prime, to cause the Silent Blight?"

"The metaspells I am casting prevent misspelling only in Language Prime. Los's metaspells prevent error of any kind."

Nicodemus blinked.

"Life is self-perpetuating language," the demon said and pointed to Nicodemus. "Living things like you are made of Language Prime, but all living things are mortal and vie with each other. Dying and killing are vital to propagating life. Language Prime is inherently chaotic. To generate originality, Language Prime needs death to cull its chaos. A Language Prime error that is too great causes disease. A Language Prime error that provides advantage allows that text to destroy other texts. Death propagates that change. You are written in mortal words."

The demon pointed to himself. "But we, the deities and demons, are not written in Language Prime. We are written in languages that have no inherent chaos. We are self-aware language. The originality for our language comes from the intellects that design us. Because error does not generate our creativity, we do not need death to cull us. On the ancient continent, religious doctrine held that the Creator made humanity and humanity made the deities. Deities were servants of the empire."

Typhon held up a pale finger. "Los refused to recognize humanity as holy. He held that there was no Creator and therefore deities need not serve humanity. He wanted to create a world populated by self-aware language, by immortal language."

Nicodemus cleared his throat. "So the Disjunction is an attempt to end death?"

The demon smiled. "Precisely. By replacing Language Prime with self-aware language, the Disjunction will bring about an eternal golden age."

"Golden, unless you happen to be alive."

"Ahh, hence your cousin and your lover," Typhon said with a pale smile. "Originally, Los wanted to eradicate Language Prime. Until ten years ago, I had a similar goal. The storybook dragon I wrote was meant to fly across the ocean and revive Los. But Fellwroth squandered that dragon. So after you helped me to destroy Fellwroth, I fled into the savanna in Deirdre's body. When I encountered the Walker and recognized that he was an imperial—although an imperfect one—I used the Emerald of Aarahest to partially transform him into a dragon who could bring about the Disjunction by crossing the ocean."

Nicodemus balled his hands into fists as he remembered nearly killing his cousin. "But he resisted you?"

The demon shrugged. "Nothing I couldn't overcome. But it was his cacographic mind that was weak. I had depleted half of the emerald's strength. I was nowhere close to producing a viable dragon; to do that I would have had to recharge the emerald by touching it to you. But I knew you would train to avoid just that outcome. I needed to convert you."

Nicodemus swallowed. "So using the emerald's remaining strength and a ghost, you created Francesca and imbued her with Language Prime so that I would think that she was human? So she might seduce me?"

"Francesca was not written to seduce you; she was written to love you."

"So that I would fall in love with her? So she could talk me into helping you complete the Savanna Walker or the second dragon?"

The demon sighed. "Ah, the second dragon. Before I answer that question, let me tell you that after you helped me escape Fellwroth, I realized the Disjunction might not be a war. Death is the agony of mortality. If the Disjunction seeks to end death, why shouldn't humanity join us?"

Somewhere above them, men began to shout. Typhon turned and pointed to the two fleets of airships now moving toward each other. "Avel's rebellion begins. My son, you must understand that dragons are hybrids of Language Prime and magical language. They are never only one thing but always many potential things. So why not create a dragon that would bring humans and demons closer together? I set out to write a dragon who could create a hybrid race. A dragon who would begin the Disjunction on this continent." The demon paused. "Of course, I needed an intellect with a superb understanding of the living body, an intellect that understood human disease and mortality."

Nicodemus frowned. He remembered Francesca's warning: that Typhon would claim that she had betrayed him. And yet what the demon was proposing sounded plausible. "Francesca, being a physician, was supposed to convince me to help complete this second dragon?" Nicodemus asked.

The demon chuckled. "There is no need to convince you. You have already completed the second dragon."

Nicodemus felt his heart grow cold. "How? Francesca touched the emerald to my skin when I was sleeping and then took the gem to you?"

Typhon shook his head. "It is far simpler than that. I did not need a physician as an intermediary. Here." The demon cast something at Nicodemus with a backhanded flick of his wrist. "This will give you brief fluency in my language."

Nicodemus stood perfectly still. Nothing happened. Then suddenly he understood why the demon had used the word "intermediary," and they both came within his ability to perceive.

One instant, he and Typhon were alone. The next, beside the demon stood a latticework of sentences, luminescent with deep ruby light and forming long bones and muscles. As Nicodemus's comprehension of the text advanced, he saw how the sentences were part of a massive body, James Berr's body.

Now Nicodemus could look past the deep red words and see his cousin's true shape: Berr had grown to fifteen feet in height; and yet, for all his size, Berr seemed lean, almost delicate. The scales that covered him from tail to top shone nacreous white. Expansive wings folded neatly behind his back. His lips were pulled back to reveal long curved teeth. He stared with eyes large and opalescent.

But surrounding Nicodemus was a being larger still and even harder to perceive. She too was written in the deep red language, and initially he could see only the sentences in her long curving bones, her powerful muscles. The massive chambers of her heart contracted to a slow power rhythm. With every beat, her heart blazed with dazzling brightness.

Slowly, Nicodemus began to perceive the rest of her. For a moment he could see both her body and the sentences shining through sinew and scales, the text in the body.

Her scales glowed a deep auburn, almost brown, but on her face flashed flecks of coppery red in the same pattern that freckles had punctuated her human face. Her eyes, very dark brown, were fixed on the other dragon. She had protectively curled her body and long tail around Nicodemus. Her long black claws were splayed across the tile as she crouched.

The demon looked at her. "So you see, Francesca did not need to take your ability to create the second dragon"—he paused to smile at her as if she were his child—"because she is the second dragon."

THE FLEET COMMANDER placed the *Queen's Lance* at the top of the vanguard along with the *Pike*, an Osprey-class cruiser written on cotton sails. Cyrus had expected this but still felt his stomach tighten as he and Izem held formation beside the *Pike* and waited as the two other Ospreys—the *Shark* and the *Kraken*—took up escort position beside the *Cyclone* and the *Thunder,* two Storm-class carriers. In Lurrikara, the *Queen's Lance* had refreshed its cloth and picked up two more crew members.

The two lines of battle were facing off. Cyrus's fleet, the monotheist fleet, boasted four cruisers and two carriers. The defending polytheistic fleet had only three destroyers, all of them Eagle class. Larger and more durable, Eagles had made up most of the polytheist air forces during the Civil War. Though the polytheistic airships were both outnumbered and outclassed, they were escorted by two-score lofting kites.

As Cyrus watched, a wing of three black kites broke formation and glided with the wind to the other side of the enemy line of battle. Presently the polytheistic fleet flew just above the city's northern perimeter wall, waiting to strike out and force the attacking carriers to deploy their warkites as far from the sanctuary as possible, ensuring that the constructs spent most of their text reaching the sanctuary.

The *Queen's Lance* and the *Pike* would push a frontal attack, trying to rip up the wide lofting sails that billowed above each Eagle's hull and kept it flying. If that was not possible, they were to try to disperse the Eagles to allow the carriers to reach the sanctuary.

Because Cyrus knew the winds around Avel, Captain Izem had appointed him the primary pilot. "Remember," Izem shouted, "few in the city fleet have flown against a Kestrel. They won't know how fast we are, but they'll quickly adapt."

A cry sounded from the hull. Cyrus turned and saw the *Kraken,* as the flagship, had let fly the signal to attack.

"All crew to slip!" Cyrus yelled, weaving himself into the hull. He folded the *Queen's Lance* into the lancelike conformation and, with a textual burn, thrust the ship toward the easternmost enemy destroyer. The *Pike* moved to follow.

Three wings of enemy lofting kites cast out jumpchutes to pull themselves windward and intercept the *Queen's Lance.*

Cyrus held course and within moments met the interceptors. The kite pilots converted their chutes into canopies and turned toward the *Queen's Lance.* But as Izem had guessed, the kite pilots misjudged their target's speed. Cyrus doubled thrust and shot past the would-be boarders.

The enemy destroyer before them unfurled more lofting sails and was climbing to present its better-defended underside. This time-honored tactic would have worked against most cruisers, but not a Kestrel. Cyrus burned on all aft sails, shooting them higher than their opponent. "Impact!" Izem bellowed the instant before their foresails punched through the Eagle's lofting sails.

A blast of air buffeted Cyrus as they loosed much of the enemy's text into the air. Then they were free and climbing into the sky.

Cyrus banked the ship to come around. But no sooner did he look down than he saw an eruption of jumpchutes flying up at him. Two lofting kites struck the *Queen's Lance*, their canopies wrapping around her side sails, trying to cut into them. With sheets of blazing blue language, the two extra crew members were working to repel the kites.

Cyrus dropped the *Queen's Lance* into a dive. Below him, the enemy destroyer had closed the hole the *Queen's Lance* had punched into their lofting sails, but not before losing altitude. As Cyrus dove, the *Pike* struck the enemy, tearing through a side sail and ricocheting off the hull.

Izem cheered as the polytheistic destroyer twisted and its lofting sail began to spill wind. Cyrus slowed their descent so the *Pike* could fly clear, but then enemy lofting kites began swarming around the *Queen's Lance*. Some of the kites landed on their hull and began cutting into the silk. Cyrus threw the *Queen's Lance* into a barrel spin, throwing off a few boarders.

At last the *Pike* was clear. Cyrus engaged all aft sails, and they shot downward, jolting forward whenever the increased wind velocity pulled a boarder off his ship.

The enemy destroyer loomed in their vision. "Impact!" Cyrus yelled and pulled up hard so that the *Queen's Lance* struck the enemy's lofting sail at the bottom of her curving trajectory, slicing through a maximum amount of cloth. Deconstructing hierophantic language—vividly blue even against a blue sky—exploded around them.

They emerged into a chaos of lofting kites, all slamming their canopies into the *Queen's Lance*. Cyrus put the ship into another tight barrel roll. Cloth and sky and savanna—white, blue, and green—spun around until he felt the last boarder thrown off and leveled out the *Queen's Lance*.

Izem cried out triumphantly, and Cyrus looked back to see the enemy destroyer breaking up as it fell toward the savanna. Her pilots were cutting free sections of sail to make emergency jumpchutes. The lycanthropes would be waiting below.

Izem's cry died, and he pointed down. The *Pike* was in a tight barrel roll, trying and failing to throw off boarders. She was losing altitude fast. Cyrus began to bring the *Queen's Lance* around, but Izem yelled, "We can't help her." He pointed north. "Bigger problems."

Cyrus followed his finger back to the remaining polytheist fleet, still holding a line of battle above the city walls. The monotheist fleet was advancing. The *Kraken* and the *Shark* had matched off against the two enemy destroyers. It would have been an advantageous position for the monotheist fleet, if the complement of enemy lofting kites hadn't increased.

Then Cyrus saw it: a flock of fresh lofting kites that had taken wing from the sanctuary. The polytheists had more pilots than they'd lofted. They'd been deliberately drawing the carriers into attack.

Cyrus engaged all aft sails. Unless they could quickly cut down the remaining enemy destroyers, the kites would force the carriers to deploy too soon and the demon worshipers would escape almost unscathed.

SHOCK FRACTURED NICODEMUS'S every thought. He stared into a face that was draconic and yet still Francesca's. He tried to step backward, but his boot struck her hind claw.

"She is the second dragon," Typhon repeated patiently. "Until last night, she was a half dragon like your cousin. She is a creature of intuitive language and Language Prime. She needed to touch an Imperial of intuitive and chaotic language before she could assume her full potential."

Nicodemus looked at the demon. "I . . . I don't . . ."

"My plan was to wound you so that only she could heal you. That would bring you into physical contact, transforming both of you. All dragons induce quaternary cognition. She was written to change how you see life and language, to make you love her and the Disjunction that she represents."

Nicodemus understood every idea the demon described and yet felt as if he hadn't heard the demon speak. "What?" he said. "I don't . . ." He looked at the dragon. "Fran . . ."

With alarming speed, Francesca more tightly encircled him. She snarled at the Savanna Walker.

"Our problem," Typhon said, "is that I had never thought to complete both dragons. Ja Ambher, like you, is a cacographer. So even with the emerald, I could not complete his draconic transformation. You saw the grotesque shapes he took as a half-formed cacographic dragon. However, with Francesca I faced no such problem. While I was hunting you, it seemed impossible that both dragons should be realized."

Nicodemus swallowed. "Vivian?"

The demon nodded. "When your half sister snuck into my city, I saw a shortcut. I didn't need to wait for Francesca and you to touch. I simply set the Savanna Walker on Vivian. Deirdre blocked the first attempt with her suicide. We shall miss her."

Here the demon paused, his pale face slack as if in genuine regret. "But your cousin caught your half sister the same night that you devoted yourself to Francesca. Now your lover does not want your cousin to live. You see, the two dragons are the embodiment of different conceptions of the Disjunction. Your cousin represents Los's conception: replacing Language Prime with divine language. Your lover, my conception: interlacing Language Prime with demonic language until all intellects are divine."

The demon sighed. "There shouldn't be a conflict between the two; they will both produce the same result." His voice became weary, almost resigned. "We should send your cousin across the ocean to revive Los. Look at his form now: wings, scales, claws, everything necessary to cross the ocean, to revive Los, to bring the demonic host to this continent."

The demon looked from the Savanna Walker to Nicodemus. "We should send your cousin flying across the ocean and return Francesca to her human form. Then we could cart you and Francesca off to Starfall Island, where you can set about creating a new society." He looked at Francesca. "But before that can happen, your lover has a few . . . stipulations."

Francesca leaned forward and narrowed her eyes.

The demon continued to speak to Nicodemus, though he did not look away from the dragon. "She is my masterpiece. Greater even than you, Nicodemus. I could not stop her from killing the Savanna Walker without sacrificing myself." His expression seemed to be trying to communicate something to Francesca. "I would pay any price to see that all of my creations coexist. Your lover has agreed to swear on the Creator's name that she will accept coexistence if you give your consent."

Typhon turned to face Nicodemus. "The humans who unknowingly wrote the first deities created us so that our unerring nature would be exposed when we swear on the Creator's name. No god or goddess or demon has been able to break an oath sworn on the Creator's name."

The demon turned to Nicodemus. "Humans, composed of erratic Language Prime, have no such trouble. Your kind can swear on the fount of divinity to never commit a sin again and then torture an entire kingdom. Nicodemus Weal, what is needed out of that chaotic mind of yours is grace." He paused and looked to the Savanna Walker. "Grace to allow another form of the Disjunction to manifest itself. You and Francesca shall inherit the League of Starfall. You will bring in a new Age of Wonders, with multiplying gods and goddesses and demigods. Your lands will be safe from Los. The demons shall not threaten your society but allow you to grow over the centuries until you have evolved past death and can join them. That is what I offer, Nicodemus. Will you accept?"

Nicodemus stared uncomprehendingly at the demon. How could Typhon even ask such a question? A low rumble filled the air and made the floor vibrate. It took Nicodemus a moment to realize it was caused by Francesca's growl. She took a half step toward Typhon.

The demon sighed. "No," he said to her. "I haven't forgotten. Nicodemus, your lover wants you to have this." The demon held up his hand, and in it glinted a small tear-shaped emerald.

The missing part of his mind.

The emerald was the focal point of his every desire for the past ten years. And yet, if demons could not err and his disability filled the world around him with error, perhaps he should reconsider relinquishing it.

Typhon was studying him now. "It's a bribe, no denying that. Prove to me that you are devoted to Francesca, and I will return what I took from you so long ago. Will you accept?"

Francesca stared at Nicodemus. He remembered her words back in Coldlock Harbor, that she had not betrayed him, that he must accept Typhon's every offer.

Had she worked some spell on his mind, given him quaternary cognition? Was he already lost to the Disjunction? Then he remembered her eyes when she had left him. Nicodemus looked at Typhon. "I will accept."

The demon smiled. He stood from the throne. "Then come here, my son. Let me look into your thoughts."

Francesca swung her tail away, and Nicodemus climbed the dais to Typhon. Both the Savanna Walker and Cala watched the proceedings without expression.

"Kneel," the demon ordered. Nicodemus obeyed. Typhon pressed an alabaster palm to his cheek. The demon could crush his skull with that hand. Suddenly Nicodemus's every thought and every intimate emotion swirled around his mind in a nauseating blur. Then the demon's hand left his cheek. Strangely weak, Nicodemus fell forward onto the dais.

"My son," Typhon said in a low voice, "it is done." Fighting the dizziness and nausea, Nicodemus stood up straight. The demon was looking down at him, all-black eyes wide with what seemed like exhilaration. "Francesca has you spellbound."

And then the demon looked to Francesca. "Swear on the Creator's name?" A blur of Numinous text flashed between them.

Then the demon's massive white arms were around Nicodemus's neck fastening a thin chain, at the end of which dangled the Emerald of Aarahest.

Nicodemus grasped the gem. As it had been when he had briefly possessed the gem ten years before, he felt no different. There was no flash or rush of energy, but even so his mind was now complete. So long as his skin was touching the emerald, he was not cacographic.

Nicodemus walked down the dais and stood next to Francesca.

"Excellent," Typhon rumbled as he sat on the throne. "When the siege begins, we shall send Ja Ambher to the ancient continent. Nicodemus, your escort of druids and highsmiths will awaken and see you and Francesca in her human form attacking me. We will make it appear that you have driven me off. Their testimony will assure your ascendency in the League of Starfall. I will disappear, and most of my followers who control this city will be killed or captured, giving your half sister and Celeste the impression they destroyed the demonic threat until I resurface."

The demon turned to the Savanna Walker and began speaking. Just then a Numinous script hit Nicodemus's shoulder. He translated it: *"Stand beside me."* He looked up to see Francesca staring at him.

Typhon was still speaking, but Nicodemus backed away until he stood next to Francesca. *"Typhon did not anticipate what your cacography can do to me,"* she wrote to him. *"Separate yourself from the emerald so it doesn't touch your skin. Then lay your hand on me."*

Nicodemus swallowed and brought his hand up to grasp the emerald. Careful not to attract the demon's attention, he pulled down hard and broke the thin necklace from which it hung. Above him Francesca tossed her head, perhaps to distract Typhon. Nicodemus brought his hand down to his waist and then tucked the emerald into his belt purse, away from his skin.

Typhon was still issuing instructions to the Savanna Walker.

Nicodemus pressed his palm to Francesca's side. It was almost painfully hot. Now he saw into her Language Prime texts, how infinitely complex they were, how they had become entwined with magical language.

He also felt how his cacography could shift her text. Unlike a being of pure Language Prime or pure magical runes, she resisted all but subtle changes caused by his touch.

A Numinous message appeared on the back of Nicodemus's hand. He translated it, *"We've mispeled the part of my mind that must obey an oath sworn on the Craetor's name. Should we braek the oath?"*

Instantly he replied, *"Yes!"*

No sooner had he cast this text than Francesca kicked with her hind legs, cracking terracotta tiles and launching herself forward. Wings outstretched and roaring thunderously, she crashed into Typhon.

fifty-one

The *Queen's Lance* had covered half the distance to the line of battle when a crewman shouted. Izem looked back. "Our target went down into the savanna. But the *Pike* lost an aft sail. They're ditching her in the lake."

Cyrus glanced back to see *Pike's* long white hull crumple onto the reservoir. Jumpchutes, mostly extemporized from the hull, bulged up as the crew tried to jump away from the impact. Some might reach the docks. Others would have to tread water or face the lycanthropes waiting on the banks.

But Cyrus had no time to worry. Ahead, the *Kraken* and the *Shark* were turning away from the engagement. "What are they doing?" he called and pointed.

The two remaining polytheist destroyers, now bolstered by more lofting kites, were advancing on the monotheist fleet.

"Reduce aft sails!" Izem shouted. "The carriers are editing some of the warkites to engage anything in the air that—"

Before the captain could finish, Cyrus saw it drop from the *Cyclone*: a storm of seething white cloth and flashing steal. Simultaneously, all the warkites bulged wide to catch the wind, each setting its sail at exactly the same angle. Cyrus extended the lateral wings, gliding the *Queen's Lance* toward the *Kraken*.

A cheer went up from the polytheist fleet. They had forced a carrier to start deploying prematurely. Cyrus grimaced. Their devotion to their city would have to border on fanatical for them to celebrate an air-to-air warkite engagement. As if to prove their zeal, every last enemy lofting kite cast out jumpchutes to intercept the warkites. They engaged just as Cyrus brought the *Queen's Lance* into company with the *Kraken*. There were maybe two hundred monotheist warkites, half that number of lofting kites. As they neared an enemy, the warkites changed from large, floating sails to serpentine streamers, talons flashing. Some fell upon the lofting-kite canopies, cutting and slashing. Five or six pilots went plummeting down to the city. Other warkites attacked the pilots suspended below the canopies, their talons slashing against flesh. Still, the majority of pilots were using their canopies to enfold and incorporate the warkites into their canopies.

"They're dropping crew!" Izem called out, pointing to the two remaining enemy destroyers. Cyrus saw green-clad figures, each followed by a chute only large enough to slow their fall to less than terminal velocity.

"They're pulling windward," Cyrus yelled. "Insanity!" The destroyers advanced into the fray between lofting kite and warkite. The warship's broad sails pushed the smaller combatants aside and sent them tumbling in their wake.

Cyrus looked over at the captain. "What are they doing?"

"It doesn't make any sense."

Some of the warkites began cutting into the destroyer's lofting sails. But whatever pilots remained onboard paid this no mind. Wounded, but still pulling fast windward, the destroyers broke out of the fray. They were only a mile distant from the *Cyclone*. "They're going to ram the carrier!" Izem yelled. "The others can't get there in time." He pointed, and indeed the *Kraken* had let fly the flags for attack, but she was coming around too slowly. The *Shark* was even farther away.

Cyrus dropped the *Queen's Lance* into a dive to pick up speed and then brought her around and engaged all aft sails. "We'll get only one pass," Izem shouted. "Then they'll hit the carriers."

Cyrus glanced back and saw that both carriers had spread all their canvas in an attempt to pull themselves up. If they could gain enough height, they might float over the destroyers to the sanctuary.

The *Queen's Lance* closed the distance to the nearest enemy destroyer. Cyrus called out before impact and pulled up, trying to turn within the sail. But he struck too soon, punched clear through the top of the canopy, and then punched through its lateral aspect: two holes rather than one long tear.

He looked back at the destroyer and cheered when he saw it was sinking. The two holes had been enough to disable the underpiloted airship. Its lofting sail blew ragged, and its hull pointed down toward the Auburn Mountains.

But the other destroyer had stayed its course and risen just as fast as the *Cyclone*. They were only moments away from impact. Cyrus prayed for mercy as the doomed carrier deployed its full complement of warkites. The constructs took wing for the sanctuary like a swarm of locusts.

FRANCESCA PINNED TYPHON with her right forepaw and then with a backhand swipe sent him flying into a pillar. His alabaster body fractured the stone.

Francesca lunged at the Savanna Walker. The pearly white dragon leapt at her, widening his maw to show translucent fangs. Francesca dodged left and raked her claws down his scales, trying to find purchase. He clamped his teeth on her shoulder even as she did likewise to his neck. They tumbled backward, rolling tail over top scale. He struck a pillar. A redwood beam crashed down on her hindleg. She snarled and kicked it off.

Though Francesca could not see the language in which he was working, she could feel the Savanna Walker casting spell after spell against her mind, trying to interrupt her perception. But her mind, like his, was now draconic—halfway between human and demonic.

The Savanna Walker screamed, and Francesca realized that she had sensed textual signals move from his mind to his throat and chest. She had known he was going to scream the instant before he had. Her quaternary cognition allowed her to prognosticate his action.

A signal shot from the Walker's brain to his left hind leg to cock it back and kick her head away from his neck. The instant he began this action, she twisted her jaws and slammed her left wing forward, rolling him onto his right side and rendering his action useless.

The Walker intended to open his mouth and bite her neck, but the moment he unclenched his jaw, she brought her left foreleg up and smashed it into his eye. The Walker's head snapped back, and all signals to his body momentarily stopped. Then he sent a score of signals down to his tail, commanding it to swing around to knock out her legs. She pinned his tail down with her right foreleg. His eyes were as wide as dinner plates, as nacreous as abalone shell. He knew.

The Walker went limp, his head hanging slack in submission. Francesca readjusted her jaws and made ready to crush his windpipe. But just before she clenched her jaws, the topography of the future sunk all around her. It was as if she had been walking on a fog-covered coast and the fog to her right suddenly vanished to reveal a massive canyon. Before her stretched wide, gaping futures she had not perceived until now.

She had just enough time to tense before an explosive force detonated against her left breast and tossed her into the ceiling. The carved redwood splintered under the force of her body.

The next instant she fell back to the floor, landing on all four feet. Typhon charged her, both fists blazing dazzling red. He cocked one hand back. She lashed out with her tail, knocked him flat. The demon's red wartext flew from his hand and blasted through a pillar ten yards away. An instant later an avalanche of plaster and wood crashed down.

Typhon struggled to his feet and bellowed, "Fly!" The Savanna Walker bared his teeth and backed away, preparing to flee. In that instant, Francesca understood what Typhon had done to alter the future. If she pursued the Savanna Walker, the demon would cast another blasting text. He couldn't hope to defeat her, but he could detain her long enough for his other creation to escape. That would mean subjecting himself to her full strength. He was willing to sacrifice.

The demon cast his second blasting text, aiming for her chest. She ducked and bunched her wings above her. The resulting detonation jammed her down, driving her claws through the tiles and into the plaster and wood below.

After pulling her paws free, she reared up on her hind legs and brought her foreclaws down on Typhon. They struck a textual shield he had written around himself. "Fly!" Typhon screamed. The Savanna Walker bolted for the outer wall and the open sky beyond. Francesca couldn't chase the Walker or Typhon would strike her with another detonating text.

She again brought her claws smashing down onto the protective text that Typhon had written around himself. Growing frantic, she reared up again. Just before she started to come down, a lance of Numinous prose struck Typhon's protective text. Francesca glanced left and saw Nicodemus, his hand still outstretched from the spell he had cast. Her lover had put his skin back into contact with the emerald. He was the Halcyon again, capable of infinitely complex spells.

Francesca brought her claws down again. All of the demon's text, now weakened by Nicodemus's disspell, crumbled under her force. She felt the demon fold under her claws.

When she pulled her claws back, she saw the demon's body broken open, brilliant ruby light bleeding out of his abdomen. This stone body was his ark, the physical seat of his soul. Leaning forward, she drove a single claw into the demon's skull. It burst into an eruption of bloody light.

The rubicund shockwave dazzled her mind with the sensations of burning and passion and injury and ecstasy and a hundred other sensations that seemed the incarnation of deep, deep red.

In the next instant, the synesthesia passed and she found herself with her author's remains beneath her claws. She shook with primal hunger. A gallon of caustic saliva gushed into her mouth. She bit into the demon. Text burned and shifted within her mouth as she chewed the divine language down to fragments.

Years ago, Fellwroth had betrayed Typhon and cut him into sentences. Still, the demon had infected Boann's ark and returned to his full strength. Francesca would ensure that did not happen now. She ground him with her teeth until not one of Typhon's runes was connected to another. She took the second bite of the ark and chewed that into nothing before swallowing it as well.

Then she saw her lover.

Nicodemus had lowered his hands. He was surrounded now by revived druids, highsmiths, and wizards. They stared at her and then at him. But Nicodemus looked nowhere but at her, and in his wide green eyes she saw naked shock at what she had just done.

She froze and looked into the landscape of the future. Time seemed almost flat save for the now-retreating possibility of catching James Berr.

"*The Walker!*" she cast to Nicodemus. "*I must try to stop him. Keep yourself alive. I will come back for you.*"

Nicodemus caught and read this. With the speed of a Halcyon, he wrote a response. But before he could cast it to her, the hallway was flooded by a seething riot of sailcloth and steel talons.

Warkites.

WITH THE SKY clear of enemy airships, Izem retook control of the *Queen's Lance* and joined company with the *Kraken*.

The suicide destroyer had brought down the *Cyclone*. Their combined wreckage had crashed into the Auburn Mountains on the far shore of the reservoir. A square mile of giant trees now stood shrouded by torn sailcloth and dead or dying pilots.

However, the *Thunder* was still flying with its full complement of warkites. What was more, the *Cyclone*'s warkites had reached the sanctuary and were swarming all about the dome, attacking any source of magical text they could detect.

By now, every enemy lofting kite should have flown flags of surrender. But only half the polytheist pilots had done so. The rest were rallying to the sanctuary, trying to fight off the warkites; however, with the *Thunder* now flying nearly on top of them, it was hopeless.

"Do you think they want to become martyrs?" Izem asked.

"What, those pilots?" Cyrus asked while watching the bloody chaos that surrounded the dome. "Martyrs for polytheism? It seems insane for a devotee to Cala to care—"

His voice died as a large swath of the flying cloth—both warkites and lofting kites—lost the blue glow of hierophantic language. Like mundane sheets, they fluttered down toward the ground. "Captain, look!" he pointed.

"What under heaven?"

The vanishing language continued upward through the chaos, leaving a trail of mundane cloth. "Some kind of massive disspell?" Cyrus asked before jumping slightly.

Izem looked at him. "What do you see?"

He pointed. "There. It's a blind spot. Look there, you won't see anything."

"Cyrus, what are—" his voice died as something large and dark took to the air from the base of the sanctuary.

At first Cyrus thought it was an airship made of dark sailcloth, but then it flapped its wings and rose fast up into the air. It was heading west, toward the ocean. Sunlight glinted off its brassy scales.

"Captain," Cyrus yelled, "that creature is important to polytheistic rebellion. I suggest we investigate."

Izem edited the passages that controlled the airship's flag signals. "I can't say I like the idea, but judging by its speed, we may be the only ship able to follow it. Let's see if the fleet commander agrees with you."

A moment later from the *Kraken* flew a signal to break formation. With a grunt, Izem dropped the *Queen's Lance* into a sharp dive and flew in pursuit of the dragon.

As THE HALL filled with seething warkites, Nicodemus was surrounded by spellwrights.

The highsmiths' plate armor spun itself into an ornate, airy meshwork that extended out from their bodies and interlocked into a cagelike construct. From their hands sprang blades and spears composed of wire-thin steel. Bellowing war cries for their king and their metallic god, the highsmiths attacked. The warkites dashed their steel talons onto the highsmiths' meshwork armor, penetrating only a few layers into the defense. In return the highsmiths thrust their weapons into the constructs, small bolts of lightning flaring out from the point of contact, scorching their sailcloth.

At first they beat back the warkites, but then a flurry of talon blows cut through the meshwork covering the lead highsmith's shoulder and jammed a talon into his neck. He jerked sidewise and fell.

When two highsmiths fought close together, their meshwork armor intertwined, forming a common barrier around them. Nicodemus began forging Magnus attack spells down his arms, but in the next instant the highsmiths had formed a circle around him and had covered him with their steel.

Wild cries came from outside this protective ring, and through the storm of white cloth he could make out druids. Some were covered with thorny skin and wielded jagged blades of polished wood. Others were covered with coats of splitters that approximated fur, their faces covered with wolf or bear masks and their hands tipped by glowing claws.

A sheet of steel emerged from the cage enclosing Nicodemus and pushed him hard on the shoulder. He stumbled to his right and then realized that the whole party was retreating farther into the hall.

"Stop; I can cast a protective text!" he yelled. "I'm the Halcyon now."

No one seemed to hear him over the battle cries. Then they were stumbling over rubble. Amid the chaos he saw a few flashes of silver and golden text; some of the wizards still lived.

A warkite's talons broke through the meshwork near a young highsmith and filled the air around him with a spray of blood. He fell into the meshwork, no longer connected to its textual structure. The razor lattice cut him into eight pieces.

Then they reached an expansive wall of sandstone. A broad recess with a low ceiling extended into the wall. One of the highsmiths pointed at the cove and shouted. The metal mages could move freely within their lattice, thrusting outside of it with their swords or spears. One metal mage directed the group into the alcove. Once inside, they broke formation and cast their meshwork of metal and spells from the floor to the alcove's ceiling, forming a barrier to keep out the warkites. Periodically, one of them dashed through to pull a wizard or a druid back to the other side.

Of the five druids who had left the station with Nicodemus, he now counted three; of the four wizards, only DeGarn and one young woman survived; of the seven highsmiths, four now worked to maintain the meshwork barrier that was barely keeping the warkites back, and they could not hold the line much longer. The riot of slashing talons struck repeatedly against the meshwork, slowly cutting through it.

Nicodemus tightened his grip around the emerald and tried to imagine what he might write to keep the kites at bay.

A highsmith screamed as a warkite cut through one end of the barrier. The man jumped away, avoiding a talon by inches.

The kite was wriggling into the enclosed space. Nicodemus drew his hand back and was just about to cast when the sandstone ceiling seemed to melt. A long, fluid sheet of stone fell from the opening of the recess. Instantly, the sandstone enclosed Nicodemus and the survivors in pitch blackness.

AFTER A LONG, desperate sprint through the air, Francesca caught the Savanna Walker's tail over the Auburn Mountains and pulled them both down to crash into the redwood forest.

She saw him smash into the ancient timber, massive trunks bending slowly and then snapping with a sudden jolt that sent their branches waving in every direction. The pale dragon rolled into the wrecked timber, and she fell upon him.

But even as she flapped hard with her wings and swung her hind claws around to slash the Savanna Walker's back, she gasped for breath.

Her claws sank into his hindquarters, and Francesca felt his left hip bend to near a dislocating angle under her pressure. Bellowing, he threw both of his wings back, striking her in the chest, keeping her from falling forward to rake him with her claws.

He squirmed free and scampered up the mountain of broken redwood. She chased but could not fill her lungs with enough air. Her mind swam with a hunger for air.

The Savanna Walker spun around and slashed at her with a foreclaw, connecting with her neck and tearing lines of pain down to her shoulder. Head spinning, she fell into a bank of ferns. As if from a far distance, she watched the Savanna Walker take flight. She gasped again, sucking so much air into her draconic maw that it uprooted a nearby fern. She spat it out.

Then Francesca realized what had happened. Typhon's texts had detonated too close to her. At the time, she had worried only about how each explosion had tossed her about. She had not thought about the shockwaves coursing through her solid muscles and organs until they reached the delicate sacs of tissue in her lungs. The shockwaves damaged the sacs so that she had started to slowly leak blood and fluid into her lungs. It was a condition called blast lung. She had seen it most often in survivors of explosive lycanthrope spells. They would arrive in the infirmary, frightened or confused but otherwise healthy. Moments later they would suffer severe breathlessness and then drown in their own bodily fluid.

Typhon must have known that he could not harm her outright. He knew he could not affect his immediate future but that he could prevent her from chasing down the Savanna Walker.

And indeed, the demon's sacrifice had succeeded. She now lay in a bed of ferns, gasping for air. The demonic texts of her body leapt into action as they realized she was in mortal danger. Her divine spells would convert the great mass of her dragon's body into energetic prose and return her to an unharmed human form.

As the transformation began, she lost her quaternary cognition. The future became merely an abstract thought: "those things that are yet to come." She could no longer imagine how she had ever seen the future as a landscape.

Her vision began to dim. She saw only a blurry outline of dark trees against a vivid sky. Then, faintly, she saw something large and dark hovering in the air. It produced, she thought, an outline similar to that of the *Queen's Lance*.

Something like sleep washed over her, and she could see no image other than that of the Savanna Walker. The pearly dragon, bleeding down his back, his hind leg held at a painful angle.

The beast, its destiny finally come around, was now flying over the deep ocean, winging its way to the ancient continent, where it would ensure that Los be reborn.

ONE OF THE druids produced a white flame from a wooden object in her hand. For a moment Nicodemus couldn't understand who was standing before him. The woman was dressed like a Spirish noble and had textured red-brown skin. Her eyes, shockingly, were composed of linear bands of tawny, tan, white, and dark gray.

Then he realized she had to be the only creature who could have made sandstone liquid. He bowed. "Canonist Cala?"

She nodded. "Nicodemus Weal."

He returned her nod.

"You may tell your foreign spellwrights to put away their curses." She turned her strange eyes to the druids and highsmiths. The metal mages bristled with blades and fine mesh armor while the tree worshipers were all thorns and spiny fur.

Nicodemus held up his hand, unsure if they would care a whit for what he did. But blessedly the sharp words, wood, and metal were blunted.

The canonist returned her strange eyes to Nicodemus. "My sanctuary is running with blood. Several thousand warkites swarm over its dome and through its halls. Maybe a dozen of my devotees are left alive. Of those, perhaps two knew the extent to which the demon Typhon usurped my rule of this city. And they weren't honest to begin with."

She looked at the other spellwrights. "Indeed, I do not know of any other witnesses save for those here who can swear that a demon ruled within these walls. A fleet loyal to the high goddess, Celeste, flies above my city. Within the hour that fleet will dock and declare martial law. I have no doubt that ships and caravans filled with the soldiers of the Queen's army are now making their way from Dar. If I am to survive, if I am to continue to keep the dam and perimeter walls standing, I need others to corroborate my account of what took place today."

Nicodemus cleared his throat. "Canonist, we will swear to bear witness. In return, I would ask—"

She held up her hand. "You don't need to ask, Nicodemus Weal. You are the scion of the League of Starfall in a city soon to be occupied by forces sympathetic to your half sister." Again she looked at the druids and high-smiths. "If any of you want to live long enough to smuggle your champion out of this kingdom, you will bend a knee to him now and take on his oath to be my witness."

Without hesitation, every spellwright knelt.

CHAPTER

fifty-two

Shannon woke when someone took his hand. He had been dreaming of his Trillinonish mother, her dark skin, the banyan tree near his childhood home. But now someone was talking to him, and he woke to remember the pain in his gut, his age, his failing health. But he also remembered that his ghost had returned, that they were again one being.

Blinking, Shannon sat up and formed a textual connection with Azure so that he could see through her eyes. And suddenly he was looking at Nicodemus, dressed in a heavy blue cloak. The boy was kneeling beside him. They were in a tent with the sound of rain striking the taut canvas.

"Magister. Magister," Nicodemus kept saying. "Magister. It's me. It's done. Magister." The boy wore the most peculiar expression as if he could not decide to be jubilant or sad.

Suddenly the last of the sleep washed out of Shannon's mind and he understood. "Creator!" he swore. "You came back?"

Nicodemus nodded and squeezed his arm.

Suddenly Shannon saw through Azure's eyes Nicodemus's bare hand on his own forearm. With a feeble cry, Shannon tried to pull away. But the boy only laughed and held out his other hand; on it lay a tear-shaped emerald. "Your canker curse is gone."

Through Azure, Shannon stared at the gem in confusion.

"I'm sorry to rush you, Magister, but we need to move quickly. Things are happening fast in Avel. I'm taking you into the city right away. I've already spoken to Vein, Jasp, and Flint. I'm sending them back to the Pinnacle Mountains. They've fought long enough for our cause. They'll leave tonight, disguised and riding with a few of our Lornish messengers."

"Our Lornish messengers," Shannon repeated as he suddenly became aware of the noises from outside the tent. Jasp was calling excitedly to Vein.

For the first time, Nicodemus's expression became more serious. "Magister, I am sorry, but we have to get back to the city right now. My half sister is moving with astonishing speed. And the book I left with you, the one with your ghost—I need it back. You still have that of course? Yes?"

"Of course," Shannon said and gestured to a small chest at the other end of the tent. "It's right there."

As Nicodemus hurried to retrieve the codex, Shannon pressed a hand to his stomach. It still hurt. "But, Nicodemus . . . I don't feel any . . . different."

With the book in his arms Nicodemus returned to his bedside. His expression was now somber. "With the emerald I could remove all of your cankers, but I could not reverse the damage they had done." He paused. "I'm afraid your . . . age . . . limited what I could do. Language Prime texts change as they age. All living creatures have mortality written into their texts, and I couldn't . . ."

Shannon nodded. "You couldn't make me into a young man." Then he laughed. "Here you are, returned alive, with a cure for my cankers and all I can do is complain."

"No, Magister. It's—"

Shannon interrupted him by reaching out for Nicodemus's hand. Now it was the boy's turn to reflexively flinch away. They both laughed.

Tentatively, Nicodemus brought his hand back and, for the first time in a decade, teacher and student clasped hands.

FRANCESCA STOOD IN front of the window and looked up into the rainstorm.

She had returned to consciousness on the *Queen's Lance*. Cyrus had tended to her while Izem flew them back to Avel. Chills and a sense of spinning had plagued her. Her frail human body felt confining, infinitely more vulnerable than the glory she had been.

They had returned to a city in a surprising state of order. The bloodshed had been contained to the air and the sanctuary, sparing most of the population.

After they had docked and Captain Izem reported to the fleet commander, Cyrus had taken Francesca to a Holy District tavern that had been commandeered by the fleet. In a private room on the top floor, she had fallen into a sleep filled with troubling dreams of the Savanna Walker flying over the ocean.

Sometime later, she'd woken to the soft black-and-white sound of rain on the roof. Rain clouds had blown in from the ocean and made the evening sky dark. A young man, one of the tavern owner's sons, had brought her a bowl of lentils. He tried to tell her something, his words flashing every color from magenta to manila. She told him that she couldn't hear. When he left, she devoured the lentils and fell back to sleep.

She'd woken the following morning feeling weak and feverish. It was still raining. Breakfast was flatbread and cheese. A young hierophant had brought her two messages. The first was written in Cyrus's cramped hand, stating that he would visit as soon as he could possibly escape his duties. The second was a simple Numinous script from Nicodemus: *"May I see you?"*

Her response spilled out of her arms and read, *"You God-of-gods damn better see me soon, or I'll bite your head off. And I mean that in the nonmetaphorical, dragon-based decapitation sense."* But then she remembered his shocked expression when he had seen her devouring Typhon. She wrote simply *"Hurry to me"* and sent it off with the young hierophant.

She spent the time waiting, napping. She bathed with a basin of firewarmed water, changed into a clean set of clothes with a fine lavender longvest. She found a comb to tame her tangled hair into its long, dark curls. Now it was near midday. The sun had broken through a few times, but presently the rain was coming down in sheets. Despite this, two of the massive airships flew from tethers on the sanctuary's dome. A third ship, the *Queen's Lance* she thought, was flying slow circuits around the city, no doubt meant to demonstrate that a new power occupied the sanctuary.

Francesca stared at the ship, its wings making tiny reflexive adjustments. She let her eyes go out of focus and thought about her mind. She was not human. She never had been. Her thoughts were moving faster and faster as she regained her health. One day, she hoped, she would regain prognostic quaternary cognition. As to whether she might ever return to her draconic body, she could not say.

Three glossy black sounds flashed behind her. A knock at the door? Francesca turned to see Nicodemus standing in the threshold. He was lowering the hood of a heavy blue rain cloak. His long black hair had been combed straight back, and his green eyes were fixed on hers. His expression was intense but unreadable. Was he frightened of her now? Did he still want her?

"Well," she wrote with an airiness she did not feel, *"aren't you going to tell me I've lost weight?"*

He read this, smiled, shook his head ruefully.

She wrote another for him. *"Who knew that eating nothing but the remains of defeated demons could slim a girl's waistline?"* She turned to show him her profile.

He laughed bright orange and walked closer. *"Is there anything in this world you can't laugh at?"* His spelling was perfect; he must be touching the emerald.

Her expression became grave. *"There is only one thing so horrible that I could never laugh at it."*

He searched her face. *"What?"*

She took a breath, closed her eyes, and handed him two words: "Menstrual cramps."

"Fran!" he flicked at her. "I thought you were serious!"

She caught his hand and then his eyes. He stopped smiling. Slowly, she raised his hand to her cheek and looked at him. With trembling fingers she put a golden question into his hand: "Do you still want me?"

He pulled her close and kissed her. His embrace tightened, and she felt as if the vast potential of her mind and body were containable within the circle of his arms.

Relief flooded through her. She could feel in his mouth and see in the sound of his breath his need for her. It was how it had been in Coldlock. They fought the urge to gulp each other down as they stumbled toward her bed. Only slowly could they control their thirst for each other.

When, at last, they lay exhausted beside each other, Nicodemus looked into her eyes. "Typhon was telling the truth about your creating a second Disjunction, wasn't he?"

She took his hand. "Typhon did not realize what we are together. Your cacography and my mind changes who we can be. It makes the future fluid. I've seen it."

"You are certain?"

She scowled at him and then kissed him. "Don't be dense. Of course I'm not certain. Who can be absolutely certain of anything?"

"What if we're making a mistake? What if this is what the demons want?"

She grabbed his shoulders. "What if separating is a mistake? What if there's some prophecy out there about a charmingly dense cacographer and a beautiful she-dragon discovering how to repel the Disjunction?"

"Charmingly dense?"

She kissed him hard and rolled on top of him.

"If this is what charmingly dense earns me, what do I get if I can pull off dashingly idiotic?"

"I'd have to lock the doors to show you."

He laughed but then grew more serious. "Fran, after you defeated Typhon, you ate his body."

Shame made a cold knot in her stomach. "An instinct, nothing more. I ground him into nothing so that he could never revive himself."

"You're certain?"

"You can only play the charmingly dense card so many times."

He didn't laugh. "Fran, why didn't you just leave me in Coldlock? Why have me walk into the sanctuary ignorant of what you were?"

She brushed his hair back. "The emerald. It's all you've ever wanted. I wanted it for you . . . and yet, I wish you would not want it. I wish you would put it away."

Nicodemus nodded. *"Because without it I change you? I increase your freedom when I am cacographic?"*

"Yes, that is part of it; I can tell you are touching the gem now."

He pulled his collar down to reveal the tear-shaped emerald on a silver chain. Gently he took it off and put it on the bed beside them. She felt a rush of heat run through her body; he was cacographic again. She looked him in the eyes. *"I want us to always be as we were in Coldlock."*

He looked from her to the emerald. *"I always thuoght it was the missging part of me. But I feel no differant when I hold it."*

She ran her hand over his stomach. *"I could make you feel different."*

He laughed red. *"Mabye not just now. We have to leve for Starfall in for hours. Can you be ready?"*

"Four hours?"

He sighed. *"The Godess Celsete is fling down from Mount Spires to proclame my half sister the Halycon. I must not be in the city, or even in the relm, by the time she arives."*

"But your sister is a cacographer now."

"Aside from Lotannu and the too of us, no one else nows that the Walker stole her abilety to spell. Vivian, or whatver her true name is, has a politicel mind and all the training to rule an empire. And Trilinnon, Verdant, and Spires have decieded they must create an empire. What the world beleives her to be is more important that what she is."

Francesca thought about this. *"You would like her to be the Halcyon?"*

Nicodemus looked at the emerald. *"Haeven knows she'd be beter at it than I would."*

She thought about this. *"It's not an ability to spell that makes you unique. It never has been."*

He looked away to the window.

She took his hand. *"How will we get to Starfall?"*

"Carevan. DeGarn has sent a colaboris spell to League of Starfall agents in Starhaven. They will meet us on the road and acompany us to Highland, where a company of highsmiths and druids will join us. Can you get ready at such short notise?"

"I'm ready now."

"Good, I have a few things to atend to in the sanctary. I'll send one of the highsmiths to you. They've become rather ademant about protecting you and me. There are two outside your door right now."

Francesca frowned at the door and something crossed her mind. *"I will always be a physician, wherever we go. You need to know that. I won't stop practicing."*

He smiled. *"Why?"*

She shrugged. *"I can't imagine living without it."*

He kissed her. *"Then you shall always be a healer. I wouldn't want you any other way."*

AT LONG LAST, the signal flags flying from Avel's lofting kites commanded the *Queen's Lance* to return to the wind garden for refitting. With his muscles aching and his eyes stinging, Cyrus set the necessary texts in motion. The *Queen's Lance* broke patrol formation and headed west.

Cyrus and every other hierophant who had fought for the monotheist fleet had been working double shifts. Glancing back at Captain Izem, Cyrus saw an exhaustion in the other man's eyes that must have mirrored his own.

The winds and rain had let up, and so the flight over the Auburn Mountains took little time. But when the *Queen's Lance* flew above the lush green pass filled with wide-mouthed windcatchers, Cyrus noticed something odd about the garden tower. The jumpdeck was crowded with pilots, and ten lofting kites were flying in a chain of tethers, one atop the other. As they flew closer, Cyrus saw that each was flying the flag signal for "Victory."

From behind him Izem laughed.

"Captain?" Cyrus asked. "I've never seen anything like it."

As the *Queen's Lance* came around and made ready to dock, a roar of cheers rose from the jumpdeck.

"It's a hero's salute," Izem replied. "For the *Queen's Lance,* her crew, and most especially her pilot."

Cyrus felt his face flush warm as he realized that last title belonged to him.

"Cyrus," Izem yelled, "I hope you're not fond of being an air warden, because after this I think the air marshals are going to condemn you to be an airship captain."

WHEN THE ATTENDANT led Nicodemus into the study, he found Vivian dressed in heavy wizardly robes and wearing long black gloves. Lotannu stood a few feet behind her. They eyed him coldly.

Behind Nicodemus stood DeGarn, the captain of the surviving highmiths, and the most senior of the druids.

Nicodemus bowed. "Sister. Magister Lotannu."

Neither of them spoke for a long moment. Then she bowed her head. "Nicodemus."

"What should I call you?"

"It seems that news is already abroad about us. The wider world is calling me by my pseudonym. So you may also call me Vivian."

As she spoke, Nicodemus realized that she was a few years younger than he was. "I hope my words during our meeting with Canonist Cala were clear."

She nodded. "They were."

"There are a few things I should like to say to you in private."

She only looked at him.

"I see no reason why we should be enemies," he offered.

"You have enabled the separatists," she said coldly. "Now humanity will not stand united against the demons."

"They will not be united under your rule, but that does not preclude cooperation."

She clenched her gloved hands. "I thought you forswore political involvement."

"So I have." He paused. "Should you wish to communicate with me, I will always welcome it."

"You are gracious."

He started to turn away but then stopped. "The gloves won't keep you far enough away from others," he said.

"What's that?"

"Your disability. The gloves might keep you from giving canker curses to others, but you'll always feel too close to other living things. It will haunt you."

Her expression became stony. "Thank you for that insight."

He studied her and wondered if he was a fool to have come. "I will leave this city within the hour. We may not see each other again until the Disjunction. Maybe not even then."

"Perhaps not."

He bowed and again started to turn away, but again he stopped. "Vivian, did you know our mother?"

"Until I was seventeen, when she died."

Nicodemus felt his throat tighten. He hadn't realized that he'd been harboring a hope. "What was she like?"

Vivian pressed her lips together. "A devout woman." She studied Nicodemus for a moment longer. "She thought of you often. Whenever news came of an assassinated demonic Imperial, she would cry. Some part of her hoped you had been killed so that you might not grow up worshiping Los. Some part of her hoped that you had not been assassinated, so you might at least live to manhood."

Nicodemus nodded. "Did she look like you?"

The tension around Vivian's eyes lessened. "She was far prettier."

He studied her face for a long time. And then, he really wasn't sure why, he tossed something to her with an underhand throw.

With a shout, Lotannu cast out a Magnus spell. Instantly, the Emerald of Aarahest hung suspended by a mesh of silver words.

Vivian and Lotannu looked at each other and then at him. "What is the meaning of this?" she asked.

"I could never be a Halcyon. All my life, I've been trying to fill an emptiness inside. But that emptiness . . . I've built myself around it. Filling it in would be like filling in the empty space within a cathedral."

"But why give this to me?"

He met her green eyes. "You were raised to be the Halcyon. You believe in order and empire. Maybe you can do something worthwhile with that. Maybe you can repel the demons. I couldn't, and frankly I'd be happier with the burden on your shoulders. Without the emerald, Francesca and I are something larger than we are with it. So now, after curing Magister Shannon's canker curses, I have no more use for it."

His half sister stepped forward. She reached out for the emerald but then stopped. "I want no debts between us."

He met her eyes. "Then acknowledge that not every soul worships order as you do."

She looked from the emerald to him. "I will acknowledge that. And I will do what is best for humanity."

"Then take the emerald, and answer to your conscience."

She peeled off a glove and plucked the stone from the air. An instant later she formed an intricate, twisting passage of Numinous and let out a long sigh of relief. Lotannu approached but then stopped. "You needn't worry, Magister, she won't impart canker curses any longer."

Lotannu took Vivian's hand. They both turned to him. "You didn't have to do this," Lotannu said.

"But I am thankful I did. And you needn't worry about me; I know how to survive as a cacographer."

"Nicodemus, you've done humanity a great service," Vivian said softly. She looked at him. "Perhaps I can reciprocate. When searching Typhon's quarters we found documents naming the different organizations of demon worshipers in all six human kingdoms. They could help us eradicate the threat that is already among us. I shall have copies made and sent to your . . ." She looked at DeGarn. "To your allies."

Nicodemus bowed. "Thank you kindly, sister. We shall put them to good use." He paused. "I should also like to discuss Typhon's research spell, the one Magister Akoma discovered, the one that can change the nature of language in a large area. It is, I believe, related to the Silent Blight that is reducing Language Prime misspelling across the continent."

Neither Vivian nor Lotannu seemed surprised. Nicodemus continued: "With that metaspell and the emerald, you might make magical language more logical in the realms within your new empire. It might also tempt you to impose the same influence on the forming League of Starfall."

All warmth fell from Vivian's face.

"Before you attempted that," Nicodemus added, "I'd remind you that Magister Akoma made a copy of that metaspell and placed it in Francesca's clinical journal, which I have. I'm sure you would rather I not cast that spell with the intent of counteracting your influence."

Lotannu spoke. "Nicodemus, please listen. I have done little the past day but scrutinize that metaspell. By making magical language more logical it will increase the power of our spellwrights. It will help us repel the demons."

"And have you considered," Nicodemus asked as casually as he could, "what would happen to creatures like Francesca, who are constructed of intuitive rather than logical language?"

Lotannu blinked. "I suppose they would weaken."

"We suppose the same thing. We also suppose that creatures like Francesca would become much more powerful if I were to cast this metaspell."

Lotannu tensed as he understood where Nicodemus was going.

Nicodemus looked at Vivian. "I believe Lotannu is now foreseeing what Francesca foresaw in her draconic form. Sister, if you and I were to compete in casting this metaspell, we would split the human world. Magical language would become different in your empire and in our league. Your spellwrights would strengthen, but your constructs and deities would weaken. The opposite would happen in our lands."

Vivian nodded slowly. "It would be a schism."

"Then we shall swear not to cast these metaspells?"

She nodded. "We shall . . . but . . . practically speaking, how long do you think either empire or league can resist the temptation to invoke an advantage?"

"Hopefully long enough to prepare for the War of Disjunction," Nicodemus quickly replied. "Sadly, we do not have any foresight as to when the revived Los might bring the demonic host across the ocean. Perhaps you do?"

Vivian shook her head. "Maybe the demons come in a year, maybe in fifty." She paused. "Nicodemus, for an apolitical man, you have taken steps that have momentous political implications."

He smiled at her. "Runs in the family."

She laughed humorlessly.

He bowed. "Farewell, sister."

After a lengthy pause, she returned the bow and said in a cold tone: "Farewell, brother."

FRANCESCA WAS LOOKING out the window at the rain when the door opened. She'd hoped it was a highsmith come to take her to the caravan. But Cyrus stepped into her room. His turban was unwound, his veil lowered to reveal his short black beard. His eyes seemed solemn even though he wore a slight smile—the expression of someone recalling a bittersweet memory.

"Hello Cyrus," she said nervously and watched the colors of his name roll away from her mouth. He began speaking blurry rainbows. She shook her head and said, "I can't understand you."

He grabbed the skirt of his robes and a square of cloth cut itself free. She understood and pointed to the room's small writing desk. He sat and dipped a corner of the cloth into the inkwell. The dark stain ran up into the cloth. He spread the sheet on the desk to reveal a sentence: *"I heard you're leaving with Nicodemus for Starfall."*

She nodded.

His eyes fixed on hers.

Using her finger, she wrote on the cloth: *"Are you coming through all the chaos okay?"*

He smiled his bittersweet smile and wrote, *"The air marshal of the western fleet promoted me to captain. I will have a ship far sooner than I ever expected."*

Francesca laughed bright orange. *"Cyrus, that's wonderful! Congratulations! What kind of ship?"*

He looked at her soberly. *"Astrophell has commissioned a new Kestrel so it may serve diplomatic duty to their new archchancellor, the woman who it seems will soon be empress."*

Francesca's smile wilted. *"You'll captain Vivian's airship?"*

He nodded. His expression had become solemn. *"I shall be captain of the new empire's command ship."*

"Cyrus!" she wrote hastily. *"Vivian will use your knowledge of Nicodemus. That must be why she's promoting you."*

He frowned. *"She's promoting me because I assisted her investigation and brought down two rebel destroyers in the Second Siege of Avel."*

"Yes, of course," Francesca wrote. *"You are the hero of the siege. I don't doubt it . . . but, don't you see that Vivian and Nicodemus are bound to clash? You would be opposing us."*

Cyrus stared at her for a long moment. *"Us?"*

She felt a chill move through her. She nodded.

"You and Nicodemus?"

"Yes."

"Does he feel the same way?"

"I hope so."

Cyrus held very still for a long while. *"I always loved you, and I never understood why."*

She felt cold, ill.

His hands were shaking as he worked on the sheet. *"Everything was turbulence and trouble with you, like flying through a storm. I thought I was staying with you despite the turbulence, but maybe it was because of it. Maybe I was drawn to you for the same reason I was drawn to the sky. I left you for thermals and ridge lifts, and I should have stayed away. I wish—"* He glanced at her, eyes hard with anger. His expression softened. *"I'm sorry,"* he wrote. *"Perhaps it is best that we be on opposite sides of the coming divide."*

Francesca nodded stiffly, trying to keep her expression even, her eyes dry. *"I am sorry as well."*

Just then a green sound came from the doorway. Francesca turned and saw a young highsmith standing in the threshold. *"I must go,"* she wrote. *"Our caravan is leaving."*

Cyrus looked at the highsmith and then wrote again on his sheet. *"Take care of yourself. It may be a very long time until we meet again."*

Francesca took in a deep breath. *"I wish you joy, Cyrus. I will smile whenever I think of you flying."* She paused before adding, *"But if you're commanding Vivian's warship, I hope that we never meet again."*

Epilog

Starfall Island rose out of the blue horizon. Its forested slopes climbed steeply to become craggy mountains shrouded by flocks of seabirds. On a high plateau of the northern slope sat several rectangular white towers. As Francesca watched, a golden colaboris spell erupted from the tallest tower and flew over the western horizon.

Starfall Keep was tiny compared with Astrophell's domes, and it lacked the grandeur of Starhaven's inhumanly tall spires; even so, Francesca thought it beautiful. Nicodemus stood beside her on the bow. She tried to focus on the wooded island, the ancient academy, but nausea sloshed through her like wine in a jug. She had sailed many times before but had never suffered from such horrible seasickness. Some days, shortly after eating breakfast, she had to bend over the railing and be sick into the swells. Blessedly, the queasiness usually dissipated in the afternoon.

Now, after fifty-three days, their journey to Starfall was almost complete. Francesca felt weary in a way she had not thought possible. Most highsmiths and druids recognized Nicodemus as their champion, but radical elements in both Lorn and Dral—wanting to prevent the League of Starfall from forming so they might continue their ancient war against each other—had focused their violence on Nicodemus.

In the Skywood, their caravan had barely survived the attack of a Dralish forest god: a massive treelike being with archers loosing arrows from his boughs and rootlike limbs burrowing into the flesh of Nicodemus's party. In the City of Rain, a highsmith assassin stabbed Nicodemus's back. Fortuitously, his cacographic nature disspelled the knife's metallic spells before they could punch a meshwork of needles though his body.

After that, the Lord Governor of Rain assigned a company of horsemen and a seraph—one of Lorn's genderless subgods bound to their metal god—to escort Nicodemus down the River Road. But ten days outside the city, a troop of antileague border guards pulled down a section of Richard's Wall, letting out the lycanthropes of the Tulgety Forest. The wolves killed two of Nicodemus's company and overturned several caravan wagons. In the fray, Shannon broke his left collar bone—a painful injury for a man already in a fragile state. Whenever they could, Nicodemus and Francesca attended to Shannon.

In Skydoc, rioters set fire to the ship meant to sail them to Starfall. The next night the governor snuck the party aboard a Lornish warship leaving on the morning tide. Once at sea, Francesca and Nicodemus finally had time to discuss what they had discovered in Avel. Twice, they hotly debated if they were destined to instigate Typhon's Disjunction. Nicodemus thought it was possible; Francesca didn't.

As hard as the seasickness was for Francesca, it was worse for Shannon. His already-small appetite diminished, and his collarbone was slow in mending. When a cough went around among the sailors, Shannon ran a fever and began coughing up dark phlegm. Francesca attended the old man, and Nicodemus kept him company. That morning, Shannon's fever had worsened, and she and Nicodemus had been at his side until a cry of landfall had brought them above deck.

"*I fear for Shannon,*" Francesca wrote as they entered the broad harbor lying beneath Starfall. On the far shore, two-score rectangular houses—white walls, thatched roofs—made up the island's largest port town.

Nicodemus looked at her. "*Was I rong? Did I fale to remove all of his canckers?*"

"*No, you removed them all. But as you suspected, you could not restore the health that was lost during a decade of fighting the disease. The curse accelerated his physical age. I can feel how the valves of his heart have stiffened, and the beating muscle itself is dilating. His body is hard-pressed to fight the infection in his lungs.*"

"*What can we do?*"

She turned to face Nicodemus. "*I'm afraid there is little to do but keep him comfortable and pray.*"

"*Do you know?*" he wrote. "*From your prgonosis?*"

She shook her head. "*He may survive . . . but mortal danger will soon return to him.*"

He only nodded and held her tighter.

An hour later, two sailors rowed them to a quay lined with wizards. With typical academic pomp, they were led up to Starfall's grassy courtyards and white stone buildings. Francesca gave instructions as to how Shannon was to be transported while Nicodemus spoke with a procession of deans and dignitaries.

When she rejoined him, Nicodemus was talking to two lesser wizards; one was older and very tall, the other shorter and with thinning brown hair.

The large man's name was John of Starhaven, but he had once been known as Simple John and had lived with Nicodemus and the other Starhaven cacographers. The shorter man's name was Derrick; apparently he had been a cacographic student in Nicodemus's first and only wizardly lecture. Both men had come to Starfall Keep once the counter-prophecy faction had taken power in Starhaven. Weary though she was, Francesca was delighted to meet two men from Nicodemus's old life.

The cacographers seemed as if they would have spent the whole night talking and renewing their friendship, but when Francesca mentioned that Shannon was fairing worse, both John and Derrick excused themselves to call on their old mentor.

Nicodemus looked as if he would have liked to join them, but several grand wizards ushered him and Francesca into a long, formal dinner.

When not talking to other wizards, Nicodemus described to her the different factions he'd already discovered within in their new home; one he suspected was already taking Astrophell's coin to spy on him. Meanwhile, other factions seemed to already be spying on Vivian. One dean reported that Vivian was emptying Astrophell's treasury to build grammar schools and—almost incredibly—printing presses. Why she should invest in mundane text production was a mystery.

When the last speech was given and the last toast made, Francesca and Nicodemus were shown their new residence of an entire floor of the westernmost tower. From the balcony, she could look out on the island forests, the ocean beyond.

Shannon had been situated in one of the bedrooms and was being attended by two acolytes. Though cheered by John and Derrick's visit, Shannon remained in poor health. Francesca administered a small dose of the alcoholic tincture of Ixonian opium to suppress his cough and help him sleep. Nicodemus sat with his former teacher. Francesca excused herself, eager for a feather bed.

As she drifted off to sleep, she worried about her body. Her mind was slowly recovering her extraordinary perception of time, but her body showed no sign of regaining its draconic potential. She had foreseen futures in which she regained this capability and futures in which she did not.

She did not know what she could do to restore her draconic potential, but presently she did not mind its absence. There was some other process—healing perhaps—to which her body was dedicated.

She came halfway out of sleep when Nicodemus climbed under the sheets. He made the bed too hot, so she rolled into cooler sheets, dreaming . . . and sat bolt upright as someone grabbed her shoulder. Colorful words flashed. One of the acolytes attending to Shannon was speaking. Something had happened.

Francesca hopped out of bed and jogged toward the old man's room. Outside, the black sky was still sprayed with stars. She found Shannon breathing fast and mumbling green. His skin was cold and clammy, his pulse rapid and weak. *"What hapened?"* the question floated before her. She turned to see Nicodemus in the doorway.

She laid her hand against Shannon's chest and felt his heart bounding. *"I fear the infection is in his blood. His vessels are dilating from the shock. Talk to him. See if he is making sense."*

Nicodemus crouched next to the bed. They spoke in dim colors. *"Its hard to understnad. He's tlaking about his wife, I think,"* Nicodemus wrote. *"He says heis cold."*

Francesca draped two more blankets over Shannon. His breathing was becoming labored. Nicodemus wrapped one of the blankets around Shannon's hand and squeezed it. *"What can we do?"*

Francesca bit her lip. *"My love, there are no good options."* She began to write two paragraphs, but then noticed that Nicodemus had looked away. He didn't want to be seen. She finished her paragraphs and sat on the other side of the bed. Shannon shifted restlessly. She took his hand.

Nicodemus remained very still. Once, he wiped his eyes. She pretended not to notice.

As she always did when caring for the dying, Francesca felt as if grief surrounded her but could not touch her. And yet, as she watched Shannon shifting and murmuring, she became keenly aware that some part of her was still mortal. One day she might lie in a bed, fading into death.

Twisting inside of her was the need to move, to do, to launch into the safety of action. In her hands, she held two paragraphs. Each one described a course of treatment. But Nicodemus, not she, should decide between the two. She longed to thrust the golden words at him and demand that he read, that he decide, that he do something. But she forced herself to wait while Nicodemus hid his grief. Perhaps a quarter hour passed. It felt like a lifetime. Shannon said words of brown and orange.

Finally Nicodemus turned to his old teacher. His face was bright with tears, his mouth pulled back and quivering. He looked like a mask, like a terrified child, like a grotesque, like heartbreak.

And in that moment, Francesca felt something in herself break as she realized that there was no safety in action, that even if she threw herself into Shannon's treatment, it would be only a distraction from the truth that one day Nicodemus would die and her own face would become the mask, the child, the grotesque. She felt a strange awe at her own grief.

Nicodemus wiped his eyes. *"What are our optieons?"*

She paused, then held out her first paragraph: *"I could textually spike his shin bone, give him fluids to fill up his dilated veins, and pray he recovers before his kidneys or bowel die from lack of blood."* She waited for him to read this and then held out the second paragraph. *"Or I could give him alcoholic tincture of opium to remove his fear and shortness of breath and gentle his passing."*

When Nicodemus finished reading, he turned away again.

Suddenly it was too much for Francesca. She jumped up and began pacing. She dried her eyes on her sleeve. The two acolytes were standing out in the hall, looking at her with terror. She thought about saying something but then saw a lavender and white sound. She turned.

Nicodemus was holding out a question. *"If you spik him, what would his chnaces be?"*

"Better but . . . still poor. It might be painful."

She feared that Nicodemus would turn away again, but he talked to Shannon in dull colors. The old man's all-white eyes swung around, finding nothing.

Nicodemus looked at her and wrote a sentence. It broke in half when she took it. *"I think"* was all she got. He wrote again. *"I think we should take his pain away."*

She nodded solemnly. *"I think so too."*

She stood and felt a release from grief so powerful she made a small noise of surprise. Her actions unfolded almost automatically—pouring, mixing, helping Shannon drink the tincture. When finished, Nicodemus tensed. She went around to him and put her arms around his shoulders. *"It will take an hour,"* she wrote. *"Maybe more."*

Nicodemus held her hand and continued to talk to Shannon. She stood with him. After three quarters of an hour, Shannon's breathing began to slow. He stopped writhing. After a few more minutes, color stopped coming from the old man's mouth. Nicodemus's teacher took each breath more slowly than the last, until he did not take another.

The room went still for a moment, and then the old man's body shone with golden prose. A ghost sat up out of his author's body. Nicodemus bowed his head, and the strength seemed to drain out of his arms and back.

Magister Agwu Shannon was dead.

NICODEMUS WALKED WITH Shannon's ghost down a wide hallway toward Starfall's necropolis.

Nicodemus had known that being within a body as it died transformed a ghost. He had known that such ghosts became incoherent and longed only to enter a necropolis. But knowing of this transformation had not prepared Nicodemus to witness it.

The ghost beside him did not respond to voice and replied to few spell-written queries. Each time, the text had not answered Nicodemus's question but reminded him that a ghost rarely, if ever, emerged from a necropolis.

As they walked, Nicodemus looked over. The ghost wore a distracted expression and gazed far off to the right, even though the hallway turned left. Then the ghost turned and held out a paragraph. Nicodemus translated with as few misspellings as possible: *"It's as if I was a singer and now I am a song. But it's not like that at all. It's as if I were two signers and now I'm only one singer. But not like that ether."*

Nicodemus was unsure how to reply. But the ghost looked away, uninterested. The hallway led into a wide circular room with plane white stone walls. This was the entryway to the necropolis.

From the far wall protruded a single stone block. Atop it sat a sheet of paper covered with shifting Numinous runes. This paper extended through the wall and into the necropolis proper, the living were not permitted to enter.

Nicodemus watched as the ghost held his hand above the paper of shifting runes. The text seemed just about to press his hand down when he looked back at Nicodemus.

Man and ghost studied each other for a long time. "Good-bye, Magister," Nicodemus said.

The ghost's expression grew distant and then thoughtful. He cast a sentence to Nicodemus. *"Or mayeb the sole isn't a singer. Maybe it's a chorus."*

Then the ghost put his hand to the paper and vanished.

FRANCESCA AWOKE IN the blue hour before dawn. Nicodemus lay next to her, at last asleep. After taking Shannon's ghost down to Starfall's necropolis, they had stayed up talking about Shannon—his life, his work, his death—until exhaustion had pulled them both down into sleep.

Now Francesca got out of bed. She couldn't say what had woken her. It hadn't been a dream or a sound . . . but something that was . . . wrong.

She stood, wondering if she needed to visit the privy, but on her feet she realized that she was nauseated. She sat back down and struggled with confusion. It was as if her seasickness had returned. She stood, wondering if a drink of water would . . .

Suddenly she knew that she was going to vomit. She ran for the balcony but bent over and heaved in the hallway. Long, painful contractions. Nothing came up. She hurried the rest of the way to the balcony and retched over the side, bringing up a mouthful of bitterness.

When she could finally stand straight, breathing fast, she found the cold sea air bracing. A crowd of gulls circled over the fishing boats heading out to sea. A second wave of nausea washed through her as if she were on one of those boats.

Two seabirds, white with flashes of black in their tails, soared overhead. Suddenly Francesca understood. She hadn't caught a flux or a flu. On the ocean, she had not been seasick. The cause of her nausea was so obvious that she laughed bright red. This explained why her body had not regained its draconic potential; it was undertaking a greater work. The future she had fought so hard to win had already taken shape in the body of her next patient.

Francesca had not thought this outcome possible. She and Nicodemus were both spellwrights after all, and no two spellwrights could conceive of this happening. But then again, she was not properly a human. This rule, apparently, did not apply to her.

A lavender noise made her turn around. Nicodemus was walking toward her, blinking away sleep. *"Fran, what hapened?"* he wrote. *"Are you allright?"*

She nodded. *"I'm fine. Nausea is common in the mornings. We are just getting used to each other."*

"We?"

Francesca had not realized she'd used a plural pronoun to announce her newest patient. She took her lover's hand and laid it on her belly. Whatever ties they might have to Typhon's Disjunction, they were now radically transformed. *"Nicodemus,"* she wrote, *"I'm pregnant."*

ACKNOWLEDGMENTS

You have your whole life to write a first novel; for your second, you have a year.
So the saying goes. When I first got the wheels turning on *Spellbound*, I
had no idea how one person could possibly produce a second novel ten
times faster than the first while simultaneously attempting to grow as a
writer. I quickly discovered that it was impossible. No one author could do
it. One author plus a small army of friends and colleagues, however, just
might pull it off.

Before anything else, my small army provided the following sources of
inspiration. In chapter one, the phrase "kill as few patients as possible" is
used in homage to Dr. Oscar London's collection of humorous essays, *Kill
as Few Patients as Possible*. Also in chapter one, the cardiac massage scene
was inspired by Dr. Sherwin B. Nuland's description of the procedure in
his book *How We Die*. The treatment of a tension pneumothorax in chapter twenty-nine came to me when I was studying Dr. Frank Netter's illus-
tration of "Chest Drainage Tube Placement." The peculiar effects the
Savanna Walker has on the minds of others were inspired by many of the
cases described by Dr. Oliver Sacks in *The Man Who Mistook His Wife for a
Hat* and *Musicophilia*. The impromptu brain surgery of chapter forty-six
was inspired by D. J. Donovan, R. R. Moquin, and J. M. Ecklund in their
article "Cranial Burr Holes and Emergency Craniotomy: Review of Indica-
tions and Techniques," published in *Military Medicine* (171, no. 1 [2006]:
12–19). A very few scenes in the book were inspired by my encounters with
patients or stories told to me by medical students or physicians. I have, of
course, not included any information that might identify an actual patient. In that regard, I am fortunate that setting a novel in an imaginary
world and populating it with creatures like dragons makes it exceedingly
difficult to violate the Health Insurance Portability and Accountability
Act (HIPAA).

First on the list of those who made *Spellbound* possible is its first reader:
Dr. Asya Agulnik, who graciously provided criticism, kindness, and support. Thank you.

Many publishing professionals made invaluable contributions to this book. My two editors, Jim Frenkel at Tor and Amy McCulloch at Voyager, provided brilliant feedback. Nina Lourie found both plot flaws and their remedies before showing me how I could more fully develop all of my characters. Megan Messinger's analysis of each character's story arc helped make the conclusion an order of magnitude more satisfying. When a deadline loomed, Lindsay Ribar saved the day by reading and skillfully critiquing as fast as I could edit. I'm very lucky to have the brilliant Cassandra Ammerman as my PR agent at Tor and look forward to working with her again. Irene Gallo and Todd Lockwood produced the perfect cover for this book, despite the complications arising from "second dragon" mystery. All through the year, Matt Bialer was a good friend and marvelous literary agent. I'm very thankful for Stefani Diaz, my foreign rights agent, who has sold this trilogy in more languages than I ever dared dream.

The Stanford University School of Medicine has been the ideal home for my dual careers. In particular, I have been blessed by the mentorship and friendship of Dr. Abraham Verghese, who has given advice about medical training and provided understanding when publishing deadlines have taken me away from my duties as his research assistant. Dr. Audrey Shafer and Dr. Irvin Yalom provided not only wisdom about the life of a physician-writer but also help in seeking institutional assistance. I am deeply grateful for the support of the Stanford Medical Scholars Research Program and the program in Biomedical Ethics and Medical Humanities for their generous support of my different projects.

Many friends outside med school and publishing made vital contributions to this book. Jessica Weare, Swaroop Samant, Kevan Moffett, Josh Troke, and Nina Nuangchamnong read various drafts and provided vital insights. Saladin Ahmed helpfully critiqued the first hundred pages during a busy time. Deanna Hoak answered myriad questions about grammar. Much of the first draft was written across a coffee-shop table from Gail Carriger, who tolerated me as a writing partner even when I would hold my laptop over her head in hopes that some of her wit might spread via osmosis onto my hard drive. Kimberly Chisholm graciously read a late draft to help catch smaller errors.

And, through it all, I had the support of my father, Dr. Randy Charlton; my sister, Genevieve Johansen; my beautiful little niece, Lis Ana Johansen; and of course my wise and loving mother, Dr. Louise Buck, to whom this book is dedicated.

ABOUT THE AUTHOR

Blake Charlton's severe dyslexia kept him from reading fluently until he began sneaking fantasy novels into special-ed study hall in the seventh grade. He has been an English teacher, a biomedical technical writer, a learning-disability tutor, and a junior varsity football coach. He currently attends Stanford University School of Medicine. *Spellbound,* the sequel to *Spellwright,* is his second novel and the second book in the Spellwright Trilogy. Please visit him at www.blakecharlton.com.